FORGIVE ME, ALEX

A TONY HOOPER THRILLER

BOOK 1

LANE DIAMOND

WHAT OTHERS ARE SAYING ABOUT "FORGIVE ME, ALEX"

WINNER:
Pinnacle Book Achievement Award – Summer 2014 – Best Thriller

"This story affords us a look into the mind of a serial killer and the tremendous strength of writing in this book makes that a terrifying experience. The writing is exceptional in that it propelled me into the story and into the minds of the main characters as well as keeping me totally fixated on the story. The suspense and tension is this story is very palpable and I found myself thinking about this story long after I had finished. The main characters of Tony and Mitchell are painted with such fine precision and depth I could almost feel their presence while reading. The character of Frank Willow the adopted Grandfather of Tony and Alex is a richly defined character who contributes a great deal of emotion and compassion to the story. The other characters in this story are all unique and well defined and successfully contribute to the sentiment, understanding and underlying current of the story."
~ *The Kindle Book Review*

"Diamond does in FORGIVE ME, ALEX what I wish more contemporary authors would do: He brings me right into the story, forcing me to identify with the characters. I didn't have a choice—I would feel Tony Hooper's wrath and need for revenge, I would wallow in Mitchell Norton's desperate inability to ward off his demons. I would cheer for Diana Gregorio's unbelievable ballsiness in the face of seemingly unbeatable odds. I would weep, shedding actual tears, for Alex Hooper's childhood." ~ *Anne B. Chaconas*

"With his first novel, *Forgive Me, Alex*, Lane Diamond has initiated a crime/suspense thriller series that exhibits many of the qualities that put the likes of Lee Child and James Patterson on the bestseller lists." ~ *Lex Allen for Readers' Favorite Book Reviews*

"Suck a rubber duck if you are not blown away by this dark psychological thriller. In a world where characters are as vital as in *The Game of Thrones*, the suspense had me on the edge of my seat and holding my breath for everyone involved. Neighboring Huntley, the setting is home to me, making this all the more twisted and real for me. If you love serial killers, red herrings, the thrill of the chase, and unpredictable endings, you are in for a treat. Methodically thorough, this book came together like a well-crafted puzzle. The word choice, though coarse, is meaningful and eloquent. The switching points of view and timelines were plot-driven, not pointless. The narrator made this story come alive. I loved all of the character voices. Well, I loved all of them except one. The author created such a vile creature in the serial killer that by the end of the book, I heard his voice and wanted to throw up. Authors should look to this as a great example of the use of an epilogue and cliffhanger. In short: mind blown." ~ *Raven Reviewer*

"Psychological thrillers are my kind of books! Not only do I write them, but truly enjoy reading one that makes my skin crawl, my nerves skitter with fear and my heart thump a tad louder. This incredible novel by Lane Diamond handed me ALL of that, in spades!" ~ *Ashley Fontaine, Author*

"This book is gruesome and emotional right out of the gate. The main character, Tony, goes through some monumental losses throughout the story. These aren't the kind of losses that you can just blow off as insignificant because Lane's writing makes you really care about these people and what's going on. Lane excels in this area of sympathetic characters." ~ *Tim C. Ward, Former Executive Producer for Adventures in Sci-Fi Publishing*

"Hooked from page one & it was quite a struggle to put this one done. If you want to read a book that will stick with you long after you finish it, you need to read this one. Everything was so well described I could almost visualize the scenes." ~ *Mark Schafer*

"The characters were very believable and engrossing. The plot grabbed me from the first moment and I enjoyed following the many twists and turns along the way. If you like suspense and intrigue you will not put this down until you've reached the end!" ~ *Steve Doss*

FORGIVE ME, ALEX
Tony Hooper – Book 1
Copyright © 2011 by Lane Diamond

FIFTH EDITION SOFTCOVER (2025)
ISBN: 1622539079
ISBN-13: 978-1-62253-907-9

Editor: D.T. Conklin
Cover Artist: D. Robert Pease
Interior Designer: Lane Diamond

www.EvolvedPub.com
Evolved Publishing LLC
Butler, Wisconsin, USA

Printed in Book Antiqua font.

BOOKS BY LANE DIAMOND

TONY HOOPER SERIES
Book 1: *Forgive Me, Alex*
Book 2: *The Devils Bane* (2026)
Book 3: *Hooper's Rules* (2027)

SHORT STORY ANTHOLOGIES
Evolution Volumes I and II

SHORT STORIES (Stand-Alone)
Devane's Reality
Paradox
Well-Suited Sentry
Wind Tunnel

DEDICATION

For Darren & Rhonda Lane, and for Steven Zerkel:
They walk the walk, and they saved me.

PART 1
JUSTICE SERVED, JUSTICE DENIED

CHAPTER 1
JUNE 6, 1995:
TONY HOOPER

"...that is the soul, and whether you are a soldier, a scholar, a cook, or an apprentice in a factory, your life and your work will eventually teach you that it exists. The difference between your flesh and the animate power within, which can feel, understand, and love, in that very descending order, will be clear to you in ten thousand ways, ten thousand times over." – *Mark Helprin, "A Soldier of the Great War"*

I never expected to be a killer.

Who does?

I don't *hate* myself. Not really. It's not as if I don't recognize the face in the mirror every morning; I just don't always recognize the man to whom it belongs.

Mitchell Norton, the man responsible for making me who I am, will skip out of his final court hearing today—a mere formality according to the news. They're set to release him from the psychiatric prison after seventeen years, the thought of which has spun my mind into a whirlwind of memories I've long struggled to bury.

I killed my first man in 1975, at the age of fifteen.

Norton's actions three years later would push me deeper into my transformation, and aim me toward this place. The life I now lead. The me who isn't me.

Some things I've lost forever. Other things... well, other things I'd like to lose, but can't.

The memory refuses to drift into the eternal ether. If only I could erase the sound and the image, press a button and — *poof* — it's gone. Yet it forever haunts me, the first of far too many ghosts....

<u>August 16, 1975</u>

Crash!

The distinctive crushing of metal assaulted our Saturday afternoon, as Alex and I watched television and waited for Mom to return from the store. I jumped from the chair and looked out the living room window, but couldn't see enough of the street. I darted into the kitchen for a better angle.

Dear God, no!

I yelled to Alex while bolting to the back door. "Stay put, Hoopster! You hear me? Do *not* come outside!"

Mom was back. Almost. Our Chevy Bel Air sat right in front of our house, crushed into an impossibly condensed version of itself. A half-ton pick-up truck, its front end curled forward in a crescent moon, loomed over the windshield of our car.

I ran through the glass and the debris to the twisted wreckage, tripping over a chunk of something unknown. I fell to my knees and banged my head against the side of the car.

Shit! Oh God. Mom!

I snapped up and peered through the envelope-sized gap where the driver-side window had once been. The back of Mom's head sagged at a bizarre angle, barely visible above the crushed compartment.

"Mom, are you okay? Mom!"

I pulled my head back, reached through the gap with my left hand, and walked my fingers along the wreckage to reach her. I found her wet, sticky hair, and stretched out... farther... farther. Unable to turn her face toward me, I moved my fingers from her chin and up the far side of her face, and —

I snatched my hand back and bolted upright.

I stared at my left hand even as I used my right one to wipe away the blood and the gray matter. Everything began to spin and close in. My chest hammered with every breath, as though God had reached down and clutched the air from the world. I leaned against the car, and my hands painted two red streaks down the metal as my legs folded beneath me.

I collapsed against the jagged wreck in a dark heap — blank — and vanished for untold moments.

Life resumed when a man fell from the pick-up truck, coughed and spat on the street. He looked at me, inched forward on his hands and knees, and vomited. It took him a moment to recover, but he....

What in hell is he doing?

The rotten sonuvabitch laughed and whooped it up, as though he'd perpetrated some ingenious practical joke. His bloodshot eyes looked as if they would burst at any moment. He spewed a garbled, incoherent mush that I struggled to translate.

"Shit! I think I fucked up my truck, buddy. Can you give a fella a hand?"

He faded in and out as my last image of Mom — what was left of her — overpowered me. Everything grayed again, but as the spinning stopped and my breath returned, the full tragedy came into focus. The wicked bastard who'd crushed my mom... was drunk.

My legs had deserted me, turned to dust. I could only look around in a daze at our neighbors, who'd emerged from their houses to investigate. *What should I —*

The asshole's staccato bursts of drunken laughter again pulled me back. The very air I breathed stifled me — gas, oil, burnt rubber and a vague metallic tinge, all mingled with the sour contents of the killer's stomach poured onto the street. I raised my hands, bathed in crimson and wafting copper, before my face.

A disembodied voice spoke from the void — *my* voice. "Where did the blood come from? Did I cut myself?"

"What's that, buddy?" The murderous drunk laughed again. "Shit! You think *you* got it bad? Look at my fucking truck!"

I floated still, adrift in an endless gray ocean of broken thought, struggling to make sense of the fluid that drenched my hands.

It's... it's.... Oh, God, it's Mom's blood and brains.

The maddening, driveling voice, like a spear in my gut, stabbed me again. "For Christ's sake, kid, stop fucking around and give me a hand, will you!"

Rage burned a red sheath over my eyes.

I stood and marched to the killer, who looked up with drunken eyes that meant nothing to me. They were evil. I focused instead on his neck, called up all that I'd learned in Master Komura's martial arts classes over the previous ten years, and struck.

Though strong for a fifteen-year-old, my success rested on the fragile physiology of that small patch of neck. To crush his trachea required more precision than strength.

The slobbering murderer collapsed, clutched his ruined throat, and gasped for air that would not come. His eyes blazed in one final, sobering realization. They pleaded for mercy and begged an answer to the simplest question: *Why?*

It didn't matter. Nothing mattered.

Yet I had to make sure he understood. "You rotten fuck! Did you think you could murder my mom and get away with it?"

I shook under a roiling tremor, an earthquake of anger. I should have been crying for Mom. Why wasn't I crying? Never had such fury engulfed me. I wanted to pummel him, again and again and again and again, as he lay helpless on the street.

"What do you think now, you murdering sonuvabitch? Still feel like laughing it up? How about another drink, you miserable—"

His empty eyes, free of remorse or guilt, unburdened in death, stared back at me.

I'd meted out justice—simple, swift, final.

Now I needed to... to.... I shook off the cobwebs as my neighbors gaped in stunned silence, turned to the right, and—

Oh God. Oh God.

My little brother, Alex, knelt at the edge of our driveway with a face painted in tears, confusion and terror. Just seven years old, he wept alone on the worst of all possible days. My feet were as tree stumps sprouting from the bottoms of my legs, as I shuffled over and crouched before him. All the while, his gaze shifted between Mom's car and me, and he blinked through the tears no dam could contain.

He choked and sputtered, "I... want my... mommy. Where's Mommy? I... I... I want my mommy!"

I could barely whisper, "Me too. I want her too."

I wrapped my arms around him, and he hugged my neck as though he would fall to his death if he let go. Together we unleashed a tsunami of sorrow.

Another thought arrived through the haze: *I killed a man.* I'd thought nothing of it; I'd merely reacted. After witnessing the devastation of that horrible wreckage, the destruction of flesh and bone and tender love, I didn't even care. Yet wrapped in my arms was someone for whom I cared deeply, someone who needed me more than ever.

I stared at my bloodstained hands and clenched my fists to still the shaking.

Oh shit! I killed a man.

It occurred to me that jail would likely be my next stop. Where would my little brother be then? What would be left of his family, his life? He'd witnessed —

Oh God. Hoopster watched me kill a man.

I clutched him to my chest. "Forgive me, Alex. I'm sorry."

Return to June 6, 1995

Frozen forever in time at the age of thirty-six, Mom had given us light and wisdom, warmth and love, a path to guide our way. Who would be our rock now?

My childhood ended with her. What choice did I have? Was I ready?

It hardly mattered.

Law enforcement took rather a cursory glance at me, given both my young age and the circumstances of the event. A state-appointed psychiatrist determined that, in that moment of anguish, and in accordance with strict legal definitions, I was simply insane. Temporary insanity? Sure. Why not?

The psychiatrist thought so, and that was good enough for the judge. They declared me healthy and normal, and sent me home.

Ah yes, home.

Dad floundered and withdrew from Alex and me over the next few months. Our first holiday season without Mom, regrettably, left an indelible scar. The elephant, as they say, was not in the room; only its ghost remained. Mom's absence nearly suffocated us.

Alex's vacant brown eyes and perpetual frown, his continuous soft sigh and the musty smell of sweat and tears on his Scooby-Doo pajamas, the way his chin rested continually on his chest—these left me utterly heartbroken.

I could only pray that the dark Christmas of 1975 would slip into history as the worst I would ever experience. Surely, Dad, Alex and I would recover our happiness, our optimism, as our futures unfolded according to a new plan, albeit a motherless one.

That little executioner's waltz I'd performed on the street in front of our house in August would no doubt be my last dance.

Little did I know: more monsters roamed the world than I'd ever imagined.

They weren't finished with me.

CHAPTER 2
JUNE 6, 1995:
TONY HOOPER

Mitchell Norton, the man I've long considered *the devil*, smiles atop the courthouse steps and waves to the simmering crowd. He tilts his head back to soak in the sunshine and cool breeze of the late spring day, the tranquility of which stands in stark contrast to the circumstances of this event.

The mere sight of him pushes me to the dark edge of my mind, where sanity hangs like... like... like a balloon in a tornado!

I stand in shadow across the street, one amongst many in the crowd of curiosity-hounds gathered to watch a monster's release. As my face blazes, fists clench and teeth grind, I can easily imagine the onset of a stroke, an aneurism, a pulmonary embolism, a raging scream —

Control yourself, Tony!

I long to charge across the street to destroy him — no remorse — as if stepping on a cockroach. Only sheer force of will prevents my doing so.

For seventeen years, I assumed this day would never come. How could they even *consider* releasing this vile creature, this very personification of evil?

In 1978, Norton murdered innocent kids who'd barely tasted of life. He tortured two of them beyond the limits of rational imagination, for to imagine such deeds was to summon a devilry that we dared not face. Yet the jury held him not responsible, a victim himself to the ravages of an illness that drove him to insanity beyond our reckoning.

He thus resides forever in the darkest pit of my psyche, chained to me in perpetuity. Now only two choices remain: I must cast off those chains, or yank them tight around his neck. Yes, I *must* obtain satisfaction. The idiotic jury seventeen years ago, and today's flawed court system, has left little recourse. No one else seems willing to deliver him to justice.

I am willing. After all, this is what I do. It's who I am. Indeed, *the devil* himself made me into this hunter of monsters. What a sweet twist of fate this is, that I may still, finally, administer justice.

He descends the stairs toward his waiting car with an arrogant swagger, watching the small group of protestors, the news reporters, and the police officers here to ensure a peaceful transition, as if to challenge them. His wicked grin never waivers.

Oh, that grin. For seventeen years it has taunted me, punished me for my indecision, my incompetence. I missed my chance to kill him in 1978, to remove his damned head—simple, as if cutting a sheet of paper. It would have been a fitting end for a monster.

Why did I let him live?

Like whispers in a storm, those memories only tease at me now, here at this obscene and maddening event. I'm trying not to relive every moment of 1978. Every time I do, I feel as if swimming in quicksand, anchored by my constant companions—sorrow and guilt. I'm too damned tired; can't shake the confusion, the dread. I fear surrendering to fear.

My life teems with just such wretched ironies.

As Norton vanishes inside a black sedan—looks like standard-issue law enforcement—I dash through the crowds to my van. Despite this call to action, my mind again zeroes-in on memories of 1978. I recall the court proceedings, particularly *the devil's* own twisted testimony, as though it were yesterday. I've only relived it ten thousand times.

Then twenty-six, Norton was a man-child who'd never quite grasped the nuance of adulthood. He continued to wash dishes at a restaurant, ten years into the only job he'd ever held. He found it comfortable and unchallenging—perfect. He harbored no great yearnings, nor imagined exciting possibilities, nor sought lucrative rewards.

Then everything changed. He said that was when his new life emerged, when he became more aware, even more intelligent. He better understood the world around him. He discovered what he called

"The Purpose" in the spring of 1978, and it guided his every deed. He claimed he became *a man* that year.

I remember it quite clearly as the year he became *the devil*.

The words I wrote in my diary at the time return to me, a personal anthem more relevant than ever: *Rage flows like lava through my veins. My soul slowly roasts upon the flames. How did I ever let it come to this?*

Now mortality, as it did seventeen years ago, lingers above me like the hangman's noose. Yet it looms more ominous than ever, as if it will drop down around my neck at any moment. After all, I know the true Mitchell Norton. And whom shall I fear if not *the devil*, the grim torturer who conquered my aspirations and left me without a recognizable world of my own?

Or is it me that I fear? The man I've become? The man Norton made me?

Some fancy maneuvering is required to escape the crowds and the police at the courthouse. I manage to keep Norton in sight, zigzagging between lanes and keeping several vehicles between us, hanging back far enough to avoid detection without losing him. Uncertain emotions bubble up, some indecipherable combination of dread and anticipation, fear and excitement, vengeance and sorrow. I must know where he'll make his home, information that has been difficult to obtain, as the authorities are concerned with Norton's security.

Give me a break! They should express their security concerns not for *the devil* himself, but for his next victims.

Oh yes, I know Norton too well. He *will* torture, murder and dismember again. The temptation will be too great to resist.

I saw him up close in 1978, looked into the soul of *the devil*, as we waded through the blood and gore he'd spilled. I couldn't fathom his unrepentant pleasure, the sick thrill, his gleeful anticipation.

Now he's out of prison, again free to call up his demons, to torture the innocent, to waltz to what he once called his "symphony of screams."

The devil walks the world again.

What shall I do about it? Aye, what indeed.

PART 2

REBIRTH

CHAPTER 3
APRIL 20, 1978:
MITCHELL NORTON

Where is this strange place? Am I flyin' over it? What's he gonna do to that woman? Who is he? Maybe the better question is; what is he? I ain't no kid anymore, don't believe in monsters under the bed or demons in the closet, but.... The way he's lookin' at me gives me the fuckin' shivers. I think he... I ain't sure, but... does he want me to watch?

The woman is lyin' on a table – naked. I like that, sure enough, but I don't think I like the rest of it. Her wide eyes never blink, and her body bounces up and down like she's havin' some kinda convulsions. Sweat pours down her face and her ratty hair looks like she ain't washed it in a month. Somethin' horrible is goin' on, but fuck if I know what it is.

The demon, if that's what he is, wheels a cart over next to the table. The cart holds a bunch of weapons and tools – knives, saws, drills, scalpels, hammers and clamps.

Is he gonna perform surgery on her? He ain't no fuckin' doctor. His leathery face, his black grin, his eyes like coals from a furnace, all point to.... Fuck! I don't know, but whatever he's gonna do, I'm pretty sure he ain't plannin' to use anesthesia. He's droolin' and lickin' his chops.

He grabs a knife the size of my foot, looks up at me, and laughs. The woman screams in a high-pitched wail that pierces my ears like someone stuck a goddamn ice pick in my fuckin' brain. He moves alongside her and raises the knife like he's –

"Wait! What are you doin'?" I yell as loud as I can, but he ignores me.

He grabs her wrist and lashes down with the knife, and she screams again as blood spurts onto the floor. He turns to me, holdin' somethin' up in his hands. It's hard to see, but I think it could be a –

"My God, why did you do that?"

He roars with laughter and tosses her finger off to the side like so much trash, and walks around to the other side of the table. His eyes blaze and he smiles, exposin' long teeth that end in a point like icicles.

My head feels like someone is crushin' it in a vice. I can't believe this is happenin'. What is this place? Why can't I get out? I gotta get help. I don't wanna watch this, but I can't seem to turn away.

Holy shit, he's feelin' up her tits! How can he do that after he —

Wait, what in hell is he doin'? He's squeezin' and pullin' up with his right hand, and raisin' the knife with his left hand, like —

"Hey, what are you doin'? Stop! Stop, damn it! You can't — "

This fuckin' house of horror ruptures in an endless, stabbing scream. Blood flies everywhere like a crimson swarm from hell. The demon's gaze bores through me again, and drool drips from his dagger-like teeth as he raises his new trophy above his head.

He points his twisted finger at me. "Soon, you'll do this, Mitchell."

My blood freezes in my veins. I can't move. I can't speak.

"If you refuse, I'll put you on this table next."

God help me.

He reaches back with his right arm, like he's on a baseball mound and windin' up for his next pitch, but that ain't no fuckin' baseball in his hand. It's his new trophy, the bloody remains of what was once so appealing and —

"Here, Mitchell, catch!"

I bolted up and looked around the dark room — *my* room, *my* bed — and could almost breathe again. The cold, soaked sheets turned my body into a shivering, chattering heap.

Why did the nightmares continue to assault me? Who was that demon, and why wouldn't he leave me alone? I didn't know but—

Fuck a rubber duck! What did he mean when he said I'd be doin' that soon?

CHAPTER 4
APRIL 22, 1978:
TONY HOOPER

"Man is the only animal that laughs and weeps, for he is the only animal that is struck by the difference between what things are and what they might have been." – *William Hazlitt*

Sunlight glistened off the surface of the lake, still as a mirror, as the cloudless sky stood sentry. The spring morning harkened me back to childhood, when the blustery weather broke and we couldn't wait to get outside to play tag, catch-one/catch-all, or Batman and Robin. I thought differently now, but those memories were no less vivid, no less uplifting.

A sheer, seventy-foot wall occupied the south end of the quarry, which had officially closed three decades ago. A narrow ledge wound down to a level spot less than two feet above the waterline, where Diana and I sat. The remarkably clear, spring-fed lake wafted a faint metallic aroma that reminded me of... I couldn't place it—something that made my stomach clench.

The water swirled in ever-broadening circles around my feet, which were submerged in the reflection of my cheeks. I leaned farther over the ledge, came almost face-to-face with myself, as if the reflected me would provide some of the answers I so desperately sought.

Diana pulled me back to the moment. "Be careful," she said. "You're liable to fall into the lake." The cool temperatures and bright sun had joined forces to paint her cheeks a rosy shade of unbearably cute.

I leaned back and let the sun work its springtime magic. The season was supposed to inspire rebirth, renewal, grand dreams and revived hopes—at least according to much of the poetry I read. I aspired to such promises, yet couldn't escape the relentless melancholy. Nothing new there.

It had built throughout the winter, as if I'd been buried in an avalanche. Each time I'd dug away three inches of snow, four new inches sealed my frozen tomb.

Shit! Don't be so melodramatic all the time, Tony. Focus on Diana.

The extraordinary Miss Gregario, perhaps the future Mrs. Hooper, dominated my thoughts. We'd met at our dads' company picnic the previous Fourth of July; they were accountants with the same firm. I'd seen her around school before then, but we hadn't actually met prior to the picnic. I'd surprised myself when I mustered the courage to ask her out, as I tended to be shy about such matters. I'd bumbled my way through it with a tongue twisted into nervous paralysis, made a complete fool of myself, and she accepted!

Whenever I contemplated the prospect of life without her, I wanted to vomit. We *fit* together. I told her I was the night and she was the stars, and that she brought an unimaginable light to my life. That made me a walking, talking cliché straight out of the classical novels I read but, what the hell, a little *corny* never killed anybody.

She was my first and only love, and when I departed for college in a few months, I'd leave her behind. Every time I pondered my future, platoons of emotions waged war within me. Even at that moment, the battle thundered in my chest and a wrenching lump bounced like a cannonball in my throat.

How will I—

"Happy birthday, Baby," she said. "I still can't believe you wanted to spend it *here*, although it *is* pretty."

I smiled, unsure how to broach the subject weighing me down.

"The big *eighteen*. Wow. So how does it feel to be a man? Well, in the eyes of the law, at any rate."

I snorted. "Oh sure, and where have they been for the last three years?"

I didn't mean to take out my frustration on her. She knew that, and took it in stride. Hell, she knew me better than I knew myself.

In one of my customary fits of introspection, I'd wanted to go there to take measure of the moment, to examine my new manhood. I thought I might enjoy some time alone on my birthday. Perhaps *enjoy* was not the right word. No matter, for Diana would hear none of it. She'd insisted that I spend the day with, as she put it, "the most magnificent girlfriend the world has ever known."

I couldn't argue with the "magnificent" part, and it was apparently some kind of unwritten law that she must share the "big day" with me. I didn't know which was funnier: her words, her goofy smile and Groucho Marx eyebrow shuffle, or the ridiculous way she'd curtsied.

She squeezed my hand until I looked at her again. "You're having another one of your moments, aren't you? Pondering the changes coming up, contemplating the meaning of life, the expanse of the universe, the—"

"I love this place, especially in summer. We weren't dating long enough last summer to come out here, but I think you'll like it. This is *the* hotspot."

"What does everybody do here? Besides swim, of course."

"You name it, somebody does it here. We bring food and pop, maybe a few beers—make a day of it."

"That sounds like fun."

"Some of the kids smoke like chimneys out here, or do drugs."

"Yuck!"

"Don't worry. We'll stay away from that stuff." I loved that we shared those values. "Then, of course, there's the skinny-dipping and the sex."

"Oh my! I'll have you know that I'm a lady, sir. I'm no exhibitionist." She leaned in and kissed me. "Except with you."

She skipped her usual seductive playfulness and leaned back. She knew I wasn't in that place, that frame of mind.

She laid her head on my shoulder. "Don't you guys ever worry about your parents catching you?"

"Nah, they don't come here."

I didn't know if this place was such a big secret, or if the older folks just didn't want to deal with the half-mile hike through the brush and trees to get there from the nearest street. At any rate, they didn't bother us, which made it a popular escape spot for teenagers.

This figured to be my last summer here, and I could hardly look at Diana for fear my emotions would get away from me. She wisely refrained from dangling her feet in the lake, but I couldn't resist. The early spring water chilled my toes into dead stumps, even as the noon sun baked my face. I loved the contrast: perfect metaphors for the forces pushing and pulling at me those days.

She sighed and placed her hand on my chest. "Summer will be here before we know it."

It's time.

I maintained a light tone. "Yeah, feels like I've been waiting forever to graduate. Then I get to have one last carefree summer before...."

She squeezed my hand again. She was a year behind me, a junior.

Her voice thickened. "You're supposed to be happy, you know. It's a big event, a fun time."

"I know."

"But...."

"I know I'm supposed to feel excited about college, about my freedom, about a whole new world full of potential and adventure. Part of me... hell, I can't wait to see it. I've earned it!"

"But...."

"I hardly know where to begin." I pulled my hand from hers and laid my arm around her shoulders. "For one thing, I've been taking care of Alex for three years. He's my Shadow, and he doesn't have anyone else."

"What about your dad?"

I huffed and almost laughed.

Alex was a bright kid, enthusiastic and determined—my little man. I often told him he was a grown-up trapped in a kid's body. He loved that. I liked it too, although I knew better. He may have acted older, but he *was* just ten years old. The way he followed me around, I often worried that people would think I had him on a leash. It irritated the hell out of me.

Well, it did. Until Mom died.

Somewhere along the way, I'd become more than his big brother; I was his best buddy, hero and idol. I'd never meant for such a thing to happen, but no sense in denying it.

I stared down at the water. "I don't know what to do about Alex. Dad wants to be a good father, but since Mom died, he's been way out of his element. He escapes in his work. He's more comfortable there than at home, dealing with two kids by himself. Not exactly father of the year."

She admonished me with a stunned expression.

"I know, I know. I hate to say such a thing about my own father, but I can't help it. You haven't seen the real Hank Hooper over the last three years. Trust me, if I walk away from Alex, I'll be leaving him largely to his own devices."

I longed for the simpler, carefree days unencumbered by the baggage of adulthood: the expectations, the worries, the pressures. I wanted to ride my bike on sunny days, play baseball all day long at the park, or teach Alex the finer points of basketball. I yearned for the simple distraction of my baseball card collection, or to crank up the stereo and sing along, pretending to the throne of stardom. I rarely did those things anymore — too old for that stuff, anyway.

"Shit! It's not fair." I hated whining, *especially* when it was my own voice.

My mother, in dying; my father, in retreating; my brother, in needing: each had conspired to take from me a sizable chunk of that which I could never regain: my childhood.

Bluch! I gazed once more into the water, and my own reflection mocked me. What right did I have to wax in self-pity and selfish examination of events over which I had so little control, yet over which I was willing to assign so much blame?

The look on Diana's face drove a stake in my heart.

I squeezed her tighter, and almost lost my words in the depths of her scent. "And what shall I do about you? How in the world am I supposed to live without you?"

"It's only for a year, and you'll be able to come home for the holidays." Her unsteady voice belied her optimistic reassurances.

"A year is a long time."

She kissed me on the ear. "We'll make it."

The frigid water numbed my feet. The endless questions without answers numbed my mind.

I'd always viewed the world through what my mom had called my "looking glass." Why must it be so cloudy, so fragile? Why must I wallow in that melancholy introspection all the time? Perhaps Mom had been right: I read too much; I thought too much; I too often lost myself in deep contemplation. She'd once claimed that when Rodin created his famous sculpture, *Le Penseur*, he must have had *me* in mind.

I'd have loved to talk to her about it. God, I missed her.

I should have just goofed off like the other kids, and had fun. I should have stopped playing Atlas, carrying the weight of the world on my shoulders.

Shit! More melodrama? Knock it off and relax, already.

CHAPTER 5

MAY 3, 1978:

MITCHELL NORTON

I never understood why people worried about dreams. I'd dreamt my whole life—everyone did—but I never could remember any of the details. Until recently, that was. All of a sudden, I couldn't think about nothing else—terrible, horrifying nightmares. It turned out that not being able to remember dreams weren't such a bad thing.

They might'a been more like visions—hard to tell. I'd go to this place in my dreams, a "realm filled with unimaginable suffering." That's what the demon that lived there called it. He said he was preparing to impose evil upon the earth, and that he'd arrive on the wings of agony and the roar of death.

Yeah, whatever the fuck that meant.

Nobody else strolled in the park. It weren't exactly a park, just a little grassy area with a walkway and a few benches—didn't even have a name. I liked to dangle my fingers in the river and think about stuff, although.... *Phew!* That weren't no rose garden. More like a pile of wet leaves baking in the sun, maybe a dead skunk flattened alongside the road, or our septic tank that had overflowed last August. More like all three, mixed into a vile liquid called the Fox River.

I rubbed my fingers on my pants. "I can't believe people swim in this shit!"

At least the bench was comfortable, the sun that perfect blast of springtime warm. This was the best time of year.

"Man, I'm so fuckin' tired."

I was still recovering from last night, like someone had beaten the ever-livin' shit outta me while I slept—typical, pretty much a daily occurrence. Amazing I didn't have any bruises, the way I felt. And my head! This weren't no little headache, this eye-popping, paralyzing, someone-parked-a-Mack-truck-on-my-fuckin'-skull headache.

I rested my head on the back of the bench and closed my eyes. I could almost see the sun right through my eyelids, a reddish-gold weave.

"Man, I'm so fuckin' tired. I should...."

My whole body shivers as an army of goosebumps marches up and down my skin. I could swear the river, the Beast, has reached up and clutched me by the throat.

"Yes, I know you are the Beast. I saw it in my dream last night. The voice told me you would be important to me. I used to think you were just a river, but I'm beginnin' to understand. I now see everything differently."

Maybe I see life correctly for the first time, shedding at last the timid, naïve costume that was Mitchell Norton. A new era is mine, one of greater understanding and power. If only I could drown the persistent fear, feed it to the Beast.

"I bet you like the taste of fear. Do you have a soul? What drives you? The voice said you would be my brother in evil."

Now that my senses have grown sharper, I long to see into the river's heart. The whole world has changed, and I've taken notice almost in spite of myself. I'm eager to grasp the true meaning of the world's follies.

"Follies? What the fuck! Where do these thoughts come from? Why, all of a sudden, am I smarter than ever before? Have I always been smart? Am I merely awakened, and, if so, why?"

The Beast doesn't answer. I don't care. I like it. Understanding gives me the power to see the truth, to see things others don't, like my newest friend here.

Cruel and determined, it no longer nourishes life as it once did. It is without remorse, for it is nearly dead, and the dead needn't suffer such trivialities.

"Hoo-wee! There's a word for you. Trivialities!"

The river runs wild and leaves in its wake the reek of many silent, screaming corpses. The constant hum of traffic on the nearby bridge, the insignificant human ritual, mutes its roar. Beneath the bridge, the Beast churns in anticipation of the nearby dam and gathers speed to make its powerful leap over the wall, for it is wise. It flees its self.

I remember the story from last summer, of the arrogant boy who decided to test his swimming skills in the water too near the bridge. Oh, the thrill of that adrenaline-charged moment, when he surrendered to the chill of realization, anticipating his inevitable outcome.

The surface waters, though treacherous, breed no fear. Therein lays the Beast's true genius: the dangerous thing waits within, silent and eager.

My mind's eye sees everything so clearly.

The swimmer dangled his legs in the black depths, unaware of, or unconcerned with, the thing that lurked within, that prepared to seize him and drag him below. What an ignorant fool.

The invisible serpent from the deep grasped the unsuspecting boy and bid him "welcome" to its murky lair. The kid tumbled through the corridors of its domain in terror and in burgeoning agony. He struggled desperately for the surface and its promise of life, but the impotent kid dangled and bobbed like a human marionette.

The Beast grinned; such pleasant exercises fortified it.

It carried the boy to the end of its corridor where, like pitching human trash, it heaved him over the dam and into the churning pit. In that instant, with lungs ready to implode and hope nearly lost, the kid caught a single breath of air, a glimmer of hope, a renewed confidence.

Yet the game played on.

The Beast followed him over the edge and, like the hand of Poseidon, pressed him hard against the bottom. The violence in the pit overwhelmed him, as though he boxed a dozen heavyweights simultaneously. He suffered a constant series of blows to the head, to the body, and back to the head – relentless, powerful. It jabbed and jabbed and – Wham! – a wicked cross. A mean and determined fighter, it held the boy down with one hand and pummeled him with a dozen others.

The Beast's helpless toy could not resist its formidable strength.

It delighted in the boy's panic as he kicked and squirmed. It reveled in his terror, grew anxious as he wearily approached submission and, finally, basked in the glory and exhilaration of victory as it poured itself into the boy's lungs, and as life poured out of his feeble body.

Many have drowned at the dam in the Fox River, in my beloved Algonquin, despite the constant warnings to stay clear. Every year, one or two sports insist on sacrificing themselves to the pleasure of the unliving Beast. What a shame that, on this cool day in May, no swimmers will entertain my new friend and me.

I can't help but smile, all the same, for the impending summer promises a bounty of treacherous possibilities. Potential sacrifices linger in every corner of town.

"What the hell!" Sweat soaked my shirt and pasted my back to the bench. The park remained empty. "Fuck a rubber duck! What's with these goddamn dreams?"

I shook my head and banged it with both hands—a stranger to myself. One moment I was the same old Mitchell Norton: quiet, happy, unassuming, and, as my dad liked to say, "content to drift through life in a soup of uneventful ignorance."

The next moment I was judge, jury and executioner.

I couldn't remember exactly when it began, and I sure as hell didn't know *why* it began. I knew who was responsible, though—the demon. The Reaper. He'd told me so in my dream the night before, said I was special—supposed to be a judge in the Dark Minion's court, whatever the fuck that meant.

I lay across the bench and closed my eyes. My head pounded again.

"Son of a French whore, just what I fuckin' needed!"

I rubbed my temples, trying to remember a more peaceful time.

"Shit! I can't think straight."

A black shroud smothered my mind's eye and robbed me of its precious view. I saw only emptiness. The goosebumps returned. My lips wouldn't stop quivering. I weren't asleep, but I weren't quite awake either. I drifted somewhere in between, desperate to escape this place—dark, dangerous, disturbing.

Here comes the judge.

"Shit!"

The terrible voice echoed in my mind again—the Reaper—but I couldn't see him. I *never* saw him. I saw only flames, and burning images that wouldn't leave me in peace.

"What do you want from me?"

You know what I want, Mitchell.

"Yes, but I'm afraid."

You'll do fine. Trust me.

"Fuck a rubber duck."

PART 3
THE HUNT

CHAPTER 6
MAY 12, 1978:
MITCHELL NORTON

I was so sick and fuckin' tired of this scene: I sat on the edge of my bed and massaged the sides of my head, where it felt like an elephant had plopped his fat ass all night. Most people would have considered it late in the morning, but who gave a shit what they thought! I worked nights and usually didn't get to sleep until three or four in the morning, so it weren't no big fuckin' deal if I slept until noon.

Recently my nights hadn't been nothin' but fitful, distressing attempts to sleep, what my dad liked to call an "exercise in futility." That's what he called *my life*. What a shithead.

I often awoke from too little sleep with a splitting headache, confused about everything that happened in the dark hours, where the Reaper prowled—a mad hunter, and fuck a rubber duck if I weren't the prey. Who was he, and why did he pursue me? Beat all hell outta me, but I recognized his pure evil. He was capable of hideous, unspeakable acts—no hesitation, no pity, no remorse.

He spoke in vile words, and performed such wicked deeds that even the strongest man would cry his fuckin' eyes out, and I weren't that strong. He carried me to distant worlds where the people writhed in pain and misery. I didn't understand, but he tried to explain it last night.

For those who suffer such misery on others, the rule of the realm is pure delight. You too will reap the rewards, Mitchell. The unmistakable look of death will be upon you, and it will be a joyful grin, indeed.

Right, whatever the fuck that meant.

I struggled to keep my eyes closed when he took me, but my mind's eye zoomed into every horrifying scene. If I opened my eyes, I could piss him off, and he'd treat me like one of those wretched souls made to suffer "endless agony and unimaginable misery." The Reaper might'a become a real, physical being, free to reach out and touch me in dreadful ways—he hadn't done that... yet. If I opened my eyes, the vicious bastard wouldn't be a simple trick of the mind, but an honest-to-God, kick-you-right-in-the-teeth monster.

As long as I kept my eyes closed, that weren't gonna happen. He'd stay locked up in my nightmares. I hoped.

"Shit! Who am I kidding? What am I gonna do?"

I rubbed around my eyes and dragged myself outta bed. I desperately needed relief for my head, which felt like someone had split it with a fuckin' axe. I trudged to the bathroom and knocked on the door.

Tommy, my little brother, opened the door and pretended to be foaming at the mouth. "Grrrrr." He snorted and giggled at his toothpaste trick, which he considered clever and hilarious.

I rolled my eyes and reached past him into the medicine cabinet, and pulled out a bottle of aspirin—sweet relief. I'd been eatin' that shit like candy lately.

Tommy finished his business like I weren't even there. Officially an adult, a strong and otherwise healthy eighteen-year-old, he was still slow in the head, on an even par with most nine-year-olds. I snickered at his exaggerated brush strokes, not to mention the ridiculous gob of toothpaste he used.

Most people made me feel like shit-on-a-stick, something they scraped off the bottoms of their shoes, but not my little brother. I always felt right around good old Tommy, and I didn't mind watchin' over him while our parents were away from home.

He liked to call me the MAN, which stood for Mitchell Andrew Norton. He played that simple game to occupy his mind and help him remember people's names. He was quick to tell others that he was TEN, for Thomas Edward Norton, but it confused them. They always thought he'd announced his age, though he was obviously much older. He was also obviously slow, so people shrugged it off, smiled politely, and ignored him.

The curse for folks like Tommy: people ignored them. Sometimes it broke my heart. Mostly I wanted to stick a fork in their eye. I swore

I'd beat the snot outta the next fuckhead that called him a *retard*. He might'a been one, but that weren't for them shitburgers to say.

I leaned over the kitchen table and chased down three aspirin with a glass of grape Kool-Aid, Tommy's personal favorite. He drank about a gallon a day. I'd have preferred a shot of bourbon to wash them down, but it was too early for my Jimmy Beam. Maybe later.

I massaged my head and attempted to defeat my headache through the sheer power of determination.

"Yeah, that should work."

A small, tender lump jutted out above my left ear.

"Shit! Twenty-six years old and I'm still fighting zits. Are you fuckin' kidding me?"

My mind drifted into a foggy nowhere land, a place I visited a lot these days. It always made me think of that Beatle's song, *Nowhere Man*.

Yeah, sounded like me, making a bunch of nowhere plans for nobody. My mental strength, admittedly quite improved lately, had diminished for the moment. This sleep deprivation had drained me and turned me into milktoast again. I couldn't fuckin' concentrate.

Too bad. My newfound intellectual... *prowess* was... *invigorating*.

Some kind'a distraction sounded good, a little relaxation, an escape from the boring grind. I needed some fuckin' excitement!

CHAPTER 7
MAY 12, 1978:
TONY HOOPER

I leaned back and rested my head on the seat of my old 1967 Pontiac Bonneville—my "Bonnie"—as I waited in Diana's driveway. I'd honked my horn and she'd waved from her bedroom window to indicate she'd be out in five minutes—ten minutes ago. No matter. I'd have waited hours to get a glimpse of her, a whiff of her scent, a taste of her mouth. The delay was my fault, anyway; I'd arrived early—again—anxious and desperate to see her.

"Come on, Diana. Hurry up, would you?"

I couldn't help but think of the coming changes again—college almost a thousand miles away. I didn't know if Diana and I would survive the separation, or even if we *should*. The next stage of my life awaited me, and perhaps I should move on and never look back.

"It's what people do, isn't it?"

The yellow stain on old Bonnie's roof didn't answer me.

"No, I can't do that. I *won't*."

We had to think it through, figure out a way to remain together, even if it meant we only saw each other during holidays and school breaks. I needed to draw on a little faith.

"Faith? Sure, Tony, and why don't you sprout some wings and fly, while you're at it?"

I wanted to hold her and kiss her, activities that always washed away all the bad thoughts in the world. It was so damned easy—*inevitable*—for me to get lost in her. Ours had been a mutual journey of discovery, a vivid film that would play forever in my mind.

It had started when we first held hands, soared when we first kissed, and been etched in stone when we first made love. The frenzied ecstasy of that moment had affirmed all that I'd imagined from song and poetry, yet the emotionally-charged nature of the event had astonished me. My heart rocketed from my chest and launched me into a delicious world I never wanted to leave. Our bond thus consummated, our love thus resolved for all time, I couldn't imagine how it would affect me, or believe it possible that I could love her more deeply than I already did.

We were now and forever two parts of one whole. Nothing in the universe could compare to that, or —

"Hi, Sweetie, sorry I took so long."

Her sudden entry into the car startled me from my daydream. In adherence to her usual practice, she slid next to me, leaned over for a kiss, slipped her hand into my crotch, and squeezed. Her perfumed skin and minty mouth were like a taste of water after days in the desert.

She squeezed more insistently. "Oh, my goodness, what's that?"

Why, that's something I made just for you, my lady.

Her expression was right out of *Soap Opera 101.*

I almost wanted her to stop rubbing me. Almost. "I was thinking about our first time together. I don't know why. It just came to me."

What a smile!

Her mahogany hair flew loosely and settled halfway down her back, and her eyes teased in an intense hazel inferno. Her mere proximity was almost more than I could bear. The only thing worse would have been her absence.

Our plans involved meeting most of our senior class at a park for "Senior Ditch Day." The teachers and administrators knew about it, yet they'd apparently chosen to look the other way and make no issue of it. After all, most of them had participated in this bold and venerable tradition in their day.

Although Diana was only a junior, she was welcome as my girlfriend. She seemed to have other ideas presently, however, and if she continued to rub me as she did, *where* she did, I was liable to jump right through Bonnie's roof.

Never one to miss the perfect opportunity for a romantic gesture, I pulled a sheet of paper from my shirt pocket and unfolded it. "I wrote this for you last night."

"For me?"

She spread the sheet on her lap, and I quoted it in my mind as she read it.

> For Diana, my inspiration:
>
> In your reflective eyes, I see the future for which I long. In your smile, I see the light that guides my way. In your loving consideration and generosity, I see the thrill of hope. In your intelligence and love affair with humor, I see the joy of great potential. I see everything in you. Without you, I am blind.
>
> All my love, Tony

She pressed her lips against my ear and whispered, "We could be a little late to the picnic, you know."

Those words, coupled with her tongue probing my ear, were seductive enough. But the look on her face! This wasn't my intention. I'd wanted to let her know, in proper terms, how I felt about her. Yet how could I resist? One might as well have asked me to stop breathing.

I choked down the lump that had returned to my throat. "Absolutely!"

I steered Bonnie with my left hand as Diana nestled beside me and snuggled my right hand in her lap. Bliss lay over us like a down comforter. An enervating aroma—perfume, deodorant, sweat, and a musky, bittersweet reminder of recent activities—whirled me into recollections of this morning. I allowed it to sink in, afraid that words might overwhelm the sensory delight. Diana appeared to be of similar mind, with a gentle smile and a far-off gaze. I conjured tremendous determination, all the force of my will, to keep my eyes off her and on the road.

I would graduate in four weeks, and we'd spend one last summer vacation together before I departed for college in North Carolina. After that, who knew?

Shit!

I crashed down from the high I'd just experienced. Lately, such thoughts invaded and spoiled even the best of moments. I couldn't escape them; they bled me like leeches in the Fox River, determined to ruin an otherwise enjoyable experience.

Damn it! Why must I constantly be my own worst enemy? Knock it off!

My gloom dissipated as I turned into Flora Park for today's big event. Several of my classmates already whooped it up. I parked the car and rejoiced in Diana's laughter as she responded to Tom Coronado's antics. My good friend wore a "beer hat" and danced around like a six-foot-four-inch leprechaun in lead boots.

Tom and I had conspired to invent the beer hat at a party last New Year's Eve. Those party hats with the tight elastic chinstraps had inspired us, but instead of a conical hat, we'd strapped on a plastic cup containing as much beer as one dare place on top of one's head. Poorly balanced, it posed a high risk of spillage — the whole point of the game.

Diana hooked my arm and slid out of my side of the car while Tom danced his exaggerated slow jig up to greet us.

He offered his best Irish brogue. "Top o' de fine morn, an' a hardy welcome to ye."

He shook my hand and bowed, the preplanned result of which is the emptying of his beer hat down the front of my tee shirt. I saw it coming, but he'd trapped me against the car and I was unable to evade the spill. Everyone around got a good laugh, including me, who'd dressed with such a possibility in mind.

I played along. "Why, thank you, sir. You are a gentleman, a scholar, and a drunken bum." It was the proper response according to the rules of our game.

He became Winston Churchill. "Tit-tit, no need for that, what. I don't allow just anyone to call me a gentleman, you know."

"Please accept my sincere apologies, Lord Bum of Drunkenness."

Like a rock star from the British Invasion, he said, "Hip-hip, right-o, and all that rot."

The game thus played, party time ensued. We joined a few others who had gathered for Tom's performance, and meandered to where the rest of our group, about fifty kids, had set up.

Tom leaned down and pulled three cans of Old Style beer from a cooler. Two nineteen-year-olds in our group, being of legal drinking age, had taken up a collection yesterday, and we'd stocked up for a long party. The cops, much like the school administration, appeared to be looking the other way.

Tom handed two cans to Diana and me. "Here you go, kids. Drink up."

"Geez, you guys didn't waste any time getting sloshed." I shrugged my shoulders at Diana, who rolled her eyes and smiled.

"Don't be a wimp, Tony-Boy." He chugged half a can and expelled a burp for the ages. "Ah, breakfast of champions."

Diana laughed. "Real nice, Tom."

"Thank you, my dear, I do try." He turned to me again. "Well?"

"All right, all right, hold your horses." I popped the top off the can and took a deep breath. "Well, shit, here goes nothin'."

Diana finished talking with several other girls about whatever girls talked about, and jogged over. She plopped onto the blanket and tackled me.

"Kiss me, my prince."

"You wouldn't be getting a little tipsy, would you?" I grabbed her ass and grinded her to me.

"Yep, and happy."

"I'll drink to that."

"Not until you kiss me."

We kissed to the edge of indecency, and my hands became bolder by the second, but she pulled away and hopped up from the blanket. "I've got to go talk with Emily."

Oh sure, leave me here holding my — "If you must." I admired the view below her tied-up yellow shirt as she scooted away. She kindly threw in a couple hip flourishes.

About thirty yards beyond her, on the edge of another picnic area, two guys played catch with a Frisbee—one about our age, the other in his mid-twenties. The older one fixed his gaze upon Diana. It happened often and I tried to compose myself when it did, but it put me a little on edge. The younger one joined the festivities, and said something to the older one, who pointed toward Diana and me.

I sat up straight and my gut clenched as I squinted to bring them into better focus. Something about the older one's face bothered me — his demeanor, his pointing, his smirk.

Come on, Tony, jealousy is not your most attractive quality. Relax. No sense worrying about some harmless ogling. Let him have his fun.

I didn't want to spoil the day over nothing.

Tom wobbled in my direction with two more beers in hand, and a look on his face as if to say, *I'm gonna get you drunk, Tony-Boy.* I laughed and glanced one last time at the two voyeurs.

Screw 'em! They weren't hurting anyone. No harm, no foul.

CHAPTER 8
MAY 12, 1978:
MITCHELL NORTON

"A covetous man does nothing well 'til he dies." – *Thomas Wilson*

Tommy and I often went to Flora Park to toss around a football or, as we did now, a Frisbee. He was surprisingly good at it. I was decent enough too, when not constantly distracted. A girl wearing cut-off jean shorts and a yellow shirt tied up in the midsection, exposing her belly button and much of her shapely stomach, broke my concentration. Talk about built!

Why must girls expose themselves so... provocatively? Don't they know how that drives men out of their –

"What are you looking at, Mitchell?"

Tommy, the intruder, broke into hysterical laughter over my exaggerated leap in the air.

"I scared you, huh, Mitchell? I scared you good!"

He made a spectacle of himself, jumping up and down, laughing and clapping his hands. I attempted to calm him by assuring him that he was the "Champion Scarer of All Time." He stopped his antics to consider this new title, which he accepted with pride. Good old Tommy.

I returned my attention to the girl, who tackled her apparent boyfriend on the blanket where he sat. She kissed him, and he traced his hand down her back and grabbed her ass! I grinded my teeth and my head hammered me again.

Fuck it! I got better things to think about. "She is one seriously hot babe, Tommy."

He looked around the park like he'd just landed here from Neptune. "Who is?"

I pointed to her. "The girl over there on the left, wearing the yellow shirt."

He located her, barely smiled and shrugged—hardly a ringing endorsement. Despite his physical age, he didn't understand or appreciate the splendors of the opposite sex. Even I had limited experience in that realm, a circumstance I hoped to remedy.

Soon. Real soon.

"Tommy-boy, I'd sure like to spend some quality time with a girlfriend like that."

"You could do it. You could have any pretty girlfriend you want."

"You think so?"

"Sure. Hey, you're the MAN!"

Good old Tommy—had to love him. I'd been with only two girls, both prostitutes, but I expected that would change soon. Why shouldn't it? Everything else was changing.

The girl in yellow played around while visions flashed through my mind—visions of power and pain, of possibilities.

"Maybe you're right, Tommy-boy. We'll have to see."

I'd taken Tommy home and treated myself to a nap, but rather than waking up fresh and renewed, I awoke feeling like someone had bulldozed my ass while I slept.

I massaged my head in the hopes of easing another of my fast-becoming-famous headaches, and when I rubbed the zit, my head damn near exploded. I should have popped that disgusting thing before it turned into Mount Everest behind my ear. I also awoke with memories of demon-laden dreams, my other common occurrence these days.

At least I enjoyed one good thought: an image of me with my newfound angel. I left Tommy with Mom and returned to the park.

I couldn't get the girl in yellow outta my head. She played with her friends like she didn't have a care in the world. I sat in my lawn chair, placed strategically between and behind the front seats of my van, and relaxed. No one would see me here.

She filled the lenses of my binoculars, like I could reach out and touch her.

I wonder what you would say, sweet thing, if you knew of my... violation.

The sun dipped below the trees on the west end of the park, and I struggled to keep the binoculars focused on my spectacular subject. She stopped goofing around and rejoined her boyfriend, and they kissed. He grabbed her ass again, and they practically mauled each other.

I lowered the binoculars and stared at the floor between my feet. I didn't know that other man—that kid—but I sure wanted to rip the fucker's heart out and feed it to the crows. Then I could take a shot at the girl and make her mine.

I grinded my teeth and intensified my headache—again. "Shit! Just what I fuckin' needed."

Another girl yelled from three cars over. "Diana, stop fooling around with Tony and get your butt over here!"

Several girls gathered around that car and giggled, no doubt sharing the latest gossip. My prize in yellow stood, laughed, and jogged over to join them.

Well then, your boyfriend's name is Tony, and your name is Diana—a good name for a heavenly babe.

I slid farther back in the van to ensure the girls wouldn't see me, rested my head on the back of the lawn chair, and closed my eyes. I needed to beat this fuckin' headache. Thoughts of my angel substituted for my usual three aspirin and a shot of bourbon.

Yeah, that's good.

My mind wandered again—foggy, drifting.

She smiles and holds my hand in a vast field of fragrant flowers. We lie against one another, naked and warm, and kiss. I trace her every contour and soft curve with my gentle fingers, until I touch her at last where I've rarely touched a woman. Her radiant moisture pushes me to the edge of frenzy. She accepts me and I plunge deeper into bliss with every quiver of her body, every gentle rhythm of her movement, every pleasurable moan. Seconds turn to minutes, and minutes turn to heaven without time. She calls my name and screams, and suddenly a tidal wave washes over us as —

"What the fuck!"

I jerked my head forward and opened my eyes. I'd thought I held Diana, but that weren't *her* in my right hand. I had no idea how long I'd been at it; hadn't been aware that I *was* at it. I couldn't even remember dropping my pants.

I peered through the windshield and breathed a sigh of relief; I didn't think anyone could have seen me. A crumpled rag from the floor of the van sufficed to clean away the results of my activity, but I needed a shower.

"I'll need some fresh clothes, damn it! I can't believe I was jerking—"

I glanced around the park again.

"I wonder if the van was rocking."

This was not what I'd had in mind when I put that bumper sticker on the back door: *If the van's a-rockin', don't come a-knockin'.* The embarrassment faded and I hopped back into the driver's seat to—

Shit! I strained through the advancing darkness to find the special angel in yellow who had so fired my imagination. The crowd had thinned out to a few stragglers.

"She's gone! How will I follow her and discover where she lives? I couldn't have been distracted for *that* long. Do I have the worst fuckin' luck, or what?"

My gut rolled over and shook.

"Mitchell, if you didn't have shit for brains, you'd have no fuckin' brains at all!"

I vice-gripped the steering wheel with both hands and plunked my head down on top of them. I closed my eyes and strained to concentrate through the marching band blasting inside my skull.

"Fuck a rubber duck! What am I gonna do now?"

I had considerable experience with this kind of shit—insecurity, inferiority—but that hardly comforted.

I remembered my first glimpse of Diana, arriving in that big, slightly dinged old car. I didn't know the make, but I might have recognized it if....

I scanned the parking lot.

"Shit."

My queasy jitters returned, and my renewed sense of hope went up in fuckin' smoke. The car had vanished, and with it my latest, greatest dream.

"What now?" My pathetic whine served as an unpleasant reminder of my former, dumbass self.

A familiar voice boomed deep inside my head. *The car, Mitchell, find it, no matter how far you must go, no matter how long it takes, for it will surely lead you to the angel and your own slice of paradise.*

"Yeah! How hard can it be to find a car in this fuckin' hick town?"

You can do it, Mitchell.

"You think so?"

Hey, you're the MAN!

CHAPTER 9
JUNE 6, 1995:
TONY HOOPER

I followed *the devil* from the courthouse to his destination, so perfectly natural that I might have guessed it. Where else would Mitchell Norton go after getting out of prison but back home? His father, who'd referred to Mitchell as his "bad seed" during the trial those many years ago, died of a massive stroke shortly thereafter.

I can't imagine that Mitchell grieved.

Dear old Mom, however, never gave up on her boy, and is now doing what Mom's do: welcoming back her baby in need. Never mind that her baby is a forty-three-year-old one-time serial killer. Mitchell's brother, Tommy, a hulking brute of a man with the intellectual capacity of the average ten-year-old, is probably pleased as well.

I must often fight against nagging guilt, having played my own role in their melancholy existence. I secretly check in on them from time to time, although I don't know why in hell I should blame myself; Mitchell's actions, not mine, drove them to this place in their lives. Still, they strike me as decent, salt-of-the-earth people, in no way similar to the family monster.

They deserve better. Mrs. Norton has maintained a relatively menial job since the death of her husband. Even Tommy, with his considerable limitations, holds down a job most of the time, performing whatever simple manual labor he can find. I can hardly fault him for being thrilled at the return of his big brother, or his mom for doing her part.

Yet I fear for them, certain there will be another sad price to pay for their affiliation with Mitchell Norton—son, brother, *the devil*.

I remain down the road from their place and watch from my van for a short time. I mustn't call attention to myself, and theirs being an older and less densely populated neighborhood—a rare enough thing in Algonquin—someone seated in a van for hours on end might cause concern. If they agonize over the darkened windshield and the blacked-out windows, they might even call the local authorities.

I must avoid the cops at all costs. Time to go.

The devil's unlikely to go anywhere tonight—at least, anywhere he'll cause trouble. It's his first day out of captivity, and as I learned long ago, Mitchell Norton's not *that* stupid.

Few things beat the simple pleasure of a comfortable stool at the bar in Murphy's Irish Pub, home of the world's best corned-beef sandwich. That's according to one of the world's foremost experts on corned-beef sandwiches—me! I wash it down with a velvety Guinness stout that goes down like the class slut on prom night. Nice and easy.

That may be a bad sign. My nerves, honed to a jagged edge, rifle me into a whirl of doubt and uncertainty. What the hell, perhaps a few more of these lovelies will help. I drain the glass in a power chug and prepare to order another, but someone behind me beats me to the punch.

"Bartender," she says, "you'd better get this guy another one. He might need a few more before the night is out."

I fidget with my empty glass and stare at the bar; no need to look at her. A wisp of lilac combines with her distinctive New England voice, eliciting instant recognition. The memories flood back as the bar jockey drifts in our direction.

"And you'd better get the lady a single malt scotch, neat," I say.

I avoid eye contact as we reminisce in silence, but I can feel her gaze all over me, like spiders crawling in search of a juicy spot to bite. My damned left foot bounces as if it has a life of its own. Ditto my fingers, drumming an indeterminate tune on the bar.

What is she doing here? And what in hell am I supposed to say to her? Shit! I feel like I'm sixteen again.

The bartender arrives with a new round of liquid courage. Just in time.

I keep my head down and my eyes on the beer. "Hello, Linda, or would you prefer Special Agent Monroe?"

"Hey, it's just we two charter members of the Lonely Hearts Club here."

Her distinctive laugh, a raucous, no-holds-barred blast, conjures pleasant memories — her sense of humor, her keen intellect and insight, her passion. We have *history*.

Most recently, we crossed paths in the pursuit of our common interests, hers strictly legal and sanctioned by the Federal Bureau of Investigation, mine outside the law and capable of landing me in a six-by-eight box of concrete and steel bars.

I believe she knows enough about me to understand, though she has never spoken of it.

Halfway through my second glass of Guinness, my courage restored, I straighten up and look at her. She wears the same dark blonde hair and suffers the same perpetual slight blush. I stir in my seat. I swear those intense green eyes, like a fluttering lure drawing me to the hook, could flash through any man's defenses like lightning through rain.

Although some might not consider her a knockout, I'm sure they would nonetheless desire to sleep with her. This assumes they're men with the necessary motivations — a pulse, for example — or women who prefer a soft, sensitive touch.

Heat rushes to my face and I take a deep breath to dowse the flame. *I hope to hell she can't see that.* "How did you find me?"

She raises one eyebrow as if to say, *I don't need to answer that, do I?*

She answers anyway. "You think you're that big a mystery? Where else would you be — where else *could* you be — on the day they released Mitchell Norton? And Algonquin, Illinois, isn't exactly a metropolis."

It might be funny if it weren't so... not funny. I force a smile and nod.

She huffs and shakes her head. "Can you believe they released that *monster*?"

It's a rhetorical question.

I stare again at the sandy foam hovering over my mahogany beer. "I don't know if I properly thanked you the last time we saw each other. You could have gotten me into some real hot water, had you chosen to."

"Oh, but I did!" She pauses, apparently waiting for some response. "Don't tell me you forgot that hot shower! That would destroy my ego."

The tilt of her head, the crook of her smile, the glint of secret thrill in her eye: they tell the whole story. Oh yes, I remember that shower, and the sofa, and the bed, and the shower again. It's hard to believe Linda was forty-two and I was thirty-two. We were like teenagers.

She was mulling over a marriage proposal at the time, from some stiff congressional aide in Washington DC. She appeared entirely unenthusiastic about it three years ago.

I smile and nod in response. "I suppose you're a respectable married woman now."

She sips her drink and expels a soft sigh. "I decided to keep my freedom a little longer. Besides, in my job, with its long hours and extended absences, it would be only a matter of time before *he* cheated on me too."

The not-so-veiled reference to her first husband doesn't make her sad, exactly, though I find it difficult to read her.

"Why bother? Besides...." She pauses for a gulp of her drink. "This way I can be one of the guys—sleep around a little."

"I suppose you do that often." I think I already know the answer.

She lowers her voice and laces it with irony. "You bet. In fact, the last time was a mere three years ago."

Those clever, teasing eyes sparkle and—

I almost choke on my beer. *Three years? How in God's name is that possible?*

She might look better at forty-five than she did at twenty-eight, the *first* time we met. She exudes a certain confidence, a maturity, and shows only a couple lines around those devastating eyes that entice above the rim of her glass. The lilac of her perfume mingles with the coconut of her shampoo in an invisible cloud of delicious splendor. She possesses a certain something, the hard-to-define quality that makes one *sexy*.

She simply arouses.

In California three years ago, we pursued the same monster: Ronald Allen Stegman, serial killer. When we first crossed paths, Linda thought I might somehow be involved with Stegman. She couldn't understand why I was there.

Then he took her.

To abduct a federal agent was stupidity writ large, even for a sociopath like Stegman. When I found him — when I killed him — he was preparing to slice and dice Linda alive, the better to cook her in his sick stew.

She agreed to my one request as payment for saving her life, and we staged it to look as if *she'd* killed him after escaping, wiping out any traces of my involvement. She alone knew the truth. It may have advanced her career, or at least have compensated for her abduction, and it kept me out of the proverbial hot water.

When we saw each other at the hotel bar the next evening, we had some drinks and, as Humphrey Bogart might have said in an old movie, one thing led to another. We could barely keep our hands off each other long enough to get up to her room. We devoured one another, each yearning for the contact, the release that might rescue us from the terrible world we'd recently visited. Mutually convenient and anxious to escape our gruesome reality, we dove into a single night of carnal pleasure.

Neither of us had expected anything more, but it may have affected us at a deeper level than we'd anticipated.

I push the point further. "Dare I ask what brings you to sleepy little Algonquin?"

Both her expression and her voice are pure deadpan. "I'm on vacation."

"You're on vacation in Algonquin, Illinois? Let me guess: Newark was closed for repairs, and you couldn't get a room in Toledo."

She shrugs, drains her glass and motions to the bartender for another. Unspoken warnings buzz in my brain as silence lays over this, our third encounter.

The first occurred seventeen years ago, when I was a young man of eighteen desperate to make sense of the ungodly times. Linda was fresh out of the FBI academy with her Ph.D. in criminal psychology, assigned to a team from their Behavioral Science unit at Quantico, where she now runs a team of her own. The second time was in California — the pursuit of Stegman.

And now? That's simple enough. She's here to stop me from killing Mitchell Norton.

CHAPTER 10
MAY 19, 1978:
MITCHELL NORTON

I again spent the afternoon driving around town in search of that fuckin' Tony's invisible car. I thought it was gray or some shade of blue, a big four-door, a late 60's or early 70's model, but after a week of useless searching, I weren't certain of a goddamn thing anymore.

Algonquin was a small town and I should have spotted it by now. Maybe the driver didn't live here. I needed to look in Lake-in-the-Hills, Carpentersville and Dundee, all small enough towns. I'd find that car eventually. Then it would be only a matter of time before I found the blessed angel of my dreams.

My nightmares full of pain and agony, of torture and death, occurred less frequently now that I spent so much time thinking of my vision of beauty in yellow. My headaches weren't nearly as bad as before. Nice to get through the day without taking twenty aspirin, which helped my head but tore the shit outta my stomach. That Diana weren't just the object of my desires; she was like medicine, an angel of mercy.

I still saw her in my mind's eye, and I could see her chariot too. I'd recognize it when I saw it. I had to find it.

Fuck a rubber duck, I must *find it.*

I grabbed some lunch from The Dairy Hut, and sat in my van in the parking lot while I scarfed down my burger and fries. Classical music, which I'd thought was for pussies until recently, soothed me. I observed people walkin' in and out of the fast-food place. I dug people-watching — always had — but I did it now with what the Reaper called "serious intent."

He said I could no longer watch people "without thought or purpose." I must observe their look, their walk, their demeanor. I imagined them as our subjects and wondered what terrible agony they might suffer. The *voice* commanded it.

They participated in the cruel games of my nightmares, where they endured the demon's cutting and gouging, ripping and burning. The mere thought of that dastardly fucker terrified me, let alone the actual sight of the shit he did.

At least, he used to terrify me. Lately, I'd found it easier, even interesting, to watch the sick fucker.

Like last night.

The torrential sweat pours off my brow and the salt from it burns my already bloodshot eyes. The intense heat in this place sucks the breath right out of me and crushes me with fatigue. I finally brave opening my eyes on this nightmare journey, and the terrifying visions of my mind are no longer mere visions.

They're alive.

The demon below me dispenses terror, agony and death. These ain't no kids' games. The reaper insists there is "a particular artistry to torture." He calls himself an "artisan."

Strapped to a table before this artisan is a young man, about twenty, and the Reaper has broken all his fingers and toes and stripped the flesh right off them. Fuck a rubber duck! He cut the kid's ears and nose clean off, and his face is a mush of tissue and gore. His shattered kneecaps, exposed through torn flesh, burst into spider-webbed cracks. He soaks in the gut-wrenching stink of his own filthy fluids – blood, puke, piss and shit.

It's fuckin' fascinating! The artisan carves a patchwork design into the boy's abdomen with a serrated knife. The kid screams with eyes closed in clenched agony. This lasts for several minutes until his eyelids pop open and his face goes blank.

"Look at his face," the Reaper says. "Note his eyes – disillusioned, despairing, dead."

"It's unbelievable," I say.

"Not at all. Why did life abandon him? Were the physical injuries that severe? Was the sheer pain and terror unendurable? Was the price of continued life unattainable?"

I have to think about it for a few seconds. "Maybe death offered the only solution, the only way that fuckin' wimp could escape."

"You're learning."

The kid's face remains suspended in perpetual, agonizing terror. The Reaper looks back and forth between the boy and me, and he flares his wicked, joyful grin. I think he admires his own performance.

Why shouldn't he?

I shivered against the memory and wiped sweat from my face. Although unthinkable weeks before, I now considered the possibility of committing those horrible deeds. It was hard to fuckin' believe, but I could become an artisan of torture. My nightmare host might have been the Grim Reaper himself, speaking to me in that *voice* like a freight train bellowing its warning—the voice of power. It demanded of me something terrible.

I didn't know why he wanted these things, beyond at least the simple pleasure of them, or why he wanted *me* to do them. Not that it fuckin' mattered. He commanded it. He showed me a new way, gave me a new opportunity and new challenges. I'd damn well better succeed at those new tasks as artisan, or he'd subject me to them as victim. After everything I'd seen that monster do to his subjects, there weren't no fuckin' way I was gonna end up on one of those tables. I'd fuck a rubber duck before I'd have let that happen.

I didn't have no choice. It was outta my hands.

My mental fog cleared and I glanced around the parking lot. A woman, probably in her mid-thirties, carried a tray of milkshakes toward her car.

I whispered, "Hoo-wee, baby! You're built like a brick shit-house."

I popped a hard-on and my whole body tingled. "I wonder where she lives."

Nice choice, the Reaper said, *but you're not quite ready.*

I nodded, accepting his guidance, and tried to chase away another looming headache by cranking up the volume of the radio. Classical music formed a symphony that rattled the windows of my van.

I drove for nowhere in particular, searching for an escape—or an angel of mercy.

CHAPTER 11
MAY 20, 1978:
TONY HOOPER

"Dance beneath the dangling limbs that reach to you in whither,
But move with purpose and with quickness, daring not to dither.
Let not him lay his hands upon your spindly arms or legs,
Or it will be for life and breath that you soon come to beg.
On the summer eve, in short and sleeve,
Lay not your head upon a pillow,
Of grass beneath his drooping reach, or bitter lessons he will teach,
Of crossing Old Man Willow."
Old Man Willow verse, conceived by Tony Hooper for the neighborhood kids

Alex spun and put on his best move. "He drives the lane. No, he fakes and turns outside and goes up with the fifteen-foot jumper, and he...."

"Misses off the front of the rim," I finished. "You know, you may want to keep yourself within that ten- to twelve-foot range. Anything more is too far for you."

"But I've been practicing, Tony. I'm getting better."

"The problem is your strength. You struggle to get the basketball to the hoop from that distance, and you shoot right from the shoulder. Hoopster, *anyone* can block *that* shot."

The little guy's face was almost too much to bear. Only ten, he insisted on acting eighteen.

"Tell you what, Hoopster, why don't we get you started on a weight-lifting program? We need to build your upper body strength, perhaps your legs so you can get more air beneath you."

"No kidding? Dad thinks I'm still too young for that stuff."

"I'll speak to him and make sure he knows we won't get carried away — just some basic stuff. He'll be okay with it."

"Cool!"

We resumed our basketball contest, if you could call it that — the mismatch was severe. Nonetheless, I enjoyed shooting hoops with Alex, and I enjoyed coaching him even more. He handled the ball quite well, having learned to dribble with both hands.

He borrowed one of the shots from my own repertoire as he planted his right foot, spun first left and then right, and put up a fade-away jumper from twelve feet. *Swish!* His priceless ear-to-ear smile made me laugh. I couldn't tell which of us was more proud of his athletic development.

I'd sure miss him when I left for college.

Saturday morning meant no school, but I had to flip burgers and make sundaes at The Dairy Hut for a few hours, from four o'clock to eight o'clock. It didn't pay a heck of a lot but it was conveniently close. I could ride my bike if I wanted, and I made enough to keep my Bonnie on the road with a full gas tank.

With gas breaking forty cents per gallon, that was getting tougher. Dad provided the other necessities — shoes, clothes, food and medicine — but he insisted that if I had a car, I must maintain it myself, unless I was willing to leave it in the garage.

No chance! The Bonnie gave me freedom, the means by which I escaped the grind.

Dad rarely objected, or said much of anything, for that matter. Alex, on the other hand, preferred I pay more attention to *him*. I enjoyed spending time with the Hoopster, but all good things in moderation. I needed to get away and do my own thing occasionally. He could be a load, more work than fun, and the responsibility sometimes irritated me. He was innocent enough — only ten years old. The real source of my irritation, Dad, should have done more with Alex.

Still, when the Hoopster dragged me down, a simple escape offered the easiest way to refresh.

Diana served as my island, my paradise. It hardly mattered where we went or what we did, so long as I was with her. We hooked up with other friends to enjoy movies, restaurants, bowling, arcades, shooting darts or pool — simple activities. Some kids, cleverly turning a *Star Wars* phrase, claimed we'd gone over to the "Dork Side." Fine. We tried to stay away from the drug culture that seemed so prevalent.

My circle of friends — *real* friends — remained a relatively small one. I'd have been lost without Diana.

I left Alex to practice shooting on his own, which he could do for hours without pause, to shower and prepare for work.

I could relax and watch the Chicago Cubs game on TV for a couple hours before I had to leave. It sounded as though someone had beaten me to the punch.

"Bill Buckner lines a shot into the gap in right-center," Alex announced from the living room floor. "It rolls to the wall and he cruises into second with a stand-up double."

He enjoyed doing the play-by-play during the game, often with the TV volume off. He cracked me up, but he was getting pretty darn good at it.

The Cubs fell behind early — again. By the end of the third inning, my thoughts already drifted toward more pleasant diversions; Diana and I were going out tonight after I finished work.

She so occupied my mind these days, hard to imagine how I got anything done at all. Her face always grabbed me first, and when she smiled.... I'd get close and her scent would hit me next: perfume, shampoo, soap, breath. She always smelled so damned good. The feel of her skin, the caress of her fingers, and the taste of her mouth came next.

At that point, I must fight off thoughts of leaving for college and focus only on her. We'd draw close, closer, until I could think of nothing else, and I must —

Whoa, I'd better think of something else. Fast! This is no time to ignite the firestorm.

The phone startled me from my daydream. Perfect timing.

Frank Willow offered his best New York mob lingo, a silly attempt at humor, yet somehow hilarious coming from such an unlikely source. "Heyyy, Tony, howzya doowin?"

"Super, Frank, the Hoopster and I were watching the Cub game. Who knew we were such masochists?"

He laughed in his easy-going, Grandpa Everyman way. "Perhaps I can save you from the self-immolation."

Hah! I don't even have to look that one up. Frank loved to challenge my vocabulary.

"If you can tear yourself away to help an old man, I need some help getting an air conditioner out of my car and into the living room window."

"I have to leave for work in a little over an hour but, if that's enough time, I'd be happy to help you out."

"It won't take long at all, and I'd be most grateful."

I hung up and tried to convince Alex to come along, hinting that Frank probably had some treats for him.

"I want to watch the rest of the game."

"Geez, Hoopster, I don't feel good about leaving you here by yourself."

"Come on! Gimme a break, will ya? Besides, Dad will be home any minute. Good grief!"

It made me uneasy, but Dad *was* due home soon. I instructed Mr. Ten-going-on-Eighteen to stay put until he arrived.

He waved his hand dismissively. "Yeah, yeah. See ya later, Gator. Tell Old Man Willow I said, 'Boo!'"

It was our little joke regarding all the ridiculous rumors about Frank.

CHAPTER 12
JUNE 7, 1995:
MITCHELL NORTON

"Mankind is safer when men seek pleasure than when they seek the power and the glory." – *Geoffrey Gorer*

I'm out at last, sweet freedom seventeen years in the making. I can't believe it took so fuckin' long. I'll never recapture that lost time. Someone owes me for that.

One of my most abiding memories is of the several shrinks I saw.

I occupied the last ten years with endless apologies, acts of contrition and outright acting. *That* was a difficult game, but I had to tell them what they wanted to hear. What I truly felt was irrelevant. No big deal. They all operated from the same playbook, the same set of expectations, the same set of practiced responses and resolutions. The fuckheads made it easy.

They also started from the assumption that I was stupid. Condescending pricks! I was never dumb, just uneducated. In the end, I had seventeen years to do little else but read—hundreds and hundreds of books. It changed me, though I saw little reason to share that fact with the fuckin' shrinks—at least not every detail.

It all started because of a little tumor, a small growth in my neocortex, the outer layer of the brain that houses the intellect and the imagination. Yeah, right. I couldn't help thinking at the time that there must be more to it.

Still can't.

Last night, my first back in the old house, frustrated the shit outta me. I enjoyed my reunion with Mom and Tommy, with some conversation and a couple drinks, but later, when I needed to sleep, anxiety attacked in full force.

My life must begin anew, but where to start? Is it too soon to worry about my future? I've much to consider, and there will be prying eyes, no doubt—those fuckin' protestors at my release! Who are they to judge *me*, to condemn *me*? They know nothing, the simple fuckheads.

For hours, I lay in bed and stared at the ceiling and, despite my unwillingness, remembered those extraordinary days.

May 20, 1978

I cruised around town, searching for the car that had carried my newfound angel.

I yelled to no one, "Jackpot!"

It pulled into a driveway off Cary Road, and I immediately recognized the driver, that fuckin' Tony. I wasn't paying much attention, absentmindedly going through the motions, when it leapt into view. I spun around and parked on a little dirt trek that was barely a road, across and down the street from the house where my archenemy lived.

"What the hell do I do now?"

The Reaper chose a lousy time to go silent.

Several minutes later, as I tried to figure my next move, Tony walked back out and toward his car.

"Shit! Should I follow him? He'll eventually pick up Diana."

It would have to be another time, as the uniform he wore clearly signaled his leaving for work. I recognized it—from The Dairy Hut, a place I visited on occasion. He pulled outta the driveway and turned down the old dirt road directly across the street. It must'a been a back way to work.

I sat and stared at the house. It drew me, stirred me, beckoned me.

"Why is Tony so special to my angel? Maybe there are clues about her inside. I might find her in a different way, unless.... *Shit!* What should I do if someone is home? There's no car in the driveway. The garage is open, but it's empty. Still...."

Again, the Reaper didn't answer.

"I've got it!"

In a stroke of ingenuity, not exactly a common occurrence for me, I decided to masquerade as a newspaper delivery boy attempting to scare up subscriptions. It gave me a valid reason to knock on the door, and if nobody was home, I could do my reconnaissance. Most people didn't lock their doors in Sleepy Town.

Just one problem: at twenty-six, I might appear too old to be a newspaper delivery boy.

I struggled with it for quite a while, working through the possibilities, trying to ease my nervousness. Hell, I doubted anyone would question it. It wasn't as if anything bad ever happened in Algonquin.

I couldn't work up my courage. "Damn it! I'm so sick of being a fuckin' coward."

CHAPTER 13
MAY 20, 1978:
TONY HOOPER

In a neighborhood like ours — almost suburban and almost rural, a hybrid — kids always looked for excitement and rarely found it. They settled on the next best thing, and manufactured some of their own.

A singular row of houses occupied our side of Cary Road, considered a main thoroughfare despite its relative calm. Behind us lay a stretch of mostly open land we called "The Outland." It encompassed several square miles between Cary Road and Highway 31, in the northern part of Algonquin, high above the Fox River valley. Kids had long biked, hiked, built forts and sought adventure in the Outland. A mix of tall grass and trees of every conceivable size made it an alluring playground.

Frank lived near the edge of The Outland, two blocks away and almost directly behind our home. At seventy-one, he'd earned the moniker of "Old Man Willow," the brainchild of some unknown local from years past — no doubt stolen from J.R.R. Tolkien's *The Lord of the Rings*.

Who knew how such idiotic rumors got started, but many believed him responsible for two children who'd disappeared many years ago. Rumor had it that Frank had buried them under his roses — special fertilization for a famous garden. A child's imagination needed an outlet, with little else to do in our sleepy neighborhood.

I'd once told some of the younger kids that I'd seen tiny fingers, surely belonging to those missing children, protruding from the mud beneath Frank's roses. I'd scared the crap out of them!

Frank had thought it hilarious too, though he regretted his unfortunate reputation. I visited him a couple times a week, not counting my official duties as his lawn mower and driveway shoveler, often with Alex. He always plied us with special treats, the grandfather we'd never had, and loved us as his "adopted grandsons."

He told stories that kept us pinned to the edge of our seats, usually about the war he'd fought in or his many world travels. He'd also taught us a little something about gardening, which we enjoyed more than I would have thought possible. If there were a better gardener anywhere in the world... well, that seemed unlikely.

I'd developed a bond with Frank similar to the one I enjoyed with Alex. I'd gladly have stepped in front of a train in order to push Alex out of the way — without hesitation. I had no doubt Frank felt precisely that way about Alex and me. He showered us with gifts, fed us, and occasionally slipped us a few dollars with instructions not to tell Dad.

No one had ever enjoyed a better grandfather.

I usually rode my bike over the dirt road to his place, a pocked and uneven mess. Since I had to leave for work from there, and since I'd be picking up Diana after work, I had to drive today. I kept it to a crawl to preserve Bonnie's belly.

Grassy fields surrounded his place, with a few oddly spaced trees — huge oaks, elms, maple and birch — to guard his private sanctuary. Developers had tried to seduce him into selling off a bunch of it. No chance! The *last* thing he wanted was a bunch of noisy, nosy neighbors.

I pulled into his driveway, and he already stood behind his car with bungee cords in hand. A box protruded from the open trunk.

He offered his usual greeting. "Hey-howdy, young neighbor, and what a lovely day it is to install one of the twentieth century's most appreciated inventions."

"Hey, I'm glad you decided to *join* the twentieth century. If you don't mind my saying so, it's about time."

"Well, if this summer is the scorcher some are predicting, I want to be comfortable in my own living room. At my age, discomfort comes in many forms. The temperature in my home shouldn't be one of them."

"What about the bedroom, and the kitchen, and the bathroom?"

"The bathroom? Don't you think people might view an air conditioner in my bathroom window as excessive? A little strange?"

"Haven't you heard? It's 1978, the age of disco and lime-green polyester suits. Anything goes."

"Is that how you justify your hair?"

"Hey! What's wrong with my hair?"

"Ah, never mind." He waved his hand in surrender. "By the way, if you ever see me in a lime-green polyester suit, you'll find a shotgun in my bedroom closet. Kindly put me out of my misery."

Our biggest challenge proved to be maneuvering the box through the door. I grimaced as Frank struggled with the weight of it. He was so lively I often forgot his age.

Forty-five minutes later, he had air conditioning, and we had enough time to enjoy a glass of iced tea on his back patio before I must go to work.

I marveled at Frank's... well, it was inappropriate to call it a mere *garden*. More like a damned work of art, an extraordinary feat of engineering. Never mind the flowers; those were the least of it.

Most impressive was the manmade stream, engineered by old Gramps himself, which ran through and around his garden, entirely self-contained within his property, like something from an old Japanese palace. Frank even stocked it with fish during the warm months. The water flowed counter-clockwise at a light pace and twisted around his back yard, a liquid snake devouring its own tail.

Three evenly spaced bridges leapt the water to the center island, each wide enough for a single walker, and each carrying its own theme. One replicated a small nineteenth century covered bridge, complete with flowerpots that hung to the left and right of each end. The second looked like a ship-loading plank from the eighteenth century, with wooden floorboards and wooden posts, between which ran a sturdy rope as hand guide. Third, a bridge of concrete and stone reminiscent of the European Gothic era was guarded by miniature stone lions at one end, and rain-spitting gargoyles at the other.

He should have charged admission.

The stream began where it ended, at a three-foot waterfall that emptied into a small pool. It emerged and traveled its winding loop, guided by pumps hidden in three separate, hollowed-out tree trunks. Along the way, filters aerated the water for the benefit of the fish, which tended to remain close to the pool where Frank fed them. In the event of heavy rains, floodwaters ran off through nearly invisible micro-screen barriers that held back the fish.

The old softy had spent twenty years of his life dedicated to its creation and many improvements. Frank, the consummate grandfather who'd never had children, nonetheless doted over his baby.

I finished my tea. "Well, Gramps, I have to head into work."

"Thank you for your help, my boy, and for the extra visiting time."

"Sure. I'll be around tomorrow to mow the lawn. How does ten o'clock sound?"

"Perfect. I'll see you then."

I stopped at home long enough to bolt in and grab a clean shirt. Alex sat in his bedroom and sorted through his baseball card collection, to which I'd added a considerable stash.

"Hey, Hoopster, where's Dad?"

"He called to say he'd be home in a couple hours. He has more work than he thought."

"Are you kidding? Who's coming over to watch you?"

He gave me another one of his looks; I'd insulted him again. I couldn't afford to call in to work, so I considered asking Frank to drop by, but....

Alex is mature for his age, and this is Algonquin, not Detroit, for God's sake. "What will you do for dinner?"

He put a sly edge on his voice. "Dad's bringing home a pizza from Gerra's."

Our favorite meal.

I sighed and played along, laying it on a little thick. "That figures, and I have to work. Just as well, I suppose." I paused for further effect. "Since Diana and I are going out for burgers and a movie after work."

He gave me his *gosh-you're-lucky-to-be-old-enough-to-drive* look— such an old soul for a kid of ten. I did my business and, as I hustled toward the door, offered up my usual farewell.

"See you in a short, Sport."

CHAPTER 14
MAY 20, 1978:
MITCHELL NORTON

"Shit! That was close."

That fuckin' Tony had returned down the dirt road across the street, and turned back onto Cary Road and into his driveway, just when I'd finally worked up the courage to move forward. Just as I was about to pull across to his house.

"What the fuck is that asshole doin'? Is he goin' to work or not?"

My plans were completely screwed-up, and I had no idea what to do next. The Reaper didn't help me out; he'd gone silent as a dead whore. Some help!

Maybe Tony would leave again at some point, maybe even to visit his *girlfriend*. Fucker! I'd show him. He could lead me right to Diana, and then we'd see who—

"What the fuck?"

Tony emerged from the house—couldn't have been inside for more than a couple minutes. He tucked in his shirt—his uniform shirt—as he hustled to his car. He hopped in, backed out the driveway, turned onto Cary Road, and zipped right past.

I froze, still trying to figure out what had happened. I couldn't be sure, but maybe he'd just stopped back to change his shirt. Why would he do that? Where had he gone before?

No matter.

I'd sit here and wait a few minutes, make sure he didn't come back again.

I turned up the radio, rested my head on the top of the seat, and pictured Diana in my mind's eye.

I waited about thirty minutes to make sure the coast was clear. "It's now or never."

I parked in their driveway, hopped out of the van, and approached the back door. The main interior door sat open, and only the outer screen door blocked entry. The dull sounds of a TV echoed from somewhere in the background.

Damn, someone must be home!

If anyone had seen me, it might look suspicious if I turned around and left without knocking, so I decided to carry out my charade. A young boy appeared at the door with a puzzled look on his face, and I started my pitch.

He interrupted me. "Sorry, but my dad's not home."

I listened for any sounds above the TV. "That's all right. Can I talk to your mom?"

The look on his face ran from irritation to confusion to sorrow. He lowered his head and I could barely hear him as he sighed and mumbled, "I don't have a mom."

"Oh, sorry about that. How about an older brother or sister?"

He raised his head and spoke louder. "No. You'll have to come back later, please, when my dad is home."

Just like that, he spun on his heels and headed deeper into the house.

I started to leave and —

Hold the phone, Mitchell! This little kid is home alone. The Reaper's voice boomed like a bullhorn. *It's time, my boy, to put your recent studies to work. A new life awaits you.*

"Fuck a rubber duck," I whispered. "Am I ready for this?"

Let us find out, shall we?

My gut rumbled, giving rise to the urge to barf right on the spot. I wiped the sweat from my forehead and returned to the door. No trace of the boy. I glanced around the neighborhood to ensure that nobody was watching. The nearest house on that side sat a good fifty yards away, and the separated garage at this house blocked much of the view.

A wild power built inside me, and I stood suddenly taller, stronger.

"I think I'm ready."

You're the MAN!

The screen door opened with a whisper. I crept toward the living room, comforted by the noise of the TV, which should cover my approach, and peeked around the corner to see where he sat. I'd have to pounce like a lion and —

Shit! The living room was empty.

I turned and stalked down the hallway toward the bedrooms, and leaned around the doorframe of the first room. Empty.

In the second room, the boy lay belly down on his bed, surrounded by a bunch of baseball cards. He focused on several that lay on the far side of the bed.

I crept up on his blind side, careful to keep each step quiet, but the fuckin' floor creaked!

He turned. "Hey! Wha —"

I clasped a hand over his mouth, grabbed hold and raised him off the bed. He flailed his arms and legs — like wrestling a fuckin' tornado! I released him for a second and, before he could scream, drilled a hard punch to the left side of his head. He hit the mattress, bounced back onto the floor alongside the bed, and lay still.

I dragged him by an arm to the back door, and checked once more to ensure that no curious neighbors were watching the house. I lifted him over my right shoulder and kicked the screen door open.

He bounced on my shoulder and I almost lost him while jogging to my van. I slid the rear door open and dumped him behind the front seat, then pulled the door shut.

Fifteen seconds later, after backing out of the driveway as unobtrusively as possible, I shook my throbbing right hand in the air.

"Shit, kid, you got a hard fuckin' head, you little bastard."

He was out cold.

CHAPTER 15
JUNE 7, 1995:
TONY HOOPER

"What you really value is what you miss, not what you have." – *Jorge Luis Borges*

See you in a short, Sport.
Those words haunt me.

Long before the embers of the dawn burn, I awake to a world cloaked in darkness, mired in a storm that mirrors my essence. My dream of Alex, reduced to a puff of smoke in a gale-force wind, still cuts me to the bone. I struggle to regain my composure, but my emotions remain on edge, as though the smallest catalyst will tumble me into the abyss, the black chasm of my mind.

I've long stood upon the precipice, waiting—almost hoping—for the ledge to collapse beneath me.

I often think of Alex these days. I still remember pulling out of the driveway seventeen years ago, leaving him with his baseball cards, assured that he'd be fine until Dad arrived home from work.

Times were different then. Our neighborhood promised innocence and security, a relaxed lifestyle. Few monsters stalked our world in those days.

I departed for work without giving it another thought.

<u>May 20, 1978</u>

My supervisor tapped me on the shoulder as I took an order at the counter, and relieved me so I could take an important phone call. What was so important that someone would interrupt me at work? Then I remembered that Alex was home alone. Perhaps Dad was running later than expected and Alex was getting antsy. I picked up the phone.

"Tony, it's Dad. Do you know where Alex is?"

"Alex? You mean he's not home?"

"No. I've called a few of his friends but I can't locate him."

"That's weird. I know he was looking forward to the pizza you were bringing home for dinner." I considered the possibilities for a second. "Have you tried Frank's place?"

"Frank!" The relief almost whistled out of his mouth. "I can't believe I didn't think of that. Go on back to work and don't worry about it."

I shared his relief. The Hoopster didn't think to leave a note, but with pizza on the way he'd probably run through the door at any moment. I drudged back to work, got busy, and finished my shift without thinking any more of it. Afterward, I did a quick change in the men's room at the restaurant before I called Diana, her voice instantly recognizable by her simple, "Hullo."

"Hey, good lookin', whatsya got cookin'?"

"Hey!"

The excitement and enthusiasm in that single word provided a rush no drug could match.

"Are you coming to get me?"

"Yep, I just have to call my dad to let him know where we'll be and when I'll be home. I should be there in ten minutes. Will you be ready?"

She assured me in that *try-not-to-be-a-smartass* way that she'd be ready and I needed to get my butt in gear. She then added her customary sign-off, "Smooch-smooch."

Geez, give me a break. I looked around to ensure that nobody could hear. "Smooch-smooch."

When I phoned home to inform Dad of my plans for the night, an unexpected voice offered a simple, monotonous reply. I hesitated and waited for it to register.

"Frank, is that you?"

"Hi Tony."

"You decided to join the gang for some pizza, huh?"

Silence ensued for a few seconds. "Are you still at work?"

"Yeah, but I'm about to leave. I need to update Dad first."

"Actually, he intended to call you as soon as he got out of the bathroom. It's been rather.... Maybe you'd better cancel your plans and come on home."

What in hell is that supposed to mean? "Frank, what's going on? Where's my dad? Where's Alex?"

"Please come home right away."

He hung up.

I stared at the phone for about a half-second before I ran to my car, jumped in and sped off as though engaged in the most important race of my life. What in hell had happened? I had no idea, yet somehow my mind returned to Alex, who'd been missing earlier in the day. Might something have happened to him? Why hadn't Frank said more? Why did he sound so worried?

The short drive home usually took about four minutes. I arrived in two.

Parked in the driveway was Frank's car, in front of the open garage that contained Dad's car, to the right of.... *Oh shit!* A police cruiser.

God, this can't be good.

It had to be Alex. He was probably hurt—something minor—or in some kind of trouble. But something that required the police? What could that be?

I parked in the grass alongside the garage, bolted from the car almost before cutting the engine, and ran into the house.

It wasn't as bad as I thought, or it was worse. Alex was missing. His baseball cards were sprawled haphazardly over his bedroom floor, an ominous sign for those of us who knew the Hoopster. Nobody we knew had heard from him. His bicycle, his only mode of transportation besides walking, remained in the garage.

Dad provided Officer Sam Weaver with a recent picture of Alex, to go along with my description of what he wore when I last saw him. I explained to Weaver the earlier events and exactly why Alex had been home alone. It had seemed so reasonable at the time, so innocent. Yet at that moment, guilt and anger beat me like the proverbial redheaded stepchild. If the look on his face was any indication, Dad felt essentially the same about himself.

Sleepy little Algonquin had been enjoying one of its usual slow nights, and the police immediately began their search. Weaver took it seriously enough and assured us that they'd look throughout the night. They would also notify the county sheriff and the police departments of the small neighboring towns. He offered lighthearted encouragement, however, confident that we'd hear from Alex or one of his friend's parents any minute.

I had my doubts.

That terrible premonition clawed at me again. A shadow was building in my mind, and it would become a raging storm if I let it. I walked outside and sat in a lawn chair to escape the madness inside the house.

Nobody thought anything terrible could happen in Algonquin, but I knew Alex, Mr. Ten-going-on-Eighteen. He'd never leave the house with the TV on, the doors wide open and pizza on the way, let alone with his precious baseball cards in a mess. Not without leaving a note or making a point to call.

Emptiness and loss assaulted me. I'd known that feeling once before: I'd been fifteen and Mom's blood had dripped from my hands.

I was desperate to chase away the feeling, but it nagged me like the bugs I swatted absent-mindedly on the humid night. I rested my chin on my chest and stared unseeing at the ground. I had let Alex down. I should have protected him. I should have been out searching for him, but where should I look? What could I do?

After two hours of futile attempts, Diana got through on our phone. I cut her off in mid-yell and explained the events of the evening, the reason she got all those busy signals, the reason I forgot about her. She caught her breath, apologized and offered to help. What could she do?

Exactly what I did: nothing. I said I'd call her the next day.

Yes, that next day.

Return to June 7, 1995

Last night's dreams, the memories of seventeen years ago, are too persistent.

Earlier in the evening, I said goodbye to Linda at the bar, but first I agreed to meet her for breakfast today. She didn't invite me to her hotel room, nor did she ask to accompany me home, nor did I breach the subject in any way. There *was* an underlying tension, a thought that we might rekindle the flame from three years ago. I sure felt it, and I believe she did too, but in the end, we said goodnight and went our separate ways.

Until now.

I've anticipated this meeting from the instant she offered to buy me breakfast, yet as I drive to her hotel, the lingering effects of last night's dreams distract me. I attempt to drown them out in a blast of music from a cassette, an upbeat, kick-ass mixed tape designed to improve my mood and get me going on days like this.

Robin Zander of Cheap Trick screams that he's *All Wound Up*. I could use a little of that myself.

Linda said last night that she wanted to talk about Mitchell Norton.

What's to talk about? I want to return to the job I started seventeen years ago and failed to finish.

I want to slit his goddamned throat.

CHAPTER 16

JUNE 7, 1995:
TONY HOOPER

"I do not believe in a fate that falls on men however they act, but I do believe in a fate that falls on them unless they act."
– *G.K. Chesterton*

The eggs are so runny on the plate that I consider using a spoon to scoop them up, but the bacon is properly crisp and the pancakes perfect. Linda has no objections about her breakfast. Then again, how does one make a mess of half a grapefruit and one slice of dry wheat toast? You call that breakfast? She's probably trying to watch her figure.

I'm doing plenty of that myself — watching *her* figure. She's dressed casually in jeans and an orange blouse that hangs loose at her waist, and her hair is down and flows freely every time she moves her head, which she does often.

Is she doing that on purpose, to make her hair bounce so enticingly? Speaking of bounce, is she...? Whoa, she's not wearing a bra. I gulp down my unwelcome anticipation. *Good heavens, she looks positively yummy.*

The conversation remains relatively one-sided as she tells me about her job. She mentions a problem with a member of her team, the office politics she hates, recent cases — anything but the one subject that dominates both our minds: Mitchell Norton, *the devil*.

I've dreaded this conversation. What can I say that will satisfy her? I could lie to her, but she'd see through that in a second. She doesn't know me that well, when you get right down to it, but she caught a glimpse of me at the most critical time, shared with me the most relevant experience — in California, the death of Ronald Allen Stegman.

Now she's here right on the heels of Norton's release.

Her gaze shifts between her coffee cup and me as the conversation reaches an impasse, and I signal the waitress for more coffee. Linda may have given up on the small talk, or perhaps she's thinking it through, determining how best to approach the real reason she came to Algonquin. Her look strikes me as designed to prod the conversation. I maintain eye contact and a pleasant smile, but I don't take the bait.

I occasionally drop my eyes lower and linger for a few seconds. I know I shouldn't stare but....

Why isn't she wearing a bra, damn it? Look at — Uh-oh!

She catches me staring. I have no idea the proper reaction here, but I'm sure my rooster-in-the-henhouse grin is *not* it. She doesn't appear upset, at any rate. In fact, I'd swear she's rather pleased, if not at my staring, then at least at the "gotcha" moment, which she has the good graces not to mention.

Her smile fades and she glances around the dining room at nothing.

Keep your eyes up, Tony. Eyes up!

She takes a deep breath and exhales a heavy sigh, and returns her gaze to me. "It would be an awful shame if I had to put you in custody, if I had to be part of an investigation that lands you in jail."

I've been preparing for this. "The real shame will be when you have to notify the next of kin that Mitchell Norton has killed again."

She comes up short, and pauses to sip her coffee while she considers a response. I have difficulty reading her expression — sad resignation, perhaps.

She strains through a low voice, "It's not that simple."

"No?"

"No. There are times when I wish it were, believe me, but the laws serve many purposes, and we mustn't condone or encourage vigilantes."

"Vigilantes?"

She rolls her eyes and looks at me as though.... Yeah, she knows.

Well shit, Tony, you already knew that, didn't you? I snap at her. "I suppose you learned that in one of your seminars."

"You're damned right I did! I've also learned it repeatedly during almost twenty years on the job. They say there is no black and white, that there are only shades of gray, but in my world, the gray can lay upon you until you suffocate. It *must* be black and white! In my world, the alternative is unthinkable."

"I understand that but, and I say this with the utmost of respect and in all seriousness, you and I live in different worlds."

"I'm sorry. I forgot that *you're* above the law. *You* don't make mistakes. Therefore, *you* may do what *you* please. *You're* so *God-like*."

The sarcasm is so thick I could pour it over my pancakes. Once more, I must wonder why she's here. Perhaps she thinks she owes me.

"You forget that my ways are the only reason you're still alive." I said it too brusquely, and the cheap shot knocks her back a notch. "I'm sorry. I had no right bringing that up."

I tap my fingers on the table and squirm under her steadfast gaze and persistent silence. *Shit! This would be an excellent time to change the subject.*

"By the way, did I mention how *fantastic* you look?"

She slaps her hands on the table and rolls her eyes again—she's good at it, and getting lots of practice today.

What the hell, it was worth a try.

My smile is barely repressed laughter. I can't help myself. I laugh through what I'm sure must be one giant, shit-eating grin.

"Not buying it, huh?" Come on, Linda. Please lighten up.

She sighs and shakes her head and, in spite of herself, a slow smile sneaks to the corners of her mouth.

"You *should* buy it," I say. "I mean it. You look...."

She wants to hang onto her anger, I think, but she can't quite muster it. Her eyes grow wide as she waits for me to finish the sentence, but I don't.

"I look *what*?"

My eyes wander freely this time—no coy glances, no shame, a thorough examination. The blush that resides forever on her cheeks deepens.

I keep my voice low, private. "Yummy."

Her face remains rosy but her expression softens. Her eyes soften. Her breathing softens.

Man, she sure looks soft. I want to reach out and —

"Thank you," she says, "but you're just being nice after taking that shot at me. I'm not even wearing make-up."

"You should try that more often—not wearing make-up, I mean. That may be a problem for some women, but it sure works for you."

Now I can't take my eyes off hers—emerald wells that hold me in a trance. I wish I could tell what she's thinking, but all emotion has retreated from her face. I know what I'm thinking. I have this overwhelming urge to kiss her, but she's on the other side of the table. Perhaps I should reach for her hand.

"That's a nice compliment," she says. "Thank you."

Her smile is more evident now but I return to her eyes, which hint at something I can't quite figure—perhaps desire or expectation, perhaps sadness or regret, perhaps last night's Red Sox game. Hell, I don't know.

The waitress breaks the uneasy silence to offer us more coffee. I ask for the check.

Linda huffs. "Hey, this was *my* invitation, remember?"

"What can I say? I'm an old-fashioned guy."

"Sure, there's a shocker."

Is it more sarcasm? Is it a compliment? Does she think I'm a gentleman? Or an ape? Her face changes again and she looks at me. More like reels me in.

Her voice is the perfect extension of that look. "So, what's there to do in the greater metropolitan area of Algonquin for a girl on vacation?"

Damn, what is that she's doing with her eyes? What kind of look is that?
"Uh, figuring out a better place to vacation would be high on the list."

She laughs, a sound that conjures from my memory our night three years ago. She exudes such light and warmth. I must remind myself that she's unmarried and uninvolved. How is that possible? It's a crime against humanity—against men, at any rate. And manly women.

She wants to stop at her room before we head to a bookstore. I told her I'd be right behind her—an excellent idea. She has nice jeans, and the sort of hips one might expect to see on a forty-five-year-old woman who works hard to stay in shape. Her feminine curves work magic.

I wonder if she knows I'm staring. What am I saying? Women always know, as if they have eyes in the backs of their heads, or something.

Does she always shake her ass that much when she walks?

A woman will often complain if we stare at her ass or at her breasts. Then again, she'll also complain if we don't notice. It's hard to win sometimes.

Her room is no wellspring of luxury but it looks comfortable enough. She grabs a sweater from a drawer and sets it next to her purse on a chair. *A sweater?* It's supposed to reach the upper-eighties today.

She stands at the vanity for several seconds and stares at herself in the mirror. "Damn, it's your fault, you know?"

My jaw drops and I spread my hands out, palms up. *Geez, what did I do now?*

"I planned to put on a little make-up before going out, but...."

I step up close behind her and my nose goes reflexively to her soft, coconut-scented hair. She watches me in the mirror, and I see the desire. It's unmistakable.

I whisper through her hair, "You don't need any make-up."

I reach over her left shoulder and under her chin with my left hand, and touch her right cheek to turn her face toward me. Her blazing green eyes are pools of expectancy. Her perfume fills my senses. My left hand remains on her face as she leans into it ever so slightly, and she closes her eyes for a few seconds.

She opens them again, and pleads, and I know that she feels what I feel. We've known this desperate need before; it was but a single night three years ago. No matter. We know it again.

I caress her left hip as I lean into her face, and our lips almost touch — almost. My heart beats faster. My breath quickens. My nerves buzz. I want to enjoy the experience for a minute, and I think she feels the same, but she waits for me.

Our lips touch, and I forget where I am for a second; it could be somewhere in the Horse Head Nebula. She moans and I rush back to the moment, and she throws her arms around me and pulls me toward her. If I were any closer, I'd be inside her.

Our bodies touch from ankle to mouth, and I think she might swallow me whole. My body reacts instantly and, the way she grinds against me, there's no way I can hide it. She again moans in response, and I again swoon in space. She leans into me and pushes me backwards.

The backs of my legs hit the bed and we fall onto the mattress. I hold her to my chest as our continuing kiss sets me ablaze. She sits up and unbuttons my shirt. I do the same for her, and both shirts soon fly across the room. She grabs my wrists and guides my hands up to where they do each of us more good.

This I can handle.

I sit up and ease her farther up the bed, and I unbutton her jeans and unzip them. She arches her back to accommodate me as I pull them off, and again when I remove her panties. I stand and look at her for a few seconds before removing the rest of my clothing.

She looks yummier than ever.

I settle back over her and we kiss again, and I take my time as I trace my way down her body. I want to explore her. I want to get lost in her. She places her hand on my head and occasionally strokes my hair, and then applies slight pressure as she gently guides me. She knows what she wants, and she's not particularly shy about it.

I'm happy to oblige.

Some unknown minutes later, she sits up, pulls my head up urgently, and guides me onto my back.

Every sensation is a cannon burst up my spine. She lets escape a series of erotic sounds that excite me as much as anything we do. There's no mistaking the magic, the fire, as she places her hands on my chest and rocks rhythmically above me. My hands roam everywhere in wonder and gratitude as her burning, velvety skin transports my fingers back to that other galaxy. I can only hope she shares my extreme pleasure.

We collide in a deep, delirious destination—a place where I could remain for a long, long, long time. I might as well be swimming in lava or flying into the sun. She remains above me as she nibbles on my ear and on my neck, and we kiss again.

God, it's been so, so long.

I feel close to her, comfortable, as though we know each other much better than we do. She slides off next to me and we embrace in a silent shroud of warm, damp skin. I brush her hair with my fingers and look at her face.

Wow, look at those eyes! "This sure beats the hell out of any bookstore that I'm aware of."

She lays her head on my chest and laughs. "You'll get no argument from me."

We enjoy another minute of silence before she says, "There's one more thing I want you to do for me."

"Good heavens! Already? Don't I get a few minutes to recover?"

She laughs and slaps my chest. "Not that! I think a nice bubble bath is in order. I've got a big spa tub with lots of room." She drills me again with her eyes. "We can talk about your *recovery* in there. Care to join me?"

The bath, and our further explorations following my record recovery, lasts almost an hour. We then dress and agree to take that trip to the bookstore.

"I have so little opportunity," she says, "to read for pleasure, given the demands of my job. I'm determined to do so while on vacation."

I still don't believe that's why she's here, but I let it go. At the bookstore, she picks up two romance novels—not exactly my style. I take advantage of the opportunity to pick up Mark Helprin's latest, *Memoir from Antproof Case*.

We leave the store and stand for a moment in the warm sunshine, as though neither of us is sure what we should do next. Now fully recovered—again—I have a definite idea about that, but she has something else on her mind.

"I'm starving," she says. "Let's get some lunch, and this time *I'm* paying."

"In that case, I know where they serve an excellent steak and lobster, along with a fine, exclusive bottle of wine, of course."

Perhaps a little humor will enhance the moment.

"That sounds nice," she says.

I need to work on my timing. Some funny material would help.

At the Barn of Barrington, an upscale restaurant in an upscale town, we enjoy a spectacular late lunch that will undoubtedly double as dinner. We huddle at a nice out-of-the-way table, side-by-side instead of across from one another—she insisted on being close. Perfect. We make small talk again, and tell jokes and laugh.

Man! I can't remember the last time I felt this good.

The food is gone and we've passed on coffee, well into our second bottle of wine, and she reaches over and grabs my hand. She leans in close and squeezes my hand as her eyes burrow into mine.

She throws me a curve ball. "Tony, tell me about 1978. I want to know about Alex."

PART 4

THREE DAYS IN HELL

CHAPTER 17
JUNE 7, 1995:
TONY HOOPER

I can barely look Linda in the face. "You were there. Don't you remember?"

"I was twenty-eight, fresh out of school with my doctorate and into a new career, trying desperately to please the people for whom I worked and to make my mark." She pauses to measure her words. "I hate to admit it, but honesty compels me to say that I wasn't terribly concerned about Tony Hooper at the time. I did my job and tried to impress my new boss. I was there, but I wasn't there, because for me, *you* weren't there. Not really."

One more thing I like about Linda: she tells the truth even when it exposes her as less than the person she strives always to be — a rare bird, in my experience. Then again, my experience is more limited than I'd care to admit: jaded, cynical, solitary. My disappointment with humanity tends to inform my opinions.

Frank, ever the grandpa, recently disagreed with that self-assessment. He insisted that I'm protecting myself from further pain of loss, having experienced too much already, afraid that another such incident might push me over the edge. He said I love people without inhibition, devote myself to them with abandon, and open my emotions, thus making myself vulnerable. To guard against that vulnerability, I've built a wall to keep others out, to keep *me* safe.

Sounds like pure psychobabble to me.

Yet when I'm with Linda, I feel as though I might remove a few bricks from that wall. Maybe. In time.

"I've thought about 1978 a lot, lately," I say.

"That's only natural, under the circumstances."

I take another long sip of wine and refill our glasses. The second bottle is empty. "Nevertheless, I have a difficult time expressing my feelings about it."

"Please try, Tony. It's important."

Damn, I don't want to disappoint her.

Her soft eyes reassure me, and I'm more comfortable than I've felt in a long time — perhaps seventeen years. It might help if I open up to her. I've spoken at length with Frank and Master Komura about my memories, my psychological baggage, my loss. They've been my sounding boards throughout the years, and I trust them with my life.

It's different with Linda, more intimate. I think I trust her with my *heart*, an unusual circumstance, and a feeling I like... a lot.

I motion the waiter over and point to the empty wine bottle. "I think we need another one of these."

Linda doesn't argue.

What the hell, I may as well get drunk given the condition I'm in. "Are you sure you're ready for this?" *Say no. Please, let me off the hook.*

"Yes, I'm ready."

CHAPTER 18
MAY 21, 1978:
TONY HOOPER

I'd suffered in bed last night, staring out the window as I floated in a mean state between sleep and consciousness. Stubborn instinct had refused to stay in its hole, burrowing from deep inside to give me the inevitable news: Alex would never again share his bright disposition and carefree smile.

For the first time since Mom had died, I'd cried. I'd screamed silently at myself, at Dad, at the world, at the Hoopster, and I'd cried some more.

Finally, dawn crept mischievously out of the darkness, like the bratty kid down the block come to tease me.

Had this been a typical Sunday afternoon, I'd have watched the Cubs game on TV with Alex, or shot hoops with him. Instead, I walked around the driveway and absent-mindedly dribbled the basketball, shooting it only occasionally, caring not a whit whether I made the shot—just going through the motions. *Any* motion.

Alex should have been there with me, struggling to make a shot from far outside his range so he could feel like a big man, or at least like his big brother. I wanted to talk to him and coach him. God, I wanted to hold him.

It had been twenty-four hours since I'd walked out the door and left him alone.

Still there was no word of him.

Every tick of the clock's minute hand struck a hammer-blow to my heart. I suffered privately and quietly, refusing to speak to anyone or even to remain near them. Dad was there, Frank was there to provide comfort, and some friends and neighbors stopped by after hearing what had happened.

Intruders! They distracted me from my anguish, my self-loathing.

We knew *nothing* with certainty.

Yet I knew.

I couldn't talk to Dad. I had no confidence in his ability to handle the situation. I'd seen first-hand how he crumbled under the strain when Mom died, and I expected him to crumble again. A damned lousy attitude, but an honest one. Frank might have helped, but he focused on Dad, perhaps sensing who needed consoling the most—again.

Diana called not once, but three times that morning, and each time I had to say I'd get back to her later. Despite her disappointment and concern, I couldn't face even *her*. I didn't know how to draw the lines between my own suffering and guilt, and my need for Diana to rescue me.

Perhaps I didn't want to be rescued. I wasn't finished punishing myself.

"Shit, I hate this!" I stared at the driveway as I dribbled the ball, and then glanced around the neighborhood. "Alex, where are you? Come on home, Hoopster."

Emotions tore at my mind until I could barely think, or stand, or breathe. One crept out of my psyche to overshadow all the others: anger—persistent, pernicious, persecuting. If someone had hurt Alex, I desperately wanted to get my hands on that someone.

What would I do?

Well, I'd done it before. I'd meted out justice on the spot—killed a killer, the drunken bastard who'd murdered Mom. I'd eliminated him without any real conscious thought in what was practically an out-of-body experience.

This time, I had plenty of time to consider my actions. Could I, with absolute premeditation, kill another human being? I couldn't escape the truth, so why deny it? If someone had killed Alex, I could kill the killer—again—if I got the chance.

What an alarming realization. Was it my rage pushing me to the edge? Would I go beyond the simple consideration of the act to its fulfillment, or should I leave it to the law? Which would be worse for the criminal: a quick death, or a lifetime of wallowing in misery behind bars without hope of parole, knowing that his life was already over but that he must suffer it all the same? Which was the more enlightened approach? Which the more costly? What price, life?

What was the value of *Alex's* life?

I grasped for answers as if catching raindrops with a fork.

What morbid thoughts I dwelled on. They jabbed at me like Muhammad Ali on speed. I couldn't shake the horror, the crushing foreboding that life prepared to deal me another devastating blow, a real knockout punch. Was it selfish to think that way, to think of the impact on *me* instead of Alex? Was that the essence of mourning?

"Goddamn it, Tony! Why such dark expectations?" I glanced around to ensure that no one had heard my outburst.

My thoughts drifted back to a time when Mom, Alex and I had gone to the beach at Cedar Lake on a sweltering July day. Alex had journeyed out too far and found deep water. He flailed and yelled for me as the strength drained from his little arms. He was four years old. I raced to him and got there just as he was about to go under. I tried to hide my own fear while holding him close. He shivered and fought to hold back the tears, so I laughed and light-heartedly called him a goof, and his smile returned. He looked around and, upon realizing the depth, puffed with pride. He'd never been out so far, hanging with his big brother in what he liked to call "the big water." I wanted to squeeze him like a warm blanket.

If I'd had a calendar of favorite days, that summer steamer would have been on it.

The recollection wisped away on the warm breeze, and I slumped as though a crane had parked a wrecking ball on my head. I could stay awake no longer. Alex was missing, or worse. What would I do about it?

I'd sleep. It's all I *could* do.

I rolled the basketball into the grass alongside the garage, and staggered inside the house. I needed to leave behind the chaos, the fear and anger, and escape for a few hours into a dream world. Perhaps I could recapture there the life I'd once known—my old friend, happiness.

Yes, dreams. What else was there?

Alex is getting his curveball to work, even though he's too young to be throwing breaking pitches. He's determined to be a pitcher, which I think is a

mistake. The kid can hit! He has a fluid natural swing that generates more power than you'd think possible from his little frame. He's a good glove too, and he can play almost any position. Although he's only ten, I swear that kid has Major League Baseball written all over him. Wouldn't that be a kick?

I can imagine how he would react to playing for the Cubs. Geez, I'd never hear the end of it. That would be a gas. Alex so loves the Cubs and Wrigley Field.

We were there April 17, 1976, to see the Cubs play the Phillies.

The Cubs get off to a huge lead, 12-1, and it looks like a lock. Alex goes nuts as his favorite players get hits and score runs. He keeps eating those lousy, sixty-cent pizza slices, which fairly resemble cardboard smothered in tomato sauce and mozzarella.

He pesters Dad relentlessly. "Please, just one more slice?"

Dad furls his brow and grins. "That's what you said two slices ago."

"I promise. Just one more slice, and one more bag of peanuts, and another Pepsi. That'll be it. I promise!"

"Yeah, yeah, yeah. Sure it will be." Dad hands him the money.

"Come on, Tony!"

He's too small to go on his own, and I have to jog to keep up with him as he bounces between the other fans in the runway like an escaped pinball.

He yells over his shoulder, "Hurry up, Tony, I don't want to miss any of the action."

When the game ends and Mike Schmidt has hit four homeruns to lead the Phillies to a big comeback win, 18-16, Alex shrinks in disappointment. Until we get outside the ballpark.

His enthusiasm resurfaces like a submarine missile launch. "Hey, Dad, can we stop for a Chicago-style hotdog? And maybe an Italian Beef?"

Dad and I look at each other and laugh. Where in the world does the skinny little kid put all that food?

Alex sits alone in the backseat and plays catch by himself. He slaps the baseball into his glove, over and over and over, for the entire ninety-minute drive home.

When we get there, he jumps out of the car and runs to the end of the driveway. He yells, "Hey, Tony, do you want to play some catch?"

Man, are you kidding me? It's been a long day and I need a break. I'm exhausted. I can barely get out of the car, let alone toss a ball around. "Sure, Hoopster, I'll play for a little while."

"All right!"

CHAPTER 19
MAY 21, 1978:
REPORTS, RUMORS, AND RE-ENACTMENTS

Lou Pratt loved to fish. He found it thrilling to stand on the bank of the Fox River in the hopes of hooking a big carp or, if he was lucky, a catfish. They were about all that survived the squalid waters of the Fox. Carp were horrid, despicable fish that made for poor eating, but he was more than happy to fry up a catfish. Never mind that they scavenged for their existence in the same sludge and sewer runoff. Catfish were eating fish and that's all there was to it—the gospel according to Lou Pratt.

Sunday meant a few competitors along the banks of the river, which was fine with Lou; he enjoyed the conversation that accompanied the competition. Light pressure tugged at the fishing line. A smart one, he thought, but not smart enough for an old pro like Lou. With a short, rapid flick of the wrists, he set the hook and worked his catch toward the shore.

He whistled through his smile. "Well, salt my gravy! Ain't you the pretty one?"

Tangled around the catfish was a determined weed. Lou dragged it through the water to a small tributary that ran beside the old carnival grounds on the west side of town, several yards below the dam. It offered fewer obstacles, both above and beneath the water. He gripped the catfish in his right hand and, immersing it in the water, used his left hand to untangle and release the stubborn weed, and unhooked the fish.

He held his prize high for inspection. "I do believe you'll make a fine dinner tonight. Maybe I'll add a few of your friends to the freezer. I *am* feeling lucky and that's for sure. Then I'll—"

He gasped and jumped from the water, and instantly forgot about the catfish that just got away. He riveted his concentration on the horrifying sight before him, and, as it came into focus, he could hold his breakfast no longer. He turned and ran up the path a few yards, where he vomited into a bush off to one side. He heaved and shivered for a minute.

When he was able to control himself, the horror notwithstanding, he returned to the water and gradually focused again on the tragedy.

"God have mercy."

He leapt up the shallow bank and darted toward the main lot. His stomach churned yet again, though it must be empty. He put it out of his mind. He had to reach the payphone across the street.

Chief Bill Radlon responded to the call. His small force, with the help of a couple county sheriff's deputies, still searched for a missing ten-year-old boy. Uneasiness crawled like ants up his spine. There must have been another explanation for Lou Pratt's hysteria. It couldn't have been Alex Hooper, who'd last been seen awaiting his father and a pizza at his home on the north ridge, high above the Fox River valley.

He admonished himself for jumping to conclusions. He'd know soon enough. Doc Wenthal, semi-retired, former County Coroner and still an occasional consultant, was on his way to the river to help with the preliminaries.

The chief pulled into the empty lot that sat idle most of the year, the most notable exception being during the Founders' Day Carnival. At the end of the lot, a man waved his arms in frantic gestures, as though it were necessary to hurry in order to save the dead body.

He pulled to a stop alongside the man and got out of his car.

CHAPTER 20

MAY 20, 1978 (ONE DAY EARLIER): REPORTS, RUMORS, AND RE-ENACTMENTS

At the back of a long unused and ignored piece of farmland, north of the gravel pits and east of Crystal Lake, stood a dilapidated, nearly ancient farm shed. Mitchell Norton happened upon it accidentally one day while doing some impromptu hiking around the gravel pits, as he attempted to gather his courage and join some kids who swam in the lake there.

It struck him as a satisfactory place to escape from the world, something he did often.

Now conscious, Alex Hooper lay gagged and bound to a wooden workbench against the north wall. He stared at the ceiling and nervously watched the meaty, motionless spider suspended in its web a few feet above him. Tears slithered down his cheeks as he attempted to make no noise at all.

He knew the faint sounds that emanated from his right must be from the terrible man who'd hit him and brought him here, yet he couldn't force himself to turn his head and look. He chose the safer route, remaining perfectly still and quiet, as if doing so might make him invisible. When he'd been younger and monsters had lurked under his bed at night, this had been a most effective strategy.

Help me, Tony! Come and save me! Dad, I'm so scared!

Mitchell sat on a dusty chair in the corner of the shed, stared at the boy across from him, and agonized over how to proceed. He dreaded his next move. The demon was in charge here, and he knew all too well what the Reaper wanted. Yet he sat frozen, unable to bring himself to action, hunched over in his armchair with elbows on knees and head in hands. He massaged his temples and growled in frustration at the pain that so distracted him.

He glanced at the boy, who trembled uncontrollably, and again groaned as the demon returned in a swirling, dizzying montage. He taunted him and showed him new wickedness, the sight of which at once terrified and compelled him. Inevitably, he threatened Mitchell with unimaginable punishment should he disobey.

He could not.

He raised his head, stood and approached the bench, until the boy lay beneath him. Although the boy kept his head still, he rolled his eyes right and focused on him.

Mitchell spoke in a flat voice, without emotion, controlled by forces outside his power. "You've been trying to avoid me, I know, but I am the deliverer. You cannot hide from me."

The man blurred through a murky puddle of tears, yet Alex remained quiet, and still but for his shaking, which he was helpless to prevent. Above him stood something different from what he'd seen before. The same face watched him, the same man, but his eyes blazed like something out of those cheap, Saturday night horror movies that he and Tony loved. Though he'd never seen it in real life, he recognized the unmistakable glare of insanity.

I have to keep quiet. If I concentrate, I can disappear. I can do it.

"Tell me, son," the man continued, "are you worthy to stand in the light? Have you been a good boy? Or might you burn in the terrible fires? Do you know that I am the judge and the jury?"

Alex didn't understand. In his terror, he barely heard the words.

"I have never seen the light, but I'm told it's a place of warmth, peace and joy. However, I *have* seen the flames of despair, torture and agony, and I know most of us will end up there. My hosts have shown me these things, for I am the chosen, the dispatcher to the new world."

The wicked man stalked to a table at the edge of his sight, and opened a small duffel bag. He pulled out a knife that could double as a machete, carried it over to the bench, and held it high.

Alex groaned and emptied his bladder as he searched desperately for some sign of rescue. Fear overwhelmed him, but also profound sadness, for he knew he would soon leave Tony and his dad behind. He felt sorry for them, somehow knowing that they'd suffer the pain long after it had passed for him. A mature resignation steeled him against the horror, an understanding well beyond his years—an acceptance.

I'm sorry, Tony. I'll miss you. And you too, Dad.

His mind flashed to the many joyous experiences of his life. Tony, ever-present in those images, taught him to play baseball and basketball and football, playing catch or shooting hoops with him for hours on end. Those were his happiest moments. He loved his father too, despite his prolonged absences and distant manner. Most of all, Tony was his family and his rock, and he would miss him more than anyone.

What would happen to Tony when he was gone? Tony would be devastated, and he felt terribly sad for his big brother—a grown-up way to think, under the circumstances. Although he didn't understand the genesis of these thoughts, they pleased him.

The memories of his mother had been fading recently, but she now came to him and spoke in her soft way, with a voice pure as starlight. Her loving face shone and exuded warmth, like a soft blanket that covered him and protected him from the monster. She positively glowed, shrouded in unimaginable light.

The bad man interrupted Alex's vision. "If you see the light, be joyful that I have delivered you. If you see the fire, then know that we shall meet again, and together we shall dance the long death through the eternal flames, for those I have chosen as my own."

The mean man held up the knife for one final inspection. Alex clenched his eyes shut. He wanted to see only the happy memories. He prayed to a God in whom he trusted despite the severe punishment he faced. He didn't understand, but calm enveloped him, and again a warm light embraced him, so comforting that he forgot the threat he faced in this terrible place.

Although a mere flash in his mind, it felt to Alex like a long escape.

He relived every happy experience of his short life, more numerous than he'd realized. Aware of his memories as never before, he rejoiced as his mind opened up in ways unimaginable. His mother, laughing and loving, doted over the baby Alex as if he were the only important thing in the entire world. His big brother bragged to all his friends about his baby brother.

Searing heat and a brief explosion of pain ripped through him, but it vanished a moment after it began.

In that flash, Alex's heart and mind knew only the miracle of joy, only the light and warmth that remained. A gentle presence assured him everything would be okay. He didn't understand, but he knew he was home.

Where are we going, Mommy?

"Fuck!" Mitchell's anger rocketed. "Don't die on me, you little shit!"

He'd botched it. Where were the torture, agony and misery? He'd thrust the knife in too deeply and in the wrong location. The boy had died instantly—no wild screams, no painful grimaces, nothing!

"Fuck a rubber duck, what have I done?"

He puckered in fear and awaited the wrath of the demon.

In that instant, the old Mitchell Norton returned. He stood over the boy's blood-soaked body, clutched a blood-soaked knife, and imagined his own blood-soaked punishment.

He sought desperately to make amends. Although the boy was dead, perhaps Mitchell could still please the demon with his next act. Then he could feed his new friend, the Beast.

That might satisfy the Reaper.

CHAPTER 21
MAY 21, 1978:
REPORTS, RUMORS, AND RE-ENACTMENTS

The chief pulled a photo of Alex Hooper from a file on the front passenger seat, and shuffled around back to grab hip-waders and rubber gloves from the trunk of the cruiser. His "witness" could barely catch his breath as he introduced himself.

Lou Pratt led him down a path toward the river, explaining as they walked the events that had transpired. When he came to the part about spotting the boy, he stopped and turned. "God in Heaven, Chief, it's sure an awful sight."

Usually is, the chief thought, and nodded as they continued down the path to the small tributary. The smell of fresh vomit assaulted him, and he spotted the unpleasant source. Lou walked past it without a glance or a word, probably embarrassed by it.

No need, Chief Radlon thought. *Nothing wrong with being human during — especially during — inhuman events.*

Lou stopped before the water's edge and pointed toward the spot.

The chief looked but couldn't see anything through the sunlight reflecting off the surface. He squinted, focused, concentrated on the shallow depths....

The body came into view.

Doc Wenthal called out at that precise instant, and startled him such that he nearly jumped out of his shoes. He took minor satisfaction in noting that Lou had also leapt at the intrusion; at least he wasn't the only one on a razor's edge. He *was* supposed to be the professional, however.

He called back and waited a few seconds until the doctor arrived. "Over here, Doc." His eyes never left the submerged body.

Doc slid by Lou with a polite nod and stood next to the chief. "What do we have, Bill?" He strained his eyes to see through the glare and into the water.

Chief Radlon pointed to the spot. "Take a look."

"Dear God, he was only a child."

The chief grabbed a nearby stick and used it to scare away the fish that picked at the body. When he turned back, Lou looked blue around the gills too. He hoped the poor guy wasn't about to pass out. He had enough to deal with.

He slid into his hip-waders and put on the rubber gloves before entering the water. Lou clutched his stomach again, as if he would puke at any moment, but his eyes never wavered. It always happened that way; people were drawn to the most gruesome sights.

"Careful, Bill," Doc said. "We don't want to upset any evidence that might be found, so be gentle when moving it to the shore."

The chief nodded reflexively and bent over the body, which he noted might have remained undiscovered were the water deeper. He looked at it for several seconds, gathered his will, and grasped the small corpse under the arms to drag it carefully to the shore.

"Sonuvabitch!"

Lou and Doc soon understood the reason for his anger. They grimaced as the corpse's arms—severed at the elbows—bobbed like buoys in the muck. Bill struggled to carry it through the thick mud, and finally managed to lift the body onto dry ground.

"Ah shit."

The boy's legs, severed two inches above the knees, trailed skin and tissue. His left eye was gone, a deep gouge left in its place. Muscle and bone peeked from holes in the skin. The chief noticed, despite his wish never to look upon this body again, that the one remaining eye, though filmed over, appeared oddly content. Perhaps his imagination worked on him, a kind of wishful thinking.

He prayed the boy hadn't been required to endure the damage inflicted upon him.

Doc put on latex gloves and knelt over the body. A full examination would wait until the victim was in the morgue, but the mutilations clearly intrigued Doc. He ran his hand over the end of one of the severed legs, and sighed. He looked up and shook his head.

The chief understood. The fish in the Fox River could not do that to a body — not in twenty-four hours. Some rotten bastard had chopped off the boy's limbs.

Difficult days lay ahead for his sleepy little town.

Lou watched with ashen face and hugged himself, shaking noticeably. The chief regretted allowing the man to observe this. Civilians were not so immune to such horror.

"Did somebody do that to the boy? Did a *person* cut him into pieces?" Lou fidgeted and nearly hopped. "Dear God, that's what happened, isn't it?"

"Now listen, Mr. Pratt," the chief said, "I don't want the whole town in a panic over something we don't yet know enough about. We need time to get this investigation moving, and to examine the forensic evidence, before we jump to any conclusions. In the meantime, I'll ask you say *nothing* about this to *anyone*. Do you understand?"

Lou hung his head in sorrow and whispered, "Yes, I understand. But this is Algonquin, for God's sake, not Chicago. This sort of thing isn't supposed to happen here."

The chief ignored him and pulled the picture from his shirt pocket. He studied it for a few seconds and compared it to the mutilated corpse.

"Damn it."

CHAPTER 22
MAY 21, 1978:
TONY HOOPER

Dad pulled me from a sleep filled with dreams of Alex, which included several appearances by Mom. I'd been out for hours.

"Tony, Chief of Police Bill Radlon is here and he needs to speak with us."

I emerged from my room in a pair of shorts and a tee shirt, with hair that announced my many hours in bed. The chief glared at Dad, uncomfortable with my presence. He hadn't come to speak with *me*, but Dad couldn't face this alone.

The chief declined the offer of coffee, which we now lived on, and Dad poured himself another big cup. I filled one for myself as I struggled to come awake.

Tensions ran high, as if a giant vacuum had sucked the air from the room. The three of us sat around the kitchen table and stared at one another for several seconds.

Dad cleared his throat. "So, Chief, I hope you have some good news for us."

You must be kidding me. You're smiling? Are you blind to the look in the chief's eyes?

How deep was his denial?

"Mr. Hooper, I wonder if we might speak alone."

God, there it is.

There could no longer be any doubt. Alex, the boy who'd been my Shadow, was gone. How would I survive without my Shadow?

Dad, with eyes that betrayed his devastating heartbreak, had reached the same conclusion. He stammered, "That won't be necessary, Chief. Tony should be here for this."

After a few seconds of silence and a grimace of indecision, the chief resolved to finish with it.

"Very well, I'm sorry to have to tell you this, but we've found Alex's body. I'm afraid he's been killed."

He wore the most curious expression, taken aback by our reactions.

One might easily have thought things were backwards between Dad and me, as he slumped over the table, rested his head on his arms, and sobbed uncontrollably. The chief cast his eyes down at first, unsurprised by Dad's expression of utter grief, but he now looked at me with what I could only assume was curiosity.

I'd hardly responded to his announcement because, deep in my heart, I already knew. This was not news, and I'd already cried.

I had no more tears to offer.

Dad's breakdown continued, and my sorrow for him was complete. Yet I felt more: pity, I thought. Strange that I should pity him. After all, didn't I suffer too? I walked over and held him as he sobbed. The chief observed again, perhaps thinking it odd that I should console my father, versus the other way around. He didn't know Dad.

The tears slowed to a drip as Dad raised his head and stared at the wall with blank eyes.

I stood and looked at the chief. "You said Alex was *killed*. In an accident? Or by someone?"

He looked back and forth between us, and resigned himself to the idea that I'd be doing most of the talking.

"He was murdered and...."

"And *what*?"

"And his body was dumped in the river."

"I see. Any ideas about who did it?"

A strange look again contorted his face, as if he silently demanded answers from me. They weren't so hard to read. *How can you be so casual? How can you be so cold? Do you have no heart? We're talking about your little brother here!*

"No," he said. "We found him only a short while ago. Our investigation will take some time. We won't have the coroner's report for a day or two."

Dad flinched at mention of the coroner, and I placed my hand on his shoulder. He came only partially out of his mist, and returned to the discussion. "We'll have to make arrangements. Where do we go from here?"

"Once the coroner finishes with her findings, you may claim the body."

Dad jerked under another spasm — *the body*, rather than, *Alex*.

"First things first," Chief Radlon said. "We'll need you to come to the morgue to identify the body — a formality, but a necessary one."

When Dad failed to reply, the chief turned to me.

I nodded. "I'll take care of that. When do we do it?"

He was no longer surprised. Dad clearly couldn't handle it.

He said he'd pick me up at nine o'clock the next morning, Monday. He'd drive me to the morgue, where I'd do what I already dreaded, and then he'd bring me back home. I agreed to all that as I escorted him out.

I returned to the kitchen. "Dad?"

"I want to be alone for a while, Tony."

"Okay."

I drifted into my room and lay down, and the floodgates opened again. I still had tears, after all.

CHAPTER 23
MAY 22, 1978:
TONY HOOPER

We entered the McHenry County complex, located off Highway 47 in Woodstock, and awaited an elevator in the lobby of the coroner's facility. Chief Radlon stood beside me and glanced over several times. I couldn't help but think the chief, offering the same gaze he'd worn a couple times the night before, suspected me of the unthinkable.

I squirmed and scratched the back of my neck, as if something were crawling up it.

I thought about coming right out and asking him, but this damn place was hard enough. And likely to get harder. Soon.

The elevator bell rang and the doors opened. Relief, anxiety, uncertainty, fear and dread — they formed a toxic soup on which I nearly choked.

The chief held out his hand and said, "After you."

We rode the elevator down in silence, but my heart thumped like a jackhammer in my chest, threatening to explode at any moment. I wiped a sleeve across my temples and forehead, where sweat dripped down and stung my eyes. I wanted to tell Chief Radlon this was a terrible mistake, that Dad should be doing this. I couldn't —

The elevator stopped and the doors slid open. I stepped through and halted, glancing up and down the hallway. Nowhere to escape.

The chief tapped my shoulder and said, "Right this way."

My chest tightened further as we approached two sliding glass doors, the bold letters "MORGUE" stenciled on the outside.

He put a hand out to stop me. "Listen, Tony, I'd say this is a simple exercise we're about to go through, except that I know how difficult it can be."

All I could think to do was nod in response.

"All we need," he said, "is for you to make an official identification, and then we can leave. If you want more time in there, that's fine. You just let me know. However, you shouldn't draw it out." He took a deep breath, held it for a few seconds, and sighed. "You should remember Alex as he was during your best times together. Not like this. Let's go in, get it done, and get out. Okay?"

I squeaked, "Okay," and the sound of it took my mind right to Alvin and the Chipmunks for some damned reason. I almost laughed, and I might have done so had I not been on the verge of tears, more frightened than I'd ever been.

The chief opened the door, and I gasped at the smell. The room reeked of that hospital antiseptic quality, and something more — deeper, fouler. I could think of little to which it compared: the Fox River on a particularly bad day, perhaps. Although I'd once touched Mom's corpse, I'd never *smelled* death.

The room contained two tables, each holding a body covered by a dark plastic sheet. The coroner sat at a desk at the edge of the room, and I had to do a double-take. Coroners should be fat old men with rumpled hair and heavy glasses, who removed organs with one hand while eating a tuna fish sandwich with the other. *She* was blonde, probably in her thirties, with great legs — just plain hot. A poor fit for the stereotype.

She stood and walked toward us.

"Dr. Singer," the chief said, "this is Tony Hooper. He's here to identify the boy we brought in."

She nodded and offered a polite smile. "Mr. Hooper, Chief Radlon."

She looked taken aback, undoubtedly surprised by my age. Not for the first time, I wished Dad had possessed the character to meet this responsibility.

"It's right over here," she said.

It's! It! You're calling Alex "it?"

My anger, or sorrow, or incredulity — or whatever the hell it was — must have been evident. The doctor's shoulders sagged as she sighed and averted her eyes.

Good! You should *be uncomfortable, calling Alex "it."*

She motioned to the chief, and led us to the examination table where a corpse lay under a black plastic shroud.

Oh God. That's Alex.

She guided me to the side near one end, and waited for the chief to situate himself at the head of the table.

"I'm sorry," she said. "I know this is difficult. Are you prepared?"

Unable to speak, or to find oxygen in this lifeless place, I nodded.

The doctor folded the sheet back to expose Alex's head and a few inches of his chest. I didn't move. I barely breathed. His face, grim and stiff, looked as though he'd fallen into a vat of flour. One of his eyes, though closed, appeared terribly disfigured.

I stared for several seconds, frozen, trying not to shiver beneath the goosebumps that erupted all over my body, trying to quell the shaking in my hands, the quivering in my lips, the churning in my gut.

Chief Radlon broke the silence. "Can you identify him for us?"

Once again, I nodded. I started to say something, but managed only a grunt, my words choked off by something huge and unknown in my throat. It could have been a rhinoceros.

He pressed me quietly. "Is that Alex?"

My vision blurred beneath pools of silent tears, and I nodded. Both the chief and Dr. Singer diverted their eyes at that awkward moment. I made them uncomfortable. Hell, I made *myself* uncomfortable.

I whispered, "Goodbye Hoopster," and reached under the sheet to hold Alex's hand for a minute, to touch my baby brother one last time.

Where's his hand? I pulled back the sheet to find it and— "No! No! My God, what did you do to him? No!"

"Tony, wait," Dr. Singer said. "*We* didn't do that to Alex. That's how Chief Radlon found him."

What? Someone chopped him up? Oh God, why? Alex! Oh Alex, what have I done? I'm so sorry. Alex. Alex.

The room spun and everything faded to gray. I tried to fight off whatever attacked me—like a thousand blowtorches—and stumbled backwards into the cold steel vaults. My legs buckled and I collapsed to the frigid floor, propping myself up with trembling hands, shivering and gasping, unable to breathe. The gray faded darker.

The blackness was coming for me.

"Tony! Listen to me! Look at me!"

I could barely see Dr. Singer. She leaned over and cupped my face in her hands. She smelled of mint and flowers. And death.

"You have to listen to me, Tony. This is important. Okay?"

Air. I need air.

"It's still preliminary," she said, "but there are some things I can tell you with absolute certainty. Alex died when a sharp object, probably a knife, punctured his heart. You must understand that death was *instantaneous*."

She snapped her fingers to provide effect.

"The mutilations were inflicted postmortem," she said, "*after* death. We know that by the way the blood clots. Whatever sick reason the killer had for performing those mutilations, Alex felt *none* of it. He was already gone."

She paused and watched me, waiting for a response, no doubt, or some indication that I'd heard her. I fought to regain my composure, and to let my breathing settle closer to a normal rate. The shaking diminished, but I still couldn't speak. I could only stare at her.

"It's true," she said. "As bad as it seems, it was completely painless. It *had* to be, because he would have died instantly."

I wiped the tears from my face, and took several deep breaths to regain control. A minute later, or two minutes, or a week, I pushed against the floor, and the chief helped me up.

Dr. Singer walked back to the table and began to pull the sheet over Alex.

"Please wait." I said it barely loud enough for anyone to hear. "I'm okay. Please, let me see Alex's face — just his face — one last time."

The doctor looked to the chief.

He peered into my eyes before turning to the doctor and nodding, and then produced a handkerchief from his pocket and handed it to me.

I used it to wipe my eyes and blow my nose. "Thanks." I offered it back.

He shook his head and flicked his hand as if to say, *you keep that,* and said, "You sure you're okay?"

"Yeah, I think so." I shuffled to the table and looked down at Alex.

My heart weighed a thousand pounds, and my eyes pooled with fresh tears. My throat almost closed again as I whispered, "I love you, Hoopster."

I reached out and placed my hand on Alex's left cheek. *You're so cold.* I wanted to rub his cheeks, to make my baby brother warmer.

"I've always loved you, and I always will. I know you're in the best place now. Say 'Hi' to Mom for me, okay?"

I bowed my head and allowed the tears to flow freely, and stuttered the last words I would ever speak to the most important person in my life.

"You... always were... a goo — a good boy."

I turned and stalked toward the door without raising my head, determined to forever etch in my mind the memory of Alex's warm love — *not* his cold cheek.

Across the hall in the men's room, I stood at one of the sinks and turned on the water. I looked in the mirror, seeing only Alex on that ice-cold table, and ran for one of the stalls.

I emptied my stomach — once, twice, three times — and wiped the sweat from my face again. After spitting a dozen times in hopes of getting the foul taste out of my mouth, I flushed the toilet and left the stall.

I slunk back to the sink, where the water was still running, and cupped my hands to rinse my mouth a few times. I splashed water on my face and hair, and glanced at the mirror as I leaned on the sink. I couldn't face myself, so I stared down at the water swirling down the drain, and drifted into a fog.

After some unknown seconds or minutes, I splashed more water on my face, then stood up and looked to my left for a towel. Nothing. I looked to my right, and there stood an observer, just inside the door.

"How long have you been standing there?"

"Long enough." Chief Radlon walked forward, snagged a couple paper towels out of a dispenser along the way, and handed them to me.

"Thanks. I'm sorry about losing it in there. And in here. I think I've managed to get myself together."

"You have nothing to apologize for. Take whatever time you need."

I managed a weak smile, and wiped the towels over my face and hands.

"You know," he said, "I thought you might actually have been involved in Alex's death, somehow. It was hard to imagine, but family members are the first likely suspects for a reason. Long history."

I shook my head and sighed. "I wondered about that. The way you looked at me earlier, while we were waiting for the elevator, and yesterday at the house too. I thought you looked kind of... strange. Suspicious."

"Well, after what I saw across the hall, and in here, I'm not suspicious anymore."

I didn't know how to respond.

"I mean, let's face it, nobody's *that* good an actor." He smiled.

I actually chuckled, as if a hundred pounds had rolled off my shoulders. "No, I guess not."

He patted me on the back and said, "Do you need more time?"

"No, it's okay. I'm ready to go." I pitched the wet towels into the trash. "We still have a lot to do over the next couple days but, geez! I have no idea where to begin."

"I'm sure your dad will know what to do."

Dad? Really? I don't know. Maybe.

The chief must have read my emotions. He appeared concerned, even angry. "And if you need any help at all, I'll be happy to do what I can for you. Don't hesitate to ask. Not for one second!"

He placed his hand on my shoulder, and kept it there for the entire walk back to the car. I felt suddenly smaller, crushed by the whole experience, but the chief's hand comforted me. It felt safe. Strong. Certain.

We exchanged awkward smiles, but said nothing more as we got in the police cruiser and pulled out of the county complex.

CHAPTER 24
MAY 22, 1978:
TONY HOOPER

I struggled to recapture my composure as we rode home from the morgue.

The chief let me.

When we arrived, Dad was sitting in a lawn chair at the back end of the driveway. He held a glass in one hand, a bottle of Jack Daniel's in the other. We got out of the car and I stared at him for a minute.

"Tony, why don't you go inside the house? I need to talk to your father."

"Listen, Chief, I appreciate —"

"Just go in the house, Tony. Please."

Despite his soft voice, I knew better than to argue with him. Besides, he might succeed where I would probably have failed. I nodded and started for the door without looking at Dad.

"What's the matter, Son, you don't want to talk to the old man?" He practically laughed, and added in a quiet slur, "Hell, I can't say I blame you. I wouldn't want to talk to me either."

I jogged on and entered the house. Once through the door, I stepped to the side, out of sight but still able to hear what they said.

The chief sighed and in a dry, sharp voice, said, "Mr. Hooper."

"Howdy, Chief Radlon. Hell, we're practically friends now. Forget that mister stuff and call me Hank."

"I'm not your friend, *Hank*. I might be, if you could manage to set aside your self-pity and stop being an *asshole* for a few minutes."

I couldn't help it; I had to peek around the edge to see what was happening. I remained quiet. Dad stared at the chief as emotions flashed across his face—confusion, self-pity, embarrassment, rage.

"Why you lousy, self-righteous sonuvabitch! What do you know about it, huh? Have you lost a wife? Have you lost a child? Well, have you, goddamn it?"

"There's no denying that you've had a tough time of it. So has Tony." He maintained his even tone. "Guess you've been too busy to notice."

The accusation stung my dad. He looked at the chief through those terribly bloodshot eyes, but he could muster no response.

"Your son did something today that no boy should have to do, at least no boy who has a father. That was *your* task. *You* should have been there."

Dad took another drink and stared at his feet.

The chief waited.

"Not being there is my way," Dad said. "I wasn't there, not *really* there, for the boys after my wife died. I didn't know how. Hell, Tony was more of a father to Alex. Then I wasn't there when the killer took Alex. I should have been there. He'd still be alive."

He drained his glass and almost fell out of the chair.

"Now what? I'll finally be there for Tony?" He laughed—a choking sound that dripped with disgust and self-loathing. "What can I tell you, Chief? When it comes to being a father, I pretty much suck."

He raised the bottle to pour another drink, and fell out of the chair.

The chief leaned over and placed a hand on Dad's neck. "Passed out. Shit."

CHAPTER 25
JUNE 7, 1995:
TONY HOOPER

I stare at my wine glass, relieved that the story of those terrible days in 1978 is over. The third bottle of wine is now empty. Like my heart.

Perhaps I needed to tell it at last, but the long story, filled with so much grief and sorrow, such powerful guilt, has rendered me limp. I can barely keep myself together. I have no energy left. My emotions have poured out.

Mostly.

I turn up my glass and chug the last several ounces of Cabernet, all the while struggling to slow my heart and fighting against the deluge.

Linda watches me, and the sadness I see — the caring, the tenderness, the moisture in her eyes — is the final straw. I lay my head on her shoulder and she places her arm around me.

I can do nothing more. I need a release.

For the third time in twenty years, I cry.

Alex, can you ever forgive me?

PART 5

OUT OF THE ASHES

CHAPTER 26
MAY 27, 1978:
FRANK WILLOW

"Loneliness comes in two basic varieties. When it results from a desire for solitude, loneliness is a door we close against the world. When the world instead rejects us, loneliness is an open door, unused." – *Dean Koontz, "Forever Odd"*

The sun rested on my old bones like the heating pad I kept near my La-Z-Boy, a welcome thing at my age. The sky sparkled in a hollow, pale blue—something between off-white and transparent—and the world exploded into green everywhere. Winter had drifted away, only a bad memory now, and good riddance. My garden, my living, breathing kaleidoscope, burst in color and sprayed a live perfume to please the senses.

Such a glorious day might have soothed the soul, had it not been one of the worst of all possible days. Distress ripped at my soul, and snatched my breath as though I'd taken a hard punch to the chest.

Today we'd lain to rest my grandson, Alex.

Though not related, I'd considered the Hooper boys my grandsons for many years. They'd brought joy and light to an old man, enlivened my solitary life. Now only Tony remained, a boy for whom I'd have done anything and given everything. Few things in life devastated so profoundly as a child's death, an event properly reserved for old farts like me. The world had stood before him, bracing for his bright future.

Alas, his light no longer shined.

Everything had flipped upside down. Alex should someday have stood over *my* grave and celebrated *my* life. The world would have made more sense if only I could have traded places with him, and I'd have been content to do so.

I tried never to be angry with God. On that unholy day... well, I had to try harder.

I'd attended the funeral, a fit and proper event filled with black suits, black dresses and red eyes, to say goodbye to the beloved Alex. I'd also provided a shoulder for Hank Hooper to lean on. He'd needed it.

Tony had embraced his girlfriend, the lovely young Diana, for moral support.

No real surprise; he'd handled the whole thing much better than his father had. Tony was strong. Hank was weak. That was just about the nut of it.

Hank had drifted throughout the ceremony, lost and unsure what he should say or do. Tony had stared at the ground with the slightest hint of a smile, as though voyaging through the memories of his many special experiences with Alex—*exactly* how his little brother would have liked it. That Alex was a real smart one, for a boy his age, oozing empathy to which most of us could only aspire.

Many people had gathered afterwards at the Hooper place, and I made an appearance for a short time. Some of Tony's relatives had been there, people he rarely saw and didn't much care for. Some of those folks gave me the willies. Their wooden smiles and plastic words said one thing, but their eyes said something entirely different. Phonies! I understood why Tony felt as he did, why he'd avoided them all day and had spent his time with me or with Diana and some neighborhood kids.

I'd escaped with little fanfare and without saying anything. No one would miss me. They had plenty else to worry about.

Now seated on my patio with a fine cognac in hand, I enjoyed my garden and the perfect weather. I wasn't a real big drinker, but it was okay on a day like today. I'd probably have a second. Maybe a third. I could sure as hell use it.

I flinched when the squeaky gate of mine yelled out. I needed to oil those hinges. The arrival of my visitor didn't surprise me, though he arrived sooner than I'd anticipated.

Tony plunked down in the chair next to me and looked at the garden without saying a word. I swayed gently in my rocker and took another sip of cognac, happy to oblige his desire for quiet.

After a couple minutes of silent reverie, he looked over and examined my drink. "I don't suppose you have another one of those?"

I thought about it for a minute. He was only eighteen but, what the hell — at eighteen, already in the army, I'd been drinking for two years.

"Given the circumstances," I said, "I think you're entitled. Sit tight."

A few minutes later, I returned with another snifter and a nearly full bottle of Courvoisier VSOP cognac.

I poured him a perfect two fingers. "Here you go. This is fine liquor, so no ice."

"Thanks, that sounds good."

He downed most of it in one huge gulp, and twisted his face into contortions as though I'd forced him to eat dog poop.

He stuttered through his coughing, "Wow! That's... pretty... strong stuff."

"You get used to it. It's a smooth cognac, a gentleman's drink — for sipping, not gulping. Take it a little slower."

"I'd say that advice is a few seconds late."

We chuckled, settled back and rocked for several minutes, me in a gentle, grandfatherly rhythm, him as though in the race of his life. His blank expression, as he stared at the garden, occasionally retreated under a palpable sadness. It broke my heart all over again, but I pushed it away.

He needed me to be strong for him, to stand in where his dad failed.

He took a deep breath and continued. "I don't know why exactly, but I expected it to be storming like crazy — something biblical, real Wrath of God stuff. It would have been more appropriate."

"Ah, nonsense! A boy like Alex deserves a bright and joyful day. He'd have wanted it this way, and it's how I'll always remember him. A day like today makes that easier, sort of finishes the point."

He took a deep breath, clearly trying to fight back the tears, and exhaled in a heavy sigh. "I suppose that's one way to look at it. Everybody at the house sure seems to be in a good mood. All those damned relatives laughing and reminiscing, as though it's a fucking family reunion or something, as though they gave a shit about Alex! Everybody kept coming up to me and hugging me and saying shit like, 'Oh, poor Tony, I'm so, so sorry.'"

He shook his head and nearly spit, "Aaaaah! I had to get out of there before I punched one of them in the goddamned face."

What could I say to calm him? Best let him vent, though it was unlike the boy to throw around so much profanity. He was usually so polite, but I understood. We all had our limits.

"Diana and her parents left. Then my friends took off. *Man!* After that, there was *nobody* there I wanted to be around."

I knew all too well that he included his father in that sentiment.

He waved his hands in gesture over his formal suit. "So here I am, still in this get-up, drinking cognac. Frankly, I'd prefer a beer."

"You know where the fridge is, and your legs aren't broken."

When he went inside, I couldn't help but wonder how he'd recover from this. He'd suffered so much loss for a boy his age. He'd lost his mother three years ago, and now he'd lost the boy who'd meant more to him than anyone in the world. A person my age expected a significant amount of loss, accrued over a long life, but a boy his age shouldn't have experienced such things. He'd gotten too much of a head start on life's miserable, more painful experiences.

He would graduate from high school soon, and he'd head off to college in the fall. In the meantime, I feared the impending summer would be most difficult for him.

If only I could have helped him somehow.

CHAPTER 27
MAY 27, 1978:
MITCHELL NORTON

"Men must have corrupted nature a little, for they were not born wolves, and they have become wolves." – *Voltaire*

The newspaper story said his name was Alex Scott Hooper – ASH in Tommy's name game. That was damn funny – ASH to ashes. The article listed his father as Henry Allen Hooper – HAH. Fuckin' hilarious! His brother, my nemesis, was Anthony Stephen Hooper – ASH as well. Interesting. His mother had been deceased for three years.

"Aw, aren't they a poor, sad family?"

The Reaper didn't answer. He might still have been pissed at me.

Bloodstains lingered on the workbench and on the floor of the shed, in my new work place, home of my second and much more exciting job. I performed my new duties here, though I had a shitload to learn.

I'd sent ASH to ashes, all right, but the demon had screamed in fury and frustration because I'd fucked it up so badly. I was supposed to torture the boy. He was to perish only after the pain had become too terrible to endure. Instead, the little shit had died instantly – a complete fuck-up on my part.

I was new and inexperienced at torture. I'd made a mistake.

I cut the hardheaded little fucker up though, and fed him to the Beast, which should'a counted for something with the Reaper. It served the little shit right after the way his head had hurt my hand. It *still* hurt to make a fist. Little fucker.

I'd pleaded with the Reaper and assured him I'd do better next time.

I think he believed me, but he'd stepped up my training and subjected me to grueling hours of instruction every night since. Sleep remained a vague memory; I had no time for such "trifles," according to that bastard. I had to learn my lessons well and get it right the next time, or lack of sleep, as he'd made quite clear, would be the least of my fuckin' worries.

In the meantime, I'd outfitted the shop with knives, saws, shears, a hammer, a mallet, pliers, a pick, a shovel, and plenty of plastic bags and rubber gloves. I'd stocked up on cleansers, disinfectants, sponges, a mop and a bucket. Good to go.

I doubted anybody ever came to that ancient shack, but I latched the door and put a padlock on it—just in case. If someone cut the lock off, I'd need a new workshop. I might lose my tools if that happened, but there weren't nothin' I could do about that.

Now I wanted to see how things were going at the Hooper house.

"*That* should be fun."

Trees surrounded my usual parking spot on the little gravel trek, barely more than a country alley, called Cermak Road. I parked as far back as I could while keeping a good view of the Hooper house. Cars lined the street up and down Cary Road in front of their place, and the driveway was full, as they entertained everyone who'd come to express their condolences.

"ASH to ashes and dust to dust. Too sad."

What *really* interested me was that old '67 Bonneville parked in the grass next to the garage—that fuckin' Tony's car.

"That sucker is like a ship on wheels. Probably seats about twenty."

I laughed; couldn't remember the last time I'd felt so damn good. I expected Hooper to take me to my angel today. Diana must have been there to comfort him, or else he'd go to her at some point. If it had been me, I'd—

"What the hell do we have here?"

Hooper appeared on a bicycle at the end of the dirt road, directly across the street, wearing a black suit.

"Not exactly the latest in biking attire, Tony-boy."

He looked up and down the road and hesitated, like he didn't want to go home, or like—

"Shit! He's looking right at me."

Easy, Mitchell, the Reaper said, *he can't see you through the windshield glare. Even if he could, it wouldn't matter. He has no idea who you are.*

Hooper rode to his house and jogged inside, and I settled back into my surveillance. It was kinda boring, but I tried to think about Diana. I could still see her face in my mind's eye, and I hoped like hell that fuckin' Tony would—

"Speak of the devil."

Hooper reappeared, alone and dressed more casually, and jumped into his car. He managed to skirt the sea of parked vehicles, driving through the yard and the front ditch, to make his way out.

"My, my, but ain't he determined to escape the festivities?"

I followed him like the cops did it in the movies. I couldn't get so close that he could *make* me, but I couldn't lose him, either. I had no idea where he was going—it could'a been anywhere—but I hoped to hell he'd lead me to my angel.

He turned left on Highway 31, down the hill into town, and then right at the light, toward Lake-in-the-Hills. I remained a few cars behind.

"Hell, this ain't so tough."

He turned right into an old subdivision, and I followed. Narrow roads snaked through the neighborhood and... he'd vanished! He could'a turned on any of several streets. I looked left and right, forward and back, and left and right again. My hands dampened with sweat as my customary panic welled up.

Damn it, Mitchell, if you've lost him, I'll—

"There it is!"

He sat in a driveway where a girl was already getting into the car. It happened too fast, and I couldn't quite make her out, but it *must* be Diana.

I drove to the next little crossroad and waited as he backed out of the driveway and headed off in the other direction. I turned around to follow and, as I passed her house, checked out the number on their mailbox. At the corner, I read the name on the street sign.

"All right, I have an address, but is it my *angel's* address? It must be, but there's only one way to find out for sure. Besides, I'm getting good at this, don't you think?"

The Reaper didn't answer. He was funny that way.

CHAPTER 28
MAY 27, 1978:
TONY HOOPER

I dreaded my bicycle ride home from Frank's house; too many of my damned relatives would still be at our place. I snuck around like a fidgety mouse and managed to avoid most of the commotion, changed my clothes, and hustled out to the Bonnie to escape.

Before she left our house with her parents earlier, Diana had suggested we go out tonight with some friends, to give me a chance to relax after today's insanity.

Hungover with the sorrow of my final goodbye to Alex, I *wanted* to get out and have some fun. The damned guilt clawed at me, but Frank said it was perfectly normal, a way to cope with the pain, a survival mechanism. By the time I got to Diana's place, I felt better about it.

She'd seen me drive up and was already on her way out. She jogged over and hopped into the front seat, slid over to give me a kiss, and skipped her usual playful shenanigans. The concern on her face matched that in her voice as she asked how I was doing.

I squeezed her hand. "I'm numb, as if someone has smothered my brain in a plastic bag. I need a break."

"Then let's go meet Tom and Sherri."

Author Thomas Hardy would surely have called Algonquin "far from the maddening crowd." We had no bowling alley, no multiplex movie theatre, and little in the way of restaurants.

Dull would have been the operative word.

We usually zipped to Carpentersville or Crystal Lake for something to do. Tonight we chose the bowling alley in Carpentersville, where we'd meet friends to bowl, shoot pool, play music on the jukebox, and to joke and laugh as though it were any other day.

We'd do this mere hours after putting Alex in the ground. I sure hoped the Hoopster would approve, perhaps with one of his patented *gosh-you're-so-lucky* pronouncements.

I trusted this pain would pass. Someday.

Tom and Sherri already whoopwd it up in the game room when we arrived. Tom spotted us, fixed his eyes upon me, and practically charged me. I didn't know whether to brace for impact or prepare to shake his hand. Neither, as it turned out, for he did the most unexpected thing: he hugged me.

I resisted at first, but he held tight for several seconds and I settled into it.

Teenage boys weren't supposed to do such a *not cool* thing. Might have been embarrassing under different circumstances, but it felt so damned comforting.

He stepped back and looked me in the eye. "How you holdin' up, *amigo*?"

"Okay, but I had to get out of the house and away from it all for a while. Know what I mean, *mon frére*?"

"Yeah man, the Good Shadow Alex—he'll be missed."

A brief, uneasy silence ensued, until he challenged us to a game of pool, couple against couple. Everyone agreed.

He raised his hand to command attention. "The first round of drinks is on me. You'll have a good stiff one, right, Tony? Maybe a double? So what'll it be, Pepsi or Seven-Up?"

An hour later, game four of pool proved no more successful for Diana and me than had the previous three. Sherri and Tom beat the tar out of us—again.

He strutted about like king of the world. "Geez, Tony, I hate to say it, but you suck at this."

The girls fell silent, their eyes wide, until I laughed and shook my head.

"Well, if I had a pool table in my basement like you do, we might have a different story here. What do you say we test your skills on the lanes?"

"Oh shit!"

He knew of my skill at bowling. We laughed again, grabbed our drinks and headed out to the lanes.

Three games and 622 pins later, I said, "Now that I've whipped Tom's ass and the world makes sense again, is anybody else hungry?"

We bought some burgers and chips from the grill and shot into the arcade for some fast driving and fast flying. Each of us took a turn at the wheel, as the others laughed and cheered, booed and yelled. In the middle of all the fun—all the forgetting—we talked about school and our plans for the summer. Saturday night meant the place was packed, yet somehow we created our own private sanctuary.

In the end, my four-hour escape from pain and sorrow marked the tentative beginning of rejuvenation. In the shadow of incomprehensible evil, I rediscovered joy and laughter. In the aftermath of death, I clung to life.

As Frank had said earlier, "This is our way. We survive."

A man seated at the bar watched us, most intent on examining Diana. His eyes squinted, like dark pools where light went to drown.

My gut clenched in a typical, instinctive response over which I had little control. Perhaps I overreacted, and we'd simply been making too much noise for his tastes. I felt self-conscious, gnawed by the guilt of having so much fun this soon after burying Alex. Still, *something* about him nagged at me, something familiar, unsettling, but I couldn't place him.

Geez, why am I so on edge? Relax and ignore him.

The night wound down and we said our goodbyes and hugged without any further expression of sadness, only friendship—thank heavens for that.

I started the drive back to Diana's place feeling about ninety pounds lighter than I had this afternoon.

CHAPTER 29
MAY 27, 1978:
MITCHELL NORTON

I sat in the crowded bar at the bowling alley, on a stool in the back corner, and enjoyed a few beers. Hooper, Diana and two of their friends had been laughing it up and having a grand old time, shooting pool and bowling. How the fuck could he have so much fun the same day they'd buried his little brother?

Whatever floated his boat.

I'd choked down a lousy hamburger and chips, which sat like a brick in my gut, but my fifth Old Style took the sharp edge off my mood. I hadn't intended to get drunk, but pushed right up against that fuzzy edge. Those fuckin' kids! They'd been at it for hours.

At least I'd found my angel again. I could hardly take my eyes off her, but did so occasionally to divert suspicion. Didn't want to be too obvious before having a chance to carry out my plan. Well, I didn't have a plan—yet—but something would come to me. I had to be ready for the opportunity when it presented itself.

I considered my empty beer glass. "Hey, bartender, how about a Pepsi?"

The kids yelled and laughed it up as they played in the arcade on some racing game. Shit! No one would have had any idea that Hooper had buried his little brother today unless... well, unless they knew it. I couldn't have done this if it had been Tommy.

Poor fuckin' Hooper didn't appear so terribly sad.

They got up from the game and milled around for a minute, talked and laughed a little more, and started hugging one another.

Fuck a rubber duck! It's about time you guys took off.

I already knew where Diana lived, so no need to follow them. Still, I *was* looking for an opportunity.

They headed toward the exit, and given the late hour, Hooper would likely take her home. Who could tell? They might have stopped off somewhere else.

Best to follow them. Just in case.

CHAPTER 30
MAY 27, 1978:
TONY HOOPER

Diana held my hand and leaned her head on my right shoulder. All talked out, we settled in and listened to one of our favorite cassettes — *Journey: Infinity*. Steve Perry's extraordinary voice informed us that, despite that ever-turning *Wheel in the Sky*, it was impossible to know where I'd be tomorrow. That might well have been my personal anthem had it not been for Diana, with whom I'd be tomorrow, the next day, and all the days thereafter.

Such good fortune was not lost on me. Without her, I'd probably have been isolated in my room, miserable as a stray mutt. My diary entry the night before had best summed it up: *Diana is not only my life preserver; she's the lens through which I search for a rescue boat.*

These new feelings, the way she now appeared to me, locked me in a state of perpetual confusion. Was it nothing more than my love for her, my first such experience? No, it ran deeper — to gratitude, admiration, faith and serenity. I'd never have survived those horrors without the girl of my dreams.

God, what should I do now? How can I leave her and go to college?

I pulled into her empty driveway. The house stood dark, the front porch light the only sign of life.

She kissed me on the neck and said, "My parents went to my uncle's house for dinner and Pinochle tonight. They said they'd be home late, around one o'clock."

I looked at my watch — almost eleven o'clock.

Ask the question! I want to answer. Yes. Please, yes. Yes. Oh God, yes.

"Do you want to come in?"

Warm water caressed us as we kissed and cleansed one another in the shower, and, lost in her, my escape from sorrow continued. My hands explored her soft curves, and I shook as though I hadn't eaten for days. This urgent need to consume her overwhelmed me. I'd never been this charged-up before, this out of control.

She advanced her playfulness—faster, faster, faster—in feverish determination, until the flood erupted. Caught in that burning wave, my rubber knees nearly collapsed me in a heap in the shower. She grabbed me, held tight, and kissed me as though our lips must touch for us to breathe.

It took me a moment to recover. "Why did you do that? What about you? Don't you want to go to your room?"

"Uh-huh. I'm guessing—hoping—you have plenty more where that came from. Besides, you needed that."

"You could tell, huh?" I almost buckled again under her wicked smile and Grinch-like roll of the eyes.

"You weren't doing a very good job of hiding it."

"What can I say? Damn thing has a mind of its own."

Our laughter echoed off the tiles as I dropped my head down to kiss the tops of her breasts, and brushed my fingers up and down her ass. She was right. I could have done this one more time. Or two. Maybe twelve. This continuing need, this extraordinary urgency, had erupted like nothing I'd ever experienced—a kind of metaphysical starvation.

She slapped me on the ass. "Let's clean up and go to my room."

I almost laughed to myself. *This poor girl has no idea what she's in for.*

No one else existed on Earth during this excursion, as we melded into one being. Fire blazed inside us as we rushed toward release together, our passion burning off all other concerns—even, for now, my sorrow and pain. Only love remained. Our appetite for it consumed our every thought and deed.

Minutes collapsed into seconds, immovable, suspended like stars on a perpetual clear night. Diana clawed into my back, craned her neck, and groaned in bursts like a steam-engine train. We spent all that we had, and I collapsed alongside her in deep embrace, grateful for all we had or would ever have, assured by the certainty of our future. Every bittersweet scent enveloped me and only heightened the sensation. Her smooth skin pressed to mine, warmed me, secured me.

I thought back to our many remarkable experiences together, including some amazing lovemaking, yet this moment towered like Everest over the foothills of those journeys. I'd never known such happiness or, indeed, that such unrestrained joy was even possible. My heart would burst at any moment.

How can this be possible on such a terrible day?

We gradually succumbed to sheer bliss, and Diana rolled her head to the side. Her soft breath of sleep whispered a lullaby and pushed me to the edge of slumber myself. Then it hit me: her parents would be home soon.

Crap! I don't want to go. Ever! I want to hold her through the night. Why can't I do that? Her parents were already married at our age. How could anyone think that what we have is anything but appropriate? It's perfect.

I kissed her forehead and gently stroked her face. She stirred without opening her eyes and said, "I love you, baby," and drifted off again. I could have sat there for hours, to watch her sleep, to brush her velvet skin, to breathe of her breath.

Damn it.

I got up, pulled the covers over her, and dressed. I kissed her again but she lay still. Hesitation linked with desire to shackle me to the floor. I couldn't take my eyes off her. Never had I felt so physically spent, and yet never had my yearning for her been stronger. I feared perishing from existence the instant I left her room, as though a hungry black hole awaited me outside her bedroom door.

The door whispered shut behind me, so as not to wake her.

If I died on the way out, I'd at least take comfort that I'd experienced the best life had to offer. It could never be better. That would have been impossible.

My chest hurt with that realization, and because, as I strolled to my car, I saw only visions of Diana lying warm in bed—without me beside her.

I should have stayed with her. I desperately, desperately needed to hold her.

CHAPTER 31

MAY 27, 1978:
MITCHELL NORTON

They'd been in the house *forever*, most of it with the lights off. I assumed her parents were out since there weren't no other cars in the driveway. There could be little doubt about what they were doing in there.

Shit! My head damn near burst into flames. I *hated* that fuckin' Hooper! Maybe I should kill him and get him outta the way; then I could move in on my angel without worrying about him.

Easy, Mitchell, remember the plan, the Reaper said. *All good things....*

"Right, stick to the plan. Still, it would be a fuckload of fun to do some serious work on my nemesis. Maybe later."

I'd parked on the side of the street, uncommon around here, and looked around the neighborhood. No telling what people would find curious or unnerving while looking out their windows at night. Another quick glance showed nothing worrisome, nothing obvious.

"What would I say if a cop suddenly pulled up? Let me see...."

I jumped when Tony's car engine fired up and the lights came on.

Damn it, Mitchell, pay attention!

He backed out of the driveway and pulled to the corner, where, under the streetlight, his lone silhouette filled the car.

"Is that it? Is the night over?"

The house remained dark except for the light over the entrance, and Diana's parents hadn't come home yet.

"Where could *they* be? What time will they arrive? Does Diana have brothers or sisters in the house?"

I didn't think so, or she and Tony wouldn't have been.... What else *could* they have been doing in the dark all that time?

"Does that mean she's alone?"

If she *did* have brothers or sisters, they must have been asleep.

"Is she sleeping too? What should I do? How much time do I have? What happens if her parents arrive while I'm inside the house? Should I take a weapon? Just in case?"

Act Mitchell! Or don't act! Make up your fucking mind and do it now! You don't have time to fuck around here!

PART 6
PLANS FORMED, FATES TESTED

CHAPTER 32
JUNE 8, 1995:
MITCHELL NORTON

My mom's cheap, weak coffee tastes like shit, worse than even the crap we had at the nuthouse. Since I have a few bucks burning a hole in my pocket, I'm gonna check out some new place called Starbucks. I snag Stephen King's *The Dark Half* off my mom's bookshelf to pass the time at the coffee shop.

I have some significant thinking to do. I need to find a job of some sort, but I doubt many people will be willing to give a reformed multi-murderer a chance. Fuckwads.

I educated myself while a ward of the state. They offered a remarkable library, damned curious given the nature of the facility and the idiots who resided there. They even provided computer classes on site.

I'm ready for the modern office. But are *they* ready for *me*?

I don't need to make much money. It's not like I got any bills, and Mom says I may live at home for as long as I wish. At sixty-three, she appreciates having me here to help around the house.

Tommy helps, but he has limits. He's amazed that I've read over a thousand books, fiction and non-fiction, a fair number of them twice. He thinks I'm the smartest man ever. Good old Tommy.

I'd like to do something from home, as Tommy does, like landscaping. I wouldn't have to answer to some annoying shithead boss, but I'd have to deal with clients. I can imagine the reaction of prospective clients when they find out who I am. What a fuckin' joke *that* is.

Whatever. I'll worry about it later.

Mom carpools to work with Mrs. Reinhart from down the street, so until I get a new van she's allowed me to use her car, ostensibly for job interviews. I should probably get my driver's license first. To hell with it. Coffee and a book isn't what Mom had in mind, but I need the diversion.

I've concentrated my first two days of freedom on catching up with Mom and Tommy. Prior to that, I had three intense days of final interviews at the hospital, and this five-day stretch without reading is the longest I've endured in fifteen years. I feel something akin to withdrawal. What a kick in the head that would be for people who knew me when I was a kid.

I always had the brains; I just never gave a shit. Why should I have, given how people treated me? They always made me feel like....

Ah, fuck it!

The short drive past Lake-in-the-Hills to Randall Road, only a couple miles, takes longer than expected. With some new stores and housing developments to accommodate the population explosion, and the traffic lights necessitated by that growth, traffic has quadrupled since 1978.

Starbucks is a small place, not exactly what I expected. It contains one sofa and two easy chairs, and a series of small wooden tables with wooden, unpadded chairs that look like real ass-busters. I toss my book onto an available easy chair to reserve it before walking to the counter.

"I'll have your strongest coffee please."

The pimply-faced clerk says, "Tall, grande or venti?"

"Excuse me?"

"What size?"

"Oh, I'll have a large."

"One venti coffee."

"A what?"

"Venti is the largest size."

"Uh-huh. All right then, I'll have a venti coffee."

"And you want the Sumatra?"

"The what?"

"That's our extra bold variety."

"Super. A venti Sinatra."

"Sumatra."

"Whatever."

What, coffee ain't coffee? And what's with the price? Two bucks a cup? Sure, it's a big-ass cup—uh, *venti*—but the last cup of coffee I bought cost a quarter. With unlimited refills. Bob Dylan had it right: the times are definitely a-changin'.

Old jazz standards play in the background, and combine with the comfortable easy chair to provide a pleasant atmosphere. I flinch after my first sip of coffee, strong enough to curve my spine and grow hair on the bottom of my feet, as George Carlin joked back in the '70's. Sure beats the hell out of the swill they served at the nuthou—um, I mean, *Psychiatric Care Facility.*

What a fuckin' joke.

I open *The Dark Half* with every intention of reading, but people coming into the place keep distracting me. Many of them are young, of college age or less. The girls dress provocatively with jeans or shorts that drop low below their waist, often exposing their underwear—and more. Their tops drop only slightly below their tits, exposing more of their midsection than I remember as customary. This assumes they've redefined the midsection to run right to the crack of their ass. The boys wear jeans about three sizes too big, which drop halfway down their asses, exposing their underwear for the entire world to admire. Boxers appear to be all the rage. Terrific.

A well-dressed, attractive, *adult* woman walks into the store, and it's all I can do to take my eyes off her. It's been so long since I've been with a woman. Would I remember what to do? Shit, a man never forgets *that*. I hope.

She glances around the shop while she waits in line. I turn away; don't wanna get caught staring.

I look back and, although I can't quite place her, there's *something* familiar about her.

She takes her coffee and heads in my direction, to the chair opposite me. She leans over to set her cup down on the small table, and I get a quick glance down her blouse. Nice cleavage. She glances over and flashes an automatic smile, then grabs her coffee.

Almost immediately, her eyes return to me, wider and brighter. Her smile has disappeared.

Shit! She recognizes me.

I look down at my book and attempt to ignore her. I've been worried about precisely this sort of occurrence. People don't understand the realities of my situation. They know only that I murdered some kids. They're repulsed and frightened, unwilling to consider the mitigating circumstances, or giving me a second chance.

Well, fuck 'em!

I look up from the book to catch her still staring. Her face suggests disgust and anger, and something else. Could it be amusement? How do I know this woman? I study her face and eyes — nice eyes — but I can't make the connection. That's hardly unexpected; it will have been at least seventeen years since I last saw her.

"Well, well," she says. "Look what the cat dragged in."

Gee, I never heard that one before. I offer no response.

"You don't recognize me, do you?"

"You look vaguely familiar. I assume we've met."

"You could say that. I was on the team that hunted you seventeen years ago."

Hunted me? That makes her a cop, maybe FBI. She must have been one of the smaller players, not someone who stood out, although she is attractive. Still, I don't think she's one of those who testified at my trial.

"Special Agent Linda Monroe," she says, "with the FBI, Behavioral Science. You helped jumpstart my career."

No kidding, and now you're here in Algonquin two days following my release. "Pleased to be of service. I suppose you just happened to be in the neighborhood."

"Something like that. You needn't flatter yourself. I didn't come here for *you.*"

"Terrific. Then exactly what *are* you doing here?"

She hesitates, sips her coffee and glances toward the door, and her eyes go wide again. She jumps up and hustles toward the man entering. He scans the place as if searching for someone.

"Hey there," she says to him. "Let's go somewhere else, okay?"

"What? Why?"

His expression changes from puzzled to curious to.... He looks around and his eyes settle on mine. After seventeen years, I know that face, those eyes. He's all grown up, but no matter; I'll know them forever.

He looks at Monroe again, then back at me. His eyes narrow as he stalks in my direction.

"Tony, wait." She sighs and stares at the ceiling.

Hooper ignores her, stopping only two feet away from me. "Looky, looky, looky. Who knew that *the devil* likes coffee?"

The devil? Sure, why not?

"What in hell are you doing here?"

He asked *me*, but Monroe answers as he looks back and forth between us. "I'm here to meet you, remember? Tony, I came in, got a cup of coffee and sat down. Imagine my surprise when I look up and see Mitchell Norton seated across from me. I know how this looks, but I swear it *is* a coincidence. I promise you."

"*You* say it's a coincidence, and I'm sure you think it is, but what about *him*?"

He spits *him* in disgust. I remain quiet, and must fight to keep the shit-eatin' grin off my face, though come to think of it—who gives a flyin' fuck? *Why are these two here together?*

"He was already here when I arrived," she says. "This *is* a small town."

I don't blame him for the way he feels, given that I wrecked his world. He has every right. Still, I *hate* him. He's my fuckin' nemesis. Why is that?

He exudes such violence that I can't help but goad him on.

I offer a hearty laugh. "Hey, Tony, old-buddy-old-pal, I'm just having a cup of coffee and catching up with my old friend Linda."

Oops. He lunges forward, grabs me by the shirt and lifts me right out of the chair. I grab his arms to pull his hands off me. *Holy shit, this fucker is strong!*

"Listen up, shitbag!" His face burns red and his spittle splatters on my face. "Don't even think about it, you understand me? If you come near Linda or anyone else I know, or anyone at all, for that matter, I will destroy you. I know where you live, Norton. Are you listening? I will destroy your entire damn world! I will tear you to pieces until you *beg* me to kill you! I will heap on you a giant dose of your own sick medicine. Do you hear me?"

"Loud and clear." I squirm in a futile attempt to escape his grip—like iron hooks.

"Tony, let him go! Tony!"

What do you know; it's the FBI to my rescue—a little irony to brighten my day.

She puts a hand on his shoulder. "*Please,* Tony, let him go."

He relaxes slightly, but holds on, still intimating blood and hatred from every pore, no doubt considering whether he should kill me here and now.

I'm not ambivalent about it. I don't wanna die, but there ain't a fuckin' thing I can do about it.

He releases my shirt and pushes me down into the chair, and my elbow hits the coffee and spills it onto the floor.

"Stay away from me, shitbag." He lowers his voice. "Stay away from everyone I know. Keep your nose clean or, so help me God, you'll wish you'd never been born."

He turns and storms toward the door with Monroe chasing after him.

I almost say something, to goad him again and have a little fun. Maybe next time.

Everyone in the place is staring at me. I wonder how many recognize me from the news reports.

I need to do something about that fuckin' Hooper.

CHAPTER 33

JUNE 8, 1995:
TONY HOOPER

Man, you almost lost it there. Get a grip!

Not exactly the smartest thing I've ever done. I wanted to kill him right there in the store, and with only about a dozen witnesses. *Dumbass!* If I *do* act against him, it would be helpful if I didn't first throw the spotlight on myself.

Linda agreed to leave her car at Starbucks and ride with me to Frank's place. She's remained silent for the entire trip, upset over my antics, but I think there's more to it. I consider launching a conversation, but best give her time to sort through it.

Frank knows I'm bringing a friend, but I provided no details. I'm home only about half the time, often on the road for weeks on end. My hunts for serial killers take time, as those bastards are typically a tricky, intelligent bunch—difficult to find. I often cross paths with the FBI, whom I must carefully avoid. In fact, I've seen Linda on two separate occasions since our last meeting three years ago. She doesn't know this— can't bring myself to tell her. The FBI at-large would not appreciate my unique avocation, and Linda would be hard-pressed to do so.

Suspect's rights? I couldn't care less. Miranda? Pfft! Harsh interrogation methods? You betcha. Judge? Nah. Jury? Nah. Executioner? Yep.

Linda might look the other way because she feels indebted to me, because I saved her from a vicious death at the hands of Ronald Allen Stegman. Yet even she has limits, a line she can't cross. What would she say about my phony FBI badge and ID, or about my informant inside her august organization?

I walk quite the tightrope, and I fear I've drawn her onto it. Without a net. Perhaps *that's* what she's thinking about during this uncomfortable silence.

I take the plunge as we pull into Frank's driveway. "Here we are."

She doesn't look at me.

"How long you going to continue the silent treatment?"

"I'll let you know."

Geez, Tony, that was smooth. You do have your way with women.

I bolt from the car and hustle around to open her door, hoping a little chivalry will earn me some points. She steps out and turns toward the house before I can get there, leaving the car door open. I close it.

Yeah, nice plan! Well, if at first you don't succeed.... "I stay here when I'm in town. Frank enjoys the company, and I help him out around the house, a nice arrangement for both of us. He's not so sprite anymore, but don't let that—or his good-old-boy charm—fool you. He's still sharp as a razor. Let's see how long it takes him to charm *you* again."

She throws me another one of her silent, incredulous rebukes, shakes her head, and says, "I'm not *that* easy, you know."

I laugh and reach for her hand, the perfect opportunity to break this frosty mood, but she pulls away from me.

"Come on, Linda, what do I have to do to make things right?"

"I'm sure I'll think of something. Later."

I bounce my eyebrows and bow low with a sweep of my right hand. "I am your slave."

"You're darn right, and don't forget it."

At least she's smiling again.

We find Frank on the patio, rocking gently and reading a book, his customary diversion. He spends most of his time there when the weather is good. The aroma, like a hundred bouquets of roses, blankets us the moment we step onto the patio.

Linda spins toward the garden and gasps. "My goodness, would you look at that."

Frank smiles and stands with cane in hand, and I reintroduce them. She insists that he should remain seated.

"Nonsense," he says. "A gentleman always stands when a lady enters the room. Or the patio, as the case may be."

I smile and observe, curious to see how long it will take him to charm her.

He kisses her hand. "It's been a long time, young Linda. I must say, you're even lovelier than I remember."

She laughs and tilts her head appreciatively.

"And my goodness, your eyes are most remarkable, like two emeralds shimmering in the sunlight."

The bright white of her smile shines through the red of her cheeks. She rests her hand on his arm.

"Please, come sit next to an old man and allow me to enjoy your company. It's not often a lovely young lady visits. You must allow me to take advantage of the opportunity."

Yeah, that should do it. He guides her to the chair next to his.

When I slide a third chair over to face them both, he looks at me as though I let go an eye-watering fart. "Where are your manners, young man?"

I must look like an idiot for a few seconds, but I finally figure it out and recite the Willow household drink menu for Linda. She and Frank settle on his lemonade, rather famous in these parts, and I head into the kitchen.

Hmmm... it's early, but.... Screw it!

Norton put me in the mood, so I grab a Sprecher Black Bavarian, a dark beer from a small regional brewery in Milwaukee.

Yeah, sure. As if I won't have it drained long before that.

Though I was gone only a couple minutes, they're already laughing when I return.

Old Gramps could charm the truth out of a politician—a genuine charm, because Frank Willow hasn't a disingenuous bone in his body. Linda relaxes again, taken in by the old smoothie.

I may still pay for that incident at the coffee shop, but a temporary reprieve is nice.

We spend the next two hours touring the garden and catching up with Linda on the past seventeen years. As lunchtime approaches, I offer to grill some burgers to go along with the homemade potato salad Frank gets from Ethel Simmons, a seventy-six-year-old widow who lives across Cary Road on Geringer Road. As his part-time chef, she stops in three times a week to cook a fresh meal. She hasn't exactly taken Martha's place, the wife Frank lost to cancer in 1966, but he likes having Ethel around.

Just when I think it can't get any better, another old friend arrives and pokes his head over the rear gate.

"Howdy folks, I knocked out front but nobody answered. I saw the cars in the driveway and heard some laughter back here. I hope you don't mind."

I wave him forward. "You know better than that, Chief. Please come in. Have you had lunch yet? We're about to dig into some grilled burgers, and we'd love it if you joined us."

"Sure sounds better than the bologna sandwich I have back at the station, and I'd just about kill for one of Frank's lemonades."

I pour him a glass and reintroduce him to Linda, reminding him of her involvement in the Norton case back in '78. He smiles and says he remembers her quite well, and lets it go at that. No "What brings you to Algonquin?" No "Are you here because of Norton?" No "Why is the FBI back in my back yard?" Indeed, the crafty old codger shows no surprise at all.

I get the sick feeling that this morning's little ruckus is about to come back and bite me in the ass. Might as well cut right to the chase. "Let me guess—Mitchell Norton stopped in to see you."

"Damn it, Tony, what were you thinking? Hell, back in '78, I wanted to take Norton to a field somewhere and put a bullet in him myself. I have little sympathy for the bastard. If a bus turns him into roadkill tomorrow, that will be fine with me." He directs his next statement at Linda. "Sorry if that sounds coarse."

She shrugs it off.

He shakes his head and turns back to me. "You know, that sonuvabitch has the names and phone numbers of three witnesses from Starbucks, each of whom will support his claim against you."

"What's that mean, his claim against me? Has he filed an actual complaint?"

"Not yet, but he's prepared to do so, and to get a lawyer, and to issue a restraining order." He huffs in exasperation. "He said he'd hold off on that if I speak with you and issue a *stern* warning to stay away from him. I swear to Holy God, I wanted to knock the smirk right off his face."

"I didn't go looking for him, Chief. He was just there. Even then, I'd have left him alone, but he made a comment about having coffee with Linda. I understood the implication, the threat. He was pushing my buttons, and I let him."

"I understand," he says. "Nonetheless, you need to tread lightly. Damn, how could they let that sicko out of prison? At least they could have waited one more year, until I'm retired and cruising around in my RV."

"What, and miss out on all this fun?"

"Yeah, right."

"Let's relax and have some lunch." I throw in all the cheer I can muster. Three of my favorite people are here. "It's a gorgeous day."

Screw Norton! He'll get his soon enough.

CHAPTER 34
MAY 28, 1978:
TONY HOOPER

Sunday arrived in near silence, and I lamented my only companions: loneliness and sorrow. The TV was off, the stereo off, the washer and dryer idle, Dad was out of the house somewhere, and....

Alex was gone forever.

An aroma drew me to the kitchen counter, where a pot of coffee cooked thicker by the minute. I poured a tall cup in hopes it would help clear my head. The label on the can read "Good to the last drop." Sure. I sipped the burnt coffee and struggled to reconcile the dichotomy of yesterday: two distinct days, two distinct worlds.

World 1: One of the worst days of my life, we'd buried Alex, the Hoopster, my Shadow, ranking right up there with the day we lost Mom.

World 2: Against all odds, I'd experienced the best night of my life with Diana.

She'd persisted in my mind deep into the night, until I awoke and wrote in my diary: *Even when we're apart, Diana fuels my desire, the instinctive fire, the roar of primeval yearning. Sleep will not come easy, yet more than the usual thoughts – sex, sex and, oh yeah, sex – distract me. Something greater stirs me: the certainty that we'll be together forever, that we'll marry, have children and grow old together. This is our future.*

Yet how could I make that happen? If I departed for college and left her behind, our separation might tear us apart. Marriage was out of the question, with her having a year of high school remaining, and me just getting out – no advanced education, no training, no prospects.

I could postpone Duke and go to a local school for a year, after which we could go to school together, perhaps at Duke, if they accepted her and allowed me to defer for a year. If not, we'd go somewhere else.

So much for my plans for the future.

I had nothing on the agenda today beyond mowing the lawn, which I hadn't finished yesterday for obvious reasons. That would take me only a couple hours, and then I must do something — *anything* — to get out of the house.

Diana and I hadn't talked about it last night because she'd passed out. I'd have to tease her about flipping that particular cliché on its head — the man always wanted to sleep afterwards, and the woman wanted to talk. After last night's performance, I was surprised I *hadn't* passed out. Would we ever have another night like it?

God, I hoped so.

I jumped when the phone rang, hoping Diana had made the psychic link she liked to think we possessed. I snatched the phone from the cradle and answered.

"Hi." The deep voice at the other end hesitated. "Is this Tony?"

Recognition spun my brain into a three-alarm warning. "Yes it is."

"This is Mr. Gregario."

His tone conjured visions of a long whip, and I steeled myself against the lashing.

"Is Diana with you?"

Whew, this isn't about last night. "Uh... no, Mr. Gregario, she isn't here."

"She's not? When did you last see her?"

"Last night, when I dropped her off at home." Almost the truth.

"That's odd. We assumed she got up early and went off with you, and forgot to leave us a note."

"Maybe she's with other friends."

"I suppose, but she must have left early. We thought she was sleeping late, and when we went in to rouse her, she was already gone. She must have headed out by eight o'clock, pretty unusual for a Sunday."

I'll say, especially after last night, I couldn't add.

"She didn't leave a note, hasn't called — no word at all. Ah! I'll call around to her friends. Sorry to bother you on a Sunday morning."

"No problem, Mr. G. I was wondering, can you have her call me when you track her down?"

"I don't know. Looks like we'll miss church because of her irresponsibility. She'll probably be grounded, meaning no phone privileges."

Shit, this might be worth a week.

After a few seconds' hesitation, he said, "I suppose one quick call will be okay, but just a quick one."

"Yes sir. Thank you."

She'd probably gone to see Cindi Bronte, her best friend and confidante, to tell her about last night. Why must girls share all the personal details of their lives with friends? Cindi probably knew everything about me, right down to the size and shape of my.... I didn't like it much. If I'd wanted Cindi to know of my prowess as a lover, I'd have had sex with her.

Hmmm, she is hot. A threesome would be.... Sure, as if Diana would ever agree to that! Get it together, Tony.

It felt good to push the mower around the yard. I needed the exercise to unwind, especially since I'd missed my usual Friday afternoon session with Master Komura.

We studied many different martial arts, including aikido, jujitsu, karate and ninjutsu. We also spent considerable time training with swords, as demanded by Ben Komura's family history, deeply ensconced in the samurai tradition. My mentor, amazing for his martial arts expertise, to be sure, but also because of his extraordinary calm and mental discipline, was the man I most hoped to emulate. Of course, I'd have tossed in a healthy dose of Frank's country charm and tender heart.

I hadn't mowed the lawn by myself for two years, not without help from my Shadow. I thought of Alex and let the memories flood me for some time, until the pain and depression resurfaced. I pushed it away and concentrated instead on Diana, specifically on how we could stay together during the coming school year.

I should postpone Duke for a year.

Shit! Am I ready to take that leap?

At some deep, subconscious level, I'd probably decided that the instant it popped into my head, but I felt better for having considered it rationally and intellectually, separated from my emotions.

Yeah, like that's possible.

After finishing in the yard, I showered, dressed, and prepared for lunch. I failed to convince Dad to come in from the garage, where he puttered around with whatever he could get his hands on, trying to stay busy. He barely acknowledged me, insisting he had too much to do.

His Jack Daniel's sat on the workbench — no glass, just the three-quarters-full bottle.

He *had* buried a son yesterday. My choice would have been different, perhaps a kick-ass workout, but twenty-five years from now I might have developed a different attitude. He'd come out of it soon. He had to.

I called Diana again but got a busy signal. I desperately needed to get of the house, to do something, to talk to someone.

I returned to the garage to roll my bicycle out, and glanced over my shoulder at Dad. He ignored me and took another gulp of his drink.

I hopped on my bike and sped toward Frank's place.

CHAPTER 35
JUNE 11, 1995:
REPORTS, RUMORS, AND RE-ENACTMENTS

"I'd kill you, but first I'd tell anybody that'd listen about how you pissed yourself and stood there crying with snot running out of your nose." — *Stephen King, "The Dead Zone"*

Quiet, idyllic Algonquin suffered so little crime that few residents gave security a second thought. Indeed, they'd enjoyed nearly two decades of uninterrupted peace.

Then a judge released the notorious killer, Mitchell Norton, from custody after seventeen years, a widely publicized event. Despite tight-lipped authorities, small-town America worked its usual magic, and all of Algonquin knew precisely where Norton lived and what he looked like.

Not that Norton went to any great lengths to hide.

Residents kept one eye on their routine, the other peeled for a serial killer, particularly at night. Many avoided situations that might appeal to the imagination of a killer: stay in groups, remain in well-lighted areas, and lock the house up tight at night. Many women carried mace — more than usual — and some folks cuddled a loaded gun under their pillows.

If the courts would no longer provide security from Norton, they would protect themselves.

They'd heard the reports of how psychiatrists had cleared Norton, of how an unfortunate tumor had caused his killing spree. Still, the things he had done! Could a tumor make a monster? There *must* have been at least a tendency toward that sort of thing already lurking inside. Most God-fearing, law-abiding, kindly-to-neighbors, patriotic Americans couldn't imagine themselves becoming such a monster under *any* circumstance.

Nothing as simple as a tumor would do it.

That accurately summed up Melody Nesmith's attitude about the matter. At forty-six and recently divorced, Melody lived alone. She often hated that fact and longed to have a man around, someone to help with household repairs, to do yard work, to maintain the car, to make love to her on lonely nights. These were a man's responsibility.

Security was another of those things. A man was supposed to protect her.

She considered her attitude neither clichéd nor archaic, merely practical. At 5'4" tall and 140 pounds, whom could she fight off? She even wished, at times, that she'd not insisted on a divorce from that cheating-bastard-of-a-husband after twenty years of marriage. Okay, so she wasn't exactly a supermodel. Who was he: Sean Connery?

She walked throughout the house to ensure that she'd locked the doors and first floor windows. Since Mitchell Norton couldn't enter the house on the second floor, she could comfortably leave those windows open for fresh air. A good dog would be nice, like a Doberman pinscher or German shepherd, and she resolved to look into that soon. Libby, her cat, kept her company but didn't keep her safe against anything more than a mouse, if that.

In the meantime, the extra deadbolts on the doors soothed her. She left a light on in the downstairs living room, another deterrent, and used a small nightlight in the upstairs hallway outside her bedroom. Despite the general nervousness she'd experienced since her separation, she felt reasonably secure.

She lay down for the night after the late news and switched on the television in her bedroom, to watch "The Tonight Show," with Johnny Carson. She always went to bed with Johnny. A cool breeze entered through her window, comforting after the warm day.

Thirty minutes later, she turned off the television and drifted into slumber.

Night shadows lurked beneath the crescent moon, with nary a streetlight to defeat the darkness. Tall oaks and pines surrounded the house and provided further cover.

He knew it well.

He'd arrived through a thin stretch of woodlands that ran right up behind the house. His black clothing and black ski mask rendered him virtually invisible as he stalked, yet he struggled against nervousness and fear. He stopped often to look around and listen, relatively certain that no one would see him at two o'clock in the morning, but preferring to take no chances. Despite the desires that burned within him, he wasn't sure he could go through with it.

Yet he couldn't deny his longing—a deep, almost painful yearning.

He knew precisely where Melody kept her spare keys hidden, as he'd spied on her once when she'd used it. A small rock lay between the hedge and the sidewalk near her back door, away from prying eyes even during the day. Beneath it laid two keys, wrapped in a sandwich bag to keep them clean and dry.

His hands shook as he picked them up.

He paused to check the only tools he carried for his work—a hatchet and hunting knife, both hanging from his tool belt—and took a deep breath. He pressed his ear to the door and listened for any sound inside or out.

Crickets screaming, and a frog belching somewhere in the trees.

Another glance around the neighborhood verified the absence of movement or threat.

He was ready.

He got the keys right on the first try, one for the doorknob and one for the deadbolt, and the door swung open with the faint creaking of rusted hinges. He paused to listen again, stepped inside, eased the door closed behind him, and stood in a utility room off the kitchen.

Inside the kitchen, a cat sat before a food dish and stared at him. He feared it would start mewing or bolt upstairs to wake Melody, but it returned to its late meal and ignored him altogether. He bent down to pet it as he walked by. He always liked cats. It leaned into him, rubbed against his leg and purred, and returned to its late-night dining.

Nice kitty.

He snuck from the kitchen into the living room, where a small lamp cast dull light into the room. He switched it off, willed his hands to stop shaking, and paused to let his eyes adjust to the dark. He took another deep breath and stared at the floor, waiting, reassured by the quiet.

He stepped past the bathroom and a small den, found the stairs at the end of the short hallway, and started up. The first stair creaked.

Freeze!

Silence. Careful to walk on the outside edges of the stairs, he continued with less noise to the top, where a nightlight defeated the darkness. The upstairs level contained three bedrooms, two at the front of the house, and a master bedroom at the rear, six feet from where he stood. That must be Melody's room.

He approached it and smiled at the steady tempo of light snoring. Perfect. He needed to keep her quiet while he worked.

He paused again to consider his next step—his plan. How could he go through with it? Fidgety and uncertain, he chewed on a fingernail. He *had* to do it. How else could he get what he wanted, what he so desperately needed? He was sick and tired of his circumstances, which he'd endured for too long.

He pulled the knife from its sheath and clutched it in his hand, close to his face. He liked the look of it, the energy it infused in him—powerful, fierce.

Yes, he could do what he must.

He flinched and launched into a short, startled leap. Something had brushed against his leg with hardly a sound. He looked down, trembling again, to discover the cat rubbing against his leg, purring. He caught his breath and relaxed, and leaned over to pet it once more.

Nice kitty.

He stepped into the room, tiptoed to the side of the bed, and stared at the sleeping Melody. Another long, deep breath puffed up his chest, and his resolve.

He raised the knife.

CHAPTER 36

MAY 28, 1978:

TONY HOOPER

Frank's empty rocker swayed in the light breeze on the back patio, so I knocked and poked my head inside the door and called out.

"Come on in, Tony," he yelled. "I'm in the den."

I plopped on the sofa adjacent to his La-Z-Boy, where he reclined and watched the baseball game on WGN-TV.

"You're in for a good one, young man. The Cubs are ahead 3-1."

"Don't worry," I said. "It's only the fourth inning—still plenty of time for them to lose."

He rolled his eyes and laughed at the misery we diehard Cub fans loved to share, and we kicked back to watch the game.

When the game ended and the Cubs had lost 5-3, I offered-up my best 'I told you so' look.

He shook his head. "You know what I think? I think the Cubs lost because you *expected* them to lose."

"Wow, who knew I had that kind of power?"

"The world is what you make of it."

Give me a break! "I'll keep that in mind."

We walked into the kitchen, and he pulled a package of white paper from the fridge, opened it at the counter, and nodded at the two rib-eye steaks. "These will go perfectly with asparagus and sautéed mushrooms. Think your dad will mind if you stay for dinner?"

"I doubt he'd know the difference at this point."

"Come on, Tony, give your old man a break. He just needs a little time."

"He hit the booze early today, probably passed out already."

He tried to hide his concern—fat chance—as he pulled out the vegetables and set them next to the sink. His eyes narrowed in thought, but no sense in pressing him, even though I hoped he'd talk to Dad.

I'd thought about talking to Dad myself, but that probably wouldn't have accomplished much beyond pissing him off. On the other hand, he might listen to Gramps; he respected Frank.

We agreed to eat out on the patio, provided the threatening clouds didn't dump rain on us. A few minutes later, after preparing the vegetables and setting the steaks in Frank's special marinade—light Worcestershire sauce and minced garlic in red wine—we lounged at the table and enjoyed a glass of Cabernet Sauvignon. Frank had planned to leave the wine for dinner but, after opening the bottle to let it breathe, he couldn't resist.

Worked for me. I settled in for the fine food and company. I'd probably have been happier living here than in my own home. Crazy.

He slapped the table. "So, how are things going with your lovely Diana?"

I leapt out of my seat. "Holy cats! I forgot all about her. She's probably been trying to call me all afternoon. Geez, I'm a dead man."

Frank let me use his phone, and it barely completed the first ring before Mrs. Gregario's strained voice responded.

"Hello, Mrs. G., this is Tony. I haven't been home to take Diana's calls. I imagine she's been trying to get in touch with me."

"No, Tony, I'm sorry." She released a five-second sigh. "I was hoping she might have ended up with you."

"You mean you still haven't found her?"

"No. I've never been so worried, and I don't know what to do. Steven is out looking for her at some of her regular haunts. I hate to do it, but we may need to call the sheriff's office. This isn't like our girl. I can't imagine what's gotten into her, or what might have happened."

Her palpable fear mirrored my sheer panic.

What in hell is going on? How could she be missing?

Missing: a simple word, an all too familiar state of being. A week ago, Alex had gone missing. Yesterday we'd buried him.

Now Diana was missing. It must be something simple, an innocent mistake. It *must* be.

Mrs. G. ran out of ideas about where Diana might be, and she paused, expecting me to offer some enlightenment. I could only offer to think about and call her later, or perhaps stop by their house.

"Okay." Her voice, flat and utterly helpless, vanished with a click.

Barely able to move, or breathe, I could only stare into unseen space, until Frank grabbed my attention with a tap on the shoulder.

"Tony, what's going on?"

I stared at him dumbly for a few seconds, and then filled him in on the events.

"*What?* What in the world is...? How long has she been missing?"

"I'm not sure." I recalled the earlier conversation with Mr. Gregario. "Since before eight o'clock this morning, less than eight hours after I left her at home. They don't know beyond that."

"Good heavens."

We flopped into our seats at the kitchen table and simultaneously chugged our wine. I stared through my empty glass, paralyzed but for my shaking hands.

It must be something simple. She has to be okay.

He reached across the table and patted the top of my hand. "I assume you must go, but you need to eat something. No more wine. Let's grill the steaks and get something into your stomach."

"What? No, I can't eat."

"I know, but you will. It won't take long. Then you'll do what you must. Come on."

As usual, Frank had been right. My body had demanded the energy, as though instructing me to fuel-up in preparation for tough times ahead. After that, unable to stand it anymore, I left for the Gregario house in the hopes of helping, although I'd no idea how.

Once I arrived there... well, who could know?

I pulled up toward their house, and to a familiar sight—a cruiser with the red-and-blues flashing on the roof, this time belonging to the McHenry County Sheriff's Department, who oversaw tiny Lake-in-the-Hills.

My heart weighed eight thousand pounds.

Mrs. G. answered the door in a frantic state, barely said hello, and led me into the kitchen. She glanced back and said, "We're speaking with Deputy Ricks from the sheriff's department. He has some questions for you."

"For me?"

The deputy and Mr. G. halted their discussion when we entered the room, and the deputy stopped writing on his pad. My colon puckered under Mr. G.'s glare as Mrs. G. introduced me to Deputy Ricks. She confirmed that I'd been with Diana last night—the last one to see her.

He shook my hand and held it for a few seconds, then furled his brow. "Hooper, Hooper, Tony Hooper." He paused, his eyes lit-up with recognition. "That's right, the case with the young boy. What was his name? Alex?"

"My little brother."

"I'm sorry, Mr. Hooper." He seemed sincere, formal, but something else lurked underneath.

I nodded.

"Isn't that odd? Someone took your brother... what, a week ago? He ends up.... Well, and now your girlfriend is missing. You seem to be the common link in all of this, Mr. Hooper."

"Common link? What do you mean?"

"I mean there are two disappearances, one we know about, one we don't, and both of the individuals involved were close to you. In fact, weren't you the last one to see each of them?"

I hesitated and swallowed the lump in my throat. "Yeah."

"Tell me, did you drop Diana off in the driveway last night or walk her to the door? Or was there more to it than that?"

Accusatorial looks attacked me from three directions. Four, if one counted my colon again. *Does he think I had something to do with Diana's disappearance? Does he think I murdered my own little brother? Is he insane!*

Should I tell them the truth about last night? Mr. and Mrs. Gregario might have wanted my head, but it could be important—timelines and what not. Deputy Ricks continued to stare at me as I wiped the sweat from my forehead. I couldn't get my nerves under control, though not for the reasons he thought.

Damn it!

I took a deep breath. "There was a little more to it."

Mr. G. took a quick step forward. "What the hell did you do?"

"Diana asked me to come in, and we were... together for a while."

"Together? What the hell does that mean?"

"Steven," Mrs. G. said, "what do you think it means? Do you think they're somehow different from every other teenager? Different from how we were? Come now."

"What are you saying? In my house? In my goddamn house!"

"Would you prefer they do it in a field, or in the back of the car?"

"Goddamn it!" He spun around and glared out the kitchen window. "And you knew about this, Heather?"

"Steven, really."

"I see." The deputy returned to the conversation, rescuing me from Mr. G., at least for the moment. "And what times were those, from when you arrived here until you left?"

"We got back around eleven o'clock. I left around twelve-thirty or so."

"And where was Diana when you left?"

"Asleep."

Mr. G. grunted and threw his hands up.

The deputy nodded, his suspicion more obvious than ever, and said, "In her bed."

Not exactly a question, but I lowered my head and said, "Yes."

Mr. G. yelled, "That's it, huh? You had your fun and took off?"

"It wasn't like that! I wanted to stay, but I didn't think you'd approve."

"You *think*? I want you out of my house right now, goddamn it!"

"Mr. G., it's not what you think. We love each other." When he didn't respond, I pleaded with Mrs. G. "Don't you understand? I know we're still young and that we have time, but I want to marry Diana and spend the rest of my life with her."

Her sad smile, both thoughtful and accepting, made it clear she already knew. Perhaps they'd talked about it—a mother and daughter thing. Good old Dad, on the other hand, appeared ready to disembowel me and eat my liver.

He yelled again. "She's seventeen, for crying out loud!"

"You were our age when you married, weren't you?"

"Bah!" He dismissed me with a wave of the hand. "Times were different then. Leave, Tony. You need to go."

Times were different then? What in hell does that mean? It was eighteen years ago, for God's sake, not a hundred!

Ricks watched me with continued unease but said nothing.

I had one last question. "Deputy Ricks, is it possible that someone is trying to hurt *me*, by hurting those I love most? How is this happening? It makes no sense."

"Let's not jump to any conclusions or assume the worst here. She may have lost track of time with some friends — probably walk in any minute." He paused as if to examine my reaction. "Teenagers have been known to do crazier things."

He said it with a straight face. Cops always tried to put the family at ease, but he didn't know Diana. Besides, there could be no doubt who topped his suspect list.

Couldn't blame him for that.

I said nothing more, but as they fidgeted about, I could easily imagine Mr. G. spontaneously combusting, or Mrs. G. collapsing with a broken heart. My own panic and fear exploded, as though I dangled above a deep, deep hole, hanging onto the edge with my last fingernail.

Mr. G. nudged me toward the front of the house, and didn't look *at* me so much as *through* me. He followed me to the door and slammed it behind me.

I stood on the stoop for a minute, trying to determine my next move, waiting for some divine inspiration as I stared at my car parked in the street. Nothing.

Still nothing.

I stared at my feet, trying to think while walking down the street, then stopped, looked around, and turned back to my car fifteen feet behind me.

I'd been sitting in my car, in my driveway with the engine running, for many minutes. I had no idea how long — didn't even remember driving home.

I needed to go somewhere. Diana was out there.

I must find her before... before....

I dropped my head into my right hand, and heat radiated from my face. I couldn't stop my hand from shaking or my teeth from grinding.

I'm gonna kill the sonuvabitch that did this! I'll rip his damn heart out!

CHAPTER 37
MAY 27, 1978 (THE NIGHT BEFORE): MITCHELL NORTON

I couldn't believe my boldness, this decisiveness. The rush of power fired every nerve in my body.

I'd figured out which room was Diana's by the light while I was outside. They made it nice and easy by leaving the front door unlocked.

Thanks, Tony, you're a real pal.

Diana slept quietly, and adrenaline buzzed through my body. Shit, I sported a hard-on to make a porn star gasp.

I crept to the edge of her bed and gently clasped my right hand over her mouth. She responded with a smile and pleasant groan at first—must have thought it was her precious boyfriend. Her eyes drifted open and it took her a second to focus on me.

Her body shot rigid, her eyes wide. She tried to jump and yell but I forced her back down. With my left hand, I held the knife up where she could see it.

I placed it at her neck and whispered, "I don't want to cut your throat, but I sure-as-hell will if I have to. Don't make me do it. *Capiche?*"

No response, except to ease her grip and remove her nails from the back of my hand. She'd scratched the hell outta me. No biggie.

"I don't want to kill you, but I'll do it if you scream. Got it?"

She nodded.

"You can't get away from me. I'm too quick and too strong, so don't even think about running. And keep your fucking mouth shut or you're dead."

I pulled the covers back and.... *Holy Curly, Moe and Joe!* I wiggled the knife over her and pressed the flat edge to her left tit, the blade close to her nipple. She stopped breathing for a moment.

"Get up and get dressed. Be quick about it, and quiet. If you try anything, it will take me about two seconds to stick you. Move!"

A strange smell made me anxious as she rose naked from bed. I stayed close to keep her from trying anything stupid. She put on panties, jeans, a tee shirt and sneakers.

Damn, sex with her would have been amazing. No time now, but maybe we'd have some fun later.

I closed her bedroom door behind us, held to the back of her jeans, and pressed the knife into her back as we walked outside — to reiterate my threat.

Once she hopped into the back of my van, I tied her hands to a rope loop welded into the wall. Easy. Nobody cruised the street at this late hour, and still no sign of her parents.

The clock in my workshop ticked past one o'clock. It hadn't occurred to me to put a little bed in here, a simple mattress in case I had to spend the night. Should I have left Diana here alone? Not yet. Too risky. I didn't want to hurt her, but she didn't know that. Best keep it that way for now — gave me all the power, and kept her under control.

She sat on a blanket in the corner, with hands tied behind her back and ankles tied together.

I needed another blanket to use as a bedroll.

"I have to go out to the van for a minute, but the same rules apply. You should know the nearest house is quite a ways off. I doubt they could hear you scream, so I won't bother gagging you, but if you try it, I'll cut you."

Terror filled her eyes, but also a hint of doubt, maybe anger.

"You see all these tools hanging around? I use them to do my work. It's the Reaper's work, but you might say I'm his apprentice. You can inflict amazing damage to a human body without killing the person. Eventually, the pain becomes too severe to tolerate. Then it's lights out, dirt-nap city. That can take a long time though, and you can inflict *a shitload* of pain before death. I happen to be a master."

Why tell her the truth? I'd develop my skill soon enough.

Her eyes widened as she gazed at the various implements of destruction. She looked convinced, but one more bit of information should cement the deal.

"I didn't quite get it right with Alex Hooper, but I've learned a lot since then."

Her eyes bulged — damn near popped right out of her head. Kinda funny.

"If you're a good girl, we can dispense with that stuff. Obey my orders, and you won't have to experience those awful things — pain like you can't imagine. Understand?"

She closed her eyes and dropped her head.

"I said do you understand?"

She nodded.

"I'll be back in about ten minutes. Gotta work on the van, but I'll be right outside."

She weren't goin' nowhere. Hell, she was scared to death.

I grabbed the bucket and walked down to the lake to get some water for cleaning up. I took a leak in some bushes along the way, and it occurred to me that I didn't have no toilet paper in the shop.

Shit!

I hadn't considered how Diana would go to the bathroom, or how I would take a dump. The old me still popped up every once in awhile, complete with shit for brains. It frustrated me more than ever, now that I was different. Now that I was smarter.

The three-quarter moon provided enough light for the grueling walk back to the shop. The fuckin' bucket of water weighed about a million pounds! Crickets chirped, lightning bugs flashed everywhere, and something huge buzzed by my head. Fuckin' bugs!

I snatched the blanket from the back of my van before entering the shop. Diana huddled in the corner with her head down on her knees, crying.

A bolt of energy shot through me at first — thought I might pop another woody — but then my stomach churned a bit. I chewed on a fingernail for a few seconds; didn't think the Reaper would like it if I felt sorry for her.

I glanced around the shop — weren't no way she'd be able to go to the bathroom in here. I'd brought a few rags in with my supplies, one of which I'd need to gag her.

"Do you need to go to the bathroom?"

She raised her head, and blinked several times before looking around the shop, then dropped into her slouch again without responding.

"You'll have to do it outside. There's a good spot nearby. You can use these rags — they're clean — since there ain't no toilet paper. I'll pick up some TP tomorrow."

A couple tears fell, and she shrugged at her bound hands.

"I'll untie you so you can go, but I gotta go out with you to make sure you don't try to run off. I'll stay a few feet away to give you a little privacy. Don't try nothin' stupid, and we'll get along fine."

Again, she didn't respond. Bitch was starting to piss me off.

"So, do you want to go, or do you want to sit there in your own stinkin' mess? Answer me!"

She cringed. "I want to go."

"All right, I have four rags. They gotta last you 'til tomorrow, so use 'em accordingly. I'll untie you, but be damn careful. Don't think for a second you can outrun me. Don't make me hurt you. Understand?"

No response, but she shook like a streaker on a winter day.

She pissed behind a tree where she had a little privacy, but where I could see if she made a run for it. I was tempted to watch. Why shouldn't I? Would that have been wrong? Fuck it! Besides, too dark to see anything.

I stayed close behind as she stumbled back to the shop, and put my hand on her shoulder when we entered; didn't want her grabbing one of my tools and attacking me.

She washed herself from the bucket — just a little, without removing any clothes. I tied her up again, with her hands in front this time, and she lay down and wrapped herself in the blanket. She turned and faced the wall. I understood. She was nervous and frightened, trying to avoid me.

No worries. She'd pay attention to me soon enough.

CHAPTER 38
MAY 28, 1978:
MITCHELL NORTON

"Man is not the creature of circumstances; circumstances are the creature of man." – *Benjamin Disraeli*

Diana had finally slept last night, at least a little, curled up in her blanket in the corner. She cried a few times.

I'd been too nervous to sleep much, and had plans to consider and supplies to pick up, like toilet paper and toothpaste and deodorant... and clothes.

I'd prodded Diana's sizes out of her before leaving the shop, then gagged her and tied her to the shed. The tight bindings had probably hurt her, but.... Whatever.

I didn't plan to be gone long—still too nervous about leaving her alone.

Mom, Dad and Tommy were out at church when I stopped at home. I took a fast shower, changed clothes, and grabbed some money from my secret stash. I left a note to keep my parents from prying.

> *Mom and Dad,*
> *I'm spending a couple days with a friend, so don't worry. I'll see you soon.*
> *Be good, Tommy-boy.*
> *Mitchell*

I'd done it before, whenever I hung with Frankie Walters for a weekend to drink, smoke dope, and listen to music or his comedy albums: Bill Cosby, George Carlin and Cheech & Chong—some funny shit!

The folks would be okay for a day or two, and I'd figure things out from there.

I packed a bag with enough stuff to last me two or three days, loaded it and an empty ice chest into the van, and zipped out the driveway before the folks got home and started asking questions. They'd have to arrange for somebody else to watch Tommy.

Whatever. I couldn't be there for him *all* the time.

I stopped at Sears in Crystal Lake to buy a couple more tools and clothes for Diana. I picked up two sets of everything for her: jeans, tee shirts, panties, socks... but no bras. I liked her better without one.

I popped into Dominick's down the street to load-up on sandwich stuff, chips and pickles, some pop, two five-gallon bottles of water, the bathroom stuff we needed, a bag of plastic forks and spoons and knives, a bag of ice to put in the cooler.... We wouldn't exactly be dining at the Ritz, as my dad liked to say, but we'd get by.

I returned to the shop feeling much better about things, anxious to see my angel.

I untied Diana and let her clean up a little before we sat down to eat. I tried to start a conversation, but she weren't responding, weren't having a good time yet.

She would. Soon.

I loved nighttime—the darkness, the ability to hide in plain sight, the perfect opportunity to move forward with the next part of my plan. This was my second chance; couldn't screw this up or I'd be in deep shit with the Reaper.

Once again, I'd left Diana tied-up and gagged back at the shop. She was kind of a pain in the ass, but she was also gonna be sweet. Sweet and tasty.

Shit! Can't think about that now.

This grocery store in Crystal Lake weren't the one I usually shopped; didn't want to run into anyone who might recognize me. It was almost closing time, so I'd try for one of the employees. I didn't give a hot shit if it was a woman or man, though a woman would have been easier to handle.

I parked next to a group of cars on the edge of the lot furthest from the doors, presumably where employees park, to give me plenty of opportunities.

Seated in the van, with my lawn chair pulled close to the rear doors, I enjoyed a wide view through the rear windows. With one of the doors open, but pulled to, I could jump out in a snap, and without a sound. I removed the bulb from the overhead interior light, and fingered the hilt of the hunting knife sheathed on my belt, and the hammer wedged under the belt. I clenched a baseball bat in my right hand too—plenty of weapons. A gun would have been good, but where would I have gotten one without raising suspicions or leaving a trail?

A woman walked from the store without bags and headed this way, probably an employee. My right foot bounced, my teeth grinded, and my grip tightened on the baseball bat. Sweat beaded above my eyebrows and on the back of my neck.

Get ready, Mitchell. Holy shit! This could be.... Fuck! I need to take a leak.

She stopped and looked back when a boy jogged toward her, undoubtedly another employee, and they walked together to their cars, parked side-by-side fifteen feet away from where I sat. They said goodnight before driving off.

The missed opportunity had me amped-up, but I gradually stopped twitching.

Patience, the voice in my head said.

Two more people left the store, a young man pushing a loaded grocery cart and an old woman right behind him. They approached a car parked near the entrance, he helped her load the groceries, and she drove off as he jogged back inside the store.

Three minutes later, a figure emerged from the store, the same kid who'd helped the old woman. He looked to be seventeen or eighteen, with long blond hair and a bounce in his step, and he whistled a tune. As he came closer, he stopped whistling and started singing *Back in the Saddle* by Aerosmith.

He walked toward one of the nearby cars, directly across from me and less than ten feet away.

I glanced back at the store. Nobody else coming. I gripped the bat and stepped out of the van, and he launched into the chorus line from the song, blaring it out for the whole world to hear.

We'll see who's back in the saddle again, dumbass!

I rushed right up behind him and swung the bat, catching him at the base of his head and across his shoulders. I wanted to knock him out, not kill him.

He grunted, dropped his keys and hit the pavement hard. He squirmed, barely conscious, so I gave him one more light swing of the bat. The poor schmuck would have *two* nasty lumps.

Tough shit!

In a little while, that would be the least of his fuckin' worries, assuming I hadn't killed him. I felt the pulse on the side of his neck. Still breathing.

Still nobody came from the store. I leaned the bat against the car, raised him up and threw him over my right shoulder.

"You're damn heavy for a skinny shit."

I grabbed the bat with my left hand and walked toward my van. Halfway there, I almost lost him, and strained my back while trying to hang on.

"That hurts, you lousy fucker!"

I dumped him in the van like a sack of useless shit. Okay, so he wasn't useless—we'd have some real fun later. Back inside the van, I breathed a sigh of relief and grabbed my handcuffs, a little something from an adult-only store off I-94 up in Wisconsin.

I'd expected to use them for other purposes, something a prostitute taught me once. That hadn't happened, but they sure came in handy now.

I covered the kid's mouth with duct tape and ran a rope through the handcuffs, and tied them up through the loop on the upper wall. I then dragged the unconscious blob of shit into a sitting position.

He couldn't go anywhere or make any loud noises. Perfect!

I froze. Laughter echoed across the parking lot. Careful to keep the van still, I crawled to the window. Three boys laughed it up as they approached the nearby cars.

"Hey," one of them said, "I thought Dan already left."

"He did," said another.

"Then why is his car still here?"

"Who gives a shit? He probably went back inside. Let's get out of here."

One by one, they drove off.

If one of them had walked over to—Dan, was it?—his car, they might'a found his keys. That would'a been trouble. I should have picked them up earlier, but now that it was clear, I darted over and scooped them up.

I jumped into the driver's seat and took one last look around the parking lot.

"All right, Danny-boy, we're ready to go."

No response. Still unconscious.

"What's the matter, don't feel like talking?"

I laughed, unable to keep my legs still as the excitement builds. Time for a good song.

"I'M BAAAACK!"

The kid remained unconscious, tied to the workbench.

I allowed Diana to go to the bathroom and wash up, and then we munched some sandwiches—a little PB&J to keep our energy up.

My energy was definitely up!

She now sat in a chair alongside the workbench, her hands tied behind her and her feet taped to the chair. Whatever. At least she could appreciate a ringside seat.

Time to wake up Danny-boy.

I had a knife in one hand and needle-nosed pliers in the other, and I danced around like a fool. I couldn't help it—barely able to contain myself. I had a hard-on that would shock that *Deep Throat* chick. I couldn't stop staring at Diana's magnificent tits, at her rock-hard nipples.

She's excited too! Man, I want to get all over that! Maybe I should let Danny-Boy wait and —

He groaned and flipped his head from side to side.

I walked to the bench and leaned down, my face a few inches away as his eyes struggled open. He tried to speak before realizing I had his mouth taped. He raised his head and looked down the table at the rest of himself, all tied and taped and... naked.

His eyes pleaded with me.

I held up my hands to display the knife and the pliers, and offered my biggest smile and a hearty laugh. "Hey, Danny-boy, we're gonna have some serious fun tonight. I have plenty of other cool tools too. Wanna see 'em?"

I reached behind me and rotated through the selections: hammer, saw, ice pick, hand-drill, before returning to the knife and pliers. "Let's start with these. Don't worry, we'll enjoy every one of them. Gotta be patient."

He screamed behind his tape, then his head rolled over and he saw Diana.

She'd already started crying, and made eye contact for only a second before dropping her head.

"No you don't, Diana. You gotta watch every single bit of this, you hear me? If you don't, I'll put *you* on the table next. Got it?"

Tears streamed down her face, but she nodded.

Why in hell is she crying like a baby?

"One more thing: if you scream, I'll cut something off." I reached over and squeezed her right tit, and pinched her nipple. "Maybe I'll start with this one."

That got her attention.

Holy shit, did that feel good or what!

"Okay then, shall we get started?"

Danny-boy tried screaming again behind the tape. What a stupid fucker.

Wow! I'd gotten it right this time. Danny-boy had spewed twice during the fun. I hadn't expected that. It was like he'd enjoyed it while I sliced, ripped, sawed, drilled and stabbed. He'd lasted twenty minutes, screaming behind the tape the whole time.

Problem was we had a stinking, fucking mess, with piss and shit and blood everywhere, including all over me. Wow!

I stepped in front of Diana, nice and close. I couldn't stand it anymore—needed a release—but she was tied-up. I'd just have to do it myself. Whatever.

"Okay, Diana, I have one more thing for you to watch tonight."

CHAPTER 39
MAY 29, 1978:
TONY HOOPER

*"'Come to the edge,' he said. They said, 'We are afraid.'
'Come to the edge,' he said. They came... he pushed them... and
they flew." – Guillaume Apollinaire*

Memorial Day meant no school, a damned good thing. No way
could I face classes today, let alone the other students. Dad went into
the office despite the holiday. No surprise.

Frank would understand my plight, and he might be able to help
me figure things out and decide what to do next. Gramps was my rock.

What would I do tomorrow? Or the next day? Or the day after
that? Hell, I didn't know. Only one thing drove me—I must find
Diana... somehow.

"We need to backtrack a little," Frank said, "to see if we can find
something useful, something suspicious. You may have ignored it at
the time because there was no reason to do otherwise."

"Shouldn't we go to the police?"

"What do you have to offer them?"

I thought about that for a minute. I didn't have a damned thing.

"Do you trust me?"

"Yes sir."

"I have some skills you're not aware of, and which I can't explain
yet. We'll get to it when the time is right. In the meantime, stick with
me on this. Okay?"

I nodded as he paused to refuel on doughnuts and coffee. He'd gone to Dunkin' Donuts early this morning — liked theirs better than the stuff he brewed at home — to pick up four doughnuts and a box of coffee. Should have us walking on the ceiling soon.

Lord knew I guzzled it now like a man on a mission. "Where do we start?"

"First, I think we should agree that it's no coincidence that someone abducted Diana a week after someone abducted and killed Alex. The sheriff's deputy was right, you know. You *are* the common link."

"He was suspicious of me."

"You *would* be the likely suspect for anyone who didn't know better. Don't worry about that. They'll get past it at some point." His eyes squinted in thought as he took another sip of coffee. "In the meantime, someone out there is snatching up people closest to you. Alex's murder and Diana's abduction must be the work of the same person, assuming it's one man. This guy must know you in some way, maybe a friend."

"Friend! Are you kidding? Besides, no one I know is capable of such a thing."

"Well, this person *has* to know you in some way. It's too coincidental otherwise. Perhaps someone has fixated on you for some reason."

I could only stare at him with my mouth hanging open like an idiot. He wanted ideas from me, but my brain could conjure nothing more than panic and terror. I felt helpless and inadequate, at the mercy of something — some*one* — beyond my wildest imagination.

"This is too bizarre," I said at last, "like something out of a Sherlock Holmes story. It's not as though I have *enemies* or anything."

"Oh? The person doing this is not exactly your biggest fan."

"No kidding, but why? I haven't done anything to anyone." That almost stuck in my throat. "Well, I was in a couple fights at school my sophomore year, but they were little things. Those guys wouldn't do something like this."

"Nothing else?"

I'd almost forgotten about the big one.

"Of course, there was that drunk who killed my mom, but he was a single guy with no kids, no siblings — just a dog. His father was deceased, and his mother had mush for a brain. She passed away in a nursing home shortly after the incident. I talked about that in therapy with the shrink, who said those facts made it easier for me to cope with what I'd done. The killer didn't leave anybody behind — nobody who'd suffer because of my actions, or who might want to exact revenge."

"All right, let's forget about that angle for now, but I want you to think about it during the rest of the day. Keep it in the back of your mind, floating around in your subconscious, and maybe something will pop up."

"Okay. Now what do we do?"

He leaned in closer and placed his arms on the table. "Attempt to determine which *stranger* might be doing this."

"Uh... Frank... how do we do that? We don't even know where to begin. That's kind of the definition of stranger."

"You'd be surprised. You see, the subconscious mind is an extraordinary machine, storing information of which we're not even aware. With proper training and techniques, it's possible to draw that information into the conscious mind."

"Training? Techniques? Come on, Frank, Diana's missing and she needs help *now*. There's no time for *training*."

"It takes less time than you imagine. There are reasonably quick methods that offer a high degree of certainty. We'll get to that. For now, let's make some assumptions to get us started."

"How do you know about such things?"

"As I said earlier, you need to trust me on this."

I sighed and waited as he sipped his coffee and gathered his thoughts.

"First, when did it start? He took Alex only a week ago, and already he's taken Diana. That's quick work, especially given the fact that the police are right in the middle of an investigation. I'd bet this guy got the idea only recently, so let's retrace your last few weeks and see what we find."

I walked to the counter to refill my coffee cup, then did the same for Frank. I kept hoping the coffee would fire-up my mind, to help me follow what he was doing. He wanted to know how my routine had changed in the past several weeks, and rattled off several questions in succession. Had there been any special events? Did I have any new hangouts? Had I met new people? Still clueless, I nodded and waited for him to guide me through the process.

"Think about that for a minute while I make a quick phone call."

He didn't use the phone in the kitchen or the one in the living room. He stepped into his bedroom and shut the door, which made me a little nervous. Why didn't he want to talk in front of me?

On Tuesday, I was supposed to be at school but... fat chance! My every thought roared for Diana, a million-ton freight train flying downhill, a sharp turn in the tracks just ahead.

Graduation would arrive in less than two weeks, but I'd be all right.

Dad had left the house earlier than usual, before I typically headed out to school, so he didn't know I'd ditched.

Not that he'd have cared.

Shit! Go easy on him, Tony.

Frank understood, pretending to be my grandfather when he'd called into school and told them I'd be absent today.

He and I talked for two hours yesterday, examining every possibility. On several occasions he'd nodded and said, "Uh-huh, that could be important," and expanded the notes he jotted down. I hadn't understood any of it, but accepted that he'd clue me in when ready. He'd wanted me to relax last night and let my subconscious mind sort things out.

Sure. Relax. What a sick joke.

I tried last night to speak with Mrs. Gregario, but Mr. G. answered every time I'd called. He'd refused to speak with me no matter how much I pleaded. In the three calls I made, it never took him more than ten seconds to hang up on me. On the third, he'd made clear that he didn't want to hear from me again.

Don't call again? Are you kidding? How am I supposed to know what's happening with Diana?

He'd decided that this was *my* fault.

And here we sat, back at Frank's kitchen table, reviewing yesterday's notes and once again drinking coffee, though lousy decaf for some reason. He said I had to lay off the caffeine. Was he nuts?

Well, he was the boss.

The doorbell rang, and he insisted I remain seated as he answered it. A muffled conversation murmured from near the front door.

A moment later, he returned to the kitchen escorting another man. "Tony, I'd like you to meet Dr. Art Reynolds, a former colleague of mine."

He was old, not quite Frank's age, mostly bald and with pop-bottle glasses, behind which football-like eyes blinked. Unlike Frank, he walked stooped over, defeated by a lifetime of gravity and whatever other forces he'd endured. He carried a small black bag, like something a doctor carried during a house call in one of those movies from the '40's. Frank had called him doctor. And a former colleague? What did that mean? Frank, a doctor? No.

Perhaps Frank was sick and.... New panic bubbled to the surface—just what I needed.

"I asked Art to help us with our dilemma," Frank said. He turned to Art. "Did you get what you needed?"

"Yes, I still have one connection back at..." He paused and looked at me. "Anyway, I can't say he was happy about giving it to me, but I got enough to do the job."

Frank nodded.

I was utterly lost. "I don't understand. How can a doctor help?"

"Actually," Art said, "I'm a psychiatrist."

I shot bullets and flames from my eyes, right at Frank. "A *psychiatrist*?"

He raised his hands in defense. "Now hold on, Tony, it's not what you're thinking. Art isn't here to psychoanalyze you. He has a certain *specialty* that will be helpful to us—to dig deep inside your subconscious mind to find answers."

Still lost, I waited for more.

"I'll let Art explain it."

Art asked without preamble, "Are you familiar with hypnosis, Tony?"

"Hypnosis? As in, 'keep your eye on the gold watch and count backwards from a hundred,' hypnosis?"

He laughed. "It's more complicated, but yes, something like that."

"You plan to hypnotize me? Seriously? *Why*?"

Frank responded. "After our conversation yesterday, Art and I had a nice long conversation. We reviewed my notes and he agreed that some interesting kernels jumped out. We'd like to explore those a little further, but you're murky on the details. Your memory isn't quite giving us what we need."

Right, so I wasn't just confused, I was also stupid.

"You see, Tony, you told me about a man who watched Diana at the park that day... um... what did you call it?"

"You mean Senior Ditch Day?"

"Yes, that's right. You didn't know him, and hadn't seen him either before or since, but something about him disturbed you. You brushed aside that thought. You also mentioned a man who glared at you at the bowling alley the night you were there with Diana and your other friends. Once again, something about the man made you uneasy. You thought he was familiar."

He paused, and I tried to think back to those guys. I remembered, but I couldn't see any details.

Frank shook his head. "The truth is that those could have been perfectly innocent occurrences, with neither of those men having anything to do with Alex or Diana. The problem is, and Art agrees with me here, we found no other occurrences in your last few weeks that were, shall we say, out of the ordinary. Art will check on that too, however, while you're under."

"Under?"

"Hypnosis," Art said.

"I see." I did, sort of, though it sounded like a hell of a long shot. It couldn't hurt anything. Besides, what else could I have done at this point? *Damn it, I hate feeling this helpless!* "Okay, what now?"

Frank nodded to Art, who opened his doctor's bag and pulled out two vials of clear liquid and two hypodermic needles.

"You intend to give me a shot?"

"Two shots."

"Why?"

"To relax you and open your mind to the experience, to the possibilities. It will help us — help *you* — find truths you didn't even know existed."

"Those must be some crazy drugs." I tried to laugh, but it seemed a tree trunk had lodged in my throat. "Nothing I can get hooked on, I presume?" I *hated* drugs.

"That's right. These will be small doses, nothing to worry about." Art offered a friendly, reassuring smile. "The first is secobarbitol. Most people think of it as a sedative, but it's also what we call a *hypnotic*, as is the second, sodium amobarbitol, which you may have seen referred to as *truth serum* in the movies."

"Are you serious? Sounds like one of those Robert Ludlum spy novels. Why is all that necessary? Can't you just swing a watch in front of me and count back from a hundred, or something like that?"

Art turned to Frank, who answered. "First of all, don't believe everything you see in the movies. Second, as I said earlier, we have some experience with this. You're a strong-willed young man—one might say stubborn. These will help. Please, you need to trust me."

"Fine!"

Art smiled again, which started to wear on me, then stuck a needle into one of the vials, drew some liquid, and stood over the sink to squirt a small amount from it. He repeated the procedure with the other needle and vial, and gave me the shots.

It took time for them to take effect; couldn't guess how long.

My head grew heavy, and darkness closed in like Godzilla's shadow. *Hah! Godzilla... shadow... some shadow... only the shadow knows.*

A bright light shone somewhere at the distant end of a tunnel, and everything blurred into mist without form. *Why am I here? What are these images? Wait... what's that noise?*

A voice called from the other side of the table, a thousand miles out the other side of the tunnel.

No idea what he said, but I answered. I thought. "Am I speaking aloud? Can you hear me?"

Darkness deepened as the mile-wide tunnel shrunk, shrunk, shrunk—small enough to fit on the head of a pin. I tried to lift my hand in front of my face, but it weighed sixteen tons. *Hah! Sixteen tons... sixteen tons... what am I gonna get?... ANOTHER DAY OLDER AND DEEPER IN DEBT.*

Couldn't know for sure, but it felt a lot like dying. Not so terrible.

"Welcome back to reality."

Frank's voice whispered from the shadows, where the darkness receded and light returned to the world. He gradually came into focus seated in his La-Z-Boy.

I lay on the sofa next to him. When I sat up, my head weighed about three hundred pounds, felt as if I'd gone fifteen rounds with George Foreman, me the loser by unanimous decision. I looked around the room as my eyes regained focus, and fifty pounds of fuzz fell off my head.

I barely managed to ask Frank about Art. My voice scratched across gravel, as though I'd been singing for twelve hours straight.

"Art's gone," he said, "had to get back home."

"Why do I get the feeling there's something you're not telling me?"

He laughed. "That, my boy, is because you're *very* smart."

"And that's it?"

"I'm afraid so... for now."

"What about the hypnosis? How did you know about that? How did you know which questions to ask? Did anything useful come out of it?"

Even before he answered, I had a sense of new memories—hazy, lingering at the edges, waiting me to grab onto them. Strange sensation.

"Why don't we find out?" Frank's voice jerked me out of my thoughts.

I stared at him, waiting, but he just stared back for a few seconds.

Then he finally said, "Diana is a precious jewel."

"Huh? Sure, that's one way of... of putting...." *What the hell!*

New data flooded into my mind: faces, words spoken, smells, sounds, textures. My brain suffered a kind of information overload as memories poured in from every direction.

Where in hell did they come from?

Frank nodded and picked up his note pad. "I see you've responded to the trigger."

"Trigger?"

"Yes, 'Diana is a precious jewel.' You remembered a number of things under hypnosis, and we wanted to ease you into remembering them consciously as well. We *instructed* you not to remember them until the moment we provided the trigger. You'd have remembered anyway, in short order, but this made it easier for you upon first waking up."

I didn't know what to say.

"Let's see where that gets us. Are you ready?"

I shrugged my shoulders. "Okay."

"Good. Do you remember Senior Ditch Day at Flora Park, and the man who held a Frisbee and stared at Diana?"

"Yes."

"Do you remember that night at the bowling alley, and the man who glowered at you and your friends?"

I hesitated. "Yes."

He paused again to review his notes.

"On the day of Alex's funeral, you rode your bike home from here. Do you remember the man parked across the street, seated in the van?"

Wait! Is it possible? "Yes."

"On those three occasions, were those three different faces, or one face?"

Everything remained unconnected, without context, yet I saw that face! It was as though I'd known the nameless man my entire life. "*One face.*"

He watched me as I considered the implications.

"My God, it was the same guy on all three occasions: the park, the bowling alley, and... wait a minute. I didn't remember that van across the street. I mean, I do remember it, but I don't.... Man, this is weird!"

"I told you, the subconscious is where the human mind dumps its refuse. There's more in there, so it takes the right person, with the proper knowledge, to dig through that refuse and make sense of it. Otherwise, there could be consequences."

Consequences? What in hell does that mean?

He recognized my concern. "Don't worry. You have nothing to worry about. We had the right person in Art."

The weight of it hit me. "Frank, it was the *same guy* each time! That has to mean...."

He nodded. I couldn't say anything more. Rage boiled like a cauldron somewhere inside. Then Frank held up a drawing, a penciled sketch of a face.

"Where did you get that?"

"Art drew it based on your descriptions," he said. "So what's your verdict? Is Art as good an artist as I think he is?"

"I'd say so. The detail is amazing, and that's definitely the face."

He handed it to me, and I raised the sketch within inches of my eyes—quite a professional rendering. There could be no question: it *must* be the face of a killer, and it *must* be the face of a kidnapper.

Frank agreed that this man was likely responsible for both Alex and Diana. We didn't believe in extraordinary coincidences.

"What are these three letters on the bottom of the page? It looks like my handwriting."

He pursed his lips and tilted his head in a near shrug. "As a matter of fact, those are the first three letters of the license plate on the killer's van."

CHAPTER 40
MAY 29, 1978:
TONY HOOPER

"The letters are from his license plate? Are you serious?"

"You wrote them down," Franks said. "Don't you remember?"

"Well... sort of. It's strange, as if I remember things that never happened, except I know they *did* happen. Hard to explain."

"That's the lingering effect of the hypnosis and the drugs. By tomorrow it will feel quite natural, as your conscious mind accepts them—a few more memories amongst thousands."

I'd never experienced anything like this. I was still groggy, but when Frank said the hypnosis had lasted for an hour, and that I'd slept for four hours afterward, I almost lost it.

"Half the day is gone already!"

"Sorry," Frank said, "but there was little choice. Those drugs were sedatives, and you needed to sleep them off. It's part of the process, and we'd know nothing had we not tried it."

Perhaps, but my frustration remained.

I stood and paced on still-wobbly legs, my mind drifting back to what we knew. "We have the killer's picture—I mean sketch—and a description of his van, and the first three letters of his license plate. With all that, the police should have no trouble finding him."

"We may not be able to proceed in quite that way."

"Huh? How else *can* we proceed?"

"You have options. While you were out, I was able to get additional information through Art's contact. He hasn't been retired for as long as I have, and he's still in touch with one guy in the game who's willing to help him out occasionally."

"Game? What did you guys retire from? And what information did you get?"

"Never mind the first part. That will have to—"

"Yeah, as if I can't guess."

"Anyway, as to the information, we obtained the rest of his license plate. That led us to his name and address."

My head reeled. "We need to call Chief Radlon right away." I reached for his phone.

"One minute, Tony, we must discuss some things first."

"What things? We have him. We can save Diana!"

"Sit awhile."

"Look, Frank, we have to—"

"I said *sit down*, Tony." His voice, soft but firm, matched his serious look.

I'd never seen him act this way. I did as he said, confused and anxious, scared and angry, needing to *do* something.

He took a deep breath and let it out slowly. "Look, I know you're anxious to move on this, but we obtained the information through unorthodox means. If pressed by the police, I'll have to say I know nothing about it. Art doesn't exist."

"*What?* Who is he? Who are *you*? Are you some kind of *spooks* or something?"

"I wish I could tell you more. You must trust me. I've never lied to you, and I sure don't want to start, but certain obligations I cannot ignore. Some things must remain unsaid."

"Damn it, I can't believe this! Don't tell me we're back to this crap out of a James Bond movie. If we can't use the information, then why did we go through this in the first place? How are we supposed to save Diana?"

"I didn't say we can't use the information. In fact, I said you have options. We need to discuss those before you act."

"Fine! What are my options?"

I'd lost Alex. I could still lose Diana, if she wasn't gone already. How far behind could my sanity be?

Frank's contacts, not to mention their methods, had to remain under the radar. I'd wanted to know the truth, but he wouldn't tell me. Too much clandestine crap! Nonetheless, after our discussion and some rehearsal, I was ready to proceed.

A phone call to Chief Radlon had produced an appointment for five o'clock. More time lost, but I hoped it would get things moving in a positive direction.

I drove past the murdering bastard's house — Mitchell Norton was his name — on the way to meet the chief. That might have been foolish, but I couldn't resist. What would I have done if I'd spotted him? I didn't have any weapons, though I probably wouldn't need one. No matter. I saw no sign of his van, so he must have been out.

I couldn't help but imagine what he might have been doing to my poor Diana. It made my stomach churn. Still, I stuck with the plan Frank and I had agreed on — no mention of Art, or the hypnosis, or the sodium-whatever-the-hell-it-was — the truth serum. The sketch of Norton was also off-limits, because Art was off-limits.

I couldn't claim credit for it because I couldn't draw, something they'd discover if they took a hard look, especially if this ended up in court. I couldn't provide the license plate or Mitchell's full name and address — too suspicious, information I couldn't reasonably explain given that I couldn't mention the hypnosis.

That didn't leave much, but I prayed it would be enough.

The police station sat on the west corner of Algonquin Road and Main Street, right in front of Towne Park, where on weekends I often played basketball in pick-up games. The desk sergeant, a woman whose name badge said J.P. Harker, took me to the hallway and pointed me toward the chief's office.

He waited at his door when I arrived. "Hello, Tony." He shook my hand and guided me to a chair in front of his desk. "How are you holding up these days?"

I got a good feeling from the chief, who seemed like a regular Joe, one of the nice guys. "Well, sir, it's been pretty tough. I don't know if you've heard, but my girlfriend, Diana Gregario, was abducted from her home in Lake-in-the-Hills late Saturday night or early Sunday morning."

"As a matter of fact, Deputy Ricks called me about it. He wanted to talk about Alex's case to see if there might be a connection. He didn't mention abduction, however."

"She wouldn't run off. It *had* to be abduction, given the hour she disappeared. I think he and Mr. G.—Mr. Gregario—suspect I had something to do with it."

"Yes, that possibility did come up in the conversation."

His straight face displayed little emotion.

I pressed on. "Well, the deputy said something that made me think, something about me being the common link. First Alex, then Diana, and each time I was the last one to see them. He's right about *that*, but wrong about the rest of it."

"I see, and where does that put us?"

"Well, sir, as I said, it made me think. I lay in bed last night and thought about everything. That's when I remembered."

I paused for effect, as Frank had suggested.

He straightened up. "Remembered what?"

"There was this creepy guy. Diana and I saw him at Flora Park on Senior Ditch Day. He was there with a guy about our age, but *he* was older—mid-twenties, perhaps. The two of them tossed around a Frisbee... when he wasn't *staring* at Diana. As I said, he was creepy."

He never took his eyes off me as he waited for me to continue.

"I got a pretty good look at him, but there's more. I remembered the younger one calling him Mitchell. Then I went out with friends the night of Alex's funeral, to try to relax. I know how that sounds, but I needed to get away."

I hung my head and acted as though ashamed of it. Not much of a stretch.

"I'm sure that's a perfectly normal reaction," he said. "Please continue."

"Diana and I met a couple friends at the bowling alley in Carpentersville to shoot pool, bowl, play arcade games, that kind of stuff. We whooped it up pretty good and made a lot of noise. You know how it is. This guy glared at us as if we were a bunch of rowdy kids who needed to shut up. That was at first. Then he stared at Diana a lot, which put me a little on edge. That's when it hit me. It was the *same* guy, the one from Flora Park. What are the odds of that?"

"Might be something, might be nothing. Was there anything else?"

"Yes sir. When we left, Diana and I were in my car getting ready to leave, laughing at something Tom said—he's one of our other friends—when this guy, this Mitchell character, walked out. He looked around as if he was trying to find someone, and when he spotted us, he stared for a minute. Then he walked to a van—dark blue, I think. We took off after that."

I stopped to let the chief consider everything I'd said.

"Have you seen him anywhere since then?"

"No sir."

"Okay, someone by the name of Mitchell, in a dark blue van.... Do you know what the make of the van was?"

"I'm not sure, but I think it was a Chevy, kind of beat up."

"I see." He made a few notes. "One more thing: Do you think you'd recognize him if you saw him?"

"I've thought about that a lot since last night. I pictured his face and everything. Yes, sir, I'm sure I would."

"It's too bad you didn't get a license plate."

I have it! I also have his full name. I can take you right to him!

"Still," he said, "I think we have plenty to start with. How many guys named Mitchell, driving a beat-up, old, dark blue Chevy van, can there be in the area? We'll track him down."

"That's great! I wasn't sure."

"You must remember, Tony, that just because you ran into this guy twice and he was 'creepy,' as you say, that doesn't mean he had anything to do with Alex or Diana."

"I understand."

"Nonetheless, we'll take a look. Okay?"

"Yes sir. Thank you."

"No need to thank me. It's my job. Thank *you* for coming in."

"Yes sir. Uh... sir... I was wondering if you could keep me posted on things. Mr. G. and Deputy Ricks are... well, they won't tell me anything, and I'm so worried about Diana."

He stared at me for a moment. "Tony, I need you to trust me to take care of things, okay? However, if we hear anything about Diana, I'm sure you'll be one of the first ones to know."

"Okay. Thank you."

He walked me to the front door and shook my hand again. Given the funny look on his face, for the life of me, I couldn't tell if he suspected me or not.

Frank had said earlier that I must give the chief a little time and be patient.

Be patient, my ass! If that sonuvabitch Norton kills Diana, I'll have his head!

Now to someone who might help me with my plan, which I'd been considering since I awoke this afternoon following the hypnosis. I hadn't told Frank—not sure how he'd take it—but I needed to do something myself. I couldn't sit around and wait for the police. Diana might die while they went through the motions.

I couldn't let that happen, not if there was any way to prevent it. I needed to prepare for my own move against Norton, but a little advice would help.

It was time to see Master Komura.

CHAPTER 41
JUNE 13, 1995:
MITCHELL NORTON

The police station buzzes with activity, with cops running about as though in the midst of some crisis. I stopped in to follow up on the big scene at the coffee shop, that little dance with that fuckin' Hooper. I'm determined to hold Chief Radlon's feet to the fire on this.

I ain't takin' no more shit from Hooper.

Feels like a thousand eyes glare at me, and the cops whisper to one another as they look in my direction. It sucks being so recognizable, and they sure-as-shit don't suffer any pretense of discretion. Feels a little like being a Hatfield upon entering a room full of McCoys, or like a storm cloud has entered the room, threatening a deluge of suspicion, disgust and anger.

The desk sergeant puts the phone down and barely looks at me before leading me back to an interrogation room. This ain't exactly where I'd hoped to end up. Bad memoires. I ask the sergeant for something to drink before he leaves, but he feigns not hearing me and closes the door behind him.

I might not get satisfaction here. Maybe I should have gone right to a lawyer. Yet somehow, I have a desire to play the game with these cops. Why is that?

Whatever. Might be fun.

A window of one-way glass dominates one wall. I use the mirror — this side of the window — to comb my hair and straighten my tie. I decided to dress for the occasion and show the proper respect — all part of the game.

Why did they bring me to this room instead of the chief's office? Do they wanna observe me for some reason? I got a strong sensation that someone is already watching me from the other side of the glass.

What the hell, if I'm gonna have fun with this, I might as well get started.

I walk right up to the glass, press my forehead against it, and cup my hands around my face to cut the glare, like I can see through it. Then I back up and give 'em my biggest smile.

Two wire-mesh circles—microphones—jut from the wall to the left and right of the glass. I lean toward them and say cheerily, "How are you doing back there? Do I look all right?"

What's the worst that can happen? If nobody hides back there, no harm done—one can only make a fool of one's self before witnesses. If someone *is* there, then maybe I've irritated them a teensy bit. Fun stuff.

I sit again and fold my arms on the table. Patience.

Two minutes later, Chief Radlon enters the room with a deputy sheriff.

"Howdy, Chief," I say. "I appreciate you seeing me."

"This is Deputy McAllister from the sheriff's office."

We nod at each other. "You involved the sheriff's department in this, Chief? Glad to see you're taking it seriously."

He looks at me like I have a booger dangling from my nose. Maybe he's waiting for me to say something more.

"I take it you've spoken to Hooper," I say.

"I have. I'm sure he won't be looking for you, Mr. Norton, but you must remember that this is a small town. It's conceivable—likely, in fact—that you'll bump into one another from time to time. Just keep to yourself when it happens. He's assured me he'll do the same."

"All right, I guess that'll do it—nice and simple."

I slide my chair back, but the chief continues.

"Before you go, we'd like to take this opportunity to ask you a few questions, if you don't mind. We planned on paying you a visit, but you can save us a trip."

"I'm not looking for trouble with Hooper. I just want him to leave me alone."

"This isn't about Tony Hooper. It's about you. As you might imagine, a lot of people are nervous about you being out of prison and back in the community."

"Yeah, I've read the newspaper reports. Whatever. I've been cleared, and I have every right to a fresh start."

"No one is arguing that," he says. "Nonetheless, in a small town like this, we need to be mindful of community concerns. You can help us in this regard."

"Oh? And how can I do that?"

I look at the deputy. *Why are you here? And why does the chief act like he gives one shit about me?*

"It shouldn't take long," Radlon says.

"How does this concern you, Deputy, if you don't mind my asking?"

Radlon holds his hand up and answers for him. "Deputy McAllister is the county's chief murder investigator. He assists us here in Algonquin on those rare occasions."

"Murder? Come on, it's been seventeen years — case tried, sentence served, game over. Don't you think we ought'a give it a rest?"

"If you'll bear with me, we'll get through this in no time."

We all stare at each other for a few seconds, and he continues.

"First, have you found a job yet? If not, do you have any prospects?"

"Not yet."

"Are you planning to stay with your mother?"

"Probably, at least until I get a few paychecks in the pocket. Is that a problem, Chief?"

"Not at all. How have you been adjusting to life back at home? Is everything going all right?"

Come on! What the hell is this about? "Everything is peachy."

"Are you keeping yourself busy? Perhaps pursuing a hobby?"

"I just got out, Chief, haven't had time for anything but catching up with Mom and Tommy." I pause for only a second and hunch forward. "You wanna tell me what this is *really* about?"

He says he has to complete a formality, and pulls a Miranda card from his pocket and reads me my rights, assuring me it's no big deal.

Sure.

I waive my right to an attorney. For now.

He continues. "Can you tell us, Mitchell, where you were the night before last?"

He's calling me Mitchell now; must make us best buds.

"I was home, catching up with the family, watching a little TV."

"And what were you doing between the hours of one and four in the morning?"

"Uh... sleeping."

"And where were you last night, during the same timeframe?"

"Sleeping again. I'm funny that way." I couldn't resist, but the gentlemen don't find it terribly amusing. No sense of humor.

"Can anyone confirm that?"

"My mom and my brother."

"They saw you during those hours?"

"Gee whiz, Chief, they might'a been sleeping themselves. They're *also* funny that way. My mommy-wommy didn't tuck me into my blanky-wanky and then check on me every hour, if that's what you're getting at."

Not so much as a smile from either of them.

"Please tell me how you know Mrs. Melody Nesmith," he says.

"I don't. Never heard of her."

"And do you know Mr. John Adams?"

"Who doesn't? He was the second president of the United States."

The deputy bores holes in me with his gaze, but leaves all conversation to the chief. "Are you saying you didn't know either of those two individuals?"

"That's right. Are you gonna tell me what's going on here?"

He turns to the deputy and shrugs, then looks at me again. "It'll hit the news shortly, anyway, and people will jump to their own conclusions. Two nights ago, someone murdered Melody Nesmith in the middle of the night, though we didn't discover it until this morning. Also this morning, we discovered that someone murdered John Adams in his home last night."

"Damn, I suppose we'll need a new president."

Neither man so much as blinks, like two statues. Maybe I should lay off the smartass comments. Such serious circumstances call for a measure of decorum.

"You realize," he says, "what people are likely to think. This attitude will make things tougher on you, Mitchell. Why don't you help us to help you?"

"That sounds real hunky-dory. How can I do that?"

He and the deputy don smiles, like they're my new best pals. "Take a polygraph to confirm what you've told us about your non-involvement in these cases. Remove yourself from suspicion."

Condescending asshole!

I've read about polygraphs. Not entirely reliable—they can be beat, or wrong. Many factors can affect the results, everything from not enough sleep to too much booze or drugs prior to a test. There's a reason courts don't allow polygraphs as evidence. If I fail, these cops will never leave me in peace. If I pass, will they leave me alone?

No way. They'll assume I beat it. No upside for me. Besides, they're pissing me off. "Polygraphs are not reliable, as everyone knows."

"Wouldn't you like to remove yourself from the suspect list? We're offering this for your benefit, Mitchell. With your history, you know what everyone will think. Wouldn't you like us to tell the public that we have reason to believe you're not involved with these murders?"

"People beat polygraphs all the time. You know it and I know it. You'll keep me on your suspect list until you have someone else in mind, regardless of the results."

"We're trying to help you here, Mitchell. Why don't you let us help you?"

"Do you think I'm an idiot, Chief? Sorry to disappoint you, but I'm not, and I'm getting a little tired of playing this game of yours. I came here to follow up on Hooper's attack, not to sit through an interrogation. You know, I hear you and Hooper are thick as thieves. I don't suppose that has anything to do with this, does it?"

He no longer smiles, nor does the deputy, whose jaw muscles and temples appear ready to jump off his face, run across the table, and choke the snot outta me.

"You realize," the chief says, "that this reinforces our suspicions."

"Take your polygraph and shove it! We both know—excuse me, all *three* of us know—you've already made up your mind. This is bullshit! You'd be judge, jury and executioner if you had your way."

"That's something you know about, isn't it, Mitchell?"

Now he's laid the cards on the table. The chief has let down his guard, but I don't respond.

"Seventeen years is a long time to go without getting your jollies. What's the matter, did you get the itch already?"

I raise my left arm and scratch my armpit. "Yep, right here."

"Perhaps you chose Melody Nesmith and John Adams at random, without knowing their names. That fits your history, doesn't it?"

"Christ, you're a laugh a minute, Chief. Am I under arrest?"

"Why don't you want to help us with this, Mitchell? What do you expect us to think when you respond this way? Be smart. It's in your best interest to help us."

I can't help but laugh. "Once again you treat me like I'm an idiot. I think my best interests, as you put it, would best be served by ignoring your ridiculous accusations."

They don't like me much. Whatever. I ain't even sure if the deputy has blinked yet.

A knock on the door interrupts us, and a woman enters the room a second later. She looks different from our previous encounter, with her hair up and wearing make-up. The fun might truly begin now.

"My, my, my," I say. "Look, everyone, Special Agent Linda Monroe of the FBI has joined us. Have you been on the other side of the glass? Are you the type that likes to watch, darling? That's so kinky. I like it."

"I'm so glad you find this amusing, Mitchell," she says. "I don't think you understand the gravity of the situation. We're trying to help you here."

"Do you folks all work from the same playbook or something? Abbott and Costello. Excuse me, Deputy, the Three Stooges, or maybe the Marx Brothers — you do talk about as much as Harpo. Hey, where's your horn? Beep, beep!"

No smile. No blink. Nothing. Someone needs to check that guy's pulse.

"You picked up a sense of humor in prison," Ms. FBI says. "You must have liked it there. Perhaps you can't adjust to life outside. It happens. I suppose you're looking forward to going back."

Bitch!

Everyone remains quiet for several seconds, and I smile, determined not to give any of them the satisfaction. This entire day has turned right to shit! The chief defers to Ms. FBI. Apparently, the feds get to do all the talking.

"Run out of funny things to say, Mitchell?"

"Just protecting myself against a lynch mob. That's my constitutionally protected right, unless you guys already have a rope and a tree out back."

"Yep, you're a real funny guy. Why do you insist on this course of action? Perhaps you think this is a big game, or that you're smarter than we are. You should give us a little more credit, and you should help yourself. Make things easier on yourself."

"But the game is such fun, don't you think, Ms. FBI?"

"Is that what this is about, Mitchell? Is that why you killed those people, tortured and sliced them up, because it's such fun for you?"

"Nice try, Ms. FBI." I laugh at the three of them. Poor things. They aren't having nearly as much fun as I am. "And now, if you're arresting me, I'll say no more until I get my lawyer. If not, then y'all have a nice day, y'heah."

I stand and walk to the door. Nobody stops me.

"Be sure to stay in the area, Mitchell," Ms. FBI says. "I'm sure we'll be seeing you soon."

"I'll look forward to it."

PART 7

HELL BENT

CHAPTER 42
JUNE 13, 1995:
TONY HOOPER

"Whenever anyone is against his will, this is to him a prison." – *Epictetus*

I received the call from Linda a few minutes ago.

All of Algonquin will soon understand that their nightmare has truly returned. Mitchell Norton is back in business. The two victims of torture, murder and dismemberment—shades of the reign of terror that gripped Algonquin in 1978—bring to an end the seventeen-year respite.

Why does this not surprise me? I still remember the eyes of *the devil*. I knew he couldn't help himself. Now two additional deaths, two more innocent victims, pile onto my already heavy conscience.

Well join the frickin' party!

"I know you're not blaming yourself for this," Frank says from his La-Z-Boy.

I swear he can read my mind.

He holds his gaze. "This isn't like the other cases. This one is personal and everyone knows it. There are too many eyes on you this time. Let the authorities handle it."

"If I'd done what I should have done seventeen years ago, they wouldn't *have* to handle it, and Melody Nesmith and John Adams would still be alive."

"You must let it go. You did what was right at that time and place. You did what a person of conscience does."

I jump up and start pacing around his living room, and laugh. "Oh? So what does that say about what I've been doing since then? About my special avocation?"

"That's unfair. You know what I mean. You were only eighteen, still a *boy*. It would have been unfair to expect you to kill Mitchell Norton. That was too much to ask of an eighteen-year-old. How long will you go down that road?"

"I'll go down that road until I hear his last terrified breath, and that won't be much longer."

"Tony, please be careful. There are too many people paying attention this time. They're watching Mitchell Norton, most assuredly, and possibly watching you as well. You always take frightful chances when you do what you do, but the risk will be even greater this time."

"I'll be careful to remain in the shadows. If the police catch him first, that's fine with me. As long as they lock him up and he can't kill again, I can live with it. But goddammit, the law doesn't always work. I know the chief is a good cop and Linda is a good cop, and that most cops are good cops, but the law is another matter. It focuses too heavily on the rights of bastards like Norton. I don't have to deal with the restraints the cops have to deal with."

"Sure, as long as you're willing to pay the price if you get caught. The law will not forgive you. Nor will most cops, for that matter."

"I've always been willing to accept the risks."

He looks at me with genuine concern, perhaps a touch of sadness. He's long expected the hammer to fall and to hear that I'm in custody. He says nothing.

"How are the finances doing, by the way? I'll need a fresh infusion of cash."

Uh-oh.

I don't like the look on his face. Frank has given me money for so long—paid my way—that I've come to take it for granted. What happens when there's no more money? I've never held a *real* job, not as an adult at any rate. I don't even know where to begin, if I *must* begin. What shall I do about my calling? How shall I walk the road I've chosen? Hell, it's more accurate to say the road chose me.

I plop back down onto the sofa. "Is money a problem?" I ask. "I always assumed.... I don't know exactly *what* I assumed. I took too much for granted."

"No, no, I was just thinking. I'm eighty-eight years old and I'm winding down, Son. I feel it in my bones, in my muscles, in my heart — everywhere. It should hardly be a surprise."

"What are you talking about? You'll probably make a hundred."

"I doubt that. At any rate, I've put this off for too long already. It's too risky to postpone it any longer. We need to talk about some things, to plan for the future."

I've wondered about Frank's past since I was a kid, but my emotions are mixed at this point. However strong my curiosity, or the prudence of discussing it, this talk, as if he faces his imminent end, is not my idea of a good time. He can't live forever but, given the dangers inherent in my avocation, I thought he might actually outlive me. Always the indestructible force, he's a mere mortal after all.

"Okay." What else can I say? The rest is for him.

"I know you've been curious for a long time, and that you've had your suspicions, especially after that hypnosis episode with Art Reynolds back in 1978. The things I'm about to tell you may be difficult to believe, and may even bring to mind those spy novels you love so much. Try to keep your imagination in check and bear with me. Okay?"

"Okay."

"Art worked with the CIA, and I worked with him until I retired in 1959. He passed a few years back, by the way. I never mentioned it."

CIA? Yeah. Why am I not surprised? "I'm sorry. Was he a friend?"

"Yeah, we worked together starting right after the war — that would be World War II. We came out of the OSS, which was the wartime precursor to the CIA. They recruited me during the war to do some fieldwork and...." He scratches his palm. "Dear me, suddenly I'm nervous."

Color rushes to his face, and a tremor has attacked his hands. He's eighty-eight, sure — but he's Frank! He swallows hard.

"It's okay, Gramps. You know you can tell me anything."

"I know." He takes a deep breath. "I was what the OSS called an *asset*. I'm German, Son, or at least I was. I obtained American citizenship in 1950. My real name, the one I was born with, was Franz Wollman. I worked as a psychiatrist with the German army during the war. They forced me to do some... unpleasant things, to participate in ungodly experiments."

"My God, are you telling me you were a Nazi?"

He clasps his hands together in an apparent attempt to control the shaking, and squeezes. His jaw muscles begin popping and he looks as if he's about ready to stroke-out.

Damn! I should—

"I was hardly a fervent believer. They *forced* me. I had two options: participate or die. They would have killed Marta—that was Martha's real name—as well."

He pauses again to take yet another deep breath, and closes his eyes as if remembering.

He opens them again, and says, "I complained about it at the time, quietly and in tight circles, which ultimately attracted the OSS agent to me. He offered to smuggle Marta and me to America, but first I had to provide what he called *vital information*. I jumped at the opportunity, but those next six months were the most difficult of my life.

"I was torn about betraying my country, but witnessing the savagery of the Nazis made that easier. Many people went along, but they did so out of fear and misguided patriotism, at least in the beginning. Those were such desperate times. After the war, most good folks felt ashamed and guilty, maybe a little angry, and many struggled against a new onslaught of nightmares.

"I begged my handler to get me out of Germany *immediately*, but they needed me where I was. The things I saw and, God help me, the programs in which I participated. I pray every day for forgiveness, and I must trust that God has heard those prayers. I must also trust that I helped to defeat that terrible evil in my own small way, and by doing so helped save many more lives. I *must* believe these things. The pain would be too much to endure otherwise."

He pulls a handkerchief from his pocket and wipes his face and neck. The handkerchief lingers a few seconds at his eyes, holding back the tears, I think.

I've never seen him so distraught.

"When Marta and I escaped and came to this country in 1943," he says, "the OSS put me to work with their intelligence officers. They were attempting to understand the German mindset and determine how they'd react to certain events, to make best use of the Nazi psyche during the war. I had insight into such matters."

"You weren't a Nazi at all," I say. "You worked against your own country. Even though it was the right thing to do, it must have been difficult."

He nods and sighs, as though the vice that had been gripping his heart just eased back. "Indeed. My conscience is mostly clear, though it would be more so, had they allowed me to leave prior to those horrifying six months. I'm not an overtly emotional man, as you know, part of my rigid German upbringing, I suppose...."

Yeah, sure... not emotional.

"...Nonetheless, I often awoke screaming and crying afterwards. I spent many therapy sessions working with Art, and he helped me recover from those horrors. He was a young man then, recently out of school, but wise and talented beyond his years."

He leans back, takes his deepest breath yet, and his shoulders relax into his chair, the tremors in his hands gone. "Truman disbanded the OSS after the war, but it wasn't long before they created the CIA. I joined them and performed various duties, always related to psychiatry. That was it, until I retired in '59."

"This is unbelievable," I say, "real movie-making material. The one thing I don't understand is the money. Were you wealthy in Germany?"

A half-smile overtakes his face, and he laughs under his breath. "No, that's another story of which I'm not particularly proud, but one for which I've tried to make amends. Before I left Germany, I stole from one of the Nazis, who were themselves stealing from all over Europe and North Africa. They took whatever they could get their hands on: paintings, sculptures, jewelry, gold and silver, money, valuable trinkets of any kind. They were murderers, to be sure, but they were also *thieves*."

"I've read about that," I say.

"It was true. One field marshal assigned to our headquarters had built quite a little stash for himself. I got a peek at it accidentally one day. The last thing I did before being smuggled out of Germany was break into his office and steal his hidden stash, all of which was ill-gotten in ways I dared not imagine."

"Stash," I say. "What in the world are you talking about?"

"It will be easier to show you. Walk with me."

Frank accepts my arm and stands gingerly, more fragile than usual, as though talking about this, remembering it, further stresses an old and tired body and mind. We meander through the kitchen and out the back door.

A blast of heat radiates off the patio, and the humidity glues my shirt to my chest within seconds. As always happens when we step outside his house, an invisible aromatic mist—some weird mixture of field grass, fresh-cut lawn, and more than a dozen flower varieties—lay over us like nature's perfume.

He points us toward the garden and leads the way, and although I'm unsure how this relates to our discussion, I follow.

We cross the gothic bridge and he stops before a tree trunk. "Remember how I put the pumps for the stream into sawed-off tree trunks?"

"Yeah, but this isn't one of those."

"It's special in another way. You see that hole down there?" He points to a knotted opening—circular, approximately six inches in diameter—at the base of the trunk.

"Sure, I see it."

"Reach inside, and be careful of spiders."

Spiders? Crap, I hate spiders! I stoop down on one knee to look inside before reaching into the hole. "What's this metal lever?"

"Pull that straight out toward you."

When I do so, the top of the trunk rises to a slight angle. "What in the world is this?"

"Now lift the top until it's straight up."

The hollowed-out trunk, constructed differently from those Frank created for his stream pumps, contains one item: a black box.

"Leave the box inside the trunk," he says, "but raise the lid. Inside are several velvet bags of varying colors. Grab the blue bag and open it."

"Holy smokes! Are these real sapphires?"

"Yes, and in the red bag are rubies, in the green bag emeralds, in the white bag diamonds—you get the idea."

"Good heavens, some of these stones are *huge*. How much are these worth?"

"Been several years since I last checked, so I'm not sure, but as long as you don't get carried away, and along with other investments I have, there's probably enough there to last your lifetime. I've used them sparingly and only when necessary, and I've been generous with charities from time to time, which is how I tried to make things right. Believe me, Field Marshal Kleinschmidt would have been less generous had I left them.

"It's a tradition I expect you to uphold. They belong to you now."

"What? Wait a minute. You're *giving* them to me?"

"It's time, and my needs are modest, so *you* may now give *me* money. Also, we'll make arrangements for you to take ownership of the property."

"Holy cow, this is moving too fast! I have so many questions. How do you convert the stones to cash? Is it difficult? What about the IRS?"

"It was difficult at first but I've had many years to work through it. I have three primary contacts, jewelers and dealers who move the stones. I'll make the necessary introductions soon and we'll talk about the procedures. As for the IRS, do they even know you exist?"

"Ummm...." My head is spinning, suffering a serious case of information overload. I heft the bag of sapphires and try to gauge their weight, as if that will mean a damn thing to me. "I don't know. Since I haven't officially had income for the past eleven years, and since I've filed no returns, and functioned under several different identities, I suppose not."

"There you go. We'll just maintain that circumstance."

"And what's this about the property?" I gaze about the place that's been as much Frank's baby as anything in life. "I don't want to take your home."

"It's your home too, and I planned to leave it to you in my Will, but giving it to you prior to my death offers certain advantages. Again, you'll learn all this over the next few weeks. I have an attorney to help with such matters. He's a fairly unscrupulous fellow, much more interested in money than in the law but, given the circumstances, he'll do nicely."

The mystery of Frank Willow revealed, quite a story, though there's clearly much more that I should like to learn. I suspect we'll have some interesting conversations.

"I suppose this is overwhelming," he says. He scratches his palm again, something he's been doing a lot today.

"Hell yes! This is unbelievable. Seriously, I couldn't have dreamed this up."

"Do you think less of me for what happened in the war?"

"Are you kidding? Frank, you're one of the most remarkable men I've ever known. You're Gramps. Nothing has changed. If anything, you're more remarkable than ever."

His shoulders relax and he so deflates in a huge sigh, I'm afraid his strength is going to give right out, collapsing him in a heap. I rush to put an arm around him for support.

"Thank you, Son." He pats the back of my hand and nods. "I'm glad to hear it hasn't harmed your feelings for me. I was afraid it might."

"Nothing could ever do that, Gramps."

"Good." He squeezes me tighter in our embrace. "We'll have plenty of time to talk later, assuming I don't keel over. Let's go inside. It's too damned hot and muggy out here, even for these old bones."

I was still reeling from Frank's story when I heard the car pull up. I hustled to the front door to await our visitor.

I've been anxious to see Linda, and not just to find out what's happening with Norton and the new murder investigations. I haven't seen her since the day before yesterday, which she took for herself to shop and read her books. It's only been a one-day separation and yet it's made me edgy.

How can that be? I want to hold her and smell her and kiss her and....

She smiles brightly as she walks up, watching me watch her. At the door, she leans in to hug and kiss me.

I swim in her lightly perfumed scent. *That's more like it!*

I step aside to let her in and follow her into the kitchen. She lights up when she sees Frank, and she skips around the table to kiss him on the cheek.

"Thank you, my dear," he says. "Don't you smell lovely? How is my flower garden supposed to compete with that?"

There he goes again. If I said that, it would sound corny at best, ridiculous or phony at worst. Yet from Frank it sounds like exactly what it is: sincere appreciation. She giggles and blushes slightly. Frank has an extraordinary talent for bringing out the best in people.

"Listen up, you old charmer," I say with a laugh. "Don't be making a play for my woman."

That brings her head around.

My woman? Did I say that?

I pull out a chair and she sits between us. After we all agree to some Mint Medley tea, Linda recounts her quiet day off. The highlight, a four-hour shopping spree, would have killed me. She also spent some time at the hotel pool reading one of her romance novels, which would have killed me as well.

I set the tea on the table. "It sounds as though you had a relaxing day. So today it's back to the grind?"

"Well, it's not exactly the grind. Chief Radlon did contact me and ask me to stop in to speak to your favorite neighborhood scumbag, but he lawyered-up. I didn't contribute much of anything, although I got a sense of *that man*."

She said *that man* as though the sound of it would strike fear into the hearts of children and small pets.

"You mean Norton," Frank says.

"Yes, he thinks it's a game, and he finds considerable humor in it. He fancies himself some kind of comedian. He's despicable."

"Aren't they all, my dear?"

She laughs in that way people laugh not out of humor, but out of frustration. "Yes, but his smug attitude is more annoying than many I've encountered. Many serial killers are introverted, introspective, even considerate in their own sick way. Norton, on the other hand, enjoys rubbing our faces in it."

I could have told her that. "So you have no doubt that he's responsible for these recent murders?"

She shakes her head and holds up her hand. "It's far too early for that, Tony. The evidence isn't in yet. He may be responsible, or he may be having fun with us while someone else plays the copycat. There are a few subtle differences between these murders and those of 1978, but even if someone else is guilty, he's the sort to find some fun in it."

"It *must* be him."

"Not necessarily. It does seem foolish for Norton to start again, so soon and so close to home. He strikes me as smarter than that, though he might not be able to help himself. It's possible that someone else is getting his jollies here, someone who finds this unique opportunity too good to pass up. He can have his fun in someone else's back yard—one of his own, so to speak—and let Norton take the heat for it. There are so many of them. You have no idea."

She shakes her head as she looks down at the teacup. Frank takes the opportunity to look at me as if to say, *Doesn't she know what you do?*

"It's happening too fast," I say. "The sick bastard can't resist. Someone else would have had to be in the area already. No chance."

"You'd be surprised. People would be horrified, I think, to know how many serial killers there are in this country. We know of those behind bars, and of several we're still trying to catch, but for every one we're aware of, at least one more exists — unexplained disappearances, random killings that appear unrelated, or those spread so far apart geographically that no one makes the connection.

"In fact, we believe most major cities have *at least* one serial killer working them. As the technologies and national databases continue to improve we may eventually be able to connect some of those dots, but we're not there yet, not by a long shot. 1995 is not quite Utopia. Most police forces have insufficient, overstressed staff, often trained inadequately for serial killers. Because they don't make the connections locally, they don't refer the proper cases to us. It's not their fault, at least not usually."

I try to hide my frustration. Bureaucracies never function efficiently; it's the reason — well, *part* of the reason — I do what I do.

"The problem," she continues, "is primarily systemic. We're making inroads and trying to fix the problem, but we need additional technological advances. Those are moving ahead at a breakneck pace, but it will take a few more years.

"In the meantime, too many of these beasts get away with it. Sadly, the worst psychopaths are typically intelligent, which makes things tougher. We know from several recent arrests, for example, that they often keep up with the technologies and try to work around them."

She spins her drink around to mix it, takes a sip, and stares into space. "Damn!"

"It's clearly frustrating for you," Frank says.

She nods. "We've had instances where we knew who the culprit was — I mean we *knew* it — but we didn't have the necessary evidence to obtain warrants and make an arrest."

"So you had to wait until more people died?" he asks.

Linda jolts, taken aback by the question.

"I'm sorry, my dear." He places his hand over hers. "I don't think that sounded quite right. I didn't mean to accuse you of sitting by and watching idly. I meant that you were frustrated by the legal process, the unfortunate result of which was that more people died."

She sighs. "That's the topic of a lot of heated discussions in every stationhouse, every courthouse, and every law school in the country. Ultimately, it's one of the *costs* of our freedom, I suppose. It's difficult to know where to draw that line."

"Indeed it is," he says.

Linda stares at her teacup again.

Frank stares at me again.

What did he do? Did he open some sort of door for me? She's a professional cop, near the pinnacle of her profession. I can't believe she would even consider.... No. No way. Looking the other way where I'm concerned is one thing, and probably quite difficult enough for her, but active participation?

Never.

CHAPTER 43
MAY 29, 1978:
TONY HOOPER

"There is a tide in the affairs of men, which, taken at the flood, leads on to fortune; omitted, and all the voyage of their life is bound in shallows and miseries." — *William Shakespeare, "Julius Caesar, IV, iii"*

The dojo sat north of town center on West Algonquin Road. My master, forty-two-year-old Ben Komura, was a first generation American born to Japanese parents who'd immigrated in 1922. His family had studied the martial arts for centuries. Once upon a time, his ancestors had been samurai. He took the family tradition, one he sought to pass down to me, quite seriously.

The most unassuming man I'd ever known, and almost obsessively polite, he insisted on sharing his hospitality with all who visited, whether family, friends, or someone who walked in off the street. He assured me that this was in proper respect to the Japanese culture engrained in him, along with the language, by parents determined that he not forget his history. He honored that cultural heritage while remaining fiercely patriotic toward the country of his birth.

He'd volunteered for the army during the Vietnam War, where he served two tours with the Special Forces in the mid '60s. I once found, inside a case on his bookshelf, three medals from the war—a Purple Heart with two clusters, a Bronze Star and a Silver Star. He bore nasty scars on his right leg and on his back that spoke clearly of his extraordinary deeds, yet he never spoke of them, or his courage. No surprise there.

I could easily imagine him killing an enemy in hand-to-hand combat, and then kneeling to pray for his enemy's soul.

Such was the nature of Master Ben Komura.

I stopped in for training, but also for his guidance. He'd taught me the martial arts for ten years and the ways of the samurai for the last three. He'd made me his special student; I no longer attended his regular classes, full of kids anxious to get their next belt. They improved their strength and balance, broke boards and practiced combat with their fellow students. They did this in preparation for the real thing, something he advised avoiding at all costs. Many students struggled with the concept. Why learn the martial arts, they wondered, if they should never fight? Self-defense was always acceptable, a responsibility we had to ourselves and to those who relied on us, but Master Komura would not tolerate offensive behavior. He'd refused to instruct more than one student who'd refused to accept this vital distinction.

What would he say about my plan?

The dojo sat dark but for the candles that always burned in the corners of the main room. He lived in modest comfort with his wife, Naomi, in a loft above the dojo. Naomi was pregnant and Master wore his excitement on his sleeve. He desperately wanted a son, though he would cherish a daughter.

I changed into my robes in the small locker room eight feet right of the stairs to his apartment.

Normally, after changing, I would ring the chimes to alert him to my presence, but Master already knelt in meditation on the pad in the center of the room. Despite my effort to make no sound at all, once again he'd heard me enter. We played this little game. I must enter and change clothes without him hearing. I must then use the chimes.

Though I'd never done so, I was determined to get him on that—someday.

I knelt before him and joined in the mental preparations and breathing exercises, which we always completed before starting. He slapped his legs to signal that we were ready, and I opened my eyes.

He looked at me thoughtfully. "You are troubled, my son?"

"*Hai*. These are troubling times, Master."

"You are still saddened by the loss of young Alex."

I nodded and glanced toward the floor.

"But there is more to it than that."

I nodded.

"You clearly find it difficult to speak of, yet all things may be said here, as you know. Together, we will seek answers. Then you must make your own decisions. You are my special student because I know your heart and soul. You need not fear of disappointing me."

He functioned as more than my mentor and teacher; in many respects, he served also as my confessor. I could tell him anything, and he'd give me guidance both contemplative and just. I also knew that I must *accept* his guidance—an important part of our relationship. I could argue for myself, and we would discuss all possibilities, but in the end, *his* decision somehow became *our* decision.

I'd never been disappointed by the outcome.

This time.... *Shit!* Sweat pooled in my palms, and my heart and breathing raced. I needed to consider my words carefully, explaining both my dilemma and my intended course of action, and seek his advice on how best to proceed. Yet what would I do if he counseled *against* such action?

I held a deep breath and... and farted! I stared at him for an instant, and then we broke into laughter.

Thirty minutes later, I'd explained everything. He knew of Diana's abduction at the hands of Mitchell Norton, of the hypnosis that had provided so much information, of how my life was on hold, due first to the murder of Alex and now to the possible loss of Diana. He knew of my plans to postpone school for a year, of my intention to marry Diana when the time was right, of my dad's withdrawal into a bottle. In all, I'd explained my utter frustration at the circumstances: the helplessness, the loneliness, the anger, the fear.

Lastly, I told him of how I stood at the edge of an abyss. If Norton murdered Diana, I would fall in. "I must *act*," I said. "I have to do *something* to save her."

He sat attentively throughout my speech, never breaking eye contact. Ever the stoic, his eyes nevertheless conveyed sadness and regret, understanding and love. When he looked to the floor with closed eyes, I knew he was contemplating the next step.

I joined him in meditative silence; no more need of words.

Five minutes later, he slapped his legs and sat straight. "You will remain here, my son. Continue your meditations. I will return shortly."

I nodded obeisance as he walked up to his apartment. Though still nervous, I also felt at peace now that I'd said what he needed to know. All that remained was to trust in his guidance.

When he returned, he carried several items, which he set on the floor between us before taking up his previous position.

On the pad lay three swords, one full-length samurai sword called a *katana,* and two short swords called *ninjaken,* each sheathed in black with black hilts. He'd also brought a ring called a *shobo,* with a small notch on it designed to strike pressure points on your opponent, to inflict sharp pain or temporary paralysis. There was also the traditional, at least in modern times, garb worn by the ninja, all black, called *shinobi shozoku.* It included boots called *jika-tabi,* with small spikes on the bottom called *ashiko.* The *jika-tabi* had a split-toe design to aid in gripping and climbing. He'd obviously obtained my sizes in advance. Last was the head cover, which utilized the *sanjaku-tenugui,* or three-foot cloths.

When dressed in the entirety, I would be both lethal and virtually invisible in the dark.

"I have had these things for you for several months," he said, "but I awaited the proper moment to give them to you. This, I believe, is that moment."

"It's an awful lot to accept. Are you sure I'm ready?"

"Yes, though we will continue your training with greater purpose and intensity than before. You must commit to excellence, as always."

"*Hai.*"

"Twice a week remains adequate, but the sessions must be longer. Three hours will suffice."

Talk about intense!

"Are you prepared to make this commitment, my son?"

There was no such thing as halfway with Master Komura. I would have to give every ounce of energy to the effort. Or nothing. "*Hai.*"

"Good, then these things are yours."

"Thank you, Master, this is extraordinarily generous. I understand the swords, but why have you given me the ninja garb? I'll be ready to audition for a Chuck Norris movie." I half chuckled, half swallowed my nervousness.

"Hold to your sense of humor. It will serve you well." He smiled in mock admonition. "Ninjutsu is but one of the arts we study, and you may need these items. You must use every available tool."

"I feared you would disapprove of my intentions."

"Self-defense comes in many guises, does it not? It means defending yourself, but it also means defending your family and dear friends. This is a matter of honor. We must pray that Diana is still alive and plan accordingly. Rescuing her is more than an opportunity. It is your responsibility. It is the way of the samurai."

"*Hai.*"

"This is your task, but I will assist you in any way you ask. We will start with your continued advanced training. However, you must know that if you require my assistance in the field, you have only to say the word."

"I know you would help me in this but, as you said, it's my task. My opponent is cruel, but he is unskilled. If something changes and I need your help...."

He watched me as if expecting me to say something more, then continued, "The dinner hour approaches, and Naomi will be upset if I fail to invite you. She always enjoys your visits. We will eat lightly and drink some tea, and we will speak of other things in Naomi's presence. I do not wish to upset her and, consequently, our child."

"Yes, Master. Thank you."

"Very well, we will dine before training. Then we will begin with the proper wearing of your garb before moving on to the proper use of the three swords, with which you are already familiar. We will also continue your focus on combining balance and power, but we will add the skill of invisibility, which is the true purpose of the garb. This will be important for you, I think."

"*Hai.*"

CHAPTER 44
MAY 29, 1978:
MITCHELL NORTON

Last night was huge! I'd disposed of Danny-Boy in exactly the right way, chopping him into small enough pieces to squeeze him into two plastic garbage bags. Then I'd driven down to the river near the base of Blackhawk Trail, backed right up to the boat launching area, and fed the Beast a little late-night snack.

The Reaper must'a been pleased.

I had one hell of a mess to clean up when I returned to the shop. Danny-Boy had spilled a shitload of blood and gore. It had attracted flies, damn it, and scratching noises started outside the shop, probably a critter drawn by the smell of blood. I ran out with my knife, but it had vanished by the time I reached the back of the shed.

Diana had watched it all in horror. I knew it would be difficult for her. Hell, given how frightened *I* was when the visions first started, it was hardly a surprise that *she'd* been terrified. That was inevitable.

She'd get used to it, like I had. Maybe she'd even help me, in time; then we'd truly be together. I had to take it slow for now. I hadn't had sex with her yet, though I'd sure worked myself into a hot lather — still couldn't believe I'd stroked the old missile right in front of her.

Still nervous about leaving Diana alone, I hadn't been home today. I cleaned myself from the bucket, as she had. It wasn't too bad... but it was about to get much better.

Her turn.

Man, that shapely body of hers, with the best tits ever! "I'll loosen your ties so you can clean up before we have something to eat. I always have my knife with me, so don't try anything stupid."

She nodded.

I'd already moved the rest of my tools where she couldn't reach them. Nonetheless, I'd stay inside and keep a close eye on her. She'd run or try to hurt me if I gave her half a chance. Besides, it figured to be fun.

I loosened her ties and sat a few feet away, where I'd have the best view.

She shuffled to the bench and dampened the rag as if to start, but stopped and stared at me. Poor little girl didn't want me to watch.

"Look, you know I can't leave you alone when you're free like that. You'll have to go about your business with me here."

Her eyes drooped back to the bench and her shoulders slumped.

"We do have options, you know. I could tie you up again, tear your clothes off and clean you myself. Maybe I'll leave you naked to wallow in your own stinking filth. How would that be?"

She looked at me briefly, took a deep breath, and removed her tee shirt.

Holy shit! Sweet mama!

She cleaned the top part of her body, and it was all I could do to keep my missile inside my jeans. She ignored me as she removed her jeans and panties. She turned her back to me, to keep me from seeing too much, but her plan failed when she bent over.

I leaned in for a closer look. *Fuck a rubber duck! Sex with her would be incredible.*

The Reaper said I had to wait until she was ready, until *she* wanted it too, as if that would make it so much better. *Shit!* Keepin' myself calm and controlled weren't no simple task.

She put on the new clothes, and rubbed her wrists where the bindings had discolored them. No way to avoid that. Once she got up to speed according to my plan, it wouldn't be an issue anymore.

In the meantime, maybe I could provide her with some temporary relief. "I know the ties hurt your wrists. That's unavoidable, but I'll let you sit awhile without them if you'd like. Just play it cool."

"Maybe if you put something beneath the ropes," she said, "some cloth to protect my skin."

The supplies included a small hand towel. I cut it in half lengthwise and tossed her the two pieces. Should'a thought of it sooner.

"That should do the trick, but I'll still give you a little break."

"Thank you," she said, and even smiled. Almost.

Maybe she'd come around sooner than I'd hoped.

"You're welcome. Now why don't we get to know each other a little better?"

We talked—mostly I talked and she listened—for two hours. I told her of the demons I'd seen, and the Reaper, whom I'd only heard, with his frightening voice. We had a sandwich, some chips, a pickle and a can of pop, and she ate while I spoke.

I apologized for putting her through this, explaining that the Reaper would do unimaginable things to me otherwise, that I was only following orders. He had a plan for *her* too, and I could help her, if she'd let me.

She nodded, but refused to look at me when she did.

Careful, Mitchell, the Reaper said. *You may be the MAN, but she's not quite ready to join you. It will take more time.*

That Reaper was a smart one.

I tied her up again, this time using the rags to protect her wrists, and dumped the bucket of dirty water behind the shop. "I'm going down to the lake for some fresh water. Sit tight and keep quiet. I'll be back in a few minutes."

She nodded weakly and said, "Okay," but I played it safe and gagged her. She wasn't too pleased but... whatever. She'd get over it.

I grabbed my baseball bat on the way out—never knew when the old Louisville Slugger might come in handy. It was mid-afternoon at the time of year, mid-May, when we saw some occasional hot weather. Though not exactly blazing, temperatures had risen. The sky cast a gray ghost over the area, holding back the storm.

Soon kids would show up at the gravel pit on weekends, and once school let out, they'd be here all the damned time. I'd need more buckets. I hated *buying* water—not fuckin' natural.

The trail dipped down before reaching a slight rise, beyond which lay the gravel pit, inside of which was the lake. I approached the rim of the pit and—

"Ooh, Bobby, you're a naughty boy."

I froze at the sound of the shrill voice. It took a minute for it to come again, clear and... a girl giggled. I dropped down and practically crawled to the rim.

"Do you like it when I touch you there, Jacque-Baby?" a boy said.

"Yes. Do it some more, you big stud."

What the hell? Didn't these kids know it was a school day? They'd probably skipped out so Bobby-the-Stud could dip his little finger in Jacque-Baby's love-muffin. Well that was fuckin' perfect!

The voice of the Reaper returned. *Think, Mitchell. What are you doing?*

"Learning," I whispered.

Yes?

"Training."

Yes, and what do you need to train?

Why hadn't I thought of that? "I need participants."

This must be your lucky day.

I had everything I needed, but the element of surprise would be critical. I walked through the steps in my head, hoping the Reaper would provide some instruction, but he remained silent. No matter. I figured it out.

With the bucket in my left hand and the Louisville Slugger, slung over my shoulder, in my right, I started quietly down the path to the lake. When their voices sounded close, I whistled a tune and acted nonchalant.

"Oops." I stumbled upon them. "What do we have here?"

The boy, Bobby-the-Stud, jumped up startled, embarrassed and guilty. *Yes, Bobby, I know exactly what you've been doing.*

The girl, Jacque-Baby, squirmed on the ground and tried to get her pants zipped and buckled. Quite amusing, though as I watched Jacque-Baby, I wanted to snap Bobby-the-Stud's fuckin' neck. Why was that?

He spoke in harsh, flustered tones. "What are you doing here, man? This place is supposed to be off-limits."

I figured them for sixteen or seventeen, and found his tone extremely annoying. "Now, Bobby, I could ask you the same question, though one look at Jacque here tells me all I need to know."

"How do you know our names?" Jacque-Baby asked—must be the smart one.

"Yeah!" Bobby-the-Stud, on the other hand—not too bright.

I turned my body to the right, back toward the path, then checked my balance and got a better grip on the baseball bat. "I was walking by and—"

I spun back hard and wheeled the bat squarely into the corner of Bobby-the-Stud's forehead, above and slightly to the left of his left eye. A terrible crunching sound rang out as blood flew through the air. He spun around and collapsed, not the sort of fall one would usually associate with people—more a plop into himself, as though he were made of liquid. Another loud snap echoed as a bone jumped out of his shin.

Man, that's cool!

When the girl screamed, I lunged over her and raised the bat with both hands. "Stop that screaming right now or you're next!"

She stopped—trembling, whimpering, her eyes like soccer balls—and put her hands up to protect her head.

"Be still." I lowered my voice. "No running or fighting back. I'm twice your speed and three times your strength, so don't make me kill you here." I couldn't tell her she was a dead woman regardless, awaiting a more vicious demise. "I'm gonna check on Bobby."

I took two steps to where the boy lay scrunched into a blob, and reached down to touch his neck. Nothing. I tried another spot... and another. Still nothing.

"Shucks, that's a shame. Poor Bobby-the-Stud is ready for the glue factory. He's deader than dirt."

She cried and shook violently, and seemed on the verge of screaming, so I threatened her again. When she realized *he* was dead, but *she* might still live, she calmed slightly. That old survival instinct—strong stuff—and I used it to my advantage.

I needed to keep her quiet long enough to get back to the shop. If she ran or screamed again, I'd have a problem. "I'm sorry about Bobby. Hated doing that, but right now we have to think about you, don't we?"

She nodded, her huge brown eyes bulging as if someone had pumped too much air into them.

"Okay, we're gonna take a little walk to a place I have nearby. You'll be carrying a bucket of water." That ought'a slow her down. I slapped the bat in my hands to sharpen my point. "I'll be right behind you carrying this. Walk slow and keep quiet, and everything will be fine."

"What are you going to do to me?"

"That's up to you. You want to live, don't you?"

She slobbered all over herself. "Yes."

"Then be a good girl and do what I say, and everything will be fine. I don't want to hurt you."

She wanted to—no, she *needed* to—believe it.

I *was* convincing. Hell, I almost believed it myself.

"What about Bobby?" She wiped first at her eyes and then at her nose.

"He's not going anywhere. Take that bucket down to the lake and fill it with water. Hurry up!"

My nerves fired on all pistons. If *they* were here, Bobby and Jacque, then who else might show up? Time to get back to the shop.

She filled the bucket, and we climbed out of the pit and onto the less obvious path leading to the shop. I stayed close behind her, hushing her each time she asked a question, looking around to ensure that we were alone. We needed to hurry; I still had a body to deal with.

Don't forget his car, the Reaper said.

Shit! I should have thought of that.

I prepared for my next move as we approached the shop. Jacque-Baby struggled with the bucket, so I instructed her to put it down and rest for a minute. She leaned over, and I stepped closer and raised the bat.

I hit her in about the same spot I'd hit Danny-Boy. She dropped to the ground and groaned, barely conscious. Excellent.

I laid the bat down, left the bucket of water for the moment, and threw her over my shoulder to carry her into the shop. She was damn sure lighter than Danny-Boy had been.

Diana raised her head, and her jaw almost dropped, restrained by the gag. Her eyes shot wide.

"Honey, I'm home." I laughed and dropped Jacque-Baby onto the workbench. "I brought company."

Darkness arrived with me jacked-up again on adrenaline and electric nerves. It had been a busy day already and, I had to admit, everything had gone surprisingly well.

After tying up Jacque-Baby and finding out from her where Bobby-the-Stud had parked his car, I gagged her and returned to where the poor boy remained poured in on himself. I took the car keys from his right front pocket, carried him up the hill and over to the rim of the pit—the part that looked straight down on the water like a small cliff—and laid him out there.

Then I jogged to where he'd parked his car near Cary Road.

I drove all the way around to my special path, where I always drove my van in toward the shop. That took fifteen nerve-wracking minutes.

Now it was a simple matter of doing some four-wheeling in Bobby-the-Stud's old Jeep, over the rough terrain and up to where I'd stretched him out. I buckled him into the front seat, put the gearshift into neutral, and pushed the Jeep toward the rim with every ounce of strength I could muster. When it started over the edge, it hung up for several seconds, like it would just stay there.

Shit!

That would have been something, but it found some gravity and tipped into the pit. I ran to the edge in time to see it disappear into the depths, where Bobby-the-Stud and his Jeep would likely remain hidden for a long time.

I prepared for the night's activities back at the shop, stripping Jacque-Baby down to her birthday suit by cutting away her clothes. She weren't happy about it. Too fuckin' bad! Those were the rules. Besides, it weren't like she'd need them again.

I placed a chair near the workbench for Diana. The look in her eyes, and her body language, made it clear she knew what was coming. As an afterthought, I decided to make Diana strip too. I padded her wrists and ankles, to keep her comfortable, before tying her to the chair.

I wasn't sure why I'd wanted her naked, but looking at her, I had to admit it was a brilliant idea. Hell, you could never have too many naked women around, I figured. That was one of the benefits of this new job of mine.

Two naked girls, one lying on the workbench with her legs tied apart, and one seated in a chair alongside it... whew! I had no idea when I started following the Reaper's orders that I'd enjoy such benefits. Sex was the perfect benefit, although now that I thought of it, I hadn't done the deed yet.

Fuck a rubber duck! How can I be surrounded by naked girls and not sex 'em up?

I was waiting for the right moment with Diana, because she and I would be together forever.

Jacque-Baby, on the other hand, was available. Sure, I'd have to cut her up and do the stuff the Reaper had taught me, but couldn't I have a little fun first?

I leaned right over her, close. She stunk of sweat and sex, maybe from her time with Bobby-the-Stud, which kicked me into high gear. I needed some fun myself.

She wriggled and cried behind her gag.

"What's the matter, Jacque? You told Bobby he was naughty for doing this, but that you liked it. Don't you like it now? Aren't I naughty enough for you?"

I stripped down in a rush while Diana cried and stared at the floor.

I reached under her chin and raised her head. Since she knew to be quiet, I hadn't gagged her. "I want you to watch me and Jacque-Baby. It'll be fun."

I climbed onto the workbench and over Jacque.

It didn't take long. Whatever. *I* sure felt better.

She lay perfectly still when I climbed off her. Hard to tell, but I thought she might'a liked it. How could she not? Good thing, too, because she would hate the next part.

The demons were getting restless, swirling around again, looking at me like they would gouge my fuckin' eyes out if I didn't get a move on.

"All right, Diana, I hope you enjoyed watching that as much as I enjoyed doing it. Now it's time for tonight's *real* lesson to begin."

Her eyes grew wide and filled with tears again, and she looked at Jacque-Baby in terror.

I grabbed my knife and a couple other tools, which I held up for Jacque-Baby to inspect and consider. "And what do you think, little girl? Now that we've made sweet love, are you ready for the next bit of fun?"

If her long, muffled scream were any indication, she was ready.

That was the best one yet! My first girl! I *definitely* preferred the girls. They had so much more to offer. Yeah, I'd stick with girls from now on. Whereas Danny-Boy had only lasted for twenty minutes—the fuckin' wimp—Jacque-Baby had lasted thirty. She was tough, I had to admit, but I was getting better at this too.

"What do you think, Diana? Does it get any better than that?"

She looked strange.

"Diana?"

Her eyes blinked in a slow, steady beat, like there weren't nothin' behind them.

"Diana, do you hear me?"

I shook her and tried to bring her around, but she'd wigged-out. *Shit! Now what the fuck has happened?*

CHAPTER 45
JUNE 15, 1995:
TONY HOOPER

"Necessity can make a doubtful action innocent, but it cannot make it commendable." – *Joseph Joubert*

I slide the door open, so careful to remain silent that my breath catches inside my throat, fearful of escape lest he discover me. The room is empty and dim with the smallest traces of late-afternoon sun. I creep along the wall, slip past the stairs, and ease open the door on my left.

This room is also empty, as expected.

I quietly take care of my business, exit, and move once again into the main room. I retrace my earlier path and move toward the stairs that are now on my right. My target hangs only two steps away. I will catch him this time. After all these years, I will finally have him.

"Ringing the chimes is unnecessary," the voice behind me says.

Damn it!

Master Komura stands in the back corner. He faked me out. He usually sits on the exercise pad. His grin, and that look of self-satisfaction, dig a little deeper.

"You know," I say, "I barely even breathed. So please tell me, how did you know I was here? Am I making a sound even *I* am unaware of?"

He smiles and points to the far right corner of the room, up toward the ceiling.

You must be kidding. "How long have you had cameras?"

"Naomi and Marissa have been nervous since the murders began again, so I had them installed yesterday."

An appropriate precaution, particularly since he refuses to lock the door. It must remain open, to welcome anyone who seeks knowledge.

He tells me of the monitors in his apartment, along with a chime that indicates movement. They are both cameras *and* motion detectors.

"And so you cheated," I say.

"I improvised, as any skilled samurai would."

I can't help but laugh at the simple lesson.

"You move with great stealth, Shadow."

Shadow is the nickname he gave me several years ago, when my skills advanced and I learned to walk without sound. Strange. Whenever he calls me that, memories of Alex, my own good Shadow, wash over me.

We agree that I will not upset Naomi, or his daughter Marissa, my goddaughter, by refusing to stay for dinner.

He claps his hands. "Good. So tell me, Shadow, besides a nice visit, what is it that brings you to me today? You wish to train, but I think perhaps there is something more."

"You know me too well."

He bows his head.

"He's back, Master—Mitchell Norton, *the devil*—and he's killing again."

"Why have the police not made an arrest?"

"They have insufficient evidence, but he's wasting no time. Two dead already, and he's been out of prison only a few days. His brutality knows no limits. How many more must die before he pays, before there is justice?"

"Is it justice you desire or is it vengeance?"

That's a fair enough question, but when I don't respond, he lets it pass.

"Are you certain it is him, Shadow? Do you have no doubts?"

"None."

"I see."

"This is my fault."

"On that, I see no such thing. I know what you think, that you had an opportunity to kill him seventeen years ago and if you had, he would not be killing now. You were still a boy then. You mustn't hold yourself responsible."

"I was eighteen and I was capable enough."

"You were eighteen and you had a good heart and a good soul. You chose to allow the law to take its course. That was enough."

I laugh. "You sound like Frank."

"A most generous compliment."

I sigh in frustration. "But he's at it again. Torture! Murder!"

"Then the law is to blame. We are civilized people, are we not? We rely on the law to provide justice. Yet it often fails for, like the men who created it, it is imperfect. But then you've known this for a long time."

He knows what I do. Indeed, he's the one man who knows everything about me. Even Frank is unaware of a few secrets I've kept. Master Komura knows *all*, for I can train with him only if I have no secrets. This isn't because he'd refuse, but because we must trust one another with our lives.

"*Hai*, and now I must do what I failed to do seventeen years ago," I say. "I must rid the world of another monster. I will be responsible for no more deaths."

"No more but one."

"No more *innocent* deaths. The guilty... well, justice comes in many forms, does it not?"

"Indeed, but the law will see it differently."

"Then I must ensure that the law remains ignorant of my actions."

He gives a thoughtful nod. "Difficult to accomplish these days. Technology is not your friend."

"I'm prepared to accept the consequences."

"*Hai*. You have been determined in your course and willing to pay whatever price is necessary. Still, we may discuss these things."

"Am I wrong to want this?"

"Who can say? We must protect our own. If someone were to endanger my Naomi or Marissa, or you for that matter, I would kill him without pause. I know the law is often more curative than preventative. Yet who can cure a murder victim? Is it unjust to destroy the killer before he kills? If one knows of the murderer's guilt beyond any doubt, I am prepared to accept such solutions with a clear conscience, and at whatever cost."

"As am I."

"Yet absolute certainty is difficult to obtain. Do you know more than the police, or do you merely *think* you know?"

There is logic in his question. I'm certain that Mitchell Norton kills again. Who else can it be? Yet what Linda said about copycats, about the number of serial killers out there, planted at least a seed of doubt. I know that my nagging guilt pushes me to end it.

What if I kill Norton and the killings continue?

"It's not about knowing," I say. "It's about what the police can do within the boundaries of the law. As for *the devil*, I'm ninety-five percent certain."

He holds up a finger. "Then you are uncertain. You are samurai and you know better. I think this Mitchell Norton has corrupted your mind." He pauses. "History teaches us to make no assumptions. Every mystery of the world, every hope and fear, every tangled web that man has ever woven—all of these things reside in history, in experience, in countless lifetimes that have come before us, and in all the promises kept or broken. We have long studied history together. It's as important as the physical aspect of what we do here."

He pauses again, but I know he's not done.

"You must promise me that you'll heed those lessons."

"How can I know with certainty when even the police have no proof?"

"You are samurai. You are Shadow. Does the night not hold your answers?"

I should have considered that. I've been there before. He's right; Norton has corrupted my mind. My emotional involvement in this case threatens my perspective, something Frank warned me about. You'd think I would know by now to listen to those two.

I must embrace the darkness to catch the killer in the act. "I must shadow him," I say, "and when he makes his move, I will end it."

"This is the way of the samurai. This is just. However, if you can capture him for the authorities, that would be the preferred alternative to killing him."

"Sure. Look where that got us last time."

"I think it would be different this time—strike two, you might say. It's unlikely they would release him again."

"We'll see." *I doubt it. I seriously doubt it.*

"It would be preferable, naturally, that however you end it, you do so *before* he kills again."

"Indeed. I don't know how much more my conscience can take."

"I hope this too will pass, as justice dictates. Now, let us train together. Afterwards, you may visit with Naomi and Marissa and we'll have a nice dinner." He puts his arm around me. "It is good to have you home, Shadow."

CHAPTER 46
JUNE 16, 1995:
REPORTS, RUMORS, AND RE-ENACTMENTS

The gentle breeze and mild temperature made a walk in the park the perfect distraction for Lindsey Merkham, but she chose the cemetery in lieu of the park. She did so because the cemetery sat conveniently at the corner of North Main Street and Cary Road, across the street from her apartment.

It contained several crisscrossing paths perfect for continuous power walking, her preferred method of exercise and, judging by her slender build, an effective one. She normally exercised right after work and before dinner, when she wasn't too weighed-down or too lazy for her walks.

On this night, she was out late.

Lindsey stood five-feet-six-inches tall, with short, bright red-orange hair, and a figure that more resembled a young boy than an adult woman. The unfortunate birthmark on her right cheek, and the ski jump at the end of her nose, further heightened her insecurities.

Men rarely lined up at her doorstep.

Thus, she chose to take a late walk through the cemetery, a perfectly reasonable way to kill another uneventful Friday night. She'd snuggle later with her loyal kitty, Puffer, and read a good book.

The man seated against the elm tree was also alone that Friday night, contemplating his recent actions. They'd squashed him under a heavy sorrow, but they'd also frustrated him, for they hadn't produced the desired results.

Maybe if he persisted awhile longer and increased his efforts, he'd eventually win his prize.

The woman walked toward him. He heard her before she appeared, and when he looked up to watch her stroll by on the path twenty feet away, she made no notice of him at all.

That figures, he thought. He sat in the shadows as night approached. It was a place he'd been on other occasions recently. He sought the magic, yet he knew only regret.

The woman passed beyond his sight and out of his thoughts as he attempted to make sense of his loneliness, his inadequacies and fear. He wanted more from his life. He *deserved* more.

The people in my life don't understand. I like the people in this place better. The dead aren't mean to me. The dead don't look down at me. The dead don't feel sorry for me.

For seventeen years he'd thought of little else but how to improve his circumstances, yet how could he do it? Perhaps two murders were insufficient. How many more must he kill? As always, the answers he craved eluded him and his frustration mounted.

Approaching sounds again distracted him, this time from a young couple that talked and held hands while they walked. They probably had visited a gravesite. Maybe he should kill them and get two for the price of one, he thought. Yeah, that might do the trick, but he didn't know how to accomplish that. When they walked on and the opportunity passed, his frustration grew into anger. Although he hated being angry, it happened often as a lifetime of insecurity raged within. It's why he usually carried his knife, tucked in its sheath in the back of his jeans, the way he'd seen detectives tuck guns away on television.

Gotta be ready.

He liked the cemetery for the peace and quiet, but also because it was within walking distance of his house. Walking helped him clear his head. He could sit there with only the night sounds as company and concentrate on his life. He was sure that intelligence was the result of determined effort. The more he concentrated, the more he was reassured that he would gain the happiness he'd sought for so long.

It had to happen soon. The *Voice* had to come. The Reaper couldn't avoid him forever. Surely, it wouldn't avoid him if he continued to do such an excellent job offering up new sacrifices. The Reaper *must* come and rescue him.

Another day journeyed toward history as darkness deepened in the cemetery. It bothered him that he'd done nothing special that day, for it had reached the point where he felt it necessary to kill almost every day. The Reaper couldn't ignore *that*. Yet how many more could he kill before the police caught him? He knew they were determined to capture him, that it was only a matter of time.

Maybe he'd get lucky and outsmart them, but he would need the Voice for that. It needed to come soon... or he'd be finished.

Again a nearby sound drew his attention, and as his eyes adjusted to the dark, he focused on the woman walker.

Why is she out here so late at night, in the dark? Is she crazy?

Lindsey was deep in her "zone" and she didn't want to stop, despite her nervousness, which grew with the dark in the cemetery. It was silly to be frightened of people long-since dead and buried, but the Saturday-matinee-spooky feel of it made her uneasy.

If she hadn't been out of town on business for several days, and if she'd watched or listened to the local news recently, she'd know she had good reason to be nervous.

Instead, she admonished herself for being afraid of the dark and of ghosts and ghoulies, like a baby.

This is Algonquin, for crying out loud – Quietsville, USA.

Concealed behind the tree, he looked around to see if anyone else remained in the cemetery. It was difficult to tell with certainty in the darkness. Yet he was too frustrated and angry to care, and he was tired. Drained.

He almost *wanted* the police to catch him.

Nonetheless, he hoped this would be the big night.

Lindsey Merkham had heard the approaching sound, and reacted — a second too late.

She cursed herself. *Why did you insist on walking in the dark, you idiot?*

He'd hit her so hard that she'd blacked out. Now awake, bound and gagged in some kind of shed, she almost wished she were still unconscious. A man hovered nearby and mumbled to himself incoherently. She raised her head and looked around, and noticed for the first time that she was naked. She assumed she would soon be a victim of that most heinous crime, something every woman feared at some point in her life.

Looks like you'll finally have some sex, she thought, and managed to laugh to herself despite the terror that threatened to fracture her mind.

Yet, for all its degradation and psychological damage, far more heinous crimes than rape plagued Algonquin these days. She would learn that soon enough.

Too late.

CHAPTER 47
JUNE 16, 1995:
TONY HOOPER

I stand at the edge of the trees less than a hundred yards from the Norton house. The crescent moon is insufficient to defeat the darkness. Even with my eyes properly adjusted, I strain to see anything of substance.

The temperature is unpleasantly warm in my *shinobi shozoku*, the black ninja garb. It requires focused determination to ignore it, what Master Komura calls the "skilled mind" of the samurai.

The neighborhood is quiet but for the creekity-creek of crickets and the occasional ruffling of leaves, compliments of a small nocturnal creature.

Shit, I hope it's not a black snake. Six-foot snakes, however harmless, rank low on my list of favorite things.

The houses are older in this neighborhood and slightly more "lived in," as my mom used to say. It's less than a mile from Frank's place—I should call it my place now—and only five blocks from my old house on Cary Road. The street is Mohawk Trail, and where it intersects Pioneer Road, a strip of woodlands runs east to west, separating Pioneer from Geringer Road further up the ridge to the north. Mohawk ends three blocks south at North Harrison Street, which runs parallel to the Fox River.

I've spent little time down here since I was a kid, and it has apparently shrunk from its previous enormity. For kids, everything is huge.

I parked on Geringer and walked down through the woods, most concerned about dogs that may alert to my presence, but none is present at this hour. It's eleven-thirty and only a couple neighborhood lights remain on — sleepy time for a sleepy town.

Except that there's a killer out there who likes to work in the wee hours, and if he —

What the devil is this?

A light appears in a utility shed at the back of the Norton property, and I have no idea how it happened, or who might have entered the shed — or when.

The light goes out and a figure emerges. Though it's impossible to recognize him in the darkness, I can tell by his gait and height that he's a man. That means it's either Mitchell or Tommy, both of whom are almost six feet tall. No other lights appear as the figure enters the back door.

It's as though the man arrived home this moment, though the method by which he did so is a mystery. Perhaps he just took out the garbage.

"Geez, Tony," I admonish myself. "What good is a stakeout if you don't see the bad guy when he comes out? You'd better sharpen up!"

He enters the dark house as though fearful of alerting anyone to his presence. At this late hour, Mrs. Norton is probably asleep, so it may be simple courtesy.

Hmmm, then why does the whole scene bother me?

I would have noticed if he'd emerged from the house. I'm certain of it. That means either he was in the shed the entire time — unlikely, since the lights were out except for that brief instant — or he arrived home and stopped at the shed first. In the latter case, he would have been on foot.

Shit! What if he's already murdered someone?

I'm anxious to know what answers or clues the shed contains. I'll give him plenty of time to fall asleep and then I'll slip down to investigate. Norton always was a big fan of tools, and now that he butchers people in their own homes, he must take his tools with him. That shed is important.

"Be vigilant, Tony. If you're mistaken about any of this, a murderer may still slip out during the wee hours."

My earlier conversation with Master Komura put me at ease; obtaining positive proof before moving on Norton, before *killing* him — Why is it hard to say the word? — should relieve my conscience. This one is more difficult than my previous hunts. I've considered the philosophical arguments throughout the years, asked myself more times than I remember: Am I doing the right thing? How is what I do different from what the serial killers do?

I traverse a fine line, what many would call simple rationalization, but those monsters kill the *innocent*, whereas I kill *them*. They personify guilt, blights on civilization, monsters from which there is no escape save one. Some might suggest that what I do—ending their horrifying existence—is red-hot vengeance.

Wrong. Their death is justice well served. I'm satisfied if they rot in prison *forever*, but the system fails far too often.

Case in point: the jury found Mitchell Norton not guilty due to insanity. The system eventually spit him out and put him back on the street. And more people died vicious, unimaginable deaths.

How can I have faith in a system that allows such a thing to happen?

I leave nothing to chance, when I can help it. And I sleep well at night. Mostly. Sometimes.

Yet Mitchell Norton has crawled inside my psyche like no one else before or since. It's personal.

He made it so when he took Alex. He made it more so when he took Diana. Every act he performed in 1978 was as a knife thrust into my heart. He knew it and I knew it, and he took pleasure in it.

Seventeen years later, he's already encountered Linda at the coffee shop, and he taunted me with words designed to push me into the abyss that has long threatened to swallow me whole. He's murdered two already—at *least* two—and he wants me to know he has his eye on Linda.

"Well I have *my* eye on you, Norton, and your time is very near its end."

The neighborhood remains peaceful and quiet. I observe the cars parked on the street—no apparent spies out tonight. It's easier that the police aren't watching, and yet it irritates me as well. I check my watch: 1:45.

I expected to follow a killer and destroy him tonight, but I doubt that will happen now.

Something about the incident at the shed still gnaws at my sensibility. Simple instinct.

A strange thing, instinct: the result of the conscious mind digging around in the subconscious for answers. My hypnosis seventeen years ago taught me that. Since then, I've worked hard with Master Komura to sharpen my instincts, to trust them. We've studied the subconscious mind and learned that, with proper training and practice, one can harness at least some of that power.

I take one more look around the neighborhood to ensure that I remain alone, then exit the woods and proceed toward Norton's shed. The path is unimpeded—no fences, no homes between me and my target. I remain alert to any movement or sound, including my own. I glide over the ground in a mere whisper, no simple feat, and something Master Komura spent seven years teaching me. My *shinobi shozoku* renders me virtually invisible even in the open—one more shadow cast by trees and houses on this near-moonless night.

The shed is a standard eight-by-twelve, pre-fabricated model, sturdy with a wooden frame and steel panels. The doors are hardly impenetrable, but entering without leaving a trace is the real trick. Given the two heavy padlocks, it will be challenging but not impossible.

I carry a small leather case that contains several picks designed for various types of locks. It's fortunate that these locks are key-operated. Cracking combination locks is a skill I've yet to master, something I should remedy. I find two picks adequate to the task, and work the uppermost lock. It pops with the slightest noise, yet any sound is like a marching band in the still night.

I pause for several seconds. Nothing, so I move on to the second—

I freeze. *What is that sound? Is it scratching?*

A dog—one I don't want to tangle with, by the sound of it—barks from the back of the Norton house. I reattach the lock and dart to the back of the shed. I drop low and spider-crawl away from the house, careful to keep the shed between that back room and me. Fluorescent lights flicker on both inside and outside the house as I crouch behind a good-sized tree in a neighbor's yard.

An unknown voice calls out, "What's a matter, Scooby? Did you see another rabbit, boy? You gotta learn to leave them poor little critters alone."

The dog barks again and whines, and I expect it to charge around the shed any second. I ready my *katana*. I don't want to hurt the dog, but I may have no choice.

The owner, whom I assume is Tommy, holds him back. "Come on, boy, there's nothing out there. Hush now, you hear!"

When the door closes and the lights go off, the neighborhood remains dark and quiet, apparently oblivious to the disturbance. How did I not know they have a dog?

Damn it, Tony, that's basic recon!

Norton continues to corrupt my mind. I've been unusually sloppy on this job, and I need to step back and think things through. That shed still calls to me, but it will have to wait.

I hustle back toward the trees. Perhaps Algonquin will be lucky and there will be no more torture for one night, no more murder.

I wait until three o'clock to be certain, analyzing the earlier incident at the shed over and over.

God, I hope I wasn't too late.

CHAPTER 48
MAY 30, 1978:
MITCHELL NORTON

"We know too much, and are convinced of too little." – *T.S. Eliot*

Last night I'd burned with uncertainty and anxiety. Diana was practically catatonic. She'd snapped while I worked on Jacque-Baby, unable to take the work up close, unable to adjust to the methods and accept them for what they were: elegant and exquisite.

She didn't hear the Reaper as I did, or see the demons and the visions of their wicked, joyful craft. How could she understand everything in the absence of those visions?

The Reaper had offered no explanation.

She'd had two opportunities, and still she understood nothing. There must be some way to get through to her.

Maybe I should explain my true feelings for her. She'd be my queen in the Kingdom of Unending Pain. We were the chosen royalty. Maybe she'd find pleasure in that fact, but I had to think it through carefully before speaking to her. I couldn't risk making things worse; she must come to me willingly. I couldn't stand many more days of looking at her and watching her clean up, of seeing her naked body, without making love to her. I needed her and if I didn't have her soon, I'd go insane.

How would I perform my new duties if that happened?

I had to leave the shop today to work at the restaurant. It frustrated the shit outta me, but I still had to make a living. Too bad the Reaper didn't pay. Maybe I'd stop at home afterwards to shower and sleep in my own bed. I was damn tired of sleeping on this hard floor, but still nervous about leaving Diana—even if she *was* tied up and gagged.

What would she think about during all that time alone? Would she drift further into a state of fear? I hated to consider that possibility now that everything else was on track. I'd learned my lessons well, and the demons were pleased with me. I'd become a master of torture. All that remained was to prepare my queen.

Then I'd claim my kingdom.

She sat with her head down, as she had throughout the night, but she occasionally moved around, returning to reality. She sobbed softly at times.

I'd be kind to her, show her the depth of my love. That should bring her around and make her want to be my queen.

"Diana, do you hear me?" She didn't respond. "Please answer me. Otherwise, I'll have to leave you alone for several hours. Do you hear me?"

She nodded without looking up, and whispered, "Yes."

"I have to work tonight, and then I have some things to take care of at home, so I'll be gone awhile."

She raised her head and looked in my general direction, although she wouldn't make eye contact. At least we were making progress.

"I want to give you the opportunity to get more comfortable. I'll let you go outside, then you can clean up and we'll have something to eat, maybe talk a little before I go. How does that sound?"

She nodded without enthusiasm.

"Speak to me! Do you want to do that?"

"Yes."

"Okay, first I'll untie you and take you outside."

She was listless and had difficulty standing; probably hadn't slept last night.

I looked around to ensure that the coast was clear before leading her outside to the area we used as a latrine, where I'd dug two holes for the purpose. It weren't no bed of roses, but the smell could'a been much worse. I handed her the toilet paper and stepped aside, but not too far. This time, I wanted to watch.

Either she didn't notice or she didn't care.

Back at the shop, she stood like a zombie at the edge of the table while I set out cleaning supplies. I laid two clean blankets on the floor so she could lie more comfortably.

She stripped without prodding and started cleaning herself, going through the motions as if on autopilot.

I walked by her and slid my hand across her smooth, velvety ass. So damn irresistible!

She jerked away. "Please don't. Just let me clean up. You can watch if you want."

She knew I'd watch no matter what she said, and probably figured it wouldn't hurt to offer.

It tore me up, twisted my gut into a million knots, to watch her without touching her. I looked away and strolled to the other side of the table to make us some sandwiches. Sick and tired of eating the same boring crap, I'd pick up some burgers, fries and shakes tomorrow. That would be a nice treat for Diana.

When she finished and started drying off, she gazed around, searching for some clean clothes. I hadn't set any out because she'd already used the two sets I bought.

"Where are my clothes?"

"I want to talk to you first, Diana. Please sit down on your blankets — they're clean — and we'll have some lunch."

Though nervous about sitting down naked, she did so and covered herself with the top blanket. I gave her a plate with the usual sandwich, pickle and chips on it, and handed her a can of pop. She took a tentative bite at first, but then devoured the rest of it.

"Do you want another sandwich?"

"Yes, please."

Good, she's getting her appetite back. "I won't be back until tomorrow, probably late morning. I'll bring some different food, a nice treat, along with some clean clothes and new supplies."

She ate the second sandwich like she'd already had her fill, but wasn't sure when the next meal might come along. She paid little attention to me, but she heard fine.

"I'm sorry, but I must tie you up and gag you again. I'll try to make you as comfortable as possible."

She sighed and hung her head.

"You gotta understand what we're doing here. You can't see my visions or hear the voice of the Reaper—he's the head demon—'cuz you're not special like me. Not yet. I know that makes it hard to understand, but you gotta be patient.

"The Reaper has plans for us. I can hear his voice. He says the Kingdom of Unending Pain will be mine, and that I may have a queen. You'll be my queen, Diana, and together we'll be royalty. We'll know the beauty, elegance and wonder of agony."

She stared at the floor and said, "Why are you doing this to me? Why won't you leave me alone? Why won't you let me go?"

"You're special. You're my queen. Don't you see? I'm in love with you."

She raised her head this time, a look of disgust on her face. "What? You don't even know me."

Be patient, Mitchell. "I've seen enough to know, and we've talked a little and shared some special things here. I want to take it to the next level. I want us to be together."

"What does that mean, together?"

"Together, like a king and queen, like a couple."

"Oh my God, you *are* crazy! How can you think I'll be with you after what you've done? You kidnapped me and you keep me tied-up and gagged." She shook her head. "You make me watch your sick shit while you torture people to death!"

"That's what makes it special. That's what makes *us* special."

She spit, "You sick bastard! Leave me alone! I'm in love with Tony." She jumped up, the top blanket barely covering her, and yelled, "I could *never* be with you. You're the most evil, twisted, monstrous human being I've ever known, or ever *heard* of. You're disgusting!"

I clenched my fists and shook my head. "No, don't talk like that. It's not true. You and I will be royalty. That's what the Reaper told me."

"The Reaper doesn't exist, you sick monster. It's a voice in your stupid head. You're *deluded*. Don't touch me, you sonuvabitch!"

The grinding of my teeth made my head hurt. She didn't understand, and the way she spoke to me and called me vile names made me want to hurt her.

"You're my angel and my queen, so I'll forgive you for what you said, but you have to come around to my way of thinking. We *will* be together."

"No we *won't*. Leave me alone, you evil bastard!" She lashed out at me and tried to run.

I grabbed her and slammed her down onto the blankets. "That's how you want it, bitch? That works for me. I can play rough."

I undressed in front of her, in between knocking her back down to the floor, and jumped on top of her. I grabbed her arms and held them off to the side, but she was strong for a girl. I slapped her hard across the face and she froze for a second and cried. Then she grabbed at me again, so I slapped her harder.

She'd definitely bruise after that one.

She yelled again, but it didn't matter a fuckin' bit. Nobody would hear anything.

I struggled to position myself over her as she continued to fight. The bitch wouldn't lie still and accept it!

"Enough!" I got off her and yanked the knife from the sheath on my belt. When I held it against her throat, she froze. "Do you want to die? Is that it, bitch? Sit still or I'll cut your fuckin' throat!"

She pressed her throat against the blade. "I don't give a shit! You'll kill me no matter what I do, and I can't take any more of your shit, you twisted sonuvabitch!"

"I'll have my way with you, bitch!"

She laughed and pointed at my dick, which had gone soft during the struggle. "Not with that limp little noodle, you won't."

That's not fuckin' funny! "You don't think so? We'll see about that."

I knocked her back down and grabbed the ropes to tie her up. I didn't gag her; I *wanted* her to scream. I'd show her who was boss. I tied her arms to the post on the side of the shed, and her right leg too. I tied her left leg to the table, leaving her legs spread wide.

"Hoo-wee-mama, time to have some fun and show you who's in charge."

She thrust her chin out. "Poor little baby with the tiny little limp dick. You sick fuck! You couldn't get it up if you sucked it yourself! Ooh, I bet you'd like that, you little tiny limp-dick motherfucker! You're a sick, impotent, puny-dick bastard!"

"Shut up! You hear me, you ugly bitch? What do you think of this?"

I gave her the same treatment I gave Jacque-Baby.

She squirmed, but spit more poison at me. "What's the matter, poor little baby? Is your tiny little baby-boy's-dick so soft and useless that you have to use your fingers?"

"I'm warning you, bitch, if you keep that shit up I'll make you pay."

"Fuck you, puny little limp-dick faggot! You're a faggot, aren't you? With a teensy-weensy tiny baby boy's limp dick! I probably wouldn't even feel it."

"You fucking bitch!" I lashed out with the knife and ripped open her arm in a gush of blood. "What do you think of that, bitch?"

She screamed and her tears poured out. Now she knew who was in charge.

"Go ahead and finish it, you little faggot," she yelled. "You know that teeny little limp dick of yours will never work again, so finish it!"

"Shut up!"

I punched her hard in the face and she went limp. I tied a rag around her arm to keep it from bleeding all over the place, then gagged her to keep her quiet. The foul-mouthed bitch! I should have killed her.

What had happened? Nothing was going according to plan, and the way she acted, she might never embrace being my queen.

Her open legs were so inviting. Maybe *now* I'd have my way with her.

"Fuck!"

The lousy fuckin' bitch had me so wound-up that I couldn't do it!

I had to get outta here and go somewhere I could think. Let her lie there, tied up naked without her blanket, until I came back tomorrow. That would teach her.

I'd figure out what to do with her then.

CHAPTER 49
MAY 31, 1978:
MITCHELL NORTON

Last night had been extremely difficult. I'd hated having to work—too anxious to get back to the shop and determine how to handle Diana. That situation had gone terribly wrong. Besides, washing dishes for a living struck me as remarkably pedestrian and dull. How in the world had I put up with it for ten years? How long would the *new* Mitchell be able to put up with it?

Yet last night, for all its anxieties, might have been a walk in the park compared to today.

I received an unpleasant visit from the Chief of Police.

How in the world had he connected *me* to anything? What mistakes had I made? I'd been careful to leave no fingerprints, and was sure nobody had seen me. I'd disposed of the bodies neatly, having learned from my mistake with Alex Hooper. Chop them into bite-sized pieces—only then would they vanish into the mouth of the Beast. My new friend had eaten well recently.

Yet somehow, the chief had managed to get onto me. His questions were relatively innocent. He even acted like we were pals.

I played it cool as I smiled and cooperated at every turn, shook my head in wonder, and tried to *imagine* anyone committing such horrible crimes.

I did have one potential problem, however. If he looked inside the dryer, how would I explain those girl's clothes? I would improvise, of course. Fortunately, he didn't look.

Mom might also have been surprised, but since it was typical for me to do my own laundry, she hadn't looked inside either. She did act nervous throughout the whole ordeal, however, as I'd been out of the house during the days in question.

No worries. She played the good Mom and said nothing, then left for work, leaving the chief in my hands.

He searched the house and asked me a few more questions. The subject of Flora Park came up, specifically the day all those damn high school kids were there. It was the day I'd discovered my angel.

How the fuck does he know about that? "Flora Park? Sure, I remember. Geez, there must have been a hundred or more of them. That was unusual, the sort of thing I'd remember."

"I see, and do you remember seeing Diana Gregario there?" he asked.

He watched me closely, but I kept my wits. I wouldn't give anything away. "Diana who?"

"Gregario?"

"I have no idea. I don't even know who she is. I mean, I see plenty of girls there and admire them, you know. A lot of them are damn cute. Hey, I'm a normal, red-blooded American boy, right?" I gave him my biggest, best, *awe shucks* smile.

"And were you *admiring* a girl that day?"

"Let me think about that." I paused and gave it real reflection, all part of the show. "Now that you mention it, there was this one girl wearing yellow. Tommy and I both checked her out. She was a hot little number, you know, but way too young for me. I thought Tommy might like her, but he's not too into girls. He's a little... uh... a bit slow."

"And that's it?"

"What? About the girl?"

He glared at me.

I threw my hands up. "Yeah, we watched her for a couple minutes or so, and that was that. Are you telling me that someone saw me there and remembered me? How do they know me? I don't know any of those kids." I shrugged. "At least I don't think I do."

He hesitated, but said, "Someone spotted you there and heard your brother call your name."

What the fuck? That ain't right. "To tell you the truth, Tommy and I were quite a ways from those kids. I don't know how anyone could have heard my name, and I don't know anything about a Diana Gregario."

"She was the girl in yellow."

"Oh, I didn't know that. And now she's missing?"

"That's right."

"That's a shame, but what does that have to do with the poor boy who was murdered? I read about it—such a tragic story."

He hesitated again.

I was anxious, and curious about who might'a seen me.

"I didn't say they were related," he said.

"Oh. I must have misunderstood."

He continued the search, and I thought about that day at the park. I'd pointed out Diana to Tommy. She'd been walking with Hooper and—

Holy shit! They looked at us!

Could he have recognized me? How? He didn't know me, and there sure as hell was no way he'd heard my name. Could it have been someone else? There was something damn strange about this.

"You know, Chief, I've been thinking about that day at Flora Park. Besides the girl in yellow—uh, Diana—the only other person I saw—up close, anyway—was her boyfriend. Is he the one that remembered me? I'm pretty sure I don't know... uh.... What's his name?"

His eyes flared—some suspicion there. I might have pushed it too far.

Whatever. Had to be Hooper. Nobody else there paid any attention to us.

We headed out to the shed in the back yard, and he broke his silence, this time with a smile and a polite tone of voice. "Do you ever go to the bowling alley in Carpentersville?"

"Umm... sometimes." *Fuck a rubber duck! Are you kidding me?* "What does that have to do with anything?"

"Were you there the night of May 27?"

"Four days ago?" I put a hand on my chin and scrunched up my eyes, to look like I was trying real hard to remember. "Let me think about that."

Hooper saw me again? And he remembered me? How the fuck is that possible? Does the bastard have a photographic memory or what?

"Geez, I might'a been, Chief. Think I was, actually. I go there occasionally to bowl two or three lines and have a few beers."

"And were you admiring the girls there too? Perhaps Diana Gregario?"

"What, the same girl as at the park? Hell, I don't know. There are kids there all the time, and if this Diana was among them, I didn't notice. Maybe she wore something different. I don't know. I was just minding my own business." *Son of a whore, this is bad!* "What the hell is this about, anyway? Has someone accused me of something?"

He hesitated.

"Come on, Chief, if some guy is accusing me of something, I have a right to know who he is."

"Some guy?"

"Well... *someone's* trying to pin something on me! Was it that guy she was with at the park? Her boyfriend?"

"I'm merely following up on some open questions, Mr. Norton."

Bullshit! We'll have to see about that. "This is all crap, Chief. And what does any of it have to do with that kid who was killed? What was his name? Let's see... I read about it in the paper. Harper? Hopper?"

"His name was Alex Hooper."

"That's it! Hooper. Okay, so what does any of this crap about— What's her name? Diana?—what's she have to do with this Hooper kid? And what does any of it have to do with me?"

His jaw muscles were pumping on the sides of his head. "I'm here to obtain a few answers regarding your whereabouts on the days in question. If you'll help me out with that, we can move on."

"Whatever. I already told you, and I'm tired of this bullshit."

I showed the proper amount of indignation and impatience, making clear that this was too much to put up with for a voting, tax-paying, law-abiding citizen—well, two out of three weren't bad.

He must have gotten the picture; he apologized for the intrusion and the inconvenience, and then left. He'd found nothing, and unless I missed my guess, he weren't gonna be botherin' me no more.

That fuckin' Hooper was a different matter.

How in the world had he gotten onto me? How did he know I'd been the one, the same man, at the park *and* the bowling alley?

I needed time to think about this, but I mustn't be too hasty—didn't want to raise any more suspicion. I'd need to be especially careful and watchful from here on in.

A word from the Reaper would have been nice.

Where has he been?

CHAPTER 50
MAY 31, 1978:
TONY HOOPER

Diana, my Diana, what would I do without you? I am but a drop of rain in the storm of your existence, yet I long to fill the oceans of your soul. I am but a wave upon the sea of your imagination, yet I long to roll gently upon your mind. I am but a footprint upon the beach of your desire, yet I long to walk forever in your heart. You are my living world, my paradise on Earth. Without you, I am but a glimmering mirage in the distant, endless desert.

Back in school Wednesday, I daydreamed and doodled my way through the hours. I hoped Diana would read my latest mind-burst at some point. I thought only of her.

Schoolwork was out.

I shouldn't let it go this close to graduation, or so I told myself. I didn't much give a damn—couldn't fight the guilt of being here while Diana was somewhere in the clutches of Norton... assuming she was still alive. My heart told me that if she were already dead, I'd have known it. Illogical, but it was my lifeline, kept me from drowning.

If Diana came through safely—she *must* come through this— surely the school would make allowances for her, given the circumstances, and permit her to make up the work she'd missed. One more reason for me to worry.

My few close friends had been a small comfort, approaching me to lend their moral support and offer assistance. Tom Coronado had offered to take up arms and help me "hunt down the bastard and shoot his fucking eyes out." I'd assured him that the police were making progress. I hoped that was an accurate statement.

Most of the kids looked at me strangely, unsure what to say, and therefore saying nothing at all. Everyone knew about Alex, and now they knew about Diana too.

Life in a small town.

The Dean, Mr. Kozlowski, who was also my Calculus teacher, called me into his office to "check on me." He wanted to ensure that I'd suffer no more lost time, given that I'd missed the two previous days, and three days last week during the ordeal with Alex.

I told him I'd do my best, but that a little more lost time was still a possibility.

He said he'd speak to my other teachers about it, and that they'd make accommodations, but that there was a limit. Currently third in the class, I'd finish between second and fifth, and he wanted me to finish my best, whatever the circumstances.

I thanked him and reassured him of my best efforts.

The seven-hour school day lasted about twelve days. Classes finally ended, and I kept my head down, avoided eye contact, and spoke to nobody as I walked to my car. I had neither the time nor patience to deal with more condolences.

I remained hopeful that the police would be onto Norton by now. I intended to stop in and see Chief Radlon on my way home. My boss had agreed to give me some time off from work, which I couldn't afford, but Frank had slipped me a hundred dollars last night without my asking or even hinting at it. That would keep my old Bonnie in gas. Good old Frank.

Just hang in there, Diana. Please, Sweetie, we'll be coming for you soon.

Cops zipped around the station in a frenzied state, wound tighter than usual. Kidnapping and murder occurred once every generation in Algonquin, if that. The chief was speaking with one man and one woman, who appeared official despite their plain clothes.

"Hello there, Mr. Hooper," the desk sergeant said.

"Hello, Sergeant Harker. Please, call me Tony."

"That will be fine, Tony. I suppose you're here to speak with the chief."

"Yes ma'am."

"If you don't mind having a seat and waiting, I'll let him know you're here. I know he'll want to speak with you, but he's a little busy dealing with those big shots from D.C."

"Washington, D.C.?"

"They're from Virginia, but close enough. Those are our *friends* from the FBI."

The way she emphasized the word *friends*, I got the distinct impression that if they'd asked her for the time, she'd have told them to go spit.

"What brings the FBI to little old Algonquin?"

"I'll let the chief handle that one. Why don't you have a seat for the time being?" She returned to her work, clearly signaling the end of the conversation.

The chief spotted me, gave me a nod, and held up his index finger as if to say, *one minute.* He was probably accustomed to a lot less activity around here, though he struck me as someone who knew his business. He was young for his position, perhaps in his early forties. I'd always thought a Chief of Police should be in his late fifties or early sixties, perhaps because TV always portrayed them that way.

The minutes dragged on and my anxiety grew exponentially.

The chief walked out of an office and marched in my direction. I glanced at my watch to see that I'd been waiting for.... *Good heavens, it's only been ten minutes.*

I stood as he approached.

"Hello, Tony, I wasn't expecting you today, was I? Or have I forgotten?" He shook his head, more to himself than to me. "That wouldn't surprise me at this point."

Remember, Tony, be careful not to let slip any secrets. "No, sir, I didn't have an appointment or anything. Sorry about that. I can see you're busy, but I was wondering if there's been any progress with the investigation, especially about that guy in the van, Mitchell. I'm going crazy not knowing about Diana."

"Tony, I'm afraid I can't discuss an ongoing investigation. The only thing I can tell you, I suppose, is that we have no word of Diana yet. You'll have to be patient."

I was sick and damned tired of hearing that.

"Excuse me a moment, Tony."

He walked to a man in plain clothes, one of the FBI agents, who'd motioned him over. The agent held our high school yearbook and pointed at something inside, and then looked at me. The chief nodded and they exchanged a few words.

A minute later, Chief Radlon returned as the agent headed in the other direction. "Well, Tony, as long as you're here, we'd like to talk to you about a few things. Maybe you'll even learn a little more about what's going on. Please come with me."

He extended a hand and guided me down a hallway toward the back of the building, into a room with a small conference table and four chairs. A mirror covered much of one wall, with small speakers, possibly microphones, to the left and right.

My skin crawled a bit. I knew they'd considered me a suspect from the beginning of this mess.

He slid out a chair and motioned for me to sit, and headed back to the door. "I'll be right back, Tony. Would you like some coffee or a Pepsi?"

"Pepsi sounds good, thank you."

Five minutes later, he returned with the two FBI agents. Sergeant Harker came in with refreshments and immediately left again. The chief handed me a Pepsi and made introductions all around. Special Agent-in-Charge Arnie Jackson was black, fiftyish, balding and wearing glasses, thick but not fat, with a friendly smile and pronounced southern accent. Agent Linda Monroe was white, late twenties, with exceptional green eyes and a pleasant smile.

It was a good thing I hadn't yet tried to take down Norton. I'd planned to do something tonight, but things were definitely more complicated with the FBI here. Perhaps I'd hear, at any rate, that my efforts would be unnecessary. With the information I'd provided, they must have already latched onto Norton.

"Tony," the chief began, "let me start by saying that there's been more activity recently. Three more kids have gone missing: a boy named Dan Helton, another named Bobby Keller, and a girl named Jacque Fuller."

I knew Bobby and Jacque.

"In the case of the last two, they missed school on Monday, and there's no sign of Bobby's vehicle. Dan Helton was last seen leaving work on Sunday night, but his car remained abandoned in the parking lot where he works. That's what everyone knows at this point."

He paused and glanced at the FBI agents. Special Agent Jackson blinked in a kind of eye-nod, and the chief continued. "Since kidnappings and disappearances are the FBI's bailiwick, and since this case has grown considerably in scope, we've asked for their assistance. Before I turn it over to Special Agent Jackson, there's one more thing we need to do. Tony, because you're in a police station, and because an officer is questioning you regarding direct involvement in an open case, the law says I must advise you of your rights. Okay?"

"Okay." I tried not to let on, but this brought my nerves back into action.

He went on to explain my Miranda rights, remaining friendly and informal about it, though that did little to comfort me.

I sat through it and agreed to each part as he went along—about as enjoyable as having a tooth pulled. Despite my innocence, and the chief's nonchalant tone, my hands were sweating as if I'd just shot the president.

"Thanks for bearing with me through that, Tony. Now I'll turn it over to Special Agent Jackson."

"Thank you, Chief." He threaded his fingers together and placed his hands under his chin. "Tony, I'd like to walk through a couple things to get us started. First, do you know Dan Helton, eighteen years old, who works at the Eagle Foods of Crystal Lake?"

"No, I don't think so."

"How about Bobby Keller, seventeen, who goes to your high school?"

"Sure, I know Bobby, but not well. We were both on the basketball team, but I was varsity and he was JV—junior varsity. I didn't play with him much, just some practices, and I don't hang out with him away from the court."

"And Jacque Fuller, sixteen, also from your school?"

"Sure, she's Bobby's girlfriend, but I don't know her well."

"I see. Of course, your girlfriend, Diana, has been missing since Saturday night. That makes four missing persons in a short time, all kids, in a town where such matters are rare indeed. And your brother was killed the Saturday before, isn't that right?"

It still made my gut tremor every time I thought of it. "Yes."

"And you can think of no connection to this Dan Helton boy?"

"No sir."

"Is it possible that your girlfriend, Diana, knows any of those three other kids?"

I nodded. "Bobby and Jacque are in her grade, so I imagine she's had some classes with them and that she knows them a little better. As for the other guy, I doubt it."

"All right, let's talk about your whereabouts on Sunday night, and again on Monday night."

"Come on, are we going down this road again?"

"Which road is that, Mr. Hooper?"

All three of them watched me closely, as if waiting for some earth-shattering revelation.

"The road where everyone thinks I'm involved," I said too loudly. "Do you have any idea what Alex's death has done to me? Do have any idea how much I love Diana? I would have killed or died for Alex, given the opportunity, and I would do the same for Diana. I would never — *could* never — hurt them."

"That's most admirable, but you still haven't answered my original question. Where were you on Sunday and Monday nights?"

I sighed loudly. "I was home both nights. My dad can confirm that."

"And I understand you weren't in school Monday or Tuesday."

Not a question; it was more an accusation.

"My brother was buried Saturday afternoon, and then I found out Sunday that my girlfriend was missing. I was too upset to go to school. I spent most of those two days with Frank Willow. You can check that with him."

"Frank Willow?"

"He's an old man, kind of like a grandfather to us, who lives a short ways behind me."

"I see. We'll do that, and we'll check with your father as well."

"My dad doesn't know about me skipping school. Frank called in for me, playing my grandfather."

"Is that right?" Jackson looked at the chief, who tightened up his lips and subtly shook his head, as if to say, *Don't ask, I'll tell you later.*

"All right," Jackson said, "let's talk about this Mitchell character.

Chief Radlon mentioned him briefly, but I believe we could all use an update. I think you should hear this too." He turned to the chief and nodded.

Chief Radlon sighed and returned the nod. "Right" he said, seeming none too happy about it. "First, his last name is Norton and he lives right here in Algonquin. I stopped by his house late this morning and spoke to him, and briefly to his mother. She appeared... I don't know... out of sorts. Mitchell remained steady throughout most of my questioning. He even offered—without my asking—to allow me to search the house. He was angry at the end, but that wouldn't be inconsistent with innocence."

He paused.

Across the table, both FBI agents zoomed in on me, as if waiting for me to react.

The chief continued. "I must admit, I found his offer unusual, but I took advantage of it and searched his home and the shed in his back yard. I wasn't as thorough as if I'd taken a team in there with a warrant, but I got a good look around. Despite Mr. Norton's odd behavior, and the fact that he became more resentful at the end, I found no evidence to suggest his involvement."

What are you saying? I can't believe this!

"Thank you, Chief Radlon," Jackson said. "Now, Tony, I'm sure you can see our dilemma. In our experience, family is almost always involved in—"

"You're out of your damned mind if you think I did this!" I leaned over the table, having almost jumped out of my chair. Every inch of me shook under a volcano of molten anger.

"Let us calm down, shall we?"

"*Calm down?* Is that a joke? What's wrong with you people? My brother is dead! And my girlfriend is missing! And you... you...." This was the part where, had this been a cartoon, my head would have exploded into a rainbow of confetti.

Jackson held up his hand to silence me, and leaned back in his chair. He looked at the chief, who seemed... well, I'd swear he was on my side.

Jackson sighed and said, "All right, then, let's talk about this Mitchell Norton. The chief has told us about your concerns regarding Norton, but I think it would be best if we heard it directly from you."

I glanced at the chief, who smiled almost imperceptibly and nodded. I took a deep breath and tried to relax my shoulders, which felt like nine tons of concrete, and sat back.

I recounted the entire story for them exactly as I'd told the chief, but with a special emphasis on the coincidental nature of the two encounters. It would have been a hell of a lot easier if I could have told them about the hypnosis. I was so damned tempted to do so, but I couldn't betray Frank.

There had to be another way. They had to see the truth.

"It's just that he was in those places," I said, "watching us. What other reason could there be? I mean, I suppose one instance is nothing, but two? And there was something about the guy, especially the way he looked at Diana. He was creepy."

"I'm sure you know we can't arrest someone for being *creepy*," Jackson said.

"Yeah, I think I get that!" *Geez, this guy is starting to get on my nerves!* "But can't you question him? Intimidate him, like you're doing to me?"

He gave a slight smile, like a politician about to pick my pocket. "We don't mean to intimidate you, Mr. Hooper."

Sure, Dick Tracy, whatever you say.

"Let's step back for a moment," he said. "First, there is no current evidence to support the idea that your brother's murder and these disappearances are related. I believe the chief will concur with that."

Chief Radlon nodded.

Good grief, this is hardly rocket science. Why don't you understand?

"However," Jackson continued, "neither is there evidence to preclude such a possibility. Therefore, we will keep an open mind."

Geez, don't do me any favors, Deputy Dog!

"Tell me, Mr. Hooper, why do *you* think those events are related?"

"Are you kidding?" I ticked the reasons off on my fingers. "First, my little brother is murdered. A week later, my girlfriend disappears. Shortly thereafter, three more kids disappear. You don't find that too coincidental?"

Nobody answered. They just stared at me.

"Ah geez, we're back to me being a suspect. I can't believe this is happening."

"No one has been able to confirm an alibi for you on either of those two occasions, and you yourself said you were the last to see each of them. One problem: no one can confirm that you left them safely at home."

What could I say? I stared at him for a moment.

Then it occurred to me. "What about these last three disappearances? You *will* be able to confirm my alibis for those. Are you suggesting those are also coincidental to Alex and Diana? Do you think I'm responsible for killing the two people I love more than anyone in the world, and that *someone else* is responsible for the other three? All this in sleepy little Algonquin, where such things are — What were your words? — *rare indeed*? Is that what you're suggesting?"

Nothing terribly positive happened after that. They asked me if I could think of anyone who might want to hurt me by hurting those close to me. All I could say was that I didn't think so. Since I couldn't tell them about the hypnosis, I couldn't explain how I knew — I *knew* — that it *must* be Mitchell Norton.

If they wouldn't follow him, I would, and if he hadn't killed her already, he *would* lead me to Diana. He must. I was drowning here.

You must stay alive, Diana. Please, whatever it takes, just stay alive.

CHAPTER 51
MAY 31, 1978:
MITCHELL NORTON

I ate dinner with the family again, a nice break after nothing but sandwiches with Diana. I made up a story about the previous two days, telling them that Frankie Walters and I had this marathon *Risk* tournament in the works, and that we'd probably spend a few days finishing the games.

After a quick phone call, Frankie said he'd cover for me — so long as he didn't get too stoned to remember.

I called work and said I had to deal with a family emergency. Since I rarely asked for time off, my boss said he understood, and that he'd have his idiot son cover for me.

Just after six o'clock, I packed my supplies into the van, anxious to return to the shop. With the distraction of Chief Radlon's visit, I hadn't given adequate thought to Diana.

I would do that back at the shop.

I'd keep her foul mouth gagged so she couldn't light into me with more of that vile language. Such a display! I couldn't believe she'd fucked with me like that, but lying bound, gagged and naked for the last thirty hours had probably brought some sense to her. Come to think of it, thirty hours was a long time to hold it. She'd probably pissed all over herself.

It served her right.

I climbed into the van, but something about the chief's visit still bothered me. Why was I so nervous? Everything appeared normal around the neighborhood, but my sphincter puckered like a girl about to lose her virginity.

If the police were onto me, wouldn't they be watching me? I couldn't shake the feeling.

I stepped back inside, grabbed my dad's binoculars from the den, and ran upstairs to the attic. I crawled to the south window and looked down the street. Two blocks south, someone had parked an unusual car with tinted windows, and there was definite movement inside. The driver slouched down in the seat, as if that made him the fuckin' Invisible Man.

That car did not belong in this neighborhood — must be hard to hide a car where residents rarely parked on the road, especially when the entire street was only three blocks long. Officer Dumbass down there had almost pulled it off. Almost.

Shit, I'll have to figure out how to lose him before returning to the shop.

The east and west windows looked on other homes — nothing suspicious there. I crawled to the north window and looked toward Pioneer Road.

Another car sat there with someone inside, also slouched down in his seat, but definitely watching the house.

Wait one fuckin' minute! Isn't that...? Well, I'll be damned.

I'd have recognized that old Bonneville anywhere. The cops must not have known about him; they'd never allow such a thing. My nemesis had jumped into the game.

How did you find out about the game, Hooper?

Diana would clearly have to wait. Another phone call was in order, but I'd have to be careful; couldn't let on that I knew who Hooper was.

Fifteen minutes later, things were about to get interesting. If Officer Dumbass hadn't known that the chief was stopping by, he was gonna have a cow.

I stood on the lawn as he pulled into the driveway. "Thanks for coming by, Chief."

He popped the door open and grunted as he stood up. "You said you have some urgent news about the case?"

"Not exactly, but I wasn't sure how else to get you out here."

His eyes narrowed. "Excuse me? What's going on here, Mr. Norton? Are you looking for trouble?"

"Listen, if anyone should be upset, it should be me. Your visit earlier was bad enough, quite annoying in fact, but this is over the top."

"What are you talking about?"

Without looking, I pointed up the road and put on my best *betrayed* voice. "Come on, we both know I'm talking about your men watching me. Are they supposed to follow me wherever I go?"

I thought I'd played this right, pointing out Hooper without naming him. The chief must have been trying to figure out the plural "men" now.

"And which men are those, Mr. Norton?"

"Let's see, there's that black Chevy parked south a couple blocks...." I looked down the street to point it out, but it was gone.

"What Chevy is that?"

"What the hell? It was there, and I know it was a cop."

"I think you may be confused."

Bullshit!

He must have radioed Officer Dumbass after I'd phoned in. I hadn't seen the car leave, but I damn sure knew it didn't belong in this neighborhood, and someone had been inside.

"Well done," I said. "You got me on that one, but we still have the blue Pontiac on Pioneer Road. That old bucket of bolts is a nice touch, by the way — truly undercover. I probably wouldn't have thought much of it if it weren't for your man in the Chevy." I held a hand up. "Yeah, yeah, I know. You don't know nothin' about that. What about the guy in the Pontiac?"

He looked north, and when he spotted the Bonneville, a strange look overtook his face.

This was my chance. "What's the matter, Chief, no response? Screw this shit!"

I darted toward Hooper's car before the chief could stop me.

"Wait one minute!"

"No chance," I yelled back as he followed me. "I've had enough of this harassment."

Nice indignation again, the Reaper said. *Damn, you're getting good at this.*

I approached the car, and the face of my nemesis.... How precious! He looked stunned, nervous and confused. He could only sit there and wait. Perfect.

The chief came fast on my heels and still yelled, but I ignored him and pressed on. When I got alongside the car, I smiled at Hooper. The look on his face was hilarious — like he'd tried to swallow an entire lemon. I'd have laughed my ass off if I hadn't been so fuckin' mad.

Radlon arrived three steps behind me.

"You're hiring them young, aren't you, Chief?"

He motioned for Hooper to get out of the car, and I waited for the whole thing to blow up in Hooper's face.

"Tony, what are you doing here?" The chief's voice dripped with disappointment. "I told you to leave it to us."

This was my chance. I yelled, "What? He's not a cop? Who the hell is this…. Wait a damn minute! Did you say *Tony*? That article I read about the Hooper kid — it said he had a brother named Tony and…. Are you kidding me? *He's* watching my house? *This* is Tony Hooper?"

"Calm down, Mr. Norton," the chief said. "I'll take care of this."

"Calm down? Bullshit! I want this guy arrested."

"That's quite amusing, Mitchell." A new voice — the quiet, confident voice of my nemesis — spoke.

He seemed way too calm for my tastes. "What the hell is that supposed to mean?"

The chief jumped in. "Look, I want you two to — "

"I know you recognize me, Mitchell, just as I know what you've done, even if Chief Radlon can't prove it yet."

How the hell was that possible? There was no fucking way he could know.

"Now wait one damned minute," the chief yelled. "I'll do the talking from here on in."

This was pissing me off. "But Chief — "

"Shut up, Mr. Norton! I said *I'll* do the talking and I meant it. Tony, I want you to get into your car and drive directly to the station. I'll be there shortly. Now!"

Hooper looked at him with puppy dog eyes, and with a hint of what might have been shame, but he hopped in his car and drove off.

Good. I *definitely* needed to put an end to this shit.

Radlon waited until that fuckin' Hooper was gone. "Mr. Norton, I want you to return home. I will deal with Mr. Hooper."

"And what about the officer you removed, the one in the black Chevy?"

"Are we on that again? I can't speak to a car that's not there. If you'll excuse me…." He spun back toward my house.

Fuckin' liar. "Maybe I should get myself a lawyer."

"Why do you think you need one?"

"I think I may have to file a nice lawsuit. How would that be?"

"You have no grounds for a lawsuit, but it's your money if you want to waste it."

"What I want is to go about my business undisturbed. Waste or not, the next time I spot a tail I *will* call a lawyer."

"I don't see any *tail*, Mr. Norton."

I screamed, "Bullshit! You must have called him off. I want to get on with my life without interference!"

Whoa! the Reaper said. *Easy, Mitchell, you're losing your cool.*

"Okay." The chief kept his voice low and calm, and smiled. "Why don't we leave you to that?"

"You're goddamned straight. I ain't gonna put up with no more of this shit."

Angry silence accompanied my walk back home. Radlon got in his car and backed out without even looking at me.

Free to contemplate my next move, I couldn't think straight. I needed to return to the shop, to address my special plans for Diana, but everything had gone to shit-on-a-stick.

"I gotta get rid of that bitch, make sure they never find her body."

You're good at that, aren't you, Mitchell?

"Damn straight."

I needed to give it a little time to cool down—couldn't have none of them fuckheads following me. I needed the darkness of night.

Diana would have to wait awhile longer. She'd probably piss herself some more, but that was too fuckin' bad. Suddenly, I didn't give one stinkin' pile of *shit* about the queen bitch, Diana Gregario.

"She's dead meat."

As it should be, Mitchell.

CHAPTER 52
MAY 31, 1978:
TONY HOOPER

"Ultimately, we know that the other side of every fear is a freedom." – *Marilyn Ferguson*

"Tony, what in the world do you think you're doing?"

Back in the interrogation room at the station, the chief's tone served as a good indication of his mood; he was as disappointed as he was angry. I liked him, and hated disappointing him, but Diana rose above all other considerations. If the authorities wouldn't save her, if indeed she weren't already dead, then I'd allow no one to prevent my saving her.

That included the chief.

"When I left here earlier," I said, "I had the distinct impression that nothing serious would be done about Norton. You're all determined to focus on me as your prime suspect, but the girl I love is still out there, perhaps alive and perhaps not. I cannot sit idly by and allow her to suffer."

"And you thought that we would allow that?"

I considered my response, not wishing to be insulting or just plain stupid, but if they were doing something about Norton, I was unaware of it. "I realize there's only so much you can do within the boundaries of the law. I don't blame you for that, but I'm limited by no such boundaries."

"Like *hell*! If *I* overstep those boundaries, it probably means my job. If *you* do it, you'll end up in jail. Do you hear me?" He jabbed a finger my direction. "This is not a game, Tony. This is deadly serious."

I yelled, "Don't you think I know that?" I paused for a moment to take a deep breath and relax. "I'll happily go to jail if it means getting Diana back safely."

"Damn it, Tony, you don't know what you're doing here."

He stood and paced before the mirror. Might someone, perhaps the FBI agents, be keeping us under observation on the other side of that glass? No matter.

He sat again, sighed heavily, and leaned in close. "You know, I've decided to lay it all on the table. I'll play it straight with you, but I want you to do the same for me. Okay?"

How far was I willing to go? "Yes sir."

"I've been thinking about you a lot lately, ever since that day at the morgue when you identified Alex, particularly after seeing how your father responded. I wanted to help you, but I wasn't sure how to do that."

"I know. You're one of the good guys. I knew that almost immediately."

He smiled. "Thanks. Frankly, I was amazed at how well you handled the whole situation, while your father could only manage to vanish into a bottle."

I stirred, but he held up a hand and continued. "Please understand, I don't mean to throw stones at your father. We all have our limits, and I expect that he'll come back to himself soon enough, but you... you've been a different story, impressive for someone so young and inexperienced."

How should I react to this unexpected exchange? He sure wasn't talking as someone who thought of me as a suspect. Besides, I hated compliments. "Thank you, sir."

"But here's the thing, since I'm being perfectly honest about everything: you may *not* take the law into your own hands. What would you have done if you'd followed Norton to a remote location and found Diana or one of the others?"

I shrugged. "Whatever was necessary."

"Does that include killing him?"

And there was the sixty-four-thousand-dollar question. Good thing they hadn't looked in the trunk of my car, where they'd have found my swords and black garb.

I took a deep breath and swallowed the lump in my throat. "You know, he killed Alex, and then he *butchered* him and dumped him in the river like so much chum."

"You don't *know* it was Norton."

"But don't you see? I do."

"How can you possibly know? Even we don't know that yet. There's no evidence to support it."

"To bring to trial, you mean."

"I mean no evidence, period!" He shook his head and sighed. "So please tell me how you know such a thing."

"Some things you just know."

"Dah! Something isn't jiving here, Tony. Is there something you're not telling me? We agreed to be straight with one another, remember?"

Uh-oh. What should I say? I couldn't—

"Did you also know we had a man watching Norton, prepared to follow him?"

Shit! He must have been south on Mohawk, hidden from me by the Norton house. "No. Did I screw that up?"

His frustration eased. "No, I can't put that on you since Norton apparently spotted our man right off. Then he looked around and spotted you. He thought you were one of us."

I breathed easier knowing— "Excuse me?"

"He thought you were also a police officer."

I considered that for a few seconds. "So that's what that display was outside my car. I wondered about that."

"What are you talking about?"

"Chief, do you really believe that?"

"What, that he thought you were a cop? I don't know. He appeared sincere enough, genuinely surprised by who you were."

I snorted. If everything I believed was true, and it was, then that *couldn't* be true. How could I get the chief to reach the same conclusion?

"You know," I said, "he watched Diana quite intently at that park, and he definitely saw me with her. Then at the bowling alley, once again, he saw me with her. I know because the way he stared at her made me uncomfortable, and I made eye contact. He looked right at me and held the gaze. He looked angry."

I let that sink in. "And how did he know where Diana lives? I've been thinking about that. He must have followed us from the bowling alley. I spotted him again, staring right at us as we sat in the parking lot, so there's no question he knows my car and my face."

He mulled it over while staring down at the table, then looked up and said, "You remember that much of him?"

I shrugged again. "Been thinking about it a lot lately, trying to remember. And like I said, the creepy way he watched Diana freaked me out a little."

He nodded, though he still seemed a bit suspicious—not of me as the killer, but that I wasn't telling him everything. Smart guy.

"You still believe he thought I was a cop?" I said. "That he didn't know *exactly* who I was?"

Now that I'd said it aloud, and as it came together, I understood it much better myself. He'd parked down the street from my house on the day of Alex's funeral, when Diana and I had gone to the bowling alley. I couldn't tell the chief but—

Oh shit! Norton probably followed me. He found Diana because of me. It was my *fault.*

The room started to spin, to wobble and—

"Are you all right?"

"Huh?" I focused again on the chief. "Oh... yeah, I'm fine."

I took a deep breath, and couldn't contain a huge sigh. "As I think about it out loud here, it occurs to me that he probably found me through my car. He must have seen it at the park that day. He *did* watch us awhile. So he finds *me*, hoping to discover Diana that way because he doesn't yet know who we are. I'm not sure how Alex comes into it. Perhaps he found me earlier and was watching our place. I don't know. Maybe it was—What do you call it?—a crime of opportunity."

Sonuvabitch, now it all makes sense! It had to—

Oh, Hoopster, I'm so sorry. Please forgive me, Alex.

The chief remained quiet, but I could see the wheels turning.

I stiffened up and clenched my fists below the table, digging my fingernails into my palms. "To answer your earlier question—I owe you that much—I'll say, '*Absolutely.*' If I had to, I could cut Mitchell Norton's heart out!"

He leaned back in his chair with the front legs slightly off the floor, stared at the ceiling, locked his hands with fingers intertwined, and rubbed his thumbs together.

I could almost imagine smoke piping from his ears.

When he sat forward and looked at me again, both his look and his manner had shifted. "Tell me," he said with a laugh, "did you ever consider becoming a cop?"

His lightened mood surprised me. I remained silent.

"You've painted quite a picture. Everything you've said is at least plausible, yet somehow, I have this nagging suspicion that you're still not telling me *everything*. Why is that?"

"I don't know what to tell you. I've said all I know to say."

Talk about dancing around the truth.

"Okay," he said. "I'll let it go for the moment. Excuse me."

He turned to the two-way glass and nodded, motioning with his hand for the observers on the other side to come into the room.

Only one entered, Special Agent Jackson. There was no sign of Agent Monroe. He nodded his greeting as he sat across the table, and leaned over with the hint of a smile, and with a look of determination that I didn't fully understand.

"Perhaps," he said, "I have misjudged you, young man. Whatever the merits of your theories, you don't appear to be acting as someone who might have committed these crimes."

He looked at the chief before resuming. "Do you mind if I tell Tony what you told us earlier, Bill?"

The chief shrugged, and Jackson again focused on me.

"Chief Radlon told us that after the day at the morgue, when you identified your brother's body, he no longer thought of you as a suspect. He said you were either the world's most accomplished actor, or you were truly innocent of that crime. I considered his opinion, but needed a little more prodding to accept it. You fit the bill, the natural suspect, but.... well, I've changed my mind. I think the chief had it right all along."

The chief and I exchanged a silent acknowledgement, and I responded to Jackson. "Thank you. That's all well and good, but what exactly do you plan to do about Norton and, more importantly, about getting Diana back?"

I looked back and forth between the two men.

"You know, I do believe what you said earlier," Jackson said. "I mean... you *would* kill or die for those you love, if you must. Wouldn't you?"

I figured he expected no response, and I obliged.

"You must be a good friend to have around in a pinch, yet I can't help wondering if that won't get you into hot water at some point. The law doesn't commend vigilantes, Mr. Hooper. It sends them to prison."

He still hadn't answered my question, and I didn't respond to his statement.

He returned his attention to the chief. "Okay, Bill, you had another meeting with Norton. Any new thoughts about him?"

"I considered quoting Shakespeare, but I thought it might be lost on him. He did protest far too much.'" He paused to adjust his uniform. "The man is just *off*. I wish I could give you more."

"Every good law enforcement officer develops instincts over the years, and I'm inclined to trust yours on this. All right, let's assume that Tony's theories are accurate and that Mitchell Norton is our perpetrator. Do we proceed from the assumption that he's responsible for Alex Hooper and all four missing kids?"

"I'd say so, Arnie. Once I ruled out Tony as a suspect, I assumed that one man was responsible for everything. Nothing else makes sense. I might feel differently if we were in Chicago, but not here in Algonquin."

"Of course. That's why you called us."

"Yeah." He turned up his hands. "Algonquin has made the big leagues."

Holy shit, are they suggesting Norton is a serial killer? Diana!

They continued to talk as though I wasn't in the room. I remained quiet, invisible, in the hopes that they'd continue to do so.

They discussed their options for tracking Norton, and Jackson said he'd arrange to bring in some special surveillance equipment tomorrow. They'd have a special van and two other vehicles, along with communications gear to set up a radio relay. He said they needed to put a man on the ground, meaning on foot, somewhere near the Norton house. The chief told him about the woods along Pioneer Road, which they agreed would be a good spot.

"Excellent," Jackson said. "Why don't we start fleshing this out? I'll make some calls tonight to get the equipment rolling. By tomorrow night, we ought to be able to begin our full surveillance."

Tomorrow night? Were they kidding? What about tonight?

As if reading my thoughts, Jackson continued. "Bill, can you get a man near Norton's house tonight? I'd like to put Agent Monroe with him, if that's okay."

"Consider it done."

"Very good." Jackson turned his gaze to me. "Young man, you've heard a good deal more than we typically share under such circumstances. If Norton turns out to be our man, we'll owe you our thanks. I suppose that's why I allowed you to stay."

"Thank you," I said.

"As long as we're laying it all out, I'd like to say a couple more things. I believe Norton will be nervous about today's encounters. He'll want to keep it under wraps for a while. I doubt our people will see anything tonight, and that may be a good thing given what transpired today. Norton is likely anxious to tie up any loose ends and go underground. That means it will be more dangerous for Diana if he approaches her. We definitely want to be there for that. If Diana is hidden away somewhere, it may be uncomfortable for her, but she'll last another day."

What could I say? Nothing, and so I nodded.

"I'm sorry to say it, but this assumes that she's still alive. And let us remember that there are perhaps three additional victims who require our concern. In my experience, a serial killer, if that's what we're dealing with here, kills. He doesn't hold four victims in waiting. He will sometimes hold one or two, particularly if they're special to him, or perhaps because he needs to make additional preparations, but only until he can't stand it any longer. His primary need, his most excruciating urge, is to kill. Twisted souls. They're hard to understand if you haven't had our training and experience. Even then...."

He shakes his head in disgust. "Now, I'm not trying to discourage you. I just want you to know where we stand. Let *us* take care of business. We know what we're doing. You've finished your part in this, and I don't want to hear that you're playing vigilante again. Okay?"

No sir! "Yes sir."

"After today, he'll be in a state of minor panic. His next move will take a little time and effort. I think he'll sit tight tonight, which will give us the time we need to set up more effective surveillance."

Maybe, and maybe not, but I'd leave nothing to chance.

Everyone seemed pleased now that things were moving forward. It helped that I appeared satisfied, unlikely to present them with any more difficulties.

What they didn't know wouldn't hurt me. I hoped.

CHAPTER 53
MAY 31, 1978:
TONY HOOPER

"Where most of us end up there is no knowing, but the hell-bent get where they're going." – *James Thurber*

No rest for the weary. I'd recounted the day's events and conversations to Frank, including all my conclusions, which he'd thought represented sound reasoning and not just emotional desperation. I'd learned to trust his judgment and, in this case, it comforted me. He'd also agreed to lend me his car, a black Cadillac that would blend into the darkness.

I'd ridden my bike to Frank's and left the Bonnie parked in its usual spot, in case the police drove by my house. Frank would cover for me with Dad, whom I'd told I was staying over at Frank's place.

I parked the Cadillac up on Geringer Road, about two hundred yards to the north of Pioneer Road, up the ridge and through the trees. I did a trial run, and I could reach it in about thirty seconds in an all-out run. That ridge was a real bear, and I could only hope it would be enough time to follow Norton should he head out.

If he drove south on Mohawk Trail, it would be close, but I should be able to catch up to him somewhere on North Harrison Street. If he drove north on Mohawk, I should have no problem.

This assumed that the cops didn't pick him up and follow him, in which case I'd have to leave it to them and trust in the outcome, as much as I hated the idea. I believed they'd set up at the southernmost end of Mohawk, though I couldn't be certain. A vehicle there looked like an unmarked police car, but I couldn't see anyone through the windows. It was too dark.

Would Norton be able to spot them? Would he make them for cops? Nothing I could do about that.

No matter. I couldn't pull myself away from this. If there was any chance at all, I had to stay. Diana was all that mattered. I could lose one more night of sleep.

I stood behind a tree in the woodlands along Pioneer, about seven feet inside the edge and well hidden, where Norton wouldn't spot me even if he looked in my direction. Presumably, he'd look for a vehicle and not for someone on foot, which had been the foundation for Special Agent Jackson's idea.

Tomorrow night, one of his men would be here. This was a one-night deal for me.

I wore the garb Master Komura had provided me, though I wished I'd not worn the *jika-tabi*, the boots with the thin soles through which I felt every little rock and bump. What was I supposed to do, scale walls like Spiderman? Perhaps I'd hang by my feet and strike with my sword, or perform the other ridiculous ninja movie acts that always made Master and me laugh.

I'd pick up some black tennis shoes for next time. Nonetheless, I remained a mere shadow of movement as darkness drew complete. All but the properly trained eye would look past me, and Norton possessed no such eye.

The police might be another matter, but....

The night crawled forward and laid a five-hundred-pound web over me, as though I'd just run the Boston Marathon, swam the English Channel, climbed Mount Everest, and spent four grueling, sweaty hours naked with Farrah Fawcett.

Lack of sleep completed my exhaustion, yet the thought of Diana sustained me. A Thermos of coffee — another one of Frank's good ideas — helped. Maybe. A little.

I checked my watch: 1:15. "Damn, I need to take a leak."

I watered a tree and thought back to four days ago, when I'd last seen Diana on that most spectacular and special of nights. Could she still be alive? I'd had doubts since the beginning, but as there'd been no sign of her body, I clung to the smallest hope. What Jackson had said earlier about serial killers and what drove them reinforced my nagging doubt, but Norton did appear to be fixated on Diana.

A glimmer of hope.

It tortured me to imagine what he'd done to her if she was still alive, and it made me want to kill him all over again—and again.

Whatever Norton had done, as long as she was alive and we could be together in the end, we could overcome anything. I just wanted to hold her again, to kiss her, to breathe in her essence and hear her laugh. Our love was too strong; nothing could rend it apart. Love like this was the true purpose of our existence. Without it, only the search for it made life worth living.

I couldn't give up on her. I mustn't give up.

I'd been thinking of Alex too. With all the excitement regarding Diana, he'd been lost in the shuffle. I should have thought of him more, as I should have been there to save him from an ending he should never have had to endure. Dr. Singer had said he'd felt no physical pain. Still, what must have gone through his mind? How lonely, frightened and desperate he must have been.

I choked down the lump in my throat. Damn thing was showing up so often these days, I should charge it rent.

It killed me to think of what had happened to Alex. The image— the worst possible horror flick from my imagination—stabbed an ice pick into my heart. I'd never been one for tears, but every time I thought of the Hoopster, it took every ounce of determination to hold them at bay. He'd been my little brother, not my son, yet I understood the heartbreak of a parent who'd lost a child.

Dad, I'm sorry. I'll try to understand. I'll try to help.

The night breezes provided cool comfort, a break from the season's premature hot weather. I poured myself another spot of coffee to help keep me awake. I probably wouldn't make it to school tomorrow. Who cared? With the FBI taking over tomorrow night, I needed this one last day, and then—

Wait, what's this?

Perhaps the night shadows played tricks on me. Perhaps my own mind, physically exhausted and emotionally wracked, imagined ghosts in the darkness.

I gulped down the coffee and screwed the lid back on top of the Thermos, and waited for another sign that the movement I'd seen was real.

There it is!

Someone was walking away from the Norton house along the back property lines. He headed away from Mohawk and toward Pioneer Road, and appeared to be dressed in black and wearing a ski mask — difficult to tell for sure.

I stole a quick glance back at the Norton house; his van remained in the driveway.

I looked south down the street, and the surveillance car remained dark and quiet — no sign of movement. In fact, from that location it was unlikely they'd see where Norton walked, if it *was* Mitchell. It must be.

He moved up out of the grass along the property lines that separated the back yards of the houses on Mohawk from those on Wildwood Road, and it appeared he'd walk west on Pioneer.

I stalked through the trees as if walking on glass, a few feet deeper in from Pioneer to ensure that I'd go unseen even if Norton heard me. Any sound would be minor, the nocturnal wanderings of a rabbit or a raccoon, and I'd freeze at the first flash of sound. This underbrush provided some cover, but it might be impossible to walk through without making any sound at all.

It helped that he was in a hurry to reach his destination. It also helped that crickets screamed the night away. The best symphony ever.

Norton approached Getzelman Terrace and a small park on the left. I knew that park well because a stone fountain there offered the clearest, coolest water that perpetually bubbled out of the ground. On a hot summer day, nothing beat it. For the life of me, I couldn't remember the name of that little park.

Who gives a shit? Keep your head on the mission, Tony!

He stopped to look around, standing alongside a tree for about thirty seconds. I began to worry that he'd heard me, when he turned to the right and headed.... There was no street there. Would he go into the woods and up the ridge?

It hit me: Suicide Trail. That's what we kids called the steep drainage ditch covered in loose gravel, which we often rode down on our bicycles. If one were careless, his reward might be a broken arm or, at the very least, skinned up knees and —

The mission, Tony. Keep your head on the mission. Damn it, I'm nervous.

He climbed Suicide Trail, which would bring him out on Geringer at the end of Cermak, only a block from where I'd parked the Cadillac.

I slipped to the edge of the trees and looked up just as he crested the top and turned left on Geringer.

The Cadillac sat about two hundred yards to the right.

I started up behind him, keeping to the left edge and away from the gravel to remain quiet. At the top, I peered around the last tree.

He'd crossed to the other side of the road and stopped alongside a pick-up truck that faced west.

What in hell was he doing? He dug in his pocket and—

Holy shit, he's opening the door to the truck and climbing inside.

He was smarter than I'd given him credit for.

I bolted east toward the Cadillac as he started the truck and pulled off to the west. I sprinted to the car and started it after he'd disappeared. I left the lights off and took off after him, careful not to come too close to him.

He drove past the cemetery to Cary Road, turned west to Highway 31, and then north toward Crystal Lake.

Though I couldn't let him discover me, I must stay close enough to keep him in sight. Frank had taken the time to explain to me the fine art of tailing another vehicle. I had no idea how he knew about such things, though my suspicions were growing by the hour. A little practice would have been nice, but there'd been no time.

"Just use your head," Frank had said.

I could do that.

No other vehicles appeared in the vicinity—most importantly, no additional tails. It would have been easier to remain hidden if there'd been more traffic to mingle with, yet the knowledge that we were alone comforted me. I could leave the lights off.

I had no idea where Norton was going, or if Diana was even alive. I could only hope and follow. Nothing more to do. Yet.

I breathed easy, focused like a riflescope on Norton far ahead of me. Despite the distance between us, his lights shone clearly enough that I'd know where he turned, when he turned. It helped to know the area so well, and the occasional streetlight, combined with a fair moon and a clear night, meant I could see well enough to drive.

Still no other traffic appeared, though on this often-busy street that could change, even at this hour, so I had to—

His brake lights flashed, but no turn signal. Was he aware of me back here? Was he waiting for me to approach? I let up on the gas and allowed the Caddy to drift, and just as my panic rose, he turned off to the right a few blocks ahead.

"Wait a minute, there's no road there."

Nervous again, but also committed, I drifted forward with the lights still off. I came to the general area where he'd turned, and slowed down to locate him. I used the emergency brake so my brake lights wouldn't flash.

A small dirt track led to the right, running back along a farm field. If I wasn't mistaken, it led into the old gravel pits where we often hung out during the summer.

I continued, but saw no sign of his truck. "Where in hell are you, Norton?"

The darkness here, where no streetlights shone and no pavement reflected the moonlight, made it tough. I strained to see with my chin practically resting on the steering wheel. Sweat swam on my upper lip. My stomach quivered.

Taillights flared in the distance; he must have been in a dip in the landscape. He wound up and slightly to the right, about two hundred yards ahead.

Driving this road was like skiing moguls on one-ton metal skis. Frank's poor Caddy. I alternated between the gas pedal and the emergency brake. Hard to believe anything but a farm tractor had traveled here for a long time, aside from Norton.

I rose out of the dip, and brake lights flashed again, ahead and to my right, and then vanished. He must have crested another hill.

"Come on, Norton, where are we going?"

I stopped before the crest, got out of the car, and jogged up to peer over the top, careful to remain low. Norton walked around the truck about fifty yards ahead, and pulled things from the front passenger seat. He gave no indication that he'd spotted me.

Though Frank's Cadillac hummed quietly, I ran back and turned off the engine.

Back at the top of the hill, I watched as Norton carried something to a small shed of some sort. He fiddled with something on the door, perhaps a lock — impossible to tell from here.

"You have to get closer, Tony," I whispered to myself, then gazed down at my *shinobi shozoku* and nodded. "No worries."

Several trees offered cover, and I darted from one to another, keeping low to the ground. The tall wild grass provided additional cover as I drew closer.

A light flared in the shed, and he reappeared and grabbed something else from the front of the truck. Looked like plastic bags.

Christ! Why does he need plastic bags?

I dropped down and spider-crawled toward the back of the shed. Once again, the rough ground stabbed through the thin, spiked soles of my *jika-tabi*. I ignored it.

The twenty-foot-square shed looked to be at least a century old.

How did you find this place, Norton?

I paused behind an ancient oak a few yards from the shed. A faint but foul odor, reminiscent of a sewer or septic tank, assaulted me.

Holy crap!

A voice invaded the darkness, but too far away for me to understand. I risked creeping right to the rear wall of the shed, and listened.

I recognized Norton's voice. "Looks like you pissed all over the place. Poor thing, you *have* been alone for the past thirty-six hours. I'll bet you're thirsty and hungry too. Tough shit! That's what you get for being a bitch."

Bitch? He has a woman in there! God, please let it be Diana.

"I'm surprised you didn't shit yourself while you were at it." He laughed. "Whatever. The Reaper has returned and he's told me what to do."

He paused, and the sound of a bag crinkling sent lightning bolts up my spine.

"The police are onto me. Do you believe that? Your fucking boyfriend somehow figured things out. That's right, your little boy Tony knows about me, though I don't know how the fuck he managed it."

It's Diana! Thank God!

"Who gives a fuck? I had big plans for us, you know. We were gonna be royalty, the king and queen of pain and misery, but you fucked it up. You had to be a prissy little baby. You had to call me vile names and attack me. You stupid bitch, you have no idea what you've given up, but I think you have a good idea of what will happen *now*."

It's show time.

I needed to get his attention somehow, and isolate him from Diana to minimize the risk to her. A bull-rush might get her killed.

I felt along the ground for a rock and found two suitable to my purpose.

He continued his rant. "Do you think it's better to die? Don't you know that I would have taken care of you? You were gonna be my queen. I would never have hurt you, but no, no, no. You ruined it! I'll tell you one thing though—I *will* have my way with you this time, and I'll keep you gagged so you can't fuck with my head. What do you think of that? Awe, that's right, go ahead and cry, you little fuckin' baby."

You sonuvabitch! I'll kill you!

I crept to the edge of the shed, and positioned myself where I had an easy aim at his truck.

"You stupid bitch, your tears don't mean a fuckin' thing. And you know what? You smell like shit, but I don't care. I'm gonna fuck your brains out. What do you think of that? Ooh, more tears. You're breaking my heart, stupid bitch! Boo hoo!"

I threw the smallest pebble at Norton's truck and it made a definite sound, but he apparently didn't hear it over the sound of his own voice.

Shit! What kind of weapons do you have in there, asshole?

"You know, after I have my way with you, then I'm *really* gonna have fun. That's right, I'm gonna work on you like I did on Danny-Boy and Jacque-Baby. Remember that, you stupid bitch? You remember the things I do with these tools? How do you think that will feel? The first thing I'll do is cut those rock-hard nipples right off your tits."

I threw the second stone much harder, and it crashed against the truck.

"What the hell was that?"

PART 8

HUNTER AND PREY

CHAPTER 54
JUNE 19, 1995:
MITCHELL NORTON

Shades of 1978, the police are all over me and I gotta assume they're watching me again, though I ain't seen no sign of them. Maybe they've learned some things since then. Has the Algonquin Police Department learned how to conduct surveillance in anonymity?

Shit! Anything is possible.

Besides, the FBI might be doing all the legwork. They may be better at it, and of course, lovely Linda is on the case. What's going on between her and Tony Hooper? I'd swear they have a relationship in the works. I'd love to get my hands on her; she's smokin' hot, but she'd also be the second of that fuckin' Hooper's women that I destroyed.

Wouldn't that be precious?

It's so easy to hate my old nemesis again. He appears over and over, like the proverbial bad penny. If that ain't a good reason to hate him, then no good reason exists. The real question is what I'll do about it. There *have* been three new murders in Algonquin. The thought of him as victim number four is positively exquisite, but the authorities are ever watchful. I don't wanna give them a reason to watch me more closely.

There's nothing to tie me to those three victims, the authorities' assumptions be damned, but Hooper is another story. He's the Elliott Ness to my Al Capone, the Batman to my Riddler, the Roadrunner to my Wile E. Coyote. There's too much history between us.

I can't escape the fuckwad.

Starbucks is crowded today. I came to finish the last forty pages of Stephen King's book, *The Dark Half*. Maybe *I* should write a book, since finding a decent job will be next to impossible. It could be an autobiography: *My Life and Times (and Wicked Ways)*, or maybe *I'm a New Man*, or *A Year in the Life – 1978 (The Voice of the Reaper)*. I should have thought of it sooner. I mean, shit, any knucklehead can be a writer, right?

I get a large cup—excuse me, 'venti'—of their Sumatra Extra Bold coffee, and grab a seat at a small table. Unfortunately, two irritating kids occupy the armchairs. I'll keep an eye on them and make a dash for it if one becomes available.

An hour later, two things have happened: I've finished the book, and my ass and legs have gone to sleep on this miserable wooden chair. I squirm around for a minute to get the blood circulating again, but I gotta stand to accomplish that, which proves tricky with dead legs.

I consider buying a second cup of coffee, and glance at the armchairs. I'd forgotten about them while finishing the book, but my numbed legs have brought them back into focus.

Excellent, one is empty. Occupying the other one is—

Are you fuckin' kidding me! You couldn't stay away, could you?

This may be one of Hooper's regular hangouts—perfectly innocent—yet given our history, my instincts say otherwise. Although I haven't spotted anyone, I've battled this suspicion that someone's been watching me the past couple days—like invisible mosquitoes gnawing on the back of my head.

What the hell, I may as well have a little fun with it.

I snag another cup of coffee and stroll over to sit in the available armchair. I avoid eye contact with Hooper, as though unaware of his presence, and pretend to read the book. I wanna let him have the first word or make the first move. Afterwards, depending on how crazy he gets, a call to my lawyer may be in order. I seriously want to nail this fucker.

It's been several minutes and still he hasn't uttered a single sound. If I keep grinding my teeth like this, one monster of a headache is gonna knock my dick in the dirt. It's difficult to resist the temptation, but I still ain't looked at him. Maybe he won't notice a quick glance.

I peek over the top of the book and....

The son of a whore stares right at me with a damned smile on his face! "You already finished the book, *Norton*. Give up the charade."

He must'a been watching me closely. Smart boy. We'll see about that, and I don't much care for the way he said *Norton*, like he was spitting out poison.

Gotta put on my smart cap. "It's not too bright to follow me, *Hooper*. I happen to know Chief Radlon warned you against it, and I have an attorney on call to follow up on this kind of harassment."

"Follow you? Harassment? Don't be paranoid. *You* sat next to *me*, remember? I stopped in for a cup of coffee, as I often do, though you being here is a definite bonus."

"Is that right?"

"Why not?" He raises his voice. "If you're here drinking coffee, then you're not out murdering people and chopping up their bodies."

He ensured that everyone in the store heard, and many of them look at me with that obvious question in their eyes. They wonder if I'm a killer. *The* killer. After all, everyone around here knows about my release.

The situation irritates the hell outta me, but I keep my cool and laugh lightly in response. "I guess that's supposed to get me riled up, isn't it, Hooper?"

"Whatever do you mean?"

I laugh again. Time to strike back. "How is lovely Linda, by the way? You know, I can't seem to get her off my mind recently."

"She's fantastic, as always."

"And pretty tasty, I'll bet."

He speaks softly, determined to ignore the bait. "You got that right. Positively yummy." He smiles as though we're good friends catching up on gossip.

"Yes, I can imagine that quite easily."

"Sure, you must *imagine* it, since you haven't *had* a woman in... what's it been, seventeen years? You remember," he yells again, "when you raped, murdered and butchered a woman."

I don't bother to look around. I can imagine the looks on everyone's faces, their thoughts.

My, he does seem to be getting better at this game. Maybe I underestimated him. "You know, Hooper, my lawyer can't wait to take a shot at you. He says I needn't settle for any of your bullshit."

"Why, Mr. Norton, you offend me. Can we not engage in a little friendly conversation here?"

"Oh? Right. Then let me ask you a question. Are you and Linda involved? I thought I'd ask her out."

He laughs. "Come on, Norton, you can do better than that."

"But I'm dead serious. I'd love to spend some quality time with her. I haven't been this attracted to a woman since... well, since Diana Gregario. Talk about yummy!"

He smiles, but his eyes are red-hot flames.

"What's the matter," he says. "Aren't you satisfied screwing Scooby?"

Scooby? Our dog? What the fuck does he know about Scooby? "How amusing, Hooper, if just a little fourth grade."

He shrugs and sips his coffee.

I gotta give him some credit for playing it cool, but no way am I gonna lose my temper in this child's game. I can be cool too.

"Perhaps you don't need Scooby," he says, still plenty loud enough for everyone in this little place to hear. "Perhaps you get all the thrills you need when you murder and dismember someone. That's what gets your rocks off, right?"

That's real funny, asshole! "Is this your idea of non-harassment, Hooper? A judge might disagree."

He smiles and sips his coffee.

I've had enough of this bullshit. "And now, if you'll excuse me, I do believe I have an appointment with my attorney. I bet he'd love to talk with you."

"Sure, that'll be fine. Have a nice day, *Norton*."

You lousy, miserable fucker, we'll see who has a nice day!

CHAPTER 55
JUNE 19, 1995:
TONY HOOPER

"If I die tomorrow, it will have been useless to have been afraid today." – *Mark Helprin, "A Soldier of the Great War"*

It's fortunate that I'm a natural-born creature of the night. As a boy, I often stayed up late on weekends to read with a flashlight, while the rest of the family slept. I would then sleep until after noon, causing Dad to wonder how I could sleep for fourteen hours or more. Mom knew better, as she'd caught me at my clandestine reading, even encouraged it.

I didn't have the heart to perpetuate our secret after she died. Sacrilege. Thereafter, I remained in the living room with a proper light on. Dad didn't really care.

I've always had difficulty falling asleep at a *reasonable hour*, no matter how tired, and I've always had difficulty waking at a *reasonable hour*, no matter how rested. That made school, and any other event for which I had to get up early, a challenge.

Left to my own devices, I return to the night. It's strictly physiological—I'm a night owl by genetic design.

This comes in handy while seated in the trees at one o'clock in the morning, this not-so-fine Monday night—err, Tuesday morning—while most of Algonquin is fast asleep. I watch and wait.

The devil may go out in the wee hours.

I have my coffee with me, as always, though I wonder what Master Komura would say about that. If I were up against a skilled or experienced opponent, coffee would be out of the question, as he could follow his nose right to me.

No problem; Norton possesses no such skill.

This is my second time out here in four nights.

I let the cops take the weekend shift, and refreshed myself in preparation for what may be a long week. I was here Friday night too, but too late, as I discovered Saturday.

Algonquin suffered a third murder victim, butchered inside a little work shed located in the cemetery. The groundskeeper couldn't understand all the flies, according to the reports, until he opened the shed and found poor Lindsey Merkham in too many pieces. He didn't know if he'd ever be able to eat again after his vomiting fit. Sleep might not be much of a bargain for him either, at least for a while.

I'm sorry, Lindsey, I was too late. I didn't know you but I won't forget you. I promise; your killer's days are numbered.

The police questioned Norton again. His mother swore he was home the whole time, reading in her living room while she knitted a new sweater. Linda, who accompanied Chief Radlon for the questioning, told me Mrs. Norton was adamant and more than a little upset that her boy suffered such harassment. Much to my chagrin, Linda said she believed Mrs. Norton had told the truth.

Perhaps, but something is amiss. The timelines are out of whack or something. I don't know. I know only that Algonquin is once again prey to a killer, all within days of a known serial killer's release. I'm no fan of coincidence.

I trust Linda's instincts, but she can't know everything. She's no mind reader, and I couldn't tell her that I spotted Norton coming home quietly in the dark the night of Lindsey's death. She wouldn't approve, and I'd prefer to avoid that argument.

It's a strange dynamic that we have, Linda and me. She knows exactly what I do, yet somehow she avoids it. Why? Because it would change our relationship? I think she enjoys our relationship quite a lot, as do I. The sex is... well... yowza! But there's so much more than that.

Yet our earlier conversation created a whole new bag of worms for me.

We were at Frank's place—I should get used to calling it my place—for dinner, tea and conversation. Linda and I went inside to wash the dishes afterwards, leaving Frank to enjoy his tea on the patio.

"So what are you going to do?"

I turned to Linda, and threw up my best Mr. Spock eyebrow. "Do? About what?"

"Are we going to dance around this thing again?"

Uh-oh! She meant Norton. She meant my... avocation. "I'm not much of a dancer. Perhaps if your question were more specific."

"You forget that I was there three years ago, when you saved my ass from Ronald Allen Stegman."

"And what a gorgeous ass it is, if I —"

"Don't do that! Don't deflect. I'm serious here."

Indeed, she was. Her eyes cast a mixture of fear and doubt and anxiety and — mostly fear. Her chest heaved with nervous, rapid breathing. She licked her lips and swallowed repeatedly. Classic signs of distress.

My head spun with possibilities — and damn few of them good. She was an FBI Special Agent, for God's sake. Whatever she might feel for me, how could I possibly...?

"Look," I said, "you never pushed me on Stegman, on what I was doing there, and I appreciated that. Then and now." I paused, damn near helpless before her. "But you have to know that I never intended to hold that over your head. Then or now."

She sighed and offered a sad smile. "I know. You saved me from...." Her upper body did that quick shiver that happens when one is spooked. "I can only imagine what he would have done to me."

My turn to smile. I needed to let her drive this conversation.

"And for that reason," she said, "I ignored who I was — what I did."

I nodded.

"But I'm a law enforcement officer for the FBI, a sworn officer of the court, and you're... you're...." She snorted and threw up her hands. "Am I supposed to believe that Stegman was the first time? The last time? What am I supposed to do here?"

I smiled again. "Your job. How could you do anything else?"

"But... how can I... what would...?"

I put a finger to her lips. "It's okay."

She looked utterly helpless as she closed her eyes and kissed my finger.

"You must do," I said, "whatever is required of you. Let me worry about me."

She laid her head on my shoulder and wrapped her arms around me. "You make it sound so simple."

I scan the area around Norton's house again — still no movement — and try to shake off the conversation with Linda.

We drifted into silence after that, holding each other and kissing, and tried to imagine better possibilities. I'd expected us to spend the night together, but somehow that too drifted away.

The truth is I think I'm falling in love with her.

I've made it a point during the past seventeen years *not* to fall in love, and I'm afraid I may have forgotten how. The pain I endured seventeen years ago, the only time I've ever loved, is something I vowed never to experience again. Since there are no guarantees in any relationship, I avoided the situation altogether.

Nice and safe.

Loneliness, however, remains a persistent foe, never surrendering the struggle. It wears me down like waves crashing on the beach, until I must either surrender or swim. After many long years of meaningless and unfulfilling encounters, I'm ready to fight back, ready for the real thing. It's happened quickly, but it feels as if I've been with Linda much longer.

I clearly have some important decisions to make, but first, time to close this chapter of my life. Seventeen years after the fact, the re-emergence of Norton has brought all my pain into sharp focus. I lost far too much, and while killing him won't bring any of it back, it's about more than that. It's about stopping the pain, the death; about defeating a butcher before he kills again.

I should have done it then, because now... three more people have died terribly.

I *will* do it this time. No choice. How else can I move on? It gnaws at me like a rat on old bones. Time to destroy the rat.

I shuffle through the trees to stretch my legs, toward Mohawk, to get a look south on the street to see if the police have set up surveillance. I may be only one of several keeping watch, and might have to work around them. I've done it for a long time, but it's often a difficult thing, something that requires constant vigilance and planning and the sort of improvisation that, fortunately for me, both Frank and Master Komura have helped me perfect over the years.

I'm nothing if not well trained.

I stop behind a tree near the corner where Mohawk and Pioneer intersect. There are only two cars parked on the street, both of which appear empty. The other parked cars are in driveways, of no concern as they belong to the residents of the neighborhood.

"Wait, what's that?"

What would the resident of that house say if he knew the police used his driveway for surveillance? Then again, maybe they got permission. Sneaky.

It's impossible to make out the color of the dark car in the black of night. No car expert, I'm uncertain of the make — domestic, definitely a four-door. Looks official.

Norton probably won't spot it. Hell, *I* spotted it only because of the movement in the back seat.

I reach into the pack at my hip, and pull out a small but powerful pair of binoculars. I'd hoped the moonlight would be enough to make out who it is, but it's difficult to focus without a streetlight nearby. I lower the binoculars and close my eyes tightly for two full minutes, and upon opening them, the night appears brighter — a simple old army trick to improve night vision.

I try the binoculars again.

There's definitely a man in the back seat, against the passenger-side door. He has a clear and constant view of the Norton house. I would never have spotted him if he hadn't moved, but Master trained me to spot movement. As he likes to say, "The samurai must see even the invisible."

I shift the binoculars toward the front seat, where an odd shape appears that's difficult to make out. It might be someone seated in the front but, if so, he leans back and keeps still. It takes a minute or two, but he leans forward and stretches, and long hair..... Perhaps it's not a *he.*

When Linda's face turns toward me, I say, "That's why you didn't press me to spend the night with you."

Her presence complicates things. The person in the backseat must be an FBI associate, or a local cop.

"No more vacation for you, my dear. I'm not the only one with secrets."

It's a funny thing about stakeouts, something I discovered long ago. I do tend to talk to myself, aloud, as if talking to someone else. It feels perfectly normal.

If Norton moves, I may have to cede the pursuit to Linda and her partner. It will depend on where he goes and by what means. He no longer uses a precious "shop," as he called it in 1978, though Friday night's effort at the cemetery was pretty close to his old *modus operandi*.

He killed the two previous victims in their own homes. Lindsey Merkham may have been a crime of opportunity, another thing he knows about.

It harkens memories of the Hoopster.

I try to put Alex out of my mind—not a good time—and focus again on Linda. She's—

Damn it, I almost missed it!

Movement flashed in my peripheral vision, off to the right. He's on the move, dressed in black and wearing a ski mask. It's déjà-vu all over again. That mask must be hotter than hell. He moves up out of the grass along the back property line, headed west toward Pioneer— precisely what he did in 1978.

I pull up the binoculars and take a quick look at Linda's surveillance car. Neither she nor her partner gives any indication that they've seen Norton. His house probably interferes with their line of sight.

Did they forget what he did seventeen years ago, how he eluded surveillance then? There must be another vehicle keeping watch in the area. I'll have to be careful.

I zip through the trees—reminiscent of '78—with the greatest caution. Norton may remember that little tidbit from the court testimony, and be watching for it. I must "walk on air," as Master Komura puts it.

Damn, Linda is going to be pissed!

Norton passes Getzelman Terrace and approaches Suicide Trail, keeping to routine. He stops and looks around. Though he wears the nearly invisible black clothes, he makes no additional effort to remain hidden.

That's dumb, Norton.

He heads up Suicide Trail, and I jog to catch up with him, repeatedly glancing around to ensure that no other surveillance vehicles are watching.

I parked my van above the ridge on Geringer Road in case I'd need it, as I did with Frank's Cadillac in '78.

It's like watching a rerun, but Linda's decision not to stake out this area, given what happened seventeen years ago, stumps me. She should know better. It's almost as if she—

Shit! Is this for my *benefit?*

I refocus on Norton. If he has access to a vehicle again, I should be all set. If not, he'll be walking to another house to do his business.

I come to the edge of the trees alongside the trail, and he clears the top and disappears left on Geringer.

Keeping to the old routine? Geez, Norton, I thought you were smarter than this.

I fly up the left edge of the trail and peer around the last tree at the top. He's walking along the left edge of the road. Two houses down, he stops and looks around again, waits a few seconds, then turns into the driveway on his left.

That's it then. This is different from '78. He's going into the second house.

My God, that's Ethel Simmons' place!

CHAPTER 56

MAY 31, 1978:

TONY HOOPER

"So act that your principle of action might safely be made a law for the whole world." – *Immanuel Kant*

The second stone had banged off Norton's truck, and he'd reacted, but then it grew suddenly quiet inside the shed.

I clung to the hope that he'd come out to investigate, but if he made a move to hurt Diana, all bets were off. I'd charge in and hope for the best.

He called from inside the shed. "Is someone out there?"

Why don't you find out? Come out and play.

My hand instinctively slipped to the hilt of my *katana*. I assumed he carried at least a knife, based on his threats to Diana, and knowing what he'd done to Alex. He might have an axe, or more. If he had a gun.... I could only pray he didn't. I'd be little help to Diana dead.

He yelled again. "Hello."

Come on, Norton, walk outside.

"It must be nothing. Shit, I'm getting downright jumpy."

Damn it! What would it take to get that asshole out of the shed?

I couldn't yell out since it would take him only a second to put a knife to Diana's throat. I must separate the two of them; I had an idea, but would need his incessant talking to stop first.

"Why don't we get things ready, what do you say? Do you want a little hoochy-coochy, baby? Let me clear the bench to make some room for us."

He shuffled around again but finally shut up. This was my chance.

"What's that? Did you hear that? Hey bitch, are you awake? Did you hear that? Shit!"

A brief pause. I continued scratching the base of the shed.

"Fuck! You know, it's probably some little vermin drawn by the smell of your piss. Or it could be all the blood that, despite my best efforts, is awful-fuckin'-hard to clean up."

Another pause.

"Maybe I'll feed it a little piece of *you* when I'm done. How does that sound? Hey bitch, are you listening?"

Damn it, shut the fuck up and come out here, you asshole! I scratch some more.

"Well shit, I have just the thing for that little vermin. Here, kitty-kitty-kitty, come and get yourself a nice big piece of my knife right down your fuckin' throat."

He stormed out and stalked around the side of the shed. As he did so, I slipped around the other side.

"Come and get it, kitty," he said.

He reached the rear of the shed, and I stepped lightly to the front and entered through the door. A woman lay crumpled on the floor to my left, bound and gagged, naked with her legs tied apart.

Sonuvabitch!

A bloody rag tied around her arm appeared to cover some kind of wound. She remained still and unresponsive, oblivious to my entry.

Dear God, help her.

I could barely tell, given her filthy state and matted hair, but it was definitely my Diana. Dried blood splatter covered much of the shed, and the smell of urine nearly made me gag.

You're a fucking dead man, Norton!

I heard him approach, and slid silently behind the door.

"Jesus-H.-fucking-Christ-on-a-raft," he yelled, "there's nothin' out there that I can see. Wake up! Hey, bitch, let's have some fun, you fuckin' —"

I eased a blade against his throat. "If you so much as breathe too hard, I'll cut you from one ear to the other, you rat fucker."

"Well now," he said calmly, "but ain't that a big-ass knife. Where can I get me one of those?"

"That," I said, pressing it to his throat, "is called a *ninjaken*, and it will end you with the slightest movement."

"Shit, I'd better be still."

His laugh gnawed at me.

"By the by," he said. "Your voice sounds awfully familiar."

I stood behind him with one hand on his left shoulder, my other hand draped over his right shoulder and holding the *ninjaken*. He hadn't seen my face yet, and would only see my eyes through the *sanjaku-tenugui*. Of course, he knew who I was—no hiding that—yet instinct told me that he should not see my face.

"Carefully," I said, "and real slow, drop the knife."

He hesitated, and his shoulders tensed up.

"Are you that stupid, Norton? It will take me about one second to kill you and.... You know what? I'll enjoy it immensely."

"Fuck a rubber duck, Hooper. Looks like you got me dead-to-rights. Here you go."

He dropped the knife. Still Diana hadn't moved. I'd thought she'd respond to my voice, but she'd given no indication that she'd recognized it.

I pushed him against the corner. "What have you done to her?"

"Shit, I didn't do *anything*—yet. You sort of interrupted things, if you must know. Too bad, because I had a hard-on to make a porn star blush. I think she wigged-out or something."

I found a pressure point midway between his arm and neck, and burrowed my thumb deep.

"Ahhhhh!" His knees buckled and he dropped to the floor.

"Any more shit out of you and it will get much worse. You hear me?"

He snickered. "Fine!"

I leaned in and in a near-whisper said, "Put your hands behind your head and lock your fingers. You've seen the *ninjaken*. Pray you don't see the *katana*. If that happens, your head goes bye-bye. Got it?"

"Roger and out, general!" He did as instructed, and his laughter grated at my soul.

Why is he still alive? You need to kill him. I looked at Diana, and back to Norton. *Damn it!*

I jumped over to Diana, and reached down to pull her tangled, dirty hair away from her face. A dark bruise the size of a tennis ball marred one side. I raised the edge of the rag to examine the deep, filthy cut on her arm. She stared at me without blinking or any sign of comprehension.

"Diana, do you hear me? Sweetie, I'm here to rescue you. Everything will be okay."

She remained perfectly still.

I cut the ties from her hands and legs, but they flopped back to the floor.

Norton snickered from the corner. "It's the brave boyfriend to the rescue, huh? Well la-di-fucking-da! What do you think of that? How the fuck did you find me?"

"Shut up, asshole!"

I grabbed what looked like a reasonably clean rag off the bench, and replaced the filthy one on Diana's arm. The bleeding had stopped, but the swelling and discoloration were like something out of a war movie. "I'm just going to clean this up a bit," I said, "and then I'll get you to a hospital. Okay?"

She was conscious, her eyes open and her breathing light but steady, yet she responded to nothing.

I turned my head toward Norton. "What did you do to her? Tell me the truth."

He twisted until he could see me. "What the fuck are you supposed to be, some kind of bad-ass ninja motherfucker?"

I gently laid Diana's arm down and brushed some dirt from her face.

Then, in a series of swift motions, I leapt up, pulled both *ninjaken*, spun and launched a kick over Norton's head, and brought the *ninjaken* to bear against his throat in a crossed pattern, poised as scissors to slice off his head.

I didn't know why I'd felt the need for this display, but it pleased me to see his eyes wide with terror. Still, for some reason I couldn't quite understand, I didn't kill him.

"Perhaps it's time to show you," I said.

"Whoa, no need for that! You made a believer out of me."

I pressed the blades deeper. I needed to find out what the sonuvabitch did to Diana before putting him out of his misery. And fast! "Last time I'm gonna ask, rat fucker. What did you do to Diana?"

"I told you the truth. Nothing. She wigged-out."

"Why did she wig-out? What caused her to do that?"

"Let's see, I did promise that I would do to her what I did to Danny-Boy and Jacque-Baby. She saw my work in those cases. I *was* spectacular, if I do say so myself."

I kept the questions going in rapid-fire succession. "Jacque Fuller?"

"You knew her?"

"Knew? You killed her?"

"Oh yeah, baby, but I did much more than that. I'm an artist, you see, and—"

"What does that have to do with Diana?"

"I made her watch it all, and I was magnificent!"

"You sick sonuvabitch! Where's Bobby Keller, Jacque's boyfriend?"

"Bobby-the-Stud? You know I caught him fingering Jacque?"

"Where is he?"

He laughed. "He's in his car."

"And where's his car?"

"At the bottom of the lake, in the gravel pit." He laughed again.

"And where's Jacque? And that other guy, Dan?"

"They're in a place where they'll *never* be found. I cut them up nice and tiny and fed them to the Beast. I'm pretty sure he was hungry."

Oh God. "What's the beast?"

He shook his head and broke into uproarious laughter again, and I'd had quite enough. The rest would wait for the authorities.

"Don't move or I'll cut your damned head off."

"Yes sir, General Ninja, sir!" The certifiable sonuvabitch saluted the corner.

I returned to Diana, suddenly aware that I'd allowed Norton to distract me from her for precious moments. "I'm so sorry, Sweetie."

I raised her into my arms, and checked her pulse. Norton might have told the truth; I had no way of knowing. With a raging fever, she might have suffered from dehydration and an infected arm. I needed to get her to a hospital immediately. Then I'd hand the crazier-than-batshit Norton to the police.

I wrapped her in one of the blankets, the cleaner and drier of the two, but before lifting her up, I needed to do something about Norton.

The bastard still knelt in the corner, bent upon himself like a warped little doll, giggling and swaying.

I stood, thought about it a moment, and stepped behind him.

"Goodnight, Norton."

"Yes sir, General Ninja, si—"

I struck him on the back of the neck, the *shobo* ring digging deep into a pressure point. He dropped like the sack of shit he was, which didn't bother me in the least, except that I must now carry *him* as well. I grabbed some rope from the bench and cut off two lengths to tie his hands and feet.

Diana remained perfectly still.

I left them both for a couple minutes to run back and get the car. Frank's Caddy managed the rough terrain without too much difficulty, and I parked close to the shed.

I carried Diana to the car, laid her gently in the back seat, and kissed her lightly.

That didn't leave much room for Norton.

Having a change of clothes at the ready had been one of Master Komura's first lessons, and a valuable one. I couldn't enter the hospital or deal with the police looking like a ninja movie reject.

I stashed my equipment in what I assumed would be a safe place, inside a duffel bag and under a shrub in a field off Highway 31. I'd pick them up tomorrow night. In my blue jeans and tennis shoes and with my hair straightened out, I looked almost presentable again.

I then broke every speed limit between Crystal Lake and the McHenry County Hospital in Woodstock.

The next half-hour was a mad blur. I rushed Diana into the emergency room, asked the doctor to check her for dehydration first, then the cut on her arm and a possible infection, before a more thorough examination. He asked several questions as he began working on her, but I had to leave most of them unanswered, and he eventually booted me out so he could tend to Diana.

Almost an hour later, I slumped in a chair in the waiting room, about to face another barrage of questions.

A tired, unhappy face burst through the doors of the ER and strode directly toward me. His disheveled hair, wrinkled uniform and dark circles under his eyes made him the perfect new actor in this sad, sick play.

I'd hated like hell to call him at home at two o'clock in the morning, especially after learning that he'd been asleep for only an hour after working late on the case. No choice, really. "Good morning, Chief."

"Tony, what have you done now, for God's sake?"

"Diana is in with the doctors."

His jaw relaxed and he stared at me for a few seconds. "Are you serious?"

I nodded.

"Tell me."

"I know I was supposed to stay out of it, Chief. Special Agent Jackson said some things last night that made real sense, and I was happy about it. Mostly."

"And yet you still managed to interfere with a police investigation."

"That's right. I had to do it. I saw a surveillance car, I think, and I would have let it be if they'd seen Norton when he left his house, but they didn't."

I told him the whole story, starting with watching Norton's house from the woods and ending with confronting him at the shed by the gravel pits. I said nothing of the special garb or weapons.

He listened without emotion, his face cut from stone, concealing every thought.

When I finished the tale, he said, "So if you hadn't done what you did, Diana would be dead."

"Yes."

"You're lucky he didn't kill you along with her, you know."

I shrugged.

"And what's this *beast*? Is it a dog or something?"

"He didn't say. He just said that Dan and Jacque would never be found, and somehow I believed him."

"Damn. And you say Bobby is at the bottom of the lake in the quarry?"

"Yeah, in his car."

"All right, I suppose that leaves us with the obvious question. Where's Norton? Did you kill him?"

"Let's take a little walk."

I led him through the front doors and into the parking lot. As we approached the rear of Frank's Cadillac, Norton's muffled voice shouted and cursed. I pulled the keys from my pocket and popped the trunk.

"Get me out of this fuckin' trunk! Are you trying to suffocate me, Hooper? Shit! It's not as though I cut your girlfriend up, for Christ's sake. I don't see— Oh, howdy Chief, and how are you doing?"

Chief Radlon looked at me, shook his head and sighed, and turned back to Norton. "Super. You want to tell me what you've done?"

"Hey, hey, hey, wait a minute. I just did what the Reaper and his buddy demons told me to. If you want to blame someone, blame them."

"Great."

"Will you get me out of here, Chief? I've been— Hey, Hooper, what happened to your spiffy ninja stuff?"

"Ninja stuff?" The chief turned to me with a quizzical, almost comical look.

I shrugged. "Beats me. I can't make out half of what he's saying. Maybe you'll have better luck. I'm going back inside to check on Diana. Here you go." I handed Frank's keys to him and turned to leave.

"By the way, Tony, Special Agent Jackson walked into the hospital a few seconds ago. Send him out, will you?"

I approached the doors as another car pulled up and stopper right out front. Two hysterical parents emerged and rushed in.

"Where is she?" Mr. Gregario's voice dripped with anger, but also a hint of relief. "Where is my daughter?"

"Mr. and Mrs. G., come on, I'll show you."

Mrs. G. grabbed my arm gently. "Tony, did you do this? Did you find Diana? You didn't quite make that clear on the phone."

I nodded and looked down at my feet.

She reached out and lifted up my chin. "Thank you, Honey. Thank you."

"Yeah, yeah," Mr. G. practically spit. "We wouldn't be in this mess in the first place if not for him."

He charged in ahead of us while Mrs. G. smiled sadly and silently mouthed the words again— *thank you*—before rushing in after him.

I stayed a few feet behind and listened as they spoke to the doctor. I didn't know what else to do, until the doctor came to me again with his questions. This time I must tell him everything if he was to help Diana. The full story devastated the now silent Gregarios.

The doctor said he understood, and explained his thoughts to us, quick to call them preliminary and to remind us that he still had much more to do.

LANE DIAMOND

When he finished, I returned to Frank's car and two weary cops. Norton yammered on and on about some reaper, about being the king of pain and misery, about the realm of pure delight, and about plenty of other nonsensical stuff, all of which about drove the chief right over the edge.

Jackson led me a few yards away. "The chief has filled me in, and Norton won't shut the hell up. He claims you're a *ninja assassin*, by the way. What's that about?"

I smirk—the best I can manage given the circumstances. "The guy is nuts. What can I say?"

"Yeah, he's already confessed to killing all four people, and he's rambling incessantly and incoherently. That could be a problem, but at least we know the killer is in custody. And your girlfriend is still alive. Amazing. How's she doing, by the way?"

"She's in some sort of shock according to the doctor, and dehydrated. Her arm needed stitching and she needed antibiotics for the infection, but otherwise she'll be all right. He thinks the damage is more psychological than physical. No wonder, given what that monster made her witness."

"I gathered that much from his ranting. She saw him torture two people to death. Dear God, he *made* her watch. That will be difficult to overcome. You know that, right? You must give her some time."

"Yeah, I can wait. Whatever it takes."

"You know, officially speaking, I have some real problems with what you did."

I said nothing, and a smile snuck to his face.

"But, off the record—and I'll deny this if you ever mention it—you did one hell of a job."

I shook the hand he extended. "Thanks."

"However, next time I'll arrest you." He smiled.

Agent Monroe pulled up in another car, with a local cop in the passenger side. She gave me a frustrated glance as she walked toward the Cadillac. She exchanged a few words with the chief, and then walked over and told Jackson that the chief needed to see him. She stayed behind and looked at me without her customary smile, and her sharp emerald eyes glistened in the moonlight.

"I'm sorry, Agent Monroe, but I have to ask you a question." I laughed a little nervously. "Do you ever speak?"

- 288 -

Slow to respond, she gradually chuckled right along with me.

"Occasionally I do, when I must." Her voice dripped with Boston, or somewhere in the Northeast. "Since I'm the rookie around here, I usually shut up and listen, but I make the necessary contributions when called upon."

She paused and sized me up as though deciding whether she should be upset with me. She had a right to be, since she'd been on surveillance at Norton's house and missed him.

"I think we'll probably be talking a lot," she continued, "over the next few days. There are reports to be drawn up, a case to be made, that sort of thing. You've done the hard stuff, since you beat us to the punch, but now we get to handle the boring stuff."

She loosened up and smiled again, and I found it contagious.

The stress rolled off me and fatigue hit me like a sledgehammer, but with my nerves still tightly wound, sleep would be difficult. "I think I'll go back in and see how Diana's doing."

"Good idea. You know, she's lucky. Few girls find their knight-in-shining-armor."

"Yeah, right. Maybe you could tell that to her father."

She raised her eyebrows.

"Never mind, it's nothing. Thanks."

I headed back inside with the desperate hope that I'd be able to speak with Diana. All I'd have to do was get through Mr. G.

CHAPTER 57
JUNE 2, 1978:
TONY HOOPER

Friday morning arrived with a reversal of circumstances for me, back in the police station for yet another round of questions. At least I wouldn't be a suspect this time. Chief Radlon, Special Agent Jackson and Agent Monroe appeared rested and refreshed, whereas I could barely stand up.

"Tony, you look terrible," the chief said. "Have you slept?"

"About an hour. Maybe. Too stressed-out. Too scared."

"Why would you be scared? Norton's in custody and Diana is.... Oh no, is it Diana? What's happened? I haven't had any updates."

"Physically, she'll be fine, but she hasn't spoken, is unresponsive, and doesn't even seem to recognize me or her parents. The doctor says she endured such an unimaginable psychological trauma that the only way she could cope was to *check out*. She suffered a psychotic break."

"Damn! I'm sorry, Tony. What's the prognosis?"

I shrugged. "Nobody knows."

Jackson stepped forward and placed a hand on my shoulder. "You know, this is not unheard of. The good news is that it's always temporary — well, ninety-nine percent of the time, it is. She'll come around. Give her some time. What she requires is your patience and understanding."

"That's what the doctor said, but it's awfully difficult."

"You'll get through it. Chief, do you suppose we could get this young man some coffee before we get started?"

"You bet. Cream only, Tony?"

"Yes sir. Thanks."

"Agent Monroe," Jackson said, "while we're waiting on Chief Radlon, would you please read through our notes to bring Tony up to speed on the situation with Norton?"

A few minutes later, the chief returned with my coffee — strong and bitter. Perfect.

I provided the timelines to go along with their notes, and they confirmed them with Norton's account, where he'd answered intelligibly. I added commentary where my time overlapped with his, and provided them with the full details of my efforts.

Well... *most* of the details.

Time crawled, interrupted occasionally for more coffee or a bathroom break.

At noon, a knock on the door preceded the entry of two officers. They carried bags of food and a box of soft drinks. As we ate, Jackson confirmed some important points that required only a simple yes or no.

After a half-hour break, we resumed the serious discussions. Every forty-five minutes they flipped over the cassette tape or put in a new one. A little before two o'clock, another knock on the door, and Sergeant Harker once again poked her head inside.

"I'm sorry to interrupt, Chief," she said, "but Deputy Ricks from the sheriff's department is here and he needs to see you."

"Now? Did you tell him I'm busy?" He made no attempt to hide his frustration.

"Yes sir, but I'm quite certain you'll want to speak with him."

The sergeant's serious demeanor defeated the chief's irritation.

"You guys go ahead without me," he said. "I'll be back as soon as possible."

A lot of work went into these reports; they must record every minor and seemingly insignificant detail. My lunch settled and the coffee, which I'd stopped drinking, wore off. My exhaustion grew. Although my mind whirled in a storm of memory and thought, my body was failing me. Stiff and sore, I was about to ask for a break to stand and walk around, when the chief returned looking as though his beloved dog had died.

He leaned toward Jackson and said in a quiet voice, "How much longer will you be?"

Jackson hesitated and gazed directly into the chief's eyes, and tension filled the room. "We can take a break for a while."

"Good," the chief said. "You mind turning off the tape?"

Jackson nodded at Monroe and she clicked off the tape recorder.

The chief sat next to me, spinning his chair around to face me directly from a couple feet away. He leaned in, and the smell of his aftershave mingled with his morning supply of coffee.

Suddenly frightened, my thoughts shifted immediately to Diana. Something terrible had happened. I could feel it.

"Tony, I don't know how to say this except to just say it. I'm afraid there's been an accident."

What? How? She was safe in the hospital and they said they would keep her there for several days, at least. What could have happened? Diana! Dear God, what has happened to my Diana!

"Your dad hit a bridge abutment while driving."

What?

"We don't know everything yet—how it happened—but.... Tony, I'm so sorry. Your dad died."

I couldn't say anything. My eyes watered but I didn't cry.

Why is the world ending?

CHAPTER 58
JUNE 19, 1995:
TONY HOOPER

"If we had to tolerate in others all that we permit in ourselves, life would become completely unbearable." – *Georges Courteline*

Norton is a solid minute ahead of me. He'll be inside soon, if he isn't already.

I sprint toward Ethel's house. I know she sleeps in one of the smaller bedrooms downstairs, and leaves the upstairs master bedroom available for guests, like her kids or grandkids. She started this arrangement after she strained her knee last year. Assuming Norton doesn't know this, it may give me the extra minute I need to catch up with him.

One thing is clear: the identity of the killer is no longer in question. Norton once again terrorizes Algonquin's residents.

How will he gain entry into the house? Does he have lock-picks that he's learned to use, or does he require an open window or an unlocked door? Whatever his method, I may have an opportunity to catch up to him while he addresses it.

Why did he choose Ethel's house? Was it intentional, or does he choose them at random? She's a widow, elderly and living alone, which must have entered into his thinking.

I reach her front hedges, pause a beat to prepare myself, and peer around the edge. Nothing. Norton must be going in through the back.

I dash down the driveway, less cautious now that Ethel's safety is the only concern. I'll have my *katana* out and drawn across his chest in a flash, if necessary. That doesn't mean I'll be reckless, just quick.

I clear the rear corner ready to act.

Shit! He's inside.

I unsheathe one of the *ninjaken* and run to the open rear door. Once inside, I move through the mudroom and into the kitchen, toward the front hall. I look in the dark for any sign of Norton, and listen for a telltale sound. Ethel's dog — Rex, I think — lies on the kitchen floor in a pool of blood.

Damn! You're working quickly, Norton, but I know how much you like to play with your victims.

He must prepare Ethel for his rituals, which should give me the time I need.

I do my walking-on-air thing — not a sound — and flash through the hall and into the small downstairs bedroom. There's nobody here! The bed is unruffled, still made up.

She must have decided to go back to her room upstairs.

I take them two at a time and continue down the hall, when a shrill voice cuts the night.

Ethel screams, "Oh no! My God, who are you? Don't!"

I lean around the corner of the doorway. Norton hovers at the bed and looks down at Ethel with a knife in his right hand, ready to strike.

"I'm sorry," he says.

"What?" I say. "You're *sorry*?"

He jerks his head in my direction, and I bolt into the room. His body still faces partly toward Ethel, which puts him at an awkward angle.

My plan, as conceived prior to this, has always been to use Norton's own weapon against him, if possible. It has nothing to do with irony or justice or any such thing. It's a simple matter of leaving no evidence the police can link to me.

I'll use my weapons only if I must — if there's no other way to save Ethel.

Shocked by my appearance, he freezes.

That's all the time I need. When I get within reach of him, he spins away from Ethel and slashes at me with the knife. *Perfect!* As long as he comes after me, Ethel is safe. He slashes back and forth wildly, and each time I jump back to avoid the knife.

I need only one brief opportunity, but it's not as easy as I'd imagined. The darkness makes it difficult to focus.

That changes when a light flashes on.

Good girl, Ethel!

She screams again and Norton stumbles to a halt. He then lunges for Ethel, but I catch his wrist and twist it up and over, which throws him off-balance and spins him into the wall. He grunts and swings the knife. Perfect again!

I slip my left arm inside his elbow and my right hand onto his wrist. In one swift motion, I use my left arm as a lever and my right hand as both a vice-grip, sealing the knife in his hand, and a plunger, driving the blade into his chest.

The sudden silence is marred by a single gurgle. Every horrible thing he's ever done — the people he's destroyed and the lives he's ruined — it ends here.

I can't pull my eyes from him, mesmerized as *the devil* chokes on his own blood.

With his free hand, he grabs my hand to remove it from the knife, but he has no strength. His arm drops limp to his sides.

I release him and take two steps back.

Norton's killing hand drops from his weapon, and he stares at me, his eyes pools of disbelief. He tries to say something, but chokes and spits a gob of blood out onto his chest. He slides down the wall to his knees, then topples over onto his right side.

I step forward and lean over him.

The knife in his chest rises and falls, rises and falls, with each dying gasp. He stares up at me blankly — won't be alive much longer. The knife is too deep, probably in a lung, and the blood flow too profuse.

He's crying.

"Your tears don't move me, Norton," I say. "If you weren't such an animal, or if you weren't *the devil*, it might be different, but this is *exactly* what you deserve."

He labors to breathe as blood runs from the corner of his mouth. He can't speak, but his eyes convey utter confusion.

"They never should have released you from the prison hospital. Seventeen years ago, you destroyed the life I had. Now I've destroyed yours, and you know what? I'll sleep fine. What do you think of that?"

"Tony?" Ethel's intrusion startles me. "Is that you, dear?"

"One minute, Ethel. It's almost over."

"What is that you're wearing? *You* scared me as much as *he* did. What are you doing here?" She shuffles closer and looks down at Norton. With barely a whisper, more terrified than uncertain, she says, "Would he have killed me?"

"Yes. This is the serial killer who's been terrorizing Algonquin."

"Dear God! How did you find him?" She pulls her nightgown tight. "Did... did you know he would come for me?"

"We'll talk about that later, Ethel."

Norton gasps and struggles to inhale. He tries to reach out for me, stronger than I'd given him credit for, but he can barely raise his arm. One last gasp wracks his body and his hand drops to the floor. The knife protruding from his chest quivers, then is still.

Mitchell Norton, *the devil*, is dead.

Ethel stumbles back and flops onto the edge of her bed.

I check the bedclothes and her nightgown for signs of blood or injury, but they're clean and white. "Are you okay, Ethel? Did he hurt you?"

"No, I'm fine." She stammers and her hands shake. "You stopped him in the nick of time. A few more seconds and.... Dear God."

"Good."

"Is he dead?" Her eyes are wide with fear.

"Yes, he's gone." I draw a deep, satisfied breath. "He won't hurt you or anyone else, ever again."

"Thank you so much, dear. How can I ever repay you for this? I'd be dead if not for you." A few tears trickle as the emotion hits her.

"You want to thank me?"

"Of course."

"Then here's what I need you to tell the police."

I spell it out for her and have her repeat the critical parts. She knows that if the police find out I killed him, they'll throw me in jail. My future hangs on what she tells them. It will be uncomfortable for her, perhaps embarrassing, but she says she understands and will do as I say.

"You're sure your conscience will be okay with this, Ethel?"

"My conscience will be fine. I'm only alive because of you."

"All right, give me five minutes and then call the police. Can you wait that long?"

"I don't much like having him there—just lying there. It's kind of creepy, if you know what I mean."

"Yes, I know what you mean, but it's only five minutes and he *is* dead. He can't hurt you."

"I know. It's spooky, but I can wait. You hurry on, dear."

I look again at Norton. The temptation to remove his mask is strong, the urge to see his face etched in terror and pain. Yet what's the point? Besides, I should leave everything for the police.

"Five minutes, Ethel, and remember, call me tomorrow when they're done with you. Okay?"

"All right." She recovers her composure, at least a little. "Maybe I'll stop over to Frank's and cook us a nice dinner. How does that sound?"

"That sounds fine, Ethel."

I turn to leave, but.... I can't resist. I *must* see his face.

I stoop down, careful to leave no marks, and raise the mask above his eyes. The eyes... they're the same as I remember—the same angle, the same color and texture. The rest, however—

Oh no! No, no, no, no, no. It can't be Tommy. Not Tommy Norton. It's supposed to be Mitchell! Goddammit!

I drop to a knee, clench my fists into furious balls, and press them against my forehead. My breath catches in my throat and everything grinds to a stop.

Until Ethel responds to my reaction. "What is it, dear? Who is that man?"

"It's the killer." I stand and stare at the wall, still struggling to find my breath. "That's all that matters."

Someday I may believe that.

I choke the raw emotion out of my throat. "Remember, give me five minutes."

CHAPTER 59
JUNE 20, 1995:
TONY HOOPER

When the chief called a short time ago and asked if I'd be available, I already knew the purpose of his visit: Algonquin's serial killer of 1995 is dead at the hands of a mysterious stranger. This assumed Ethel Simmons adhered to the plan.

The chief has responsibilities, and he must go through the motions, though I'm guessing he'd prefer not to delve into my possible involvement.

It must have been almost two o'clock this morning when Ethel contacted the police.

I presume that shortly thereafter, Linda received the call in her car. I can imagine her unpleasant reaction, and I'm surprised that it's taken this long for them to contact me.

I slept long and mostly well this morning, though I will confess to a mild case of the jitters. It's almost three o'clock in the afternoon and Frank and I sit on the patio, where for the past two hours we've discussed last night's events. He drinks tea and watches over me with a modicum of concern. I suck down beers at a prodigious clip.

Last night was precisely what I'd anticipated, planned for, hoped for... and a complete shock. Nonetheless, I reduced the world's ranks of serial killers by one. How terrible should I feel about that?

I continue to unwind into an alcohol-induced blur.

The chief pokes his head over the fence and says, "Mind if we come in?"

He and Linda come through the gate and plunk down in the chairs I set up for them. The chief faces Frank, Linda faces me, and I face the judgment of two friends.

I hold up my beer and say, "I know you're on duty and you can't have one of these, but I assumed you'd love one of Frank's world famous lemonades. Those are yours." I point to the two glasses I set up for them.

They nod their appreciation and grab their drinks. Everybody is silent for a moment, hesitant. Nobody wants to talk about this.

I've never been sure how much the chief knows about me, about what I do, but he's a smart man and a professional. I wouldn't be surprised if he's figured it out.

Frank breaks the uneasy silence. "How is the bright and beautiful Linda today?"

She flashes a winning smile. "You're such an old charmer."

"And how is the bright and beautiful chief today?" Frank's grin is precious.

"Very funny, old man," the chief says. "You're a laugh a minute."

The chuckles recede to a nervous halt.

"So," I ask, "to what do we owe the pleasure of this visit? You made it sound important on the phone, Chief."

He goes on to explain last night's events, and all the while, he and Linda seem to be watching to see how I'd react to the news. I express the proper shock, of course, including the revelation that Tommy Norton was the killer.

"I shouldn't tell you about any of this," he says with a smirk, "but giving you details of an investigation is becoming a habit with me."

He looks at Linda, and she nods her approval.

"Ethel claims her guardian angel descended from heaven and smote the killer with his own knife. She says he was virtually invisible, her angel, with a voice like velvet and short, curly blond hair like a lamb's."

My goodness, she really went overboard.

"She said that after he rescued her, he disappeared like a puff of white smoke, or more like a cloud." He looks right at me. "What do you think of that?"

"I'm inclined to say the old girl should lay off the brandy." I almost chuckle. Almost. Nobody else seems amused. "Still, you must admit, she sounds awfully fortunate."

"Yeah," Linda says, "I could use a guardian angel like that myself."

She keeps a straight face, but I swear there's a smile in her eyes. The chief looks at her with the same puzzled expression he had for me a few seconds ago.

I shake my head. "Tommy Norton. Who would have thought *that*? I would have bet anything that it was Norton—Mitchell, I mean."

"Yeah," he says, "I imagine we all would have put our money on Mitchell. Tommy even managed to evade surveillance last night."

Linda flinches, though I doubt the chief meant it personally. "That's my fault," she says, "since I was the one on surveillance."

"No, no, I didn't mean to blame," he says hurriedly. "I meant that Tommy Norton, of all people, didn't strike me as someone who could slip surveillance. The whole situation is odd."

"Yes," she says, "very odd."

"And you're sure," I ask, "that Tommy was responsible for *all* of the murders?"

"Yes, at least preliminarily. We have solid blood evidence on his hatchet and some blood spatter on his ski mask. We have shoe impressions that will match, I'm sure, and we have some fibers that will probably match his clothing. Lots of testing still to do. Also, it turns out he did yard work for Ethel, Melody Nesmith and John Adams, so besides the obvious connection, he may also have had easy access to their homes. We think Lindsey Merkham's murder was unplanned. All in all, I'd say it's a lock."

I almost hoped the answer would be no. That would leave open the possibility that Mitchell committed some of the murders. Something inside me still rages where he's concerned. It would give me an excuse to—

"The real clincher," he continues, "are the notes we found in his desk. They're in handwriting like a third grader's, and they explain why he started killing."

"You're kidding! He left notes?"

"Yep. He thought his big brother, Mitchell, was the smartest man around. Furthermore, he thought Mitchell's intelligence improved not just *after* he started killing in 1978, but *because* of it."

"Shit! Are you telling me that Tommy thought *killing* people would make him smarter? That he wouldn't be slow anymore?"

"That's what he wrote. The last entry explained how much he hated it, and how it made him sick to his stomach. But he was sure the Reaper would help him as a result of his killing, and make him smart like his big brother."

I remember the way he told Ethel he was *sorry* as he prepared to kill her. "Shit!"

PART 9

CLOSURE

CHAPTER 60
JULY 4, 1978:
TONY HOOPER

"The world turns aside to let any man pass who knows whither he is going." – *David S. Jordan*

Summertime was the penultimate time of year in Algonquin, with no school and with weather second only to autumn. As the Fourth of July dawned—*Why does nobody call it Independence Day anymore?*—on this bright Tuesday morning, Algonquin rested easier and more relaxed. The serial killer that had plagued them was in custody at the state psychiatric facility, where he'd remain until his trial, and probably thereafter.

For me this would be a day of relaxation after several days of packing, clearing and cleaning, selling and moving. The old house, which sold several days ago, was almost empty, with a few odds'n'ends straggling and more cleaning to do.

The sale wouldn't close for a few weeks. Frank offered to help me put the money into a mutual fund. We'd have plenty of time now that I lived with Gramps, as I took to calling him.

Dad had been well prepared to leave his financial house in order, with significant equity in the house, a generous life insurance policy, a burial plot already paid for, and a Last Will and Testament with every I dotted and T crossed. He'd made sure I'd have no *financial* worries, at least, and had provided enough to get me through college. There'd been some wrangling over the life insurance, as they'd suspected his death was a suicide, but with no note and no real evidence, the police eventually wrote it up as an accident.

Dad had left work early that Friday, and stopped at a bar to drown his sorrows in Jack Daniel's. Then, while presumably driving home, he'd struck a bridge abutment at approximately ninety miles per hour. We'd never know if it had been intentional, whatever anyone's suspicions.

I chose to believe it had been an accident.

A relatively small group of people attended the funeral: a few of Dad's extended family, one associate from his work, a few of our neighbors, Ben and Naomi Komura, Chief Radlon and his wife Kathy, Frank and me. We gathered afterwards at the old house, where Frank had arranged for caterers to provide the appropriate fare. I played the sober host who accepted everyone's condolences with solemn nods and sad smiles.

An utterly miserable day; I wouldn't have made it without Frank.

It took several more days for the investigation to wind down, and toward the end they asked a few questions of Frank, who had loaned me his car the night I saved Diana and captured Norton.

He responded in his usual manner, playing the innocent old charmer. "My grandson—he's not my true grandson; I sort of adopted him; unofficially—he asked to borrow my car. No, I didn't ask him why. I didn't need to. He's a responsible young man, which I should think is obvious by now. I trust him, so I let him borrow the car. That's about the nut of it, I reckon."

Frank had mistaken several questions for threats against me, and fired back with both barrels. Quite amusing, though it was comforting to have someone around who'd protect me at any cost. I doubted the FBI agents had bought a single bit of his story, but they let it go.

I contacted the admissions people at Duke and, with the assistance of Frank, Mr. Kozlowski and Chief Radlon, deferred my entry into school for a year.

I needed a little more time to myself, to think things through and determine what I'd do with my life.

I'd made it through high school graduation without too much excitement. Mr. Kozlowski managed, at the insistence of a stubborn neighbor and Chief of Police, to get me a pass on homework assignments for the two weeks of school I'd missed, provided I scored well on the finals. In the end, I maintained my standing and finished third in my class.

I spent most of my free time at the dojo, where Master Komura trained me to the edge of my endurance, and where he and Naomi treated me as their own son. There was love there. Chief and Kathy Radlon, too, had practically adopted me, insisting I stop by once a week for dinner, conversation, games, a ballgame on TV — some simple, caring company.

Despite the recent tragedy, I was not alone. Frank, the Komuras, the Radlons; together they constituted my new family, and I loved them all.

Diana had remained in the hospital for two weeks, after which she started to show improvement. She regained her memory, as Jackson had predicted, but she continued to be troubled and, much to my chagrin, refused to see me. Mrs. G. asked me to give her a little more time, promising that Diana would come around eventually.

I agreed to be patient and understanding for as long as was necessary, and I meant it, but that was three weeks ago.

My desperation overwhelmed me and I drove to their place last Sunday. I figured I'd at least speak with Mrs. G., even if I couldn't speak with Diana.

A massive, white and red *For Sale* sign jutted from their yard. The house was empty. Their neighbor knew nothing more than that they'd moved somewhere out west. Mr. G.'s boss, also Dad's former boss, said he couldn't speak with me about it, adding that it was none of my business. Nice.

This morning I returned to the old house to pick up the last of my clothes. I also checked the mail from yesterday, and found a letter with no return address on it, postmarked Denver, Colorado. It was addressed to me in handwriting that I knew as well as my own, and hinting at a perfume that made my head reel.

Now seated on Frank's patio, as I soaked up the warmth of the late morning sun and drank a beer, I could only stare at the unopened letter on the table — scared to death to open it. I didn't know *how* I knew, but I knew that Diana was gone forever.

I wouldn't see her again.

I faltered, utterly drained after having barely slept the past two days, certain I hadn't the strength to read the letter. Yet I couldn't walk away from it.

I downed the last of my beer, took a deep breath, let out a long sigh, and grabbed the envelope. A deep, pleasurable scent wafted up as I opened it.

My Dearest Tony,

My sweetest man, my knight in shining armor, my guardian angel, my hero, the one and only love of my life — how shall I begin? I think I should start with three simple words: I LOVE YOU! It's true, and I'm sure it will always be true. I wish that was enough, but I'm afraid it's more complicated. My ordeal has taken a terrible toll on me, and only I can heal me.

I will need a lot of time, I'm afraid.

It's not just that I can't put anyone else through that — such as you, my love — it's that I CAN'T do it unless I have the time to do it on my own, without distractions or reminders, or the many emotions that I must now fight.

I am so mad at my father for blaming you! I've told him that, and that if it weren't for you I would have suffered the most horrible death imaginable. Believe it or not, he understands and he's sorry for treating you the way he did. As for me, THANK YOU FOR GIVING ME MY LIFE! I understand that you know what Mitchell Norton did to those people, including poor Jacque, but knowing and seeing are two different things. You truly have no idea what you saved me from. THANK YOU, MY LOVE!

The truth is I feel guilty for all of this. I know it was Mitchell Norton's obsession with me that led to all the problems for you, including poor little Alex. He was innocent! He was so sweet, and Mitchell Norton found him while looking for me. I'm sorry.

How do I live with that?

The doctors tell me over and over that it's not my fault, that it was that terrible monster's fault. There's a part of me, somewhere inside, that knows that's true, but another part of me can't escape the guilt. I need time.

There's much more to it, however. I'm not whole, and until I am, I can't be with anyone, even the most wonderful man ever. That's you, my love. My emotions are a mess. My outlook is a mess. Hell, my whole life is a mess.

I am so, so sad to be apart from you. I cry day and night thinking about you. I'm crying right now. I can't stop. I still remember our last night together. It was the most amazing night of my life! Right up until that monster....

I'll always cherish that night, no matter what. I know I'll never know love like that again, and it makes me sad. God, here come the tears again.

Okay, I'm back. Maybe I'll stop crying long enough to finish this letter. I don't know how long it will take me to heal. I don't know what life has in store for me. I don't know if I'll ever see you again. I know only that I WILL LOVE YOU FOR AS LONG AS I LIVE! Wait for me, if you will, for a little while. Give me some time, but not too much. If I don't come around, then at some point you must move on. Promise me! I want you to be happy.

Please promise, right now (I'll know), that you will be happy.

God, how I long to kiss you. You are forever the love of my life,

Your Diana

CHAPTER 61
AUGUST 10, 1978:
TONY HOOPER

I'd been sitting in this damned parking lot for about an hour, staring at the sign above the door.

I didn't come for this. I came for the bookstore, but the bookstore's next-door neighbor intrigued me. They might be my answer.

I'd tried the past few weeks, without much success, to figure out what to do with myself.

Now I knew.

"Are you being a tad impulsive?" I asked myself.

"Maybe. Tough shit!"

I got out of the car and walked into the office.

The sign over the door said, *U.S. ARMY, Recruiter*.

CHAPTER 62
JUNE 28, 1995:
TONY HOOPER

"I'm an idealist; I don't know where I'm going, but I'm on my way." – *Carl Sandburg*

"Hey, Hoopster, it's been a long time. Sorry I haven't been around more often, but I was all wound up in my life. You know what I mean?"

The staff has put out flowers, and color explodes throughout the cemetery, bursting from a green so deep, it gives the illusion they plucked the very land itself from the slopes of Ireland. Above Alex's headstone, a plastic pot overflows with blossoms and heavenly scents. Perfect. Mom and Dad rest nearby, and I said a quick hello, but I came to see the Hoopster today.

A blanket of otherworldly silence shrouds the empty cemetery. I'm grateful, as it means I may speak aloud without appearing the fool. Speaking, as opposed to mere thinking, lends credibility to the proposition that Alex can hear me, as though it's inconceivable the dead can be psychic.

"It's been quite an eventful time, Alex. They let loose *the devil*, I'm sorry to say, and the killing started again. That was no surprise, except, as it turned out, it is a surprise. *The devil* didn't do it. That's a long story, so maybe I'll save that for another time.

"Frank is hanging in there, though he's wearing a bit thin these days. He still has that wit like a straight razor, and he still hides a keen intellect below that country charm. I'll be sure to tell him you said, 'Boo!' I know how much he misses his youngest grandson.

"You wouldn't recognize the old house anymore. The folks that live there destroyed much of the side yard, which they use for storage, and it looks like a junk-heap compared to our time there. Whenever I look at it and remember our days playing in that yard, I'm struck by its puny size. It was an entire world back then."

I sigh and shuffle my feet as I look around at the other graves, and continue.

"I've met someone, Hoopster, and she's smart, successful, and quite the looker. Her name is Linda, and when I'm with her, the world makes sense again. We recently spent a couple weeks together, but she returned back east to the FBI. I always knew she would. The only question is what I'll do about it. How could I let her go without me? How will I survive without her touch, her smell, her smile and those devastating green eyes? I think she could save me, if only I would let her, but some final issues are holding me back.

"I've tried to put all the tragedy and sadness behind me, to settle up old debts. I think of Diana often, even tracked her down a few years ago and found out where she lived. I checked recently — she's still there. It's relatively close, only a couple hours north, and I want to go see her but... I'm afraid. It scares the hell out of me, in fact. What will I say? How will I act? A simple 'Sorry' won't do the trick, but what will? I've been unable to figure it out, but I'll keep working on it."

I kneel on the ground beside his headstone, careful to stay off him; that would be wrong. I'm out of gas, emotionally drained, yet this one last thing is important. Once again, I've let *the devil* go, the monster that killed my little brother, except that he's apparently no longer the monster I was certain he must be.

Why am I so confused? God, I need some kind of closure.

"The truth is, this is difficult for me, Hoopster. Every time I think of you, every time I see a picture of you, every time I come here to visit, the damned guilt overwhelms me, knocks me right on my ass. I know it was my fault, and I've never been able to forgive myself."

I fidget with the grass and take a deep breath to control my watering eyes.

"Well, I think I need to. How else can I move on? I'm drowning here, Buddy, and I need your help.

"So I thought... maybe... oh hell! Alex, I'm so sorry. You know that, don't you? Come on, Hoopster, all I need is one little sign. Find my mind. I know you can do it. You always were the one with the big heart."

All these years later, I need one last thing from the boy who was my Shadow.

"Forgive me, Alex."

CHAPTER 63
AUGUST 12, 1995:
TONY HOOPER

"Character is that which reveals moral purpose, exposing the class of things a man chooses or avoids." – *Aristotle*

Circumstances change, roads turn, and life occasionally heads off down its own path, like the impetuous child who turns and says, "Come on, hurry up!" That's how I feel, as if chasing after my own life, unsure where it's going but cautiously hopeful. Contentment remains hidden—my elusive desire. In my entire adult life, I've been unable to cast it from the shadows. It's there, I know—waiting, perfectly camouflaged in the vagaries and machinations of everyday life. I have merely to reach out and grasp it.

Is it that simple? Perhaps, but I must complete one final task if ever I'm to find out.

Interstate 43 runs north out of Milwaukee, parallel to Lake Michigan on the way to Green Bay, but I approach my exit long before then. The town of Mequon is behind me and I'm passing Cedarburg—won't be long now.

I've chewed my fingernails to the edge of bleeding. My stomach is victim to a strange sensation, as if I've swallowed an army of tiny demolitions experts who've gone to work. I hope to keep it together, that I won't need to run to Diana's bathroom to evacuate all this pent-up anxiety.

Nah, that wouldn't be embarrassing at all.

I haven't felt this way since the first time I picked her up for a date. It's strange. I haven't seen Diana — talked to her or written to her — for seventeen years. The pain of that time was too much. I never understood why her father insisted on moving her out of Algonquin, far away from the horrible events, given that she survived. She endured unimaginable horrors, but she *did* endure.

She *made it*.

She underwent a lot of psychological counseling, which was hardly unexpected; one experienced such atrocities with severe consequence. Still, she made it. Yet her father wouldn't let me speak to her. He forbade my seeing her and blamed me for everything.

I accepted that at the time, up to my ears in guilt and prepared to accept responsibility for Alex, Diana, Dad, and for the terrible way limburger cheese smelled. The whole world had fallen into the shitter and it was *my* fault.

Diana's letter explained the first few weeks, perhaps even a few months. But seventeen years? Forever?

Grafton, Wisconsin, a bedroom community for Milwaukee, offers little by way of excitement. The homes are older than I expected, appropriate to a basic working middle class kind of town, not too pricey but quaint and clean. Diana lives on Sixth Street. I know from my source that she's unmarried and still using her maiden name of Gregario, but that she does have one dependent.

Okay, she had a kid somewhere along the way — nothing surprising there. I didn't expect her to join a convent. Still, why does it bother me? Is it jealousy, all these years later, even now that I have Linda in my life?

I park up the block from her small, boxy old house. It has light gray siding, darker gray roofing, a sliver of driveway without a garage, and a tailor's patch of front yard. Elbowroom is an excessive luxury in this neighborhood. A basketball hoop occupies the back end of the driveway, and a basketball rests in the grass beneath it. The bicycle that leans against the house looks like a boy's fifteen-speed.

Although it's Saturday, I wasn't sure she'd be home. I wanted to surprise her.

Right, good plan, Tony.

The driveway is empty, but a car hugs the sidewalk along the street in front of the house, an old '88 Ford Taurus with dull paint and a small dent on the passenger-side rear panel — Diana's car, exactly as my investigator indicated.

Okay, she's home. Now what? Boy, you sure thought this one through.

My stomach cartwheels again. I'd feel better if I puked first.

Right, surprise her after seventeen years with some lovely barf-breath.

As I walk down the sidewalk toward her place, I try to look relaxed, nonchalant, cool — as if somebody will call the cops or something. I'm nervous as hell, damn it, but here I am.

The doorbell emits no sound, so I also knock.

Seconds later, she opens the door and immediately dons that *oh-crap-it's-a-salesman* look. "May I help — ?" She comes up short.

I can see her search her memory and try to sort it out.

"Oh... my... God."

"Hello, Diana, it's been a long time." The ghosts of Fred Astaire and Ginger Rogers are dancing the Jitterbug in my stomach, and my emotions are about to explode my brain through my skull.

She shakes her head. "It's really you."

Her hair is shorter and dyed a light reddish-brown; it looks good on her. Her eyes are mostly the same, encircled by a few thin lines, the residue of a life that's been... difficult, I imagine. The light I remember in them lurks somewhere in the background, subdued. She carries a few extra pounds, with hips that imply children.

I drift back in time. *God, she looks good enough to....* I can't believe my heart is fluttering. How can that be? "It's me."

"My goodness, it has been such a *long* time. You look well."

Anxiety laces her words, and suspicion hangs like a hammer over the doorway.

She rifles through several questions in a vocal sprint. "Why are you here, Tony? After all this time? How did you find me? What do you want?"

She gives me little opportunity to answer. The last question is more like an accusation.

Take it easy, Tony. Just press on. "The last few weeks have been... well... difficult. A lot has happened, things that brought me back to 1978." I hesitate and attempt to recapture my nerves in a deep breath. "Mitchell Norton was released."

There, I said it. I brace for her reaction, a storm, horror.

Nothing. She already knows. Her silence is uncomfortably detached and unconcerned.

"I got drawn into this whole big drama. There were more murders in Algonquin, but it wasn't him. It wasn't Norton."

She still stares at me with that look: *Yeah, yeah, I know all that.*

"When it was over, I needed to put that life behind me, to find a way to start over. I wasn't quite ready—had to do a few things first. I suppose it's what they call closure."

She doesn't react, but her eyes remain lasered to mine.

"I needed to talk to you, Diana, about what happened back then. May I please do that?"

As she mulls it over, a new voice shatters the uneasy silence. I'd been so engrossed in the conversation that I hadn't heard the two boys come up behind us.

The nearest one looks at me as though deciding if he needs to run and get his gun. "Hey, Mom, I'm going over to Sean's to shoot some hoops. What time should I be home for dinner?"

"Six o'clock."

"Okay."

He looks at me again, then back at his mom, then shrugs and heads off. He and his friend hop onto skateboards and zip down the street.

I stare after him for several seconds. There's something familiar about him, but I can't quite put my finger on it. He's older than I'd expected, perhaps sixteen or seventeen, but that's impossible, since his mom and I—

Diana clearly recognizes my stunned concern—and the question. When she smiles, melancholy nevertheless peeks through as she shakes her head and stares at the ground. A cloud of resignation masks her expression.

I strain to hear her soft voice. "That was my son. His name is... Alex."

I can only stare at her with my mouth agape, my mind whirling in a twister of incredulity and confusion.

She nods. "Yeah, I thought you'd like that."

"You mean he's our...?" I can't believe it, yet I can. I still remember vividly our last time together, a night to surpass all other nights.

She smiles and deflates in a heavy sigh, which drips again with resignation and, if I'm not mistaken, relief.

She stands aside to make room for me. "You'd better come in. I'll put some coffee on. We have a lot to talk about."

EPILOGUE
AUGUST 13, 1995:
MITCHELL NORTON

"If pleasures are greatest in anticipation, just remember that this is also true of trouble." — *Elbert Hubbard*

The critical element to good torture, of course, is pain: unfathomable, unending, but endurable—just barely—right unto the moment of death.

When the voice of the Reaper comes to call, you'd better put on your listening cap. He's quite the work, the Reaper, dedicated to everlasting misery, the exploitation of flesh, the ecstasy of terror. If the deepest, darkest and most horrifying recesses of the human mind can conceive of it, then the Reaper has already heaped it upon the dredges of humankind, already made of it a plaything, already rollicked in the pure joy of it.

His grin can freeze your blood. His words can destroy your mind. His laugh can seize your soul and send you running hysterically, gladly into the great fires.

I know. I've been there. I escaped.

You only thought you escaped.

"Am I back?"

Yes, you're back.

"Fuck a rubber duck."

Hey, Mitchell, you're the MAN!

ACKNOWLEDGEMENTS

I must thank my little brother and his lovely wife, Darren and Rhonda Lane. Without going into all the gory details about my life taking a twisted turn, presenting me with unexpected hurdles, let me just say that Darren and Rhonda saved me. They're the real deal — fine people who understand that good deeds matter most. Thank you, guys.

When circumstances changed and I needed someone else to step up, my "brutha from a different mutha," Steven Zerkel, came to my rescue. Friends don't get any better than Steve. Thanks, Mano.

Several people had a hand in helping me work out the bumps in this story. I'm always amazed at how we writers, no matter how good we might think we are, fail to see some of our own foibles. As I've long told my editing clients, it's rather as the old saw tells us: "Forest? What forest? I don't see no stinkin' forest. All those darned trees are in the way!" We all need a little help seeing past our trees to the forest within.

Author Michael A. Gibbs was the first to provide some helpful feedback. In particular, he pointed out that I needed to shift back in time one critical scene. What a difference that made in the emotional impact of the scene! Thanks, Mike.

Then my editor, D.T. Conklin, provided an objective pair of eyes. He spotted not only the little mistakes I was blind to after so many revisions, but provided a reader's perspective to help me make some tough changes. We writers so often, as a lawyer might say, "Assume facts not in evidence." If it's in my head, then surely, it's in the reader's head. Well... no. This is one of the great services an editor provides, and one of the key reasons we all — each and every one of us — need editors. Thanks, Dan.

Thank you to the talented D. Robert Pease for this cover design, and for that of the upcoming sequel, *The Devil's Bane*.

Finally, thanks to the entire Evolved Publishing team, terrific and talented people who inspire me and give me great hope for the future.

ABOUT THE AUTHOR

Lane Diamond is the pen name for Dave Lane, who grew up in Algonquin, Illinois, where he graduated from Harry D. Jacobs High School in 1978. After a short college stint, he served in the U.S. Air Force at Ramstein AB, Germany, 1980-1982, and at Lowry AFB, Denver, CO, 1982-1983. Then it was on to real life.

For more, please visit his website: **www.LaneDiamond.com**.

Lane Diamond is also the Founder, CEO, and Managing Publisher/ Editor at Evolved Publishing, a hybrid small press publisher. For details, please visit their website: **www.EvolvedPub.com**.

These days (2025), Lane calls Transylvania home, where he lives with his beautiful wife, Mary, and enjoys his new family. Some day, he might even learn to speak their native Hungarian. Or maybe not, 'cuz that monster is just plain hard! They still travel on occasion to his old home in Las Vegas, and enjoy traveling to new destinations.

Find more from Lane Diamond online at:
Website: www.LaneDiamond.com
Publisher: www.EvolvedPub.com/LDiamond
Goodreads: Lane_Diamond
X: @ EvolvedPub
Facebook: @Lane.Diamond
LinkedIn: LaneDiamond

WHAT'S NEXT?

THE DEVIL'S BANE
Tony Hooper – Book 2

Watch for this sequel to *Forgive Me, Alex* to release in 2026 (or sometime before the apocalypse... hopefully).

A serial killer the media has dubbed "The Blue Suede Killer" plagues southwest Wisconsin, and the authorities are having a hard time tracking him down. Tony Hooper thinks he can help. After all, this is what he does. He's a hunter of monsters.

This new evil brings Tony back into the shadows where his love interest, FBI Special Agent Linda Monroe, must do her job. It also brings him close to the one woman he always assumed was meant for him, the woman he lost seventeen years earlier. Can he and Diana speak about what happened? Can they finally put it behind them? Will they move on together, or separately once again... and forever? And what will it all mean for Tony and Linda?

All the while, Tony is battling another foe, the man he's long called 'the devil,' Mitchell Norton. They've waged their personal war for seventeen years, and it's time for one – at long lost – to declare victory. 'The devil' has stolen too much from Tony, throwing his life into a whirlwind of remorse, self-doubt, and self-examination.

If Norton has his way, Tony's losses will mount even further.

MORE FROM EVOLVED PUBLISHING

We offer great books across multiple genres, featuring hiqh-quality editing (which we believe is second-to-none) and fantastic covers.

As a hybrid small press, your support as loyal readers is so important to us, and we have strived, with tireless dedication and sheer determination, to deliver on the promise of our motto: **QUALITY IS PRIORITY #1!**

Please check out all of our great books,
which you can find at the website address below.

www.EvolvedPub.com/Catalog/

Thank you!